BLOODWALKER

BLOODWALKER

L.X. Cain

FREEDOM FOX PRESS
Dancing Lemur Press, L.L.C.
Pikeville, North Carolina
www.dancinglemurpress.com

Dedication

This novel wouldn't have made it to publication without the help and support of my critique partners: Kate Larkindale, T.F. Walsh, Kim Lajevardi, Stuart R. West, David Emanuel, and last but certainly not least, Graeme Ing. Much gratitude also goes to my beta readers: Leigh Hogan, Donna Hole, Rhiannon Taylor, and Tegan Whalan. Special thanks to Breanna and Phillip Teintze for research advice and to Melinda Csikós who helped me with the Hungarian dialog.

CHAPTER ONE

Rurik
Budapest, Hungary

"School is out, no books today.
Boneyard's where the children play.
Marta's there and Peter, too,
Silent faces, cold and blue.
Shut the doors. Lock them tight.
Ratman prowls the streets tonight."

The refrain of the children's song swelled, and the winds swirled it up to the roof of an old stone church. Perched on its parapet, a line of gargoyle statues stared dead-eyed at the horizon. But one set of eyes stabbed downward. Rurik leaned over the edge, his gaze roving the street two stories below, searching for the source of the Hungarian rhyme.

The retreating sun stained Budapest red. Shadows of tree limbs and buildings bled across lawns and sidewalks. Yellow pansies bowed their heads and furled their faces closed for the night. Sparrows, pigeons, and swifts abandoned the sky.

Rurik scoured the area till he spotted the rhyme's young singers.

Three kids, probably no older than eight or nine, neared the gate of a train yard at the end of the road—the killer's hunting ground.

Forbidden things drew children. The grittier and scarier the place, the bigger the thrill. So there they went, two girls and a boy, shoving each other, squealing and laughing in fearful delight.

They didn't know four children had vanished, one by one, over the past month. Never any sign of a struggle.

Just schoolbooks found along the road.

Rurik's rooftop position afforded him a good view of Budapest's Istvantelek train depot. But as the children squeezed under the loose chain between gate and fence and wove down the path, the shadows grew. Subway cars sitting beneath electric wires seemed to lengthen on their tracks. Inch by inch, murk swallowed the tall grass and bushes that marked the boundary between the newer train warehouses and the rotting old one the children headed for.

Plenty of places for a killer to hide.

Dusk drained color from the rail yard and turned the children's cheerful sweaters to corpse gray. They huddled together, as close as the weeds that sprouted from the crumbling asphalt under their feet.

Rurik hoped they'd get nervous and run home. Doubtful anything would happen today anyway, not with the police searching the neighborhood for little Dora Tolnay who'd disappeared yesterday.

But did he want to bet the kids' lives on it? Especially after they finally overcame their fear and tiptoed through the entrance of the decrepit warehouse?.

He pulled his hood lower, shading his eyes from the dying sun's glare as he strained to catch the slightest movement around the depot.

Nothing stirred in the huge train yard.

On nearby streets, people left their offices and entered parked cars or waited at the bus stop. If any glanced up at the peculiar form crouched on the church's parapet, they'd betray no curiosity. That would be impolite—a violation of the keep-to-yourself code that held the country of radically diverse ancestries and cultures together. He'd be written off as a trick of the light or maybe an extra gargoyle. The stone monsters sat atop half the old façades in Budapest anyway.

Being mistaken for a monster was nothing new. Rurik was used to it.

The police presence and general alarm would be greater if they knew it was actually four children missing, not just one.

A little girl taken from a park in northern Italy. A boy taken from a playground in Slovenia. A girl taken from an abandoned Slovenian train station a week later. And now a girl from Budapest.

No one had put it together except Rurik. No one realized that each child had vanished on the day of the final performance of the *Zorka Cyrka*.

And the killer's appetite was increasing. Tomorrow was the circus's last show in Budapest, and already a little girl was gone. Dora Tolnay had vanished on her way to a friend's house. Her parents told the newspaper she often cut through the train yard to get there. This time, however, she never came out.

Tension crept into Rurik's shoulders, and he rolled the stiffness out. He didn't have much time before he needed to leave. The killer had to make his move soon.

Then Rurik heard it. The tiniest jingle, cutting through the sunset's stillness, like a cat's bell of warning.

A shape emerged from the trees on the far side of the warehouse. White silk shrouded the figure, giving it a ghostly glow in the dimness. But it wasn't a ghost. Far from it. It was a clown.

The oversized tunic and baggy pants bore a checkered harlequin motif although clowns rarely wore that style anymore. And Rurik hadn't seen the stiff fabric of the Elizabethan neck-ruff anywhere but old pictures. Yet there it was, like it had stepped from a silent film, accompanied not by an organ, but by bells tinkling from the tips of its three-pronged jester's hat. The figure loped in a strange see-saw motion, somewhere between a limp and a gorilla's hunched gait, its legs carrying it along almost as if they weren't jointed like a normal human's.

Surprise glued Rurik's feet to the stone parapet until a second later when the figure disappeared into the warehouse. Then he jumped, plummeting two stories to land in a crouch on the church's lawn. Pain shuddered up his oversized leg bones. He took off, sprinting across the street, vaulting the shoulder-high gate, and plunging over the railroad tracks.

Wind whistled in his ears. No, not wind. Noises like

tiny train whistles. He sped up, following the sounds of children's screams.

Inside the warehouse's doorway, he stopped short.

The last rays of light filtered through holes in the roof, illuminating trains from long ago, their twenty-foot tall engines rusted into monuments to the past. Behind them sat boxcars with wooden sides so rotted half the planks had disintegrated. Each car was a giant skeletal ribcage revealing more desiccated trains beyond. Fungus covered the timbers. Vines dangled off metal roofs. Sickly little trees grew from the dirt floor like skinny travelers frozen in time, waiting to board the trains to nowhere.

Istvantelek was a graveyard.

The shrieks had stopped. Footsteps pounded toward him, and the two girls burst into view, dashing toward the exit.

The boy wasn't with them.

One of the girls tumbled to her knees, her face upturned, glassy eyes meeting his within the darkness of his hood. Her mouth worked. A bubble of spittle popped between her lips, but no words followed. She pointed a shaky finger behind her.

Rurik bolted down the center aisle of the petrified machines, gazing left and right between cars. Halfway down the expanse, a flock of barn swallows erupted from the far end. Their white breasts streaked through the gloom, and their tumultuous wing-beats matched the thudding of his heart.

If he couldn't find the clown—and the little boy—the child would become just another mystery in the wake of the circus as it traveled across Eastern Europe. The girls' story about a clown wouldn't be believed. Everyone knew the Hungarian police were useless. The parents would be left to mourn alone. A perfect family, shattered forever.

Rurik doubled his speed.

A squeal of hinges pierced the silence. He skidded around a caboose, grabbing the railing of its back platform to stay upright. The metal strut broke off in his hand. At the end of the warehouse, a door swung in the breeze. He dove through it.

The pale figure of the clown hastened along the tracks, his off-kilter lope rocking the boy tucked in his arms, a warped caricature of a mother rocking her child.

"Stop," Rurik bellowed in his native Russian, knowing it was no Hungarian he chased.

The kidnapper didn't react. Didn't even look back. He reached a walkway that crossed above the tracks and lurched up the steps. On the far side, trees and bushes lay in deep, dark thickets. A million places he could hide and lose a pursuer.

Rurik raced after him, taking the stairs two at a time, gaining quickly. His boots clanged against the corroded metal catwalk. The whole structure vibrated beneath him.

The clown glanced over his shoulder, the red grease-paint of his smile smeared sideways on his cheek.

Rurik caught him halfway across the bridge, grabbing his arm.

The short, stocky clown spun quicker than Rurik expected. His fist swung at Rurik's head.

No stranger to fights or taking punches, Rurik ducked his chin so the blow would glance off the hard skull above his ear. But the strike slammed into him like a weighted club. It pitched him sideways, toppling him over the railing. His feet flew into the air. He fell past the railings, scrabbling for a hold. Hooking an arm around the lowest one, he caught himself and hung, legs suspended only a yard above the electric train wires—and a thousand volts of death.

By using one hand to hit Rurik, the kidnapper lost his grip on the child. The boy squirmed down the silken costume to land on the bridge. The clown bent and snatched at him.

Rurik speared his free arm through the railings and wrapped a fist around the front of the harlequin tunic. He yanked, dragging the clown to his knees.

The boy crawled away.

The clown twisted and jerked against Rurik's grip, and a snarl of frustration peeled his lips back from his teeth. Long teeth. Too long to be normal. He chopped at Rurik's hand, the punishing blows heavy as a mallet on Rurik's

11

wrist.

Rurik held on, jaw clenched against the pain raging through his forearm. He could take it. Had to give the child time to escape.

The clown switched to hammering at the arm Rurik had locked around the lower railing. Rurik's elbow went numb, and his grasp began to loosen.

Several yards away, the boy scrambled to his feet and took off down the walkway.

A howl of anger erupted from the clown. He leaned between the railings, beating his fists against Rurik's head and shoulders.

A black haze lowered across Rurik's vision, like the curtain coming down on a performance. From the corner of his eye, he caught sight of the child staggering down the last of the stairs and fleeing toward the exit gates. Farther away with every step. Too far for the clown to catch him now.

A final blow knocked Rurik loose. He fell toward the wires.

Would the thousand volts feel like the lightning?

Would they tear through his body, stiffen his muscles, and make every cell peal in agony? Would he get caught on the wires as the electrical fire ate his body from the inside out? Like the lightning, would the charge leave him alive but destroyed, stealing everything that was important to him?

He hit the ground with a wrenching thud. As his consciousness dissolved, he wondered if he had finally died. At last.

Moments later—hours later?—voices woke him. Five or six of them, drawing near, their tones confused and alarmed. He translated the Hungarian in his head.

"Did you say he was hit by a train?"

"I saw him fall off the bridge. I think someone pushed him."

"It's dark as hell out here."

"Look. Over there. I think I see something."

Rurik willed his strength to return. He had to escape.

"Why don't we just call the night watchmen?"

"Those fat guards don't leave their huts for anything. Best have a look ourselves."

"But it could be dangerous! I heard a little girl say a crazy man was on the tracks and he scared her and her friends."

"She said he kidnapped her brother!"

Rurik moved his neck. It cracked, but it worked.

"No, no. I just saw the boy. He was right there with her."

"Someone should call the police."

"There. I see him. Let's find out if he needs an ambulance first."

"You have a light?"

Rurik really had to get out of there before—

"My phone lights up. Here."

Rurik opened his eyes to a blue glow in his face.

And then the screams started.

He sat up, and the people recoiled in terror. A quick yank got his hood over his head but didn't lessen the shrieks. He gathered his feet under him and bolted across the tracks and through the waist-high weeds. The screams chased him, blending with all the others from his past, the ones that had forced him to stop performing after the last time he was struck, ten years ago. The lightning's kiss had turned the smiles of his seventeenth year into a permanent snarl, half his face and body twisted into a monstrous parody of a human.

The car. Where had he left it?

Damn. His brain felt like a rock bouncing inside his skull.

Behind the church. That's where he'd parked. He had to get to the Danube and across the bridge to Obudai Island. The circus's box office would open soon. By now, his father would be worried. Maybe even trying to get into a security uniform. That would be a disaster, and word would get back to Alyosha.

Rurik pounded down the street and finally spotted his car. He started to fish for keys and realized he had something in his hand. Under a streetlight, he slowed and uncurled his fingers.

Lying in his palm was a red pom-pom. A button. Like

the three he'd glimpsed on the front of the clown's tunic. It had torn off in the struggle.

After unlocking the car, he slid in, gunned the motor, and headed for the Arpad Bridge.

Somewhere in the *Zorka Cyrka*—his home since childhood—among the circus's tents, RVs, dressing rooms, and show trunks was a clown costume, missing a button. And he was going to find it. Find out who owned it.

And he'd never let them hurt another child.

CHAPTER TWO

Sylvie
Budapest, Hungary

> *When arriving at the deceased's house,*
> *always leave your shoes outside. No sense*
> *ruining good shoes with corpse stains.*
> *~ The Bloodwalker's Book*

Sylvie gathered her long skirt in one hand, her suitcase in the other, and wobbled down the steep train steps after her mother. She made it to the platform without tumbling on her face but then ruined any semblance of propriety when her mouth dropped open, and she gawked at Hungary's Keleti railway station.

Her entire Romanian village could have fit inside the immense building. It dwarfed the trains. Its ceiling floated a hundred feet above. Without pillars to support it. It hung as if magically suspended from the clouds.

By the time her gaze fell earthward again, her mother had vanished in the crowd.

Sylvie sprang onto tiptoe, searching for her mother's black dress and white crocheted cap. So many people. Too many. Heads bobbed. Bodies swerved. Colors blurred from the Hungarians' garish clothes. Tracksuits. T-shirts and jeans. Women in pants. A few teen girls wore shorts— right out in the open, in front of everyone.

Sylvie turned on the spot, her bulky shoes stepping all over each other in her panic, and prayed for a glimpse of her mother's cap. Thinking she'd spotted it, she pushed through the crowd, only to find a man wearing a white baseball hat.

"No, no," she whispered, swallowing the acid suddenly

15

climbing her throat. She couldn't be lost. Not on the most important day of her life.

People streamed by, jarring her shoulders, clipping her elbows. A dark-haired man gazing down at his phone banged into her, almost knocking her down. Instead of apologizing, he continued on as if nothing happened.

Other commuters dodged her, but then turned to look back with raised brows, ogling her from top to bottom.

Sylvie shrank from their gazes and examined her floor-length dress. It was clean. No stains, no dirt. Even her cuffs and long apron shone as white and pristine as when she'd left home that morning.

Was her outfit really so strange?

Or had they guessed what she was?

She clutched her suitcase to her chest, trying to avoid the prying glances and the impacts of passengers brushing past. Cowering simply produced more stares. But she felt safer behind her makeshift shield. At least it was light, although it contained all her belongings. A tiny box for a tiny life.

A hand gripped her elbow, and she gave a startled yelp.

"Where were you? You're slipperier than goose grease!" The words lashed out, and Sylvie cringed. Her mother impatiently swept a lock of flaxen hair off Sylvie's face and tucked it back under her cap. "There's no reason to be nervous. Everything will be fine."

"Of course it will," Sylvie murmured.

Her mother's eyebrows arched in the familiar I-know-you're-lying look. "Sylvie, listen to me. Your wedding will go as planned."

Though almost forty, her mother still had the rawboned look of a teenager. All Skomori women had high cheekbones and sharp chins, but on her mother, the features seemed too sharp, too pale, as if her white skin was carved from ice. She drew herself erect, and Sylvie could almost hear every chiseled vertebrae snapping into place.

In a gruff voice, her mother decreed, "I have seen it, so it will come to pass."

Whenever her mother used that authoritative tone to make predictions, Sylvie's skin prickled, but this time, the reassuring words didn't help.

Her wedding day should have been her happiest moment—yet her nerves were strung tighter than the twine she used to sew corpse's eyes shut.

"Come along, Sylvie, we're late already. Let's hope the others haven't left." Her mother took Sylvie's elbow, steered her toward the end of the platform, and then up the stairs.

Sunlight from tall windows flooded a vast foyer and bounced blindingly off its marble floor. Sylvie spotted the other two brides waiting for them by the exit doors. At their sides, their mothers fidgeted in their long black dresses, dark as grave pits, the emblem of married women.

Across the foyer, dozens of passengers flowed in and out, frowning, pushing, rushing for their trains. Their footsteps reverberated off the ceiling and walls. The sound filled the space with a loud patter as if trapped birds were throwing themselves at the windows, lured by blue sky and the promise of freedom.

Sylvie's feet dragged and then stopped altogether. The other four bloodwalkers hadn't seen her yet. She still had time to turn and run away.

"Don't let them spook you." Her mother tightened her fingers on Sylvie's arm. "They know nothing about your past. If you keep your mind clear and draw no attention to yourself, they won't notice a thing."

"But there are four of them." Sylvie's breath came in short hiccups. "One is bound to sense I'm not...like them."

"Then you'll have to convince them you *are* like them! Eighteen years of bloodwalker rules and rituals aren't good enough?" Without waiting for a reply, her mother continued. "The people back home may know, but that doesn't mean anyone else has to. You must be careful. Very careful."

"I'll try, but—" Sylvie clacked her teeth shut, locking her words inside. Across the way, the bloodwalker mothers looked around impatiently, all sharp angles and hard eyes. The dam inside her burst. "I hate this! I don't want to be here. Can't you fix it so I can go back home?" As soon as she saw her mother's appalled expression, Sylvie wished she could take it back. This disaster wasn't her mother's fault. *She* was a real bloodwalker—saw souls, heard the dead's voices, and gave messages to their families. Sylvie couldn't, no matter how hard she tried. Even when all she had to do was prepare a body...somehow, things just went wrong.

Sylvie wiped a sweaty palm on her dress. If word got back to the Skomori elders about all her mistakes, the bungled rituals, and worse, that she couldn't bloodwalk, they'd cast her out. Ban her from every clan and town. Without home, friends, or money, she'd never survive. "I'm sorry. It's all my fault."

"No..." Her mother's stony façade cracked, her features weighted down by sadness. "I should have quieted the complaints and gossip. But the talk hasn't reached the elders yet. In your new home, no one will know you. It'll be a fresh start. Just get through today without letting them suspect you." She smiled and squeezed Sylvie's hand. "Okay?"

Sylvie nodded though her heart still told her to run.

"Keep your wits about you, and everything will be all right." Her mother led the way through the mass of travelers, Sylvie trailing behind.

The other two mothers gave them curt greetings and passed judgment on their lateness with the Gaze-of-Condemnation, a staple in any Skomori woman's repertoire. Sylvie had seen it often enough in her home town.

"Liana and I left the Carpathian mountains before dawn to make it here on time," said the mother of a tall, blond bride who chewed a wad of bubblegum.

"Lowlanders." Liana stared at them and popped her gum with a loud smack.

Sylvie's eyes devoured the girl's long purple gown with its sheer sleeves and lilac ruffles at wrists and collar. Every tiny seam perfect. Store bought for sure. Sylvie fingered her hand-sewn cuffs and winced at the threads hanging from the edges.

"Don't they have clocks in whatever tiny village you're from?" The other bride's mother gave a petulant huff. "We're all here now. Go on, Ada...Ada!" She elbowed her mousy-haired daughter.

The girl, who looked about sixteen, stopped counting travelers with umbrellas and mumbling about bad omens. Pink flared in her cheeks. She dug two flowers from a pocket of her apron and handed one to Sylvie and the other to Liana. "Crocus," she said with a shy smile. "I picked them this morning."

"Thank you." Sylvie accepted the bedraggled white bloom that symbolized auspicious beginnings.

Liana made a face. "I hope our futures fare better than this did." She dropped the flower in her purse and retrieved two salt shakers. "Bees' wings and powdered ash bark, in a silver shaker." She handed one to each girl. "Sprinkle this in your bread dough and your husband's business will always prosper!"

Real silver? Sylvie cradled the gift, the metal warming in her palm. She'd never owned anything so expensive.

After the oo-ing and ah-ing from the daughters and mothers alike, it was Sylvie's turn. She knelt and opened her suitcase. Her stomach squeezed tight as she reached for the sachet packets. It had taken three months to collect the ingredients for the bloodwalkers' strongest charm. But what if the sachets weren't good enough? What if the girls didn't like them, or suspected they wouldn't work? She handed a bag to each bride and forced the ritual words past the lump in her throat.

"In the blackest of plagues, we lit the way,
From town to town, behind the dray,
Collecting the dead, from gutter and hearth,
To bury them deep, in cold, cold earth.
But when souls speak, to soothe their kin,
We open death's door, and let them in."

"For we are bloodwalkers," the others finished the recitation in a hushed tone.

"Is this really a *Farmece Arkana*?" Liana frowned at her packet. "You want us to believe you found capuci centipedes, at midnight, during a new moon?"

"Yes." It had taken weeks for Sylvie to locate them under a rotten log and then wait for the next new moon to collect the squirming six-inch creatures.

"And chicken beaks, bearberries, and bladderwort?"

Sylvie nodded. The bladderwort plant had been the hardest to find. It floated in water and ate insects and small animals. She'd found a field mouse in hers, partially digested.

"Okay. But tell me how you got a bone of a real bloodwalker from the Black Plague. That's more than five hundred years ago."

"It's from Kutna Hora, in the Czech Republic. Mama's cousin is the caretaker of the bone church." At Liana's skeptical expression, a pleading note crept into Sylvie's voice. "I did everything right. This *is* the *Farmece Arkana*. It will make us into great bloodwalkers. Perfect ones. I swear..." Words dried up as her confidence deserted her. Although she'd followed the recipe exactly and desperately wished it would work, she was certain it wouldn't. Nothing ever did.

"Pull in your claws, Liana," the girl's mother scolded. "Thank the girl."

"Yes, indeed." Ada's mother beamed. "It's such a glorious gift!"

As the others complimented Sylvie, delight warmed her cheeks, and she dropped her gaze to the marble tiles.

A rubber ball rolled under the hem of her skirt and bumped her foot. She squatted to pick it up and found a toddler careening across the floor, a grin on his face, his arms outstretched. With a smile, she placed the ball into his grasping fingers.

A shadow slid over them. A gray-haired woman bent down and slapped the ball away. She hissed Hungarian words Sylvie didn't understand.

"I-I'm sorry," Sylvie began in Romanian, but the old woman switched to badly accented Romanian and cut her off.

"Don't touch him, you filthy girl." Her eyes shrank to slits in her weathered skin, and she scooped up the boy. "Bad enough you put your unclean hands on his toy. I know what you are—Skomori ghoul!" She spat in Sylvie's face.

Sylvie reeled back and fell on her rump.

The old lady stabbed a finger at the others. "Crawl back into the disgusting graves you came from. Your kind's not welcome here!" She whirled and stalked off, the little boy peering back over her shoulder, his eyes misting, one hand outstretched toward the ball.

Sylvie struggled to her feet. The other women glanced about, fear bleaching their faces. Even Liana appeared uncertain.

"This is a terrible omen!" Ada's eyes glittered with tears.

Her mother shushed her, and the whole group barreled out of the building like criminals. Commuters dodged out of their way. On a clear patch of sidewalk away from the entrance, the woman stopped and huddled together.

Taking a handkerchief from her pocket, Sylvie's mother wiped the spittle off her face.

"I'm so sorry," Sylvie whispered. "If I hadn't touched the ball, this wouldn't have happened."

"It's not your fault," her mother said. "Some of the *Baran* are more wicked and stupid than others."

"Mongrels!" Ada's mother said. "Marrying anyone instead of keeping their line pure. That's how they end up so stupid and frail."

"May their blood become vinegar and their hair fall out!" Liana's mother spat in her hand and rubbed her fist in it, sealing the curse.

"But my groom has a shop in Miskolc," Sylvie said. "He deals with the *Baran*..." She halted beneath cutting looks.

"How do you know that?" Liana's mother snapped. "The elders chose him. You shouldn't know anything except his name."

"I told her," Sylvie's mother raised her chin. "My late husband's Aunt Cosmina, the elder who will perform the ceremony today, naturally made sure Sylvie's groom had a good livelihood."

The others' faces soured like pickles, but they held their tongues. Favoritism was rife in the Skomori clans, all depending on how closely one was related to Zora, the oldest living elder who could trace her lineage back to Ratmir of Novgorod. Zora was a bloodwalker, a powerful one. Legend had it she was born with a foot in both worlds, the living and the dead.

Ada's mother dried her daughter's tears while Liana and her mother stared daggers at Sylvie.

From across the parking lot, a silver-haired woman in a long black dress limped toward them, leaning heavily on a cane.

Sylvie's mother ran out to embrace her while the other two brides' mothers bent their heads together.

"Look," Liana's mother whispered. "The bloodwalker's curse is upon her."

"Heaven protect us from that horror!" Ada's mother crossed herself.

Sylvie's brow wrinkled. She knew every Skomori superstition and rule by heart but had never heard of a bloodwalker's curse.

As Aunt Cosmina drew closer, Sylvie straightened up and tried to clear her mind of all doubt and fear. Considering the woman was an elder, she might be as prescient as Sylvie's mother. In their village, grieving families and neighbors came all the time for advice and remarked on how her mother knew things no one could and how her predictions always came true.

The nearer the elder got, the more Sylvie's heart fluttered. If only she could make it through this one day. Her mother had promised that her groom was from a faraway city where no other Skomori lived. A man said to be modern minded. One who might not care if Sylvie forgot things, like scattering owl droppings on the hearth every month, adding spider eggs to the porridge, or hanging a rat skeleton over the bed to ensure marital harmony.

All things that the elders swore kept the Skomori strong and healthy. No Skomori ever got so much as a cold.

"Hello!" Aunt Cosmina smiled as she reached the sidewalk. "Don't you girls look lovely!" With twinkling eyes, flushed cheeks, and the smell of cherry pie wafting from her, she wasn't at all what Sylvie expected. Maybe it wouldn't be so hard to keep her weaknesses hidden after all.

"The sun pales beside your shining face, *Oma*," Sylvie and the brides recited in unison and curtsied.

After allowing the mothers to kiss her on both cheeks, Aunt Cosmina said, "A fine crop of youngsters you've brought me. Their new husbands will be well pleased."

"We are honored our girls have been chosen and are most grateful someone of your status will be performing the ceremony." Liana's mother kept nodding and bowing like an old pump handle.

"Indeed," Ada's mother chirped. "I can hardly believe our good fortune that you're doing the ritual!"

Aunt Cosmina's grin stretched wider. "Then you'll be even more pleased when I tell you we're going to Obudai Island, and someone far more important than I will perform the wedding."

The women stared at her blankly.

A chill of foreboding ran down Sylvie's back.

"We are lucky enough to have the *Zorka Cyrka* in town, and you know what that means..."

"No!" Liana's mother's eyes lit up, and she bounced on the balls of her feet.

"Yes!" Aunt Cosmina crowed. "The services will be performed by none other than Zora herself!"

Hoots of elation sounded, and the girls and their mothers hugged. Sylvie barely clung to her smile as vomit burned the back of her throat.

She could possibly fool Aunt Cosmina long enough to make it through the ritual, but her hopes shattered at the name of the Skomori woman who'd officiate the marriage.

Zora. The most powerful bloodwalker alive. The one who could uncover the lies and secrets concealed in every heart.

CHAPTER THREE

Rurik
Obudai Island, Hungary

Sausages sizzled and popped in a frying pan, spattering oil over the countertop in Rurik's RV camper. A few burning drops landed on his bare chest, but he hardly noticed. The lightning strike that seared his face and chest hadn't left many nerve endings alive.

He threw diced tomatoes into the pan. A steam cloud boiled up, and a layer of condensation fogged the window above the sink. When he fished the farmer's cheese out of the refrigerator, he sniffed it and almost gagged. Between chasing the killer, secretly combing the circus tents for the clown costume, and working, he'd forgotten groceries.

He lobbed the rank cheese into the trash can where it splattered against an empty vodka bottle.

"Katenka?" his father called in a slurred voice from the bedroom. "Make me blinis."

Katenka, Rurik's mother, had died eight years earlier, but with enough vodka, the dead could come back to life. At least in his father's mind.

"Omelet and sausage today, Papa," Rurik said.

"I want blinis..." A minute later, snores rumbled from the bedroom.

"Rurik! Rurik!" From outside, a woman's voice cut through the snores.

In three strides, Rurik crossed the dining area to the camper's door and threw it open.

Marva rushed down the line of parked RVs, her wrinkled face flushed as red as her hair. She owned the best dog act in the business and doubled as the circus nurse. Few

24

things rattled her.

Rurik's mind leaped to possible emergencies. Fire? An accident? Someone hurt? He hoped not. The circus people couldn't take any more bad luck.

"It's Ivan and Alexei." Marva arrived at the door, panting. "They're going to kill each other!"

Before she finished, Rurik whirled and shut off the stove's burner. He then dove into the pile of dirty clothes in the corner, searching for his Security shirt. Damn laundry. Another chore forgotten. A chunky mess coated the clothes, gluing them together. He sniffed. Vomit mixed with vodka. His father hadn't made it to the bathroom again.

"Hurry!" Marva called.

All his clothes reeked of alcohol. One whiff and the gossips would pounce. They'd make a beeline for the manager, Alyosha.

Rurik couldn't take the chance. If he lost this job, he'd never be hired on the outside. Not with his looks.

He sprang from the vehicle bare-chested and ran beside Marva between the dented and scratched RVs. Black-out curtains darkened almost every window despite the fact it was after noon. Circus people kept vampire hours.

Rurik glanced at the sky out of habit. Bright sun. No storm clouds. No lightning. His breathing eased slightly. "Where are they? In their tent?" he said.

"No, they're in..."–Marva paused, gasping for air–"...in Johan's workshop."

He slowed, more worried about the woman who was like a second mother to him than about Ivan and Alexei. Those two were probably fighting over something stupid.

"Don't wait...for me." Marva stopped and bent over, a hand clasped to her ribs. She waved him on with the other. "Go on! Stop that fight!"

Leaving the parked vehicles behind, he sprinted toward the next meadow. The slaps of canvas hitting poles grew louder. Two dozen tents filled the grassland. Constant exposure to the weather had faded all the tents to the same greenish gray. Silver duct tape fluttered in the wind, peeling from rips and holes in badly-patched canvas.

Sloping roofs sagged. Rusty poles propped up lopsided awnings.

On the far side, like an astounding mirage, the brilliant white and red stripes of the big top soared into the sky.

At night, strings of tiny lights transformed the circus into a fairyland, dusting everything with magic. The magic lost its sparkle in the daylight, but the gleaming big top never did. At least, not to Rurik.

Outside Johan's carpentry tent, a red pickup truck glinted in the sunshine. Tied to its bed was a motorcycle spray-painted with leaping flames and the name "Alexei" in big letters. About a dozen circus folk, some still in their bathrobes, clustered around the tent opening, peering in.

Rurik stopped. A shaky breath filled his lungs. He knew what was coming, but that didn't make it any easier. "Let me through," he demanded.

Faces swung toward him. Eyes latched onto the mass of scars ridging his chest and neck. Some lingered on his face, probing every inch of the damaged flesh as if they expected it to have changed since the last time they saw him.

It wasn't the ones who stared that bothered him most. He understood their fascination with ugliness—the same way people slowed when passing an accident on the highway, mesmerized by blood and broken limbs. Those people drove away flushed with relief, their own problems suddenly seeming small by comparison.

He didn't mind being the one who made others feel lucky.

What bothered him were the ones who wouldn't even look. Their gazes skittered away. They cringed and shuffled sideways as if afraid he'd hurt them, as if he were as vile on the inside as the outside.

Okay, he wasn't the headlining "Strongman" in the circus anymore. Didn't bask in the spotlights as the crowd roared their approval. Didn't earn a lot of money. Wouldn't marry and have children like others. The lightning had destroyed any chance of that.

But he was Chief of Security, and they had to respect the job.

"Move!" he yelled.

The group broke apart in a flurry. Two female gymnasts tripped over the Austrian horse-master. The Serbian jugglers elbowed the Latvian slackliners out of the way.

In the tent's entrance, Rurik spotted Yuri, another security guard. The overweight, balding man met his gaze, gasped, and shoved a wad of money into his pocket while whipping a pad he'd been writing on behind his back.

Taking bets. Typical. Rurik would tend to him later.

Rurik pushed past and entered the tent. The smells of fresh lumber, sawdust, and the oily odor of paint wafted up his nostrils.

A table flew through the air and clattered into a tool closet, tossed out of the way by two Russian men. Built like bulls, Ivan and Alexei circled each other, fists up, blood trickling from cuts on cheeks and eyebrows. By the sweat dripping off them and their heaving chests, Rurik figured the fight was winding down. But then, Ivan—the leader of the motorcycle act—landed an uppercut on Alexei's jaw, knocking the younger man off his feet.

"Go ahead and leave, traitor!" Ivan stood over Alexei, his swollen lips and bloodied mustache garbling his words. "But you're not taking my sign!" He picked up a large painted canvas from the ground and made it three steps toward the exit before Alexei jumped up and leaped onto his back. The sign tumbled to the floor. Ivan collapsed onto his knees, arms pinned behind him by Alexei.

"Enough!" Rurik said, but Ivan ignored him.

The older man dropped his chin, gray locks flopping onto his sweaty forehead, and then snapped his head back. His skull slammed into Alexei's face.

Alexei staggered backward, a hand flying to his nose. Blood seeped between his fingers.

Ivan climbed to his feet, spun around, and punched Alexei in the eye. "Ha! You may be able to ride your bike with one eye swelled shut—but how about both!" He cocked his arm for another punch.

Rurik leaped between the two, wrapped a fist in each shirtfront, and held them apart. All three of them topped six feet, but Rurik's abnormally dense bones made him far more powerful. "Stop it," he roared. "What the hell is wrong with you?"

"Nothing." Alexei dragged his forearm across his nose, smearing blood and mucus onto his cheek. "I just want my sign."

"*My* sign, you ungrateful ass!" Ivan tried to smack Rurik's hand away and get at Alexei, but couldn't get past Rurik's steely grip.

"Look at this!" Alexei bent down, lifted the painting, and pointed past the words *Ivan & Alexei's Globe of Death* to the picture of a man straddling a motorcycle. "This is me, not you, and I'm taking it with me, old man." He strode out the exit, shoving past Yuri and the gawking onlookers.

"When you come crawling back, you better bring it with you!" Ivan shook loose from Rurik's grip and glared at him. "A lot of help you were. You're supposed to stop thieves from taking things."

Rurik folded his arms over his chest and gave his friend the look—the one he used to scare off parking lot buskers who mooched customers from the circus.

"Don't you use your monster face on me. I'm old enough to be your father. Show some respect."

"Then act like a man who deserves respect," Rurik said.

Ivan's neck and face darkened in a flush. Throwing back his shoulders, he stomped toward the exit. "Nothing to see here! Go back to your own damn tents," he bellowed, sending people scurrying.

Marva appeared and blocked his way. "That split lip looks bad. You need stitches."

Ivan puffed out his chest. "It's nothing," he said and stalked off.

"Yuri." Rurik's menacing tone carried across the tent to where Yuri was trying to slink away with the others.

Yuri pulled his collar away from his flabby neck, and his lips tweaked up in a half-hearted smile. "Just a little sport, boss."

"Why aren't you behind the main tent, setting up for the wedding?"

"Johan and Misha are there. They can handle it."

Rurik's jaw tightened. Yuri probably hadn't even showed

up, and Johan was too old to be lifting things. "Come with me." He left the workshop and headed for the big top.

Marva fell into step beside him. "I have to talk to you," she whispered. "Privately."

He raised an eyebrow at her. "Something wrong?"

"Yes." She peered over her shoulder to where a sulky-faced Yuri plodded through the grass twenty yards behind them. "This morning I woke up to find the Petrovich trailer gone. They joined the Olympia Circus! And from the mess back there,"—she tipped her head at Johan's tent—"it seems we've lost a cyclist. Ivan will look ridiculous circling the cage by himself. Plus, the slackliners are demanding more money, and the Bartelli family is feuding and half refuse to perform tonight."

Just great. The Petrovich's defection meant five acts had left the circus in the last month. Box office receipts were lower than any year he could remember, but there wasn't a damn thing he could do about it. "You should talk to Alyosha."

"I did." Marva's tone sharpened. "But he isn't doing anything! The whole circus is coming apart, and this bloodwalker wedding is making it worse. When I was a kid and Alyosha married Zora, he could keep everyone in line. No one dared say a thing against her. But he's never around anymore except during the show, and the people are getting angry about Zora and the bloodwalkers. They're afraid tourists on the island will spot them and word will get out. The last thing we need are rumors keeping customers away. And with Alyosha changing our tour schedule every week, we can't advertise properly to begin with."

Rurik's hand rose, rubbing at the scar that ran across his temple and into his hairline. He hated to hear anything against the man who'd done so much for him. As far as he was concerned Alyosha always had everyone's best interests at heart, and it didn't sit right to hear others criticize. Not even Marva. "It's true we're in Budapest early this year, but Zora's been too ill to do a wedding for a long time. Alyosha's probably happy she's feeling good enough to do one this year."

"There's one more thing." Marva's gaze flashed around the surroundings nervously, and she lowered her voice. "Someone told the clowns you were in their tent while they were working last night. Now they're claiming things are missing... They've made threats."

Rurik's steps faltered. None of the clowns wore a costume like the killer's, but to make sure they weren't hiding it, he'd snuck in and opened every trunk and closet looking for it. He'd found nothing. "It's just gossip. It'll blow over." He feigned an indifferent shrug, but knew he'd have to be more cautious when searching the other tents and RVs.

"Rishya."

The old pet-name made him stop and turn toward her.

"Things are worse than I've ever seen them. I think there's going to be trouble, and I'm worried about you." Her eyes watered, and she swallowed hard. "You have to be careful, Rishya. Promise me!"

He reached out and gave her shoulders a gentle squeeze. Beneath his large hands, her bones felt as delicate as the *trubocki* puff pastries she liked to bake. "Don't worry. I can handle anything that comes my way. I'll be fine."

"You'd better be." She wagged a finger at him before hurrying away, swiping at her cheeks.

He shook his head. Marva was sweet, but her warning didn't change his plans. He'd been up all night thinking about how to catch the killer. The police would be patrolling Istvantelek depot after the attempted abduction yesterday. The murderer would have to find a new location. Since Rurik couldn't be everywhere, he saw only one solution. He'd stake out the island's only bridge all afternoon and turn back any circus people who tried to leave.

If the killer couldn't get off the island, Budapest's children would be safe.

He just had to make sure Yuri and Misha—his two deputy security guards—watched the bloodwalkers' ceremony and headed off any problems, so he could guard the bridge.

In a clearing behind the big top, two long tables had been set up, but nothing else. Johan and Misha crawled over a big trellis-like structure lying on the ground. Johan's white hair glistened from the gel keeping his pompadour in place. The old man was ridiculously vain about it. He might wear threadbare shirts, have sawdust under his fingernails, and stink of sweat, but his hair was always perfect.

Johan spotted Rurik and stabbed a finger at the trellis. "The damn wedding arch hasn't been used for so long the wood rotted. One of the legs collapsed."

"So just set up an awning instead. Who will know?"

"Who? *Who?* Alyosha will! And Zora." Johan shuddered, his wrinkled face puckering. "No! I'm not having them say I can't do my job. I just have to build a support base. Misha's helping." He pointed his hammer at a lanky teen who grinned at Rurik. "It'll be done in a half hour, so if Alyosha asks, you tell him everything's fine. Except I need someone to go to equipment truck three and find the plastic roses we drape on this thing."

Rurik beckoned Yuri over. "Here, explain to Yuri where—"

"Are you kidding?" Johan interrupted. "He'll disappear again, and I won't get my roses! You go."

Dammit! The killer might be getting into a car any moment and making for the bridge. But the wedding was important to Alyosha, and Yuri couldn't be trusted to search for the roses. Rurik clamped stern eyes on Yuri. "I'll get the roses. But since Misha's busy, you have to wait in the tourist's parking lot for the brides and their mothers."

"The *bloodwalkers*? Hell no. I'm not interested in babysitting those freaks."

"Are you interested in getting paid next week?"

Yuri looked down. His toe dug into the soft earth. "Yeah..."

"Then meet the women and bring them to the dressing room trailer."

"But I can't do that, boss. Madame Nadia will go crazy! She said if she sees those bloodwalker bitches—her words—near her wardrobe trailer, she'll quit."

Rurik ground his teeth. He'd never get to the bridge at this rate. "Then take the women to the public restroom building. Stay with them to make sure they're okay, and then escort them here. You got it?"

Yuri mumbled something.

"I can't hear you," Rurik bit off each word.

"All right, all right..." Yuri trudged off in the direction of the public parking lot.

Leaving Johan and Misha repairing the trellis arch, Rurik jogged to the rear of the encampment and headed down the row of semi-trucks until he found the one marked "3." His key ring held over two dozen keys, but he'd labeled them and quickly found the one for the trailer. The back doors swung open with a screech. He vaulted inside.

Dusty spotlights and spools of electrical wire and steel cable lay stacked on one side of the truck bed. On the walls, ladders, hydraulic hoses, and extra supports for the audience bleachers hung on metal hooks. He sped to the end, where cartons held props and set pieces for the acts.

Pulling open the first one to look for the plastic roses, he suddenly realized he should be looking for the clown costume, too.

When he'd come up empty in the clowns' quarters, he'd mentally cleared them from the list of suspects—but he hadn't considered the trucks. *Zorka Cyrka* traveled with six equipment trucks, two horse trailers, and a converted horse trailer for Marva's dogs.

The killer could have secreted the costume inside any of them. He could still be one of the clowns.

Rurik crushed the cardboard flap in his hand. He should have thought of it before. Now he had no time to search all six equipment trucks. It was getting late. He had to find the roses, grab some clean clothes, and stake out the bridge.

A grunt came from the rear of the trailer, and the floor dipped as a group of men climbed in.

"We hear you visit our tent last night." Silhouetted against the sunlight, the speaker was a black shape, but Rurik knew that Italian accent anywhere. Antonelli. Leader of the clowns. "Funny thing,"—Antonelli gave a snarling laugh—"we not remember inviting you."

The group cackled in appreciation.

Antonelli's tone hardened. "No one allowed in our tent.

Ever."

"As head of security, I go where I want," Rurik said, but there was really no point in arguing. The Italian comics were a nasty bunch, and nothing would stop them from what they'd come to do.

"Security." The shortest of the six spat on the floor. "You're no cop—just nosy like one. You gotta learn to mind your own business."

Six against one. Hardly a fair fight. But the clowns knew that whatever happened, Rurik wouldn't rat them out. Even if he did, they wouldn't be fired.

There were only two punishable offenses in circus life. You never messed with someone else's act, and you never, ever involved the police. Everything else was fair game.

Knowing minutes were ticking past, and he had to get to the bridge, Rurik raised his fists and tucked his chin. "Come on then."

CHAPTER FOUR

Sylvie
Obudai Island, Hungary

> *All haste must be made to reach the corpse before it*
> *stiffens.*
> *If you arrive too late, be sure you order the relatives to*
> *leave*
> *before you begin breaking the joints and snapping the*
> *sinews.*
> ~ The Bloodwalker's Book

"No. This absolutely won't do," Aunt Cosmina said as soon as she set foot inside the Obudai Island public restroom.

Sylvie and the other two brides peeked in.

Footprints from a hundred muddy shoes covered the tiled floor, the mirrors hung crooked and broken over the sinks, and the smell was enough to make even the bloodwalkers screw up their faces in disgust—and that was a rare thing. Working with dead bodies tended to drum out any squeamishness early in life.

The security guard, a fat, middle-aged man with a face as sour as tripe soup, folded his mouth in a stubborn line. "Use this or go behind bushes to change," he said, his Romanian barely understandable.

"Behind the bushes?" Ada echoed in a small voice. The youngest bride looked like she might cry again.

"Don't worry, girls." Aunt Cosmina smiled serenely. "We'll just go see Alyosha and Zora. I will explain that Mister…"—she waddled over to the guard and squinted at his nametag—"Yuri Corkov couldn't find us a clean and proper place to change. I'm sure Alyosha will find us one."

At the ringmaster's name, the man looked like he'd

34

swallowed a chicken bone. "No! I find you somewhere else." He swung away, grumbling something in Russian under his breath.

Sylvie didn't know what he said but guessed it was nasty. Zorka clan members loathed the Skomori, which made no sense considering they shared the same ancient Slavic lineage. They were practically cousins. But some wedge had driven apart the clans centuries ago. The reason was lost to time. Only the hatred remained.

The girls traipsed behind Aunt Cosmina's limping figure as the man led them across a field to several rows of parked RVs. Some had colorful lawn chairs set outside with wide awnings stretched above. Smoke from a grill spiraled into the air, bringing with it the smell of braised ribs. Instead of making Sylvie hungry, the nausea brewing in her stomach worsened with every step that took her farther from home. Farther from the life she knew. Farther from safety.

Ada tugged Sylvie's sleeve and pointed at the sky. "That cloud has a fire giant's face. Very bad luck."

Sylvie didn't bother looking up; she was more worried about the other faces.

Eyes scrutinized them from camper windows, mean eyes above angry frowns.

"Ada, stop looking for bad omens, and you'll stop finding them." Liana tossed her head, and the dyed-blond highlights in her hair glimmered in the sunlight.

That must have caused talk in her village. Skomori women didn't believe in wasting money on hair salons, cosmetics, or fancy clothes. Nonetheless, shiny high-heeled boots peeped from under Liana's long skirt, a far cry from the staid mud-plodders Sylvie and Ada wore.

"I wonder what my groom will be like." Liana trod lightly through the grass, steps bouncy, hips swinging. "I hope he's big, strong, handsome, and makes lots of money! What about you?" she said , grinning at Ada and Sylvie.

"I just want one who's kind," Ada mumbled.

"Sylvie?" Liana said . "You're the oldest, so you'll probably get the oldest groom. But what if he's decrepit and wrinkly?"

Sylvie hung her head. Dandelions burst into clouds

of fluff beneath her feet. At eighteen, she *was* old for a Skomori bride. Most married at fifteen or sixteen. But a regular village girl could say no when a boy tied a goat or pig to her family's gate, signifying what he was willing to trade for her. Bloodwalkers had to marry whomever the elders chose. "I-I'm not sure... I guess I want someone who'll love me."

Both girls blinked at her, and Aunt Cosmina threw a scandalized glance over her shoulder. "Bloodwalkers do not marry for love. That would be selfish."

"No..."—Sylvie thought fast—"I meant I wanted to bring love to a home. To the children we'd have." She ducked her head again. Children. A fine example she'd set for them when she couldn't perform Skomori and bloodwalker rites correctly to begin with. It was too difficult. She was bound to fail. What if her new husband threw her out?

A cascade of frightening thoughts ran through her mind. Bad omens. Zora seeing through her lies. Being cast out. Her stomach churned. The dandelions tangled with her feet. She staggered.

Ada grabbed her arm. "Are you okay?"

Somehow, Sylvie righted herself and gained control. *No doubts. No fear. Not today.*

"I'm fine." She held her head up and gave the others a smile.

Ada leaned in. "Don't worry. It's good luck if a bride faints on her wedding day. Even better if she throws up."

Great. Then Sylvie was well on her way to an auspicious marriage.

The guard trod past rows of parked vehicles until he reached one at the very end, sitting off by itself. The shabby RV was sun-bleached beige, its bumpers rusty, and its windows lined with dark film that was cracked and bubbled.

The man pulled at the door. When it didn't budge, he wrenched it open. Hinges cried in protest, like someone in pain. "This one is empty since Zim-Zim the Snake Charmer left." He bared his teeth in a grin. "He said he lost one or two snakes, so maybe you find them inside." His dark chuckle faded as he swaggered away.

Aunt Cosmina herded everyone up the steps. "Quick, girls, hurry and change. Being late to the ceremony is an insult to your grooms."

"But...the snakes!" Ada whimpered, hanging back in the doorway.

Liana snickered. "He's just trying to scare us, you idiot. There are no snakes." The tall girl led the way with Sylvie and the others following. She strode into the cabin, her gaze roaming the chipped countertops, ragged curtains, and stained walls. "Even snakes wouldn't live in this dump."

Sylvie agreed. Snakes wouldn't live there. Maybe frogs would, considering all the flies buzzing around. Mildew, old food, and stale sweat fought for dominance with the odor of bleach. And beneath those smells was another, a faint one that seemed familiar. Sylvie couldn't place it, but it made her uneasy.

"How do you know there are no snakes? There might be." Ada's gaze darted into every corner.

"Sylvie?" Aunt Cosmina said . "What is the first rule for bloodwalkers?"

Sylvie's heartbeats stuttered, but she answered by rote. "Bloodwalkers must never be afraid." Why had Aunt Cosmina asked her that? Had she seen through Sylvie's pretense? Had she seen her fear?

"And that includes snakes," Aunt Cosmina said to Ada and chuckled.

Sylvie practically sagged with relief. Aunt Cosmina hadn't seen inside Sylvie's mind. If she had, she'd know Sylvie had failed the fear rule many times before.

Once, a corpse's hand twitched when she was cleaning his nails, and she'd nearly wet herself. It took five minutes for her to get up the courage to approach him again, during which he'd jerked two more times. He was fresh. The fresh ones twitched.

"Take your things into the bedroom and get changed." Aunt Cosmina approached a small dining table marred by gashes, as if a butcher had used his cleaver on it. She plopped her oversized satchel on top and eyed Ada. "You are stronger than you think you are."

Liana snorted.As Ada crept past, Liana crooned, "Snaaakes," sending Ada leaping to the bedroom.

"Liana! Mind your mouth," Aunt Cosmina snapped.

When Liana rolled her eyes, Aunt Cosmina closed the gap between them and thrust her face close to Liana's. Then the woman continued in the low, hypnotic bloodwalker voice Sylvie's mother used so well.

"I know all about you, Liana Platko, with your fancy clothes and hair. You can't slink into the city time after time unnoticed. Everyone knows what you're doing. Reading palms, making *potiune magica*, and selling charms to outsiders like a common fortune teller."

Liana's mouth dropped open, and Sylvie backed up a half step. How did Aunt Cosmina know all that?

"With *Baran* money in your pocket, you think you're better than everyone else?" Aunt Cosmina brows arched wickedly over her unblinking eyes.

"Nooo..." Liana pressed herself against the kitchen counter, looking like she wanted to crawl up into the cupboards hanging above her, and Sylvie was scared enough to climb in after her.

"In half an hour, you will marry," Aunt Cosmina said in a whispery drone, like the wind rustling in a chimney flue. "You will go with your new husband to his town. If you think he'll let you sneak away to the city like a trollop, if you think he'll sit idle while you flounce around his town in pretty things bought with *your earnings*, I can assure you his fists will soon teach you otherwise."

"I—but—" Liana began.

"Silence! You will marry and become a good Skomori wife, and you will do your duty as a bloodwalker for the people in your new town. Lucky for you, your veil will hide that dyed hair or your groom would surely refuse to marry you. He may still take a scissors to it while you sleep tonight."

Liana gasped, and her hands flew to her blond locks. She dove toward the bedroom, throwing a terrified glance behind her.

Sylvie tiptoed after her, trying to escape Aunt Cosmina's attention.

"Wait, Sylvie."

Sylvie froze and slowly turned to face the inevitable.

"I have something for you." Aunt Cosmina dug in her bag and pulled out a paper-bound parcel.

Confused, Sylvie inched forward and picked it up. The wrapping fell away to reveal the most beautiful lace she'd ever seen. The veil was dark crimson, shot through with silver threads, and would match her wedding dress perfectly. And it was long. It would fall to her hips, hiding the horrible mess she'd made of her embroidery on the gown's bodice.

Aunt Cosmina patted her hand. "Don't worry, dear. Your mother mentioned your needlework was a bit lacking, but with this, no one will know."

Sylvie's hands curled around the scarlet lace. She couldn't believe it. Instead of Aunt Cosmina accusing her of something, the woman had given her a lovely, helpful gift—as if she really cared. A lump rose in Sylvie's throat. "Thank you" was the only thing she could choke out.

Aunt Cosmina smiled and pinched Sylvie's cheek. "You're such a good girl. If you have any fault at all, my dear, it's that you worry too much." Closing her cavernous satchel, she picked up her cane and hobbled to the front of the RV. "I must help decorate and keep the mothers company. For heaven's sake, don't be late!"

After the door banged shut, Sylvie began to gather up the veil when a shriek sounded from the bedroom.

"My God! It's ruined!" Ada wailed.

"Don't just stand there—go wash it!" Liana shouted.

Ada burst out of the bedroom, the puffy gold gown she'd changed into filling the doorway. She held up a length of green chiffon in front of her. Splotches of an oily substance darkened the fabric. Above the material, her eyes bulged. "My perfume. The bottle broke. What'll I do?"

"Don't let it touch your dress." Sylvie grabbed the girl's veil, taking care to keep it away from the gold satin. The kitchen's faucet handles spun uselessly, broken, so she raced to the bathroom.

At first, only dirty brown water came from the tap, but after a minute it ran clear.

A foul fishy smell filled the bathroom. Sylvie sniffed at the water, and then at the stained fabric. "This isn't perfume."

"Umm...it's not." Ada blushed. "It's a fertility potion. I'm supposed to take a teaspoon every morning. An old lady in the next town, a *Baran*, gave me the recipe and swore I'd have a baby soon—a *boy*—to make my husband happy."

"It smells like fish oil. And cloves." Sylvie gave another tentative sniff. "But what's the other odor? It's like...a barnyard."

"Bull urine."

"Oh, Ada!" Sylvie thrust the veil under the water, thinking Ada was the one who needed her head soaked. *Baran* potions never worked.

Rubbing and rinsing the material failed to clean it. Above the sink, Sylvie found soap crowded on a shelf with jars of white grease paint, black liner pencils, and red lipstick. Strange colors for a snake charmer to wear. Maybe someone else had been using the RV.

After a few minutes of scrubbing, Sylvie rinsed the veil one last time and held it at arm's length. The fish oil still showed, but had evened out so the whole veil appeared slightly darker.

"That's not too bad, Sylvie." Ada almost smiled before Liana poked her head in.

"But it's soaked," Liana said. "Anything wet will stain your dress. Aren't there any towels in here?" Liana frowned at the empty towel rack. "Guess not. Well, come here and help me pin on my veil." She swirled a length of hot pink lace in the air and turned away.

"How can we dry it?" Ada's eyes welled. "I knew this would happen. My wedding's ruined!"

Sylvie spied a hamper beside the shower stall and threw off the lid. White towels lay in the bottom. She pulled one out, delighted to find it dry to the touch, and quickly rolled the green veil inside it, squeezing as she went. With a grin, she said, "This should do the trick. Your wedding day will be saved after all."

Ada blinked back tears and gave a ghost of a smile in return.

"Come on, Sylvie," Liana called. "We can't be late...Oh! Look at this. It's gorgeous."

Sylvie emerged from the bathroom to find Liana holding the crimson and silver veil, her eyes magpie bright.

"Ohh," Ada breathed. "Is that your veil, Sylvie?"

"Yes. It's mine." Sylvie's stomach clenched as Liana put it on and paraded around.

Liana twirled and posed. The crimson veil clashed with her gown's yellow and orange ruffles, but it was the kind of clash Skomori women liked, especially bloodwalkers. After marriage, bloodwalkers could only wear black dresses, so they celebrated their wedding day with the most dazzling colors they could find. The only things they couldn't wear were beads and sequins. Those were for the Zorka and their lewd circus costumes.

Ada suddenly gasped and pointed at Sylvie's hands. "You're bleeding."

But it wasn't blood. The red smudges on her hands were lipstick. And there were smears of white grease paint, too.

Sylvie unrolled the towel, and her stomach sank.

The veil's water and oil had mixed with dried makeup that Sylvie hadn't noticed on the towel. White, red, and black colors had transferred onto the green, staining it far worse than the original oil.

Ada took the veil and held it up to the light, the hideous blotches leaving no doubt it was ruined. The girl burst into tears.

Her miserable sobs cut into Sylvie. It was all her fault. She'd been the one to take the towel and use it without checking it first. It was what she always did. Messed everything up. And poor Ada was the one to suffer.

Sylvie had to think of a way to fix this.

Sympathetic tears wet her lashes. In her blurred vision, she saw the strangest thing. The white, black, and red stains on the veil resembled a face.

A clown's face.

CHAPTER FIVE

Rurik
Obudai Island, Hungary

The sun, impaled on the highest peak of the distant big top, shone through the open doors of the semi's trailer. Rurik squinted into the light as six Italian men scrambled over piled equipment, jostling to get at him.

A slim scarecrow of a man threw the first punch. Rurik blocked it and shoved the man backward into his cohorts.

A shorter attacker zipped in from the side and struck at Rurik's ribs. With barely any effort, Rurik raised his elbow and whacked it into the scrawny clown's head, sending him tumbling into the truck's wall.

Two other men darted closer, aiming blows at his head and stomach.

Rurik dipped and dodged, deflecting each attack.

One opponent wormed his way behind and chopped at Rurik's kidneys. Rurik sidestepped but stubbed his foot on a spotlight. His guard wavered. A hard blow smacked into his chin.

The clowns, thinner and faster than Rurik, weaved around each other, like they were doing the "fire-drill" skit from their show. Surrounding him, they pressed their advantage, forcing Rurik back toward the stacked boxes at the end of the trailer.

"What's wrong, big Security Chief? A few clowns too much for you?" Antonelli smirked, standing well outside the melee.

Rurik's lips thinned. He could have finished the fight in seconds. Laid them all out like swatting flies. Except for Alyosha's rules. The ringmaster would be furious if his clowns couldn't work because of broken bones or concussions. Performers were the circus's lifeblood—they brought in the money. Rurik was just an employee. Easily replaced.

His defense-only strategy was just prolonging the fight. Consuming the time he needed to get to the bridge. He had to finish his foes without injuring them. Not too badly, anyway.

Ducking one blow, he delivered a solid punch to the tallest man's solar plexus. A loud "oof" sounded as his victim doubled over. Rurik locked his hands together and hammered the man's exposed back. The clown collapsed to the floor.

One down. Four left. And Antonelli.

Rurik grabbed his next adversary's head and slammed an open palm into his ear. The man howled and stumbled away, clutching the side of his face. Burst eardrum. Painful, but the guy could still work.

Between hits and blocks, Rurik considered each clowns' size and fighting style. The killer at the train station had been about 5'5", stocky, with an unusually strong punch, but he'd been slow, ponderous.

None of the clowns fit the bill.

Someone else was donning a harlequin costume and hiding behind a white-painted face. It could be anyone in the circus.

A stunning blow slammed into Rurik's forehead. Pain exploded across his skull. He reeled backward.

One of the clowns hooted in triumph, a metal spotlight stand held like a club in his hand.

Damn! He'd let himself get distracted.

Something trickled into his right eye. Salty, stinging. He brushed at it and saw blood coating his fingers. More ran down his face. A red pall curtained his vision. He could only see from his left eye now. Barely. The lightning scars had warped that eyelid half-closed permanently.

In seconds, the fight devolved into blurred flashes of movement and a series of punishing blows he couldn't avoid.

He swiped at his eye, clearing his vision in time to see the man swing the metal stand again.

Rurik's arm shot out. He grabbed the rod midair, ripped it from the man's grasp, and tossed it away. But from the side, someone kicked the back of his knees. He tried to save himself, arms windmilling and feet backpedalling, but toppled into the boxes. A stack collapsed onto him. Decorations and props spilled out, and a burst of glitter and confetti peppered the air.

He tried to get his feet under him, but they slid on loose cardboard and confetti, dumping him to the ground again.

The clowns booted the cartons out of the way and surrounded him, kicking his ribs and stomping on his arms and face.

He managed to catch hold of one foot and shoved it, sending its owner flying.

A boot slammed into his neck. For a second, shocks reverberated up and down his spine. Like the lightning. Adrenaline flooded his body. He sat up, swinging in every direction, pounding flesh and not caring how hard he hit.

With shouts of pain, they stopped their onslaught for a second, giving him time to struggle to his feet.

"Hold him!" Antonelli yelled.

The weight of bodies hit Rurik. One man clung to his back and wrapped an arm around his throat. Others tried to pin his arms.

Blood flowed into his eye again. His vision dimmed. He struck out, but his fists met only air.

"Take him down," Antonelli said.

A fist bashed into Rurik's jaw. The five clowns hung on him, like a pack of wolves dragging down a stag. He twisted and jerked but couldn't shake them off. Someone kicked his legs out from under him. He collapsed to his knees, and the clowns held him there.

Bloody. Battered. Blinded.

Over the rasp of heavy breathing, he heard the snick of a switchblade being flicked open.

"I add autograph to those lightning marks," Antonelli said. "Make you remember to stay out of people's tents."

Rurik gritted his teeth. Antonelli could turn his chest into a jigsaw puzzle, but he wouldn't give him the satisfaction of making a sound.

"Hey, Rurik!" Ivan's gravelly voice filled the trailer. "You having a party and forget to invite me?"

Rurik cracked his scarred eyelid and barely made out Ivan's bulk at the open end of the trailer.

"Leave, cyclist," Antonelli growled. "Keep your nose out of other people's business."

"But I'm a nosy guy. For instance, I heard you bet on the fight between Alexei and me. Fifty Euros. On Alexei! That hurt my feelings, boys. It's like you don't respect my fighting ability."

Antonelli tossed his head. "So what?"

"So this," Ivan said quietly. His hand swung out, revealing a tire iron he'd hidden behind his back. He tapped it against the side of truck. Sharp clunks echoed through the gloom. "I've had a very bad day, and I'd really like to take it out on someone. Volunteers?"

"We no have any quarrel with you," one of the clowns protested.

"This all Rurik's fault," another clown piped up. "He went in our tent!"

"So? What're you worried about?" Ivan said. "The little pharmacy you have stashed? It's obviously still there, since I could smell you cooking it after the show last night. And right now, my cousin Vadim is outside your tent. If I don't show up in five minutes, he's going into that false-bottomed trunk you think no one knows about and you can say goodbye to your midnight delight."

One clown gasped. Angry Italian words flew between them. Rurik picked out "expensive," "lose," and "son of a bitch" before he was abruptly released.

"You not worth the trouble," Antonelli said to him.

The clowns shuffled past Ivan one by one.

"I not forget this, cyclist. You neither, Security man." Antonelli glowered at Rurik before he jumped from the truck and disappeared with his cohorts.

Ivan ambled into the trailer and shoved a big spool of wire along with his foot until he reached Rurik. Giving Rurik a hand off the floor, he indicated the spool. "Sit."

Rurik swayed for a second before easing himself onto the spool. Every muscle ached. He fingered his ribs and grimaced. Bruised but not broken. His bones—exceptionally dense from generations of strongmen in his family and a bizarre growth spurt after the lightning hit him at seventeen—had protected him from serious injury.

"You look like shit." Ivan pulled a handkerchief from a pocket and handed it to Rurik. "Even worse than you usually look. Which is arguably like shit anyway."

"Thanks." Rurik dabbed the blood from his eye. "Always nice to have a fan."

"What did you think you were doing?"

"I was here looking for—oh. There they are. Toss me that box with the plastic roses." He caught the battered carton when Ivan pitched it over.

"That's not what I meant. You went in someone's tent. The Rurik I know would never do that." Ivan pulled up another large spool and sat down, stretching out his legs. After smoothing his graying mustache a few times, he speared Rurik with a keen look. "Now, tell me what the hell is really going on."

Rurik looked at his hands, his knuckles already bruised from yesterday's battle with the killer, now swollen and split from the new fight. So far he'd made no progress in finding the man he wanted. Two people searching would be better than one. Although he hated to admit it, he could use some help.

He stood. "Come. I need to go to my RV and clean up, and I'll tell you everything I know on the way."

* * *

Rurik ran past the performers' tents, trying to outrace the lengthening shadows. It was after five o'clock. Only an hour remained before sunset, and by seven-thirty, customers would begin lining up outside the main tent. There was still a chance to get to the bridge and make sure no one from the circus left the island.

During their discussion, he and Ivan decided to divide up searching the circus for the clown costume. Ivan would take tents and trucks. Rurik would take the RVs. Ivan promised to start checking the other five equipment trucks after his show that night.

After washing his wounds and unearthing a Security

shirt that wasn't too ripe, he'd thrown a black cloak over his shoulders and pulled up the hood. He usually only wore it at night—part of the circus image—but both sides of his face were damaged now. Tourists crossing the bridge didn't need to see that.

His path took him behind the big top. Johan and Misha had succeeded in erecting the trellis arch for the wedding. Mounted on a platform, the arch spanned seven feet and topped out at ten. Several women in long black dresses hovered near the tables, spreading colorful tablecloths, setting up candles, food, and drinks. Bloodwalkers. One of them carried paper cups to three light-haired men in suits standing off to the side. The Skomori grooms.

Rurik would never understand them. The Skomori were an unusually attractive people and could have blended in, even been admired in normal society. They could have gotten married. Had children. Everything that made life worth living. But they stubbornly clung to their strange ways. Proud of the fact they were different. Not interested in acceptance. It made no sense.

Johan dashed over to take the carton of roses Rurik held. "About time," the carpenter said. "Even Yuri got here before you, and Zora and Alyosha should be arriving any minute." He trotted away, pulling long vines of plastic roses from the box.

Rurik spotted Yuri standing at the rear entrance to the main tent and detoured that way. "Where are the brides?" Rurik said . "Why aren't you with them?"

Yuri shrugged. "The little princesses refused to get changed in the restroom. I had to take them to the extra RV. Zim-Zim's old one."

"Then go tell Alyosha where they are."

"I already did that. He's the one who told me to come here and guard the tent." He leaned closer. "Probably doesn't want that scum going inside and stealing anything. Don't worry, boss, it's all under control."

Rurik doubted that, but at least Yuri and Misha were there and could head off any trouble in case the bloodwalkers attracted a crowd. Turning away, he jogged around the side of big top and passed the wardrobe and make-up trailer.

The shrill voice of the wardrobe mistress, Madame Nadia, blared from inside. When he glanced in, he saw the old woman swearing in Russian at a slim blond girl. Her dowdy long dress and crocheted cap marked her as a Skomori. Undoubtedly one of the bloodwalkers. She was trying to escape out the door, but Madame Nadia had her by the wrist and was spewing angry words into her face.

He passed them and made it about ten yards farther—the distant bridge just becoming visible across the next field—before he stopped, sighed, and reversed direction.

"Madame Nadia," he called, leaping up the steps to the trailer. Brilliant bulbs surrounding the makeup mirrors reflected off dozens of sequined and beaded costumes hanging opposite them. It created an annoying glare. He pulled his hood lower. "What's going on?"

"This thief is stealing my scissors!" Madame Nadia said in Russian, her narrowed eyes almost disappearing into the crinkles of her wizened face. She'd been with the circus since before Alyosha owned it. Current wisdom alleged she'd been sewing dresses since the Stone Age.

The young blonde spun around and launched into Romanian. "Please, I need these scissors for—Oh!" The sight of his face stopped her cold. Her eyes widened as she peered beneath his hood.

Rurik steeled himself for the look of horror he knew would follow.

Instead, the girl reached out a hand and gently brushed the right side of his face. The side without the lightning scars. "You're bleeding. And your cheek is swollen. You need ice. You'd feel a lot better."

Surprise held Rurik immobile for a moment. She couldn't have missed seeing what the lightning had done to him. Why wasn't she shrieking and cringing away?

"Do you speak Romanian?" the girl said softly.

He nodded. "My friend speaks it, too." He sent a hard look to Madame Nadia. Growing up in a circus featuring acts from many countries meant everyone knew a bit of everything.

"I didn't mean to cause trouble. The other guard said

this lady would help me, but..." The girl's huge blue eyes brimmed with tears.

Yuri. That asshole knew Madame Nadia would throw a fit, but he'd sent the bloodwalker here anyway. Under his cloak, Rurik's fingers curled into fists.

"I'm to be married, but we have an emergency. I need these scissors to cut a veil in half. We can't get married without them."

"She's lying! You can't trust bloodwalkers," Madame Nadia said.

One tear spilled over the girl's lashes. It glittered like a silver sequin and slid down her cheek.

"Let her take the scissors," Rurik ordered Madame Nadia. "If they aren't returned, I'll buy you a new pair."

The woman's lip curled back, revealing yellowed teeth outnumbered by empty gaps. She released her grip on the girl's wrist.

"It's all right. You can take them," Rurik said and gestured to the door.

The girl flashed a grateful smile before rushing out of the trailer.

"I'm holding you to your promise." Madame Nadia's screech chased him as he left and ran toward the bridge. "I expect a new pair!"

In front of the big top, the circus's portable mesh fence blocked his way, stretching out for fifty yards on either side of the tent's entrance. It kept the customers cordoned off from the performers' private areas, and the circus's concessioners set up their stands and food carts along it every evening.

He slipped through the narrow gap between the fence and the side of the big top and aimed toward the field and the bridge in the distance.

"Hi Rurik," Catrina called, pouring pink sugar into the top of her cotton candy machine. Clear bags with blue cotton candy already hung atop the cart's high glass sides.

Soon, the smells of popcorn, caramel apples, fried donuts, sausages, and stuffed *pirozhki* would fill the air from all the various concession stands, enticing the customers to spend their money on snacks before entering the big top.

He waved at her over his shoulder, and when he turned forward again, he stopped dead.

From the other side of the meadow, several policemen approached.

Cops. The worst thing possible for the circus.

Alyosha worked hard to avoid problems. He greased the palms of the top officials in every town they visited, so the police always kept their distance.

This had to be because of the train depot. The children must have described the clown.

Damn. The Italian clowns were bastards, but they didn't deserve to be locked up for something they hadn't done. Plus, if the cops searched the circus for evidence, there was no telling what they might find. Doing live shows every night could be brutal. Aches, pains, and injuries were common. Many performers took painkillers—legal and illegal.

And then there were the recreational drugs.

If the police found anything, they'd close the circus and probably arrest half the performers.

Rurik had to diffuse the situation and get rid of them quickly and quietly, even if he had to swear the clowns were on the grounds all yesterday.

As the three policemen stopped in front of Rurik, he swung his cloak off one shoulder, displaying his Security patch. "I'm Chief of Security for the *Zorka Cyrka*. I can assure you all permits and documents are in order."

"I am Lieutenant Brakas," said a man with small eyes and pock-marked cheeks. "I'm not here about working papers. We have a complaint about someone from the circus making trouble."

"Our performers and employees don't leave the grounds. The management doesn't allow it," Rurik said firmly.

"There was an attempted kidnapping at the Istvantelek train station yesterday. Reliable witnesses described the suspect—a man, over six feet, and very muscular." The detective's hand darted out and flicked the hood off Rurik's head. "And they said he had scars running down his face. Sergeant! Take this man into custody."

Rurik's jaw slackened as a policeman pulled his arms behind him and closed a pair of handcuffs on his wrists.

CHAPTER SIX

Sylvie
Obudai Island, Hungary

If a body has been outside and subjected to the elements, do not collect it in plastic bin liners—corpses are not garbage!
Use a sheet from the deceased's house, and remember to bring a bucket in case some parts need to be scooped up.
~ The Bloodwalker's Book

Sylvie tiptoed back up the stairs of the circus's wardrobe trailer, the scissors tight in her grip, and peeked inside. No one was visible. Neither the scary Russian lady nor the huge man who'd saved Sylvie on her first visit. She hoped he'd found some ice. Head wounds bled faster than a spring flood, and his gash looked bad.

Well, not *that* bad when she compared it to other horrors that could befall a human body.

Once, to help earn money for his foundering farm, her neighbor Mr. Baboescu had traveled to a big co-op farm in the next county. Instead of returning with money in his pocket, he'd come back in pocket-sized pieces, having fallen in something called a "combine harvester."

And Mr. Tugurlan had been gored by his prize bull, a long-horned *sura de stepa* with a filthy temper. Poor Mr. Tugurlan had staggered back to his home, holding his stomach in place, but dragging fifteen feet of intestine behind him. He hadn't survived. When Sylvie prepared his body, she'd discovered putting intestines back inside was like trying to fill a ten-pound goose with twenty-pounds of stuffing.

Even though the tall circus man seemed self-conscious about his scars and kept pulling his hood lower, they didn't bother her at all.

Sylvie crept inside the wardrobe trailer, her eyes flitting into every corner. The Russian woman could be waiting to catch her, like some nasty old spider lurking in a web. Sylvie placed the scissors on the nearest makeup counter, and then dashed out as if her feet were on fire.

Hurrying away from the trailer and toward the RVs, she couldn't help sneak a glance back at the wedding area. The massive big top hid most of it and the people congregating there. She could only see a tall wooden arch festooned with beautiful roses.

But...if she went back and slipped around the side of the big tent, she could see the whole area—and the grooms.

It was so tempting. She was dying to know what her future husband looked like.

But it was forbidden for them to see each other before the ceremony. If anyone caught her, she'd be in big trouble. Worse, Zora would find out she'd broken the rules. And one word from the leader of the bloodwalkers would destroy any hope Sylvie had to start a new life.

So she lifted her skirt and ran the opposite way, passing green tents so fast that the few performers who saw her didn't even have time to throw a rude comment her way. By the time she reached the rows of RVs, her breath came in tired gasps, perspiration streamed down her face, and her dress was pasted to her skin.

Ugh. Too bad she didn't have time for a shower, but she was late already—all three of them were. Her steps quickened as she rounded the last row of RVs and the brides' camper came into view.

At least Ada's problem had been solved. Sylvie had cut her beautiful veil into two halves and given one to Ada. The girl had been so happy, it made Sylvie smile to think about it.

She opened the door and clambered up the step-well behind the driver's seats. "Ada, Liana? Can you help me with...?"

The girls weren't in the dining area, so she went through

to the bedroom. They weren't there. Nor in the bathroom.

The RV was empty.

The brides had vanished. Their bags, too. Only her little suitcase remained on the kitchen table. And her half of the veil *was no longer on top of it!*

"No," she whispered. They couldn't have taken it. Perhaps they'd put it away for her?

She whipped her case open. Her scarlet wedding dress lay inside next to her underthings, nightgowns, an extra apron, and the two black dresses she'd wear as a new wife.

No veil.

She darted into every room, searching for it, but only found Ada's ruined green veil crumpled in the bathroom sink.

Sylvie's hands curled into fists.

Liana. It had to be her. She'd practically drooled over Sylvie's veil. She must have taken it.

Sylvie pressed her hands to her temples and groaned. She had to have a veil. It was part of the ceremony. They'd be veiled when presented to Zora for her approval. Then the grooms would step forward and officially agree to marry them, and after Zora pronounced them wedded, the grooms would remove the colorful veils and burn them as a symbol of the end of the girls' previous lives.

Her face must be veiled. It was tradition. A bloodwalker rule.

She'd have to wear Ada's green one.

As fast as she could, Sylvie changed into her wedding gown, fled into the bathroom, and pinned on the veil. The mirror pronounced judgment.

She looked ugly. The veil was awful. Wrinkled, stained, and smelly.

Her mother would be ashamed of her. The grooms would be disgusted. And Zora would realize Sylvie wasn't worthy of being a bloodwalker or marrying.

There was only one way Sylvie could save herself—get rid of the stains. Fast.

She ripped the veil from her head. Bobby pins flew into the air and pinged off the walls. She stuck the fabric under the faucet, slathered it with soap, and rubbed like a madwoman. After rinsing it, she dug though the hamper. All the towels had splotches of makeup, but one was stained only on the bottom half.

She tucked the wet fabric in the clean half of the towel and squeezed.

The RV's door hinges squeaked. Footsteps clumped inside.

The girls? Maybe Liana had felt guilty and returned.

Sylvie stuck her head out of the bathroom.

A short man, muscled like a prizefighter, stood in profile, rifling through her suitcase.

She ducked back into the bathroom, her heart jumping in her chest.

A thief? Or worse?

Skomori girls were taught never to be alone with *Baran* men—told they'd do terrible things to lone females. Even if the man was Zorka, they despised the Skomori, too. Especially bloodwalkers.

The intruder's footsteps approached.

She leaped to the shower stall at the back of the bathroom and hid behind its half-closed curtain. Her hand rose to shut it all the way but stopped. The metal hooks would scrape on the rod. He would hear.

She pressed herself back as far as she could in the stall. The shower handles jabbed her spine. The curtain wasn't completely closed on that side either. It offered a sliver view of the intruder.

He entered the bathroom, his thighs so overdeveloped he seemed to lurch from side to side when he walked.

He swept all the makeup containers into a plastic bag. Even the soaps. He turned to the hamper and dug inside it.

Only a few feet separated them. The sour odor of his sweat seeped into the shower stall. Her mouth dried out. Her breaths came in tiny gulps.

He grabbed all the towels from the hamper—all except the half-rolled one still in her hand—and headed for the bathroom door. But he glanced over his shoulder and came back. Before she could think what to do, he bent into the shower and reached for the towel clutched in front

55

of her skirt.

His gaze went past the towel, landed on her red dress, and climbed to her face.

She stopped breathing.

His brown eyes narrowed below a heavy brow ridge. He snatched at the towel, his hand closing on its edge and yanking. She almost let it go until she remembered the veil inside. She couldn't lose it! He pulled, and she pulled back.

His teeth clenched, jaw muscles bulging.

She recognized the typical Zorka features—pale complexion, dark eyes, and a gorilla-like brow line in a square-shaped face. She'd heard Zorka people were untrustworthy, backstabbing thieves. Now she knew it was true.

With a grunt, he tore the towel from her hands and hurried out the door.

She ran after him. "No! Stop!"

He shoved all the towels under one brawny arm. The ends dangled, and the green veil slipped out from the folds and floated to the floor.

With a victorious cry, she seized it.

But then the man picked up her open suitcase, clasped it under his other arm, and hastened toward the exit.

Not her case! It had everything for her new life in it.

"No!" She plunged forward and caught its corner. "That's mine!"

He kept going, dragging her along with him. When he got to the stairs, she dropped the veil and fastened her other hand onto the case. She wouldn't let this criminal leave the RV with all her belongings. He trotted down the steps, pushed the door open with his shoulder, and stepped out.

Desperate, she jammed her feet on either side of the doorframe. Her butt hit the top step. She braced her legs and pulled. Hard.

The sudden stop jerked him around.

They fought in a tug of war.

He said something she couldn't understand. It was probably a threat. She didn't care. She wasn't letting go.

With one arm full of towels and the plastic bag of

makeup, he only had one arm to hold onto the suitcase. He dug in his heels and leaned his substantial weight backward.

With her legs straddling the opening, she leaned back, too, but his pull lifted her butt off the floor. He strained, his muscles cording across his thick shoulders and neck. Her knees began to shake, and her whole body inched inexorably toward the doorway.

"No! You're not getting my case!" she shrieked.

His eyes widened. He looked around nervously and suddenly released his hold.

Without a counterbalance, she flew backward and smacked into the kitchen counter. The case rocketed over her head and slammed into the cabinets high on the wall. Clothes rained over her.

With a popping sound, the top cabinets tipped outward, and the whole thing dipped, hanging precariously on the wall.

The man put his foot on the lowest step, his nostrils flaring, his complexion redder than the roses on her wedding arch.

Sylvie realized her mistake. Now that he had a free hand, he could use it. On her.

But he stopped and cocked his head as if he heard something. Giving her a last venomous scowl, he retreated and slammed the door so hard the whole RV shook.

With a screech of nails, the cabinet lost its grip on the wall. It fell and hit the countertop behind her. Splinters shot over her head. The cabinet doors burst open, and a bulky package wrapped in plastic tumbled into her lap.

An odor rose around her. Suddenly she knew what had been beneath the reek of mildew, rotten food, and bleach she'd noticed when first entering the RV, and why it was familiar.

It was the smell of death.

Inside the clear plastic wrapping were bones with shreds of flesh still attached. She recognized a human collarbone wedged between broken ribs and a femur, alongside other bits of bone. Many of them had been snapped in half.

She peered closer, her nose almost touching the plastic

because she couldn't believe what she saw around the bones' broken ends.

Teeth marks. They scored the area near the marrow. They weren't pointy marks, like an animal's. They were flat scrapes, made by human teeth.

The bones were small.

The size of a child.

And someone had been gnawing on them.

CHAPTER SEVEN

Rurik
Obudai Island, Hungary

After securing Rurik's handcuffs, two policemen grabbed him by the elbows and shoved him along toward the tourist parking lot.

Rurik didn't know what the police would do to him, but he sure as hell knew that if the circus left without him, the killer would prey on children in every town on the tour.

Frustration boiled inside him. The metal handcuffs bit into his thick wrists. He gave in to the temptation to test their strength. His hands fisted. Tendons strained. His upper torso tightened and burned as he began to let out his full power.

But the second he felt the slightest give of the metal links, he stopped. His abnormally strong body might break them, just as he'd bent iron bars when he used to perform. But then what?

If he escaped into Budapest, police would swarm the circus searching for him. Others would be swept up in the dragnet. The scandal would spread. The circus would be blacklisted. Alyosha would go out of business.

Rurik couldn't do that to the man who'd always treated him like a son, who gave him work when everyone else wrote him off as too damaged.

Getting the police to drop the charges was doubtful. He *had* been at the train depot and had no explanation unless he implicated the killer. *And the circus.* A lawyer cost too much. With Rurik gone, his father would need their savings. Marva or Alyosha might help. But Rurik wouldn't ask them.

Staying mute was the smartest option. The only option.

Maybe prison wouldn't be so bad. Lightning couldn't find him behind concrete walls.

But he also couldn't find the murderer.

That duty fell to Ivan now. He'd promised to search but said he'd never believe the circus could really be home to a child-killer.

The cyclist was naïve.

Rurik wasn't.

Suspicion came easy to someone who worked security. Rurik constantly saw the darker side of humanity, the people who lived in the shadows, and the things they did to each other.

As Rurik and the policemen neared the parking lot, the wind picked up, tousling Rurik's hair, whipping his cloak around his legs. Behind him, the big top's canvas snapped and its cables rang off metal poles. A last farewell.

Rurik surrendered to one final temptation. He tipped his head back and inhaled, letting the circus aromas fill his chest. The fresh sawdust from Johan's work. The spun sugar of the cotton candy. Salty buttered popcorn. Meats sizzling on grills. Even the harsh tent waterproofing blended with the other smells into a mixture that said only one thing—the circus. Rurik's home. The one he'd likely never see again.

A few paces in front of Rurik, Lieutenant Brakas glanced over his shoulder. Above the man's bulbous nose, eyes hard as agate combed Rurik's face, lingering on the injuries and scar tissue. "It will go easier if you admit being at the Istvantelek depot and having inappropriate contact with the boy." Getting no reply, the lieutenant shrugged. "If you choose not to cooperate, that's your business. But child molesters often have accidents in jail."

Rurik's lips tightened. The idea that he of all people would be branded a child molester made his skin crawl. Nothing in the world was more important to him than children. His childhood had been destroyed by the lightning. He wanted to make sure no child suffered like that.

The burly cop at his side moved ahead when they reached the police car. He yanked open the rear door and stood back. Shaggy black hair poked out from under his police cap, the tips matted against his sweaty skin. "Get in!"

Rurik bent to slide into the small car when a solid push from behind sent his head cracking into the door jamb.

"Oops," Brakas said. "Didn't realize you were so clumsy. My men will help, so you won't get hurt."

Rough hands pulled Rurik back and spun him around.

"Sit!" the same stout policeman said.

When Rurik began to lower himself backward into the seat, the cop put both hands on Rurik's shoulders and shoved, trying to ram the back of his head into the doorframe. But this time, Rurik had his legs planted apart, angled his body in a wrestler's crouch, and locked his muscles.

The cop grunted, straining, but might as well have been pushing a brick wall. A second later, he stepped back, red-faced.

Rurik eased his backside onto the seat.

The cop leaned close, his breath a toxic brew of overcooked onions and rotting teeth. "That was a mistake, you ugly piece of shit. The more you resist, the more fun we'll have breaking you."

Rurik stared at him impassively.

The crunch of gravel cut through the air. A white circus van raced down an adjacent road, a cloud of dust billowing in its wake. It sped into the parking lot and skidded to a stop near the police car.

The policemen stepped back. The black-haired one clutched the butt of his gun.

The van's passenger door burst open, and an elderly man sprang out, sunlight gleaming off his white hair. Short but barrel-chested, he brushed imaginary dust from his lapels with a dainty gesture and headed for the group of police. His black jacket was staid as a preacher's, but the vest under it blazed with cheerful red and yellow stripes, matching the big top's canvas. Behind him, two brawny bodyguards in gray tank-tops slid out of the vehicle. They crossed their chiseled arms and stood their ground on either side of the van, as hard and cold as marble bookends.

Alyosha and two of the strongmen from the Markarov

family. The ones that had replaced Rurik and his father ten years ago.

Odd that Alyosha had discovered the arrest so quickly. Then Rurik remembered it had gone down in front of all the concessioners. The news must have raced across the circus encampment.

Donning a jovial smile, Alyosha spread his arms in welcome. "Officers! I'm Alyosha Zurenko, the owner of *Zorka Cyrka*." His gaze whisked over the policemen and landed on Lieutenant Brakas's gold-starred epaulettes. "If I'd known a lieutenant was here, I'd have invited you to my home for a drink."

The lieutenant straightened to his full height. "I am here on business, taking this man into custody."

Alyosha's eyebrows rose . "Oh? On what charge, sir?"

"Trespassing and attempted kidnapping—*of a child.*" Brakas glowered.

"I can't imagine Rurik, my Chief of Security, having anything to do with such a thing." Alyosha glanced at Rurik, whose gaze fell. "Perhaps the child was mistaken. Did he or she identify Rurik?"

The detective sniffed. "I'm not at liberty to say."

"I see." Alyosha nodded sagely. "Well, uh, Lieutenant...?"

"Lieutenant Mihaly Brakas."

"Brakas? Would you happen to be related to Colonel Laszlo Brakas?"

The lieutenant's lips twitched into a slight smile. "He's my grandfather."

Alyosha grinned and smacked his hands together. "Laszlo Brakas! A great man. He and I go way back. He knew how to run this town—nothing got past him. Of course, that was when being a cop meant something. When civilians had *respect*. Now, after all the stupid reforms"—Alyosha shook his head—"the politicians and government paper-pushers have made it impossible for policemen to do their job."

Brakas and the two other policemen exchanged nods. "Damn right ," the black-haired one muttered.

"How is Laszlo these days?" Alyosha said.

"Retired, but doing well."

"Amazing man! He could drink all night in a cathouse, run the ladies ragged, and be at his post at eight, no one the wiser. A meaner, funnier bastard was never born!"

With a flash of teeth, Brakas chuckled. "True!"

"Such good old days... But tell me, Rurik has been positively identified by the child?"

"There have been some...inconsistencies in his story. But I'm sure that's due to the appearance of the suspect." The lieutenant looked down his nose at Rurik. "No doubt his face scared the children, confused them. But other witnesses at the train depot came forward. This is definitely the man."

"These witnesses saw the kidnapping?"

"Well...no. They saw him in the area, lying on the tracks."

"Ah! Then I know what happened. I sent Rurik and Dmitry"—Alyosha gestured to one of the bodyguards behind him—"to pick up some circus equipment arriving at the station. They got lost and poor Rurik had a tumble on the tracks. A bad one, as you can see by his injuries. Dmitry went to get help. That must have been when your witnesses arrived."

Dmitry nodded curtly. "That is what happened."

"But the child is alright, yes?" Alyosha said , and Brakas nodded. "So no one was hurt, and there was no kidnapping." He tilted his head. "But I agree my boys were trespassing, and the circus will take full responsibility. Might we discuss the fine for trespassing...in private?"

After a slight hesitation, Brakas ambled past the hood of the car and onto the grass. Alyosha joined him. The men murmured, Alyosha using expansive hand gestures, Brakas repeatedly shaking his head. Finally, Brakas nodded. Alyosha slid a hand in his pocket. A moment later, Brakas tucked a bulky wad inside his jacket and swung around.

"This isn't the man we're looking for." Brakas walked to the passenger door of the car and waved a hand at his men. "Release him and take me back to headquarters."

With stony faces, the policemen pulled Rurik from the car and unlocked the cuffs. While Rurik rubbed his wrists, they piled into the car, drove out of the parking lot, and across the bridge.

Alyosha approached Rurik and surveyed his face with a grimace. "You have more dings and scrapes than a used car." He clapped Rurik on the arm. "But you'll be fine. Don't worry. Alyosha takes care of everyone."

"It was a...misunderstanding," Rurik began.

The Markarov brothers, Dmitry and Viktor, came striding up.

"What's going on, Rurik?" Dmitry said . "You making trouble with the locals?"

Rurik would have apologized to Alyosha, but not with the Markarovs there. Since their arrival ten years before, they'd seized every opportunity to needle Rurik and his father about their fall from star status, like alpha dogs harrying the lesser members of the pack.

"You're lucky we're in Hungary and not Austria or Poland." Viktor's nose wrinkled in disdain. "Here, the police are easily bought."

"And lucky we got here quick or you'd be inside a cell by now." Dmitry's smirk indicated he found the idea amusing.

"Never mind," Alyosha said. He moved toward the van, speaking quickly. "We have to get Zora to the wedding. Viktor, I want you to pass the word—no one leaves camp. We can't take the chance of attracting more attention from the police. Dmitry, tell the concessioners to keep an eye on the bridge. If they see a police car, I want to be notified immediately. Rurik..." He met Rurik's gaze and frowned. "Maybe you should take tonight off. Misha and Yuri can fill in."

"No, sir. I'm fine," Rurik said.

"Not necessary. Just take care of yourself." Alyosha climbed in the passenger side and Viktor swung into the driver's seat.

Dmitry turned a contemptuous eye on Rurik. "Before you enjoy your night off, you need to pass by Madame Nadia's tent. She's got a big mouth, and she's been flapping it all over camp. Make sure she and her friends stay away from the bloodwalker ceremony." He turned on his heel, got in behind Alyosha, and the van peeled away.

Rurik exhaled long and loud. Alyosha telling him what to do was one thing, but he never thought he'd see the day when the Markarovs would weasel into the man's good graces enough to start giving Rurik orders.

On his way back to camp, Rurik avoided the concessioners. Too many questions. Too many prying eyes. In the shadow of the big top, the wardrobe trailer sat empty, so he set off for Madame Nadia's tent at the rear of the encampment.

Halfway there, a dull roar of voices reached him, growing louder as he neared her tent.

Twenty or more people stood outside, tension written in their stiff postures and jerky movements.

He paused at the back of the crowd, catching snatches of conversation.

"...an affront to our good name..."

"An affront to God! Who knows what those evil people pray to..."

"...they make trouble for everyone..."

"I heard the police were here!"

Madame Nadia's voice rang above the others. "It's true—the police took Rurik!" She stood at the opening of her tent and raised a crooked finger in the air. "That was no coincidence. Bloodwalkers always attract trouble."

"Next time, it could be any one of us!" a woman's voice called out.

Rurik needed to set them straight before it got any uglier. But as the vicious accusations multiplied, ice condensed in his belly. It flowed into his veins, stiffening his legs, gluing him to the spot. Like it always did when he had to speak to a group.

He thought of his duty to Alyosha. He set his jaw and tried to will himself forward. His legs refused to cooperate.

Then the image of the blond bloodwalker in Madame Nadia's wardrobe trailer flashed into his mind. Her eyes had been filled with kindness not judgment. If this mob got out of hand, she and the other brides would bear the brunt of it.

He raised his chin and barreled into the crowd.

Madame Nadia dominated the front of the pack, her

viperish comments stoking the fire. With her hair sticking up in raggedy tufts and her wrinkled face curled into a grotesque leer, the crone resembled the infamous *Baba Yaga*. "Those Skomori bloodwalkers will ruin us!" she said.

Rurik reached her and held up his hands, drawing the mob's attention. "As you can see, I was released. Alyosha fixed it, and there are no more problems now."

Madame Nadia's eyes popped open in surprise, but narrowed just as quickly. "Your troubles may be over,"—her voice rose—"but what about the rest of us, eh? If the police are sniffing around, the customers will stay away!"

"Yeah, and attendance is low as it is," said Minko, the boss of the bareback riders. Tall and lean, he had a red birthmark on his forehead that looked eerily like a horseshoe. He planted his hands on his hips and glared at Rurik.

More faces turned toward him. Fear and revulsion rippled over them, warring with the anger already branded on their features.

"No!" Rurik ignored the nausea curdling his stomach and plunged on. "The police are gone. I saw—"

"None of us are making money," Madame Nadia cut in. "How about you, Bartelli? You earning what you used to?" she said to the head of the trapeze artists, known for being a temperamental bastard.

"No! I have very bad income. And payment always late!" Bartelli smacked a fist into his palm.

"Me too!" someone in the back of the crowd shouted.

"Everything's more expensive, but where's our pay increase?" another demanded.

"It's all the fault of Alyosha and the old witch he married." Madame Nadia made the sign of the devil's horns and spat on the ground.

"Alyosha has never let the circus down," Rurik shouted. "He—" Angry voices drowned him out.

"What are you going to do about it?" yelled Madame Nadia.

"Tell him!"

"Kick the bloodwalkers out!"

"No getting pushed around anymore!"

"Come on!" Bartelli and his teenage sons strode away through the camp. Half the pack surged behind them.

"I'll find my riders. Bring everyone! We'll get rid of the bloodwalkers and make Alyosha give us what we want!" Minko stalked off.

The rest of the crowd broke up, heading in different directions.

Madame Nadia cackled.

Rurik flung her a dirty look before taking off toward the big top. He had to alert Yuri and Misha that trouble was coming.

CHAPTER EIGHT

Sylvie
Obudai Island, Hungary

A corpse can decay in a few days, especially in summer.
Organs putrefy. Gasses expand. Bodies explode.
Mind your community. People who live alone, die alone.
They depend on you to find and attend to them.
You are the caretaker of the dead.
~ The Bloodwalker's Book

Sylvie turned the plastic bag of flesh over and over in her hands, unable to believe what she was seeing. From every angle, the truth assaulted her. The broken bones bore human tooth marks. A dark chasm of shock opened inside her. She'd prepared many bodies for burial but never a child's. Her eyes began to sting, and her throat closed up.

The death was horrible enough, but this poor child's remains were in a shabby camper, wrapped like trash. No one had cared for the body. No one had put it safely in the ground. No one had mourned over the grave.

Who could have done such a thing?

Her mind zeroed in on the man who'd stolen the towels. He could be the killer.

She had to tell someone.

Holding the bundle in one hand, she hiked up her long skirt so she wouldn't trip over the hem, but then froze mid-motion.

If she told people, they'd raise the alarm. Someone would call the police. Knowing how much they hated the Skomori, they might even try to blame them for the murder.

The wedding would be canceled.

If she returned home unmarried, the gossip-mongers would have even more ammunition against her. It would prove she wasn't good enough.

And what about Ada and Liana? It would be catastrophic if no one could marry—all because of Sylvie. Word would spread. Her name would be synonymous with bad luck.

But then she looked at the bundle in her arms.

The dead child had no one to speak for it. No one to expose the truth or lay it to rest. No one who cared. No one except Sylvie.

The weight of the child's remains felt heavier with each passing moment of indecision.

She knew what she had to do, even if it got her in trouble. She owed the child some peace.

She started to rise when the RV door wrenched open with a squeal of hinges. Her mother tore up the steps, black dress swirling around her. Sylvie recoiled, lost her balance, and thumped back onto the floor.

"Why aren't you outside with the others?" her mother cawed like an enraged crow. "What is wrong with you? Do you want to ruin everything I've worked so hard for?"

Thoughts whirled in Sylvie's brain, but words refused to form on her tongue. She held out the package.

"What...?" Her mother bent closer, icy-blue eyes constricting into points. In the space of two breaths, all the color drained from her face. She clapped her fingers over her mouth, shuffled into the driver's compartment next to the stairs, and sank onto a seat.

A tense silence hung between them until Sylvie whispered, "Did you see the tooth marks on the bones?"

Her mother's head jerked up and down in a yes. Then she crossed herself twice in quick succession.

"We have to tell someone," Sylvie said.

"No!" Her mother sprang up, alarm slicing her face into sharp angles. "We can't tell anyone."

"Why?"

"Because we can't." Her mother's gaze darted to the door and out the windshield. "This isn't our place. What goes on here isn't our business."

"But—"

"No buts. Believe me, this is for your own good." She snatched the package from Sylvie's arms. "You must never speak a word about this. Promise me."

Sylvie blinked at her in surprise. Her mother was the one who'd taught Sylvie to respect the rights of the dead—every bloodwalker's duty—and she should have been the first to alert others and expose the tragedy.

"Promise me!" her mother said.

Disagreeing was unthinkable. "I promise," Sylvie mumbled, watching miserably as her mother carried the heart-breaking little package to the kitchen sink and shoved it into a cabinet beneath.

"We must go. Where's your veil?"

Sylvie pointed to the floor under her mother's feet.

Her mother leaped back but too late. When she picked it up, her footprints now smudged the fabric atop all the other stains. "Unbelievable. How could you let this happen?" she said. "Don't just sit there. Pack your things!"

Sylvie scrambled up and retrieved her dresses and underwear from where they lay strewn on the floor.

Her mother grabbed the nightgowns and the apron, and together, they stuffed them into the suitcase. She grabbed Sylvie's hand and bolted from the RV, towing Sylvie behind her.

"But...my veil isn't on..." Sylvie tried to pull loose.

"Don't stop!" Herding Sylvie past the other RVs, her mother pulled bobby pins from her own cap and fastened the green veil on Sylvie's head. "What is all over this? It's disgusting. And your dress—you've stained it, too!"

Sylvie looked down, but the green chiffon blurred her vision, and it took her a moment to see what her mother meant. A big wet spot marred the crimson fabric. She tried to bend closer to see what it was, but her mother was pulling her along too fast.

Performers' tents flashed by until finally, they passed the last one, and her mother yanked her to a stop.

They'd arrived at the wedding site.

Sylvie couldn't breathe.

The space was huge, about forty yards across. The performers' green tents bordered the area behind her. On her left, the massive big top soared upward, dominating the end of the clearing. In front of it, banquet tables had been set up for the celebration. Brilliant flower arrangements covered them, along with traditional wedding food: marbled *cozonac* cakes, filled crepes, gingerbread, sugar-dusted *gogosi*, cheeses, and fruits.

On her right, a rose-covered arch towered above a small stage. Light from the setting sun set the roses ablaze, making them shine like giant rubies.

It was more beautiful than Sylvie ever dreamed.

Opposite her, across the forty-yard expanse, women in white caps and long black dresses gathered behind men in suits. It was too far for Sylvie to discern faces through her veil, but one of those men was definitely her groom.

This was it! By the end of the day, she'd be a married lady, going to a modern city—to live with her new husband!

Fear and excitement tingled through her limbs.

But then a smell wafted up her nostrils, and suddenly she knew what had stained her dress. Fluid had leaked from the plastic bag holding the child's remains.

Sylvie smelled like a dead body. It was as if the child was punishing her for not helping. She deserved it.

"Quick, take off your shoes!" Her mother dug in her purse and came up with a small, lumpy pouch.

Setting down her suitcase, Sylvie untied her clunky brown shoes and slid them off. Her mother upended the pouch, dumping fifteen or twenty pebbles inside each shoe. The ritual of *indurera*. Every Skomori bride had to put rocks in her soles and wear them throughout the ceremony. It proved the bride could face the pain of childbirth, that she had the patience to run a household, and that she could hold her tongue and never complain to her husband.

But when Sylvie stepped back into her shoes, it felt like shards of glass stabbing her feet. The pain traveled all the way up her shins.

Panicking, she turned to her mother. "I-I can't—"

"Go!" Her mother jabbed a finger at the tables. "Fetch your bouquet and stand with the other brides. They're waiting for you!"

Sylvie's gaze zipped to the flowered arch. Both girls stood in front of the stage with bouquets in their hands, heads angled in her direction. Sylvie's beautiful crimson veil covered their faces. Liana shifted tenderly from foot to foot. Ada's back bowed as if she was about to crumple to the ground. They'd probably been standing there in agony for fifteen minutes, waiting for her to arrive.

"Hurry up!" Her mother gave Sylvie a firm push.

Sylvie managed one step toward the banquet tables, but her leg immediately buckled, her foot deciding that under no circumstances would it bear her weight with rocks cutting into it. A gasp whistled through her teeth. No one could walk like this. She froze into an off-kilter stoop, only too aware that everyone was staring but unable to convince herself to go on.

Her first bridal test—failed. Apparently the virtues of strength, patience, and suffering silently weren't in her repertoire.

Her mother whispered, "Put your weight on the edges of your feet and take small steps."

Sylvie forced her knees apart and struggled forward, her jaw clamped shut to trap her groans inside. Tilting her feet sideways helped a little. Thank heaven the long skirt hid the fact she was walking like a bow-legged sailor.

She minced her way across the grass, hoping the chiffon veil obscured the horrible grimaces she was making.

At the end of one table lay her bridal bouquet, traditional anthurium flowers. One shiny red petal shaped like a heart with a long pink stamen jutting from the center—just like a man's private part. It symbolized the bonding of male and female. As a child, she and her friends used to giggle, blush, and wriggle their eyebrows when brides walked past with it.

Now, the soles of her feet were too busy screaming for mercy for her to find anything funny.

As she neared the table, she noticed the fat security guard, Yuri, standing behind it alongside three other men. He gestured to her veil and said something to his friends she couldn't understand. They snickered, and one jeered, "Sexyyyy." Funny how some words were international.

They all laughed until she reached the table in front of them. Then one coughed. Another choked. Soon, they were all covering their noses and backing away with sounds of disgust.

"*Derr-mo!* You smell like dead animal!" Yuri's complexion turned green as he gagged.

A wave of heat surged up Sylvie's neck and erupted on her cheeks.

This was a disaster. Bad enough she wore the ugliest veil in history, but smelling like a corpse too? One whiff and Zora would never give her permission to marry. Sylvie would be ridiculed in front of everyone. She'd be sent away. Maybe cast out.

Sylvie wanted to crawl under the table and cry—*and take off her shoes !*—but hiding wouldn't help. What she needed was a truckload of perfume.

Or...maybe her bouquet? She picked it up and sniffed, hoping anthurium flowers had a strong enough odor to hide the stink surrounding her.

They didn't.

But all sorts of flowers decorated the table. Her gaze raked over them. Lavender, sweet pea, and azaleas all had heavy fragrances.

She sidestepped down the length of the display, gathering the purple and fuchsia blooms in a big bunch around the anthuriums, and then inhaled.

Yes! The powerful scents hid the corpse smell. She might get through this after all.

Heading for the arch to join the other brides, the agony in her feet worsened with each step. She gritted her teeth. No giving in to fear or pain. She'd solved the stench problem, and she was determined to give Zora no other reason to criticize her.

She *would* be married today.

She decided her first act as a married lady would be to tell someone about the child's body. She'd be a wife then. An adult. Her mother's equal...sort of...

Well, perhaps she could tell Aunt Cosmina without her mother knowing. Aunt Cosmina would understand about a bloodwalker's duty. She'd take action.

When Sylvie drew near the arch, Liana hissed over her shoulder, "How dare you make us wait here so long, you slug!"

Sylvie wobbled to a spot beside Ada, not even glancing Liana's way.

Ada leaned over and whispered, "She made me do it. I'm so sorry, Sylvie ."

Sylvie shook her head. "It's not your fault."

"Shh! They're coming." Liana stared across the stage.

From outside the clearing, a small procession approached. Two burly men in gray tank-tops carried a wheelchair between them. In it, a figure in a long black dress listed to one side, head drooping, swaying with each uneven step the men took. A veil of black lace hid her face, but it had to be Zora.

The elderly bloodwalker could no longer stand? But Skomori people aged well and never got sick. Even ninety-year-old women in Sylvie's village did chores and walked to Mass every morning.

Sylvie wondered if it had to do with what Liana's mother mentioned—the bloodwalker's curse. Maybe bloodwalkers aged differently than normal Skomori women. Since only one bloodwalker was allowed to live in each town, Sylvie didn't know any other bloodwalkers for comparison.

Aunt Cosmina limped along behind the wheelchair. Next to her, a white-haired man strolled, his smile brimming with overly-white teeth, his cheeks so pink they looked rouged. Despite his short stature, the jaunty tilt of his head and his puffed up rooster-strut made him seem bigger than those around him. He had to be Zora's husband, Alyosha, the owner of the Zorka Circus. His marriage long ago to Zora was supposed to heal the rift between Zorka and Skomori clans. It hadn't worked.

After lowering the wheelchair onto the wooden platform, the two muscle-men pushed it under the arch to the edge of the stage facing Sylvie and the other two brides.

Sylvie's bouquet trembled. This close, the men looked frighteningly familiar. They resembled the thief from the RV, same brown hair, Neanderthal brow, square jawline, and weight-lifter's body...except these were taller and

74

older. Otherwise, the similarity was so strong they had to be related. Did they know the thief—or killer—and about the body, too? What if there was a whole family of killers living in the circus?

Sylvie shook her head, telling herself she was overreacting.

Zora straightened in her wheelchair and clutched the armrests with blue-veined hands, their joints hugely swollen.

"As it was for our ancestors, so it continues," she said in a voice as cracked and parched as a dried-out creek bed. "Women bloodwalkers marry Skomori men, beget children, and then teach their girls to bloodwalk. Our vocation is almost 700 years old, but our line dates back to Novgorod in Rus, over 1000 years ago. Can you three carry the weight of this heritage? We shall see."

The pebbles stabbing Sylvie felt like they were growing in size and number. Although she desperately wanted to get this over with and fling her shoes off, she prayed Zora would pick another girl to go first. Her mother had explained that bloodwalker weddings included a "seeing" and a "pronouncement," but the thought of hearing her future told from a faceless shroud, in a voice that seemed to come from the depths of a tomb, terrified her.

"You. Orange dress." Zora thrust a gnarled finger at Liana. Aunt Cosmina hurried forward and murmured in Zora's ear. Zora cleared her throat. "Liana Miruna Platko, come here. Kneel before me."

Liana teetered forward, trying to keep her weight on her heels—her pebbles had probably all fallen to the toes of her boots—but the spiked high heels sank in the grass, throwing off her balance. She tripped and collapsed gracelessly onto her knees and had to crawl the last few feet to Zora.

Sylvie would have gloated if she wasn't in so much pain herself.

"A tall one...Wide hips... Good bonesss..." Zora stretched the word out as if she liked the feel of it in her mouth. After a pause, she continued. "I sense energy in you. You have ambition. Commendable—but not for a wife. You must become the fertile earth below your family's feet." Her voice rose. "Whoever marries this girl must keep her fat and pregnant!" She chuckled but it devolved into a hacking cough. Aunt Cosmina took a dark bottle from her satchel and gave it to Zora, who maneuvered it beneath her heavy veil. Slurping sounds issued before she handed it back. "Young lady, you will put your energies where you should. Into your home, household, and children."

Sylvie could imagine Liana rolling her eyes.

"Who wishes to marry this woman?" Zora called out.

A man appeared at Liana's side. Sylvie startled, realizing the grooms and families were right behind them now. Her own groom must be just feet away, but she was too scared to look.

"I am Claudiu Gogean," the man next to Liana said. Short and wiry, his suit barely closed over his paunch, and gray sprinkled his brown hair. He had to be over forty. "I own a dairy farm in Ardud, Romania. I will marry this girl."

Ardud was near Sylvie's village but a long way from the Carpathian Mountains where Liana grew up. As a milkmaid mucking out cow sheds, Liana wouldn't have time to frequent hair and nail salons anymore.

"Acceptable," Zora announced.

The man pulled a length of braided leather from his suit pocket, and when Liana extended her arms, he bound her wrists together, leaving a few feet free to hold the end in his hand.

"You are now man and wife," Zora said.

Liana's new husband hauled her up by the leather lead and pulled her in the direction of the food tables. On his way, Liana's mother handed him a fat envelope. Liana's dowry. Claudiu could probably afford a few more cows now.

From the corner of her eye, Sylvie noticed more circus people standing with Yuri behind the banquet tables, and others now lurked at the edges of the clearing. Strange that they'd be interested in a Skomori-bloodwalker wedding. It wasn't as if there'd be music or dancing. The Skomori frowned on that type of gaiety.

Aunt Cosmina remained at Zora's side and bent to her ear.

"Ada Felicia Sterescu. Come here," Zora said.

Ada slid her feet along the ground as if skating on a pond. The unusual strategy didn't seem to help, since whimpers crept out with each step. When the girl reached Zora, she fell onto her knees.

"What a little thing you are. Delicate as a bird. Soft as down." Zora fell silent and turned her head toward the growing murmur.

A bigger group of Zorka had appeared among the performers' tents. They stopped at the edge of the clearing, scowling and muttering to each other.

Zora returned her attention to Ada. "Like most birds, your voice will sing sweetest from the security of a roost. Stay close to your home, young one. Don't venture far from it. The world is filled with dangerous things. There are monsters that might like the taste of young, tender fowl."

Ada gasped.

Behind Zora, the smile drained from Alyosha's face.

A sudden dread filled Sylvie. It sounded like a reference to the tooth marks on the dead child. Did Zora know something?

"Who will marry this woman?" Zora called over the noise of the onlookers.

"I am Dragomir Popescu." A young man stepped up to stand beside Ada's small form, his blond hair as pale as moonlight. "I live in Oradea, Romania, and I work with my father, the groundskeeper for Rulikowski Cemetery. I will—"

"Ah!" Zora interrupted. "Good! A family that keeps to the old ways, not toiling on a farm or cobbling shoes like the *Baran*. We tend to the dead. If you want this girl, she is your wife from this day forward."

After a slight bow, Dragomir produced his own braided leather rope, bound Ada's wrists, and helped her up. He also received a plump envelope as he moved toward the banquet area.

"Sylvia Annamaria Dinescu," Zora said.

Perhaps it was a trick of the fading light, but it suddenly seemed colder and darker in the clearing. All the hair stood up on Sylvie's arms.

"Come here. Kneel before me." Zora ordered.

Sylvie couldn't move. Didn't want to move. Not toward *her.*

At Sylvie's hesitance, Aunt Cosmina gave her an encouraging smile and beckoned.

Sylvie swallowed and forced herself forward, her fear of what Zora might say outweighing the discomfort of walking. She made it to her knees without falling, now so close to the ancient bloodwalker that she could make out the glitter of Zora's eyes through her lace veil. Red and bloodshot, they burned into Sylvie's.

"Careful steps lead to a careful life, young one. You are practical, quiet, and thoughtful. But...you hide much within."

Prickles ran across Sylvie's neck like spiders. If Zora could see "within," she'd know all Sylvie's secrets and failures.

"In time, you will bloom like the beautiful flowers you have in..." Zora trailed off and leaned so far forward that Sylvie was afraid she'd fall off her chair. The old woman's hand shot out and captured Sylvie's wrist. "Death!" the bloodwalker howled. "I see nothing but death in your future!"

Sylvie tried to pull away, but the twisted, arthritic hand gripped hers like a steel trap.

Alyosha and Aunt Cosmina leaped to the wheelchair, whispering urgently into Zora's ears.

But Zora wasn't done.

"Wherever you shall go, tragedy will follow," the bloodwalker shrieked. "Everyone around you will come to grief and die."

Sylvie's pulse thudded in her ears. Her bouquet tumbled to the ground, and she whimpered, trying desperately to pry the old woman's hand off.

The muttering at the edges of the clearing grew into a bedlam of shouts.

Zora suddenly released her grasp, and Sylvie rocked

back on her haunches.

"Does anyone still want to marry her?" Zora cried.

No one moved to Sylvie's side. No one helped her up. Her heart squeezed inside her chest as if a fist was crushing it. This was what it felt like to be abandoned. To be less than nothing. Her life, her dreams, finished before they'd even begun.

A thunderous crash resonated behind her.

Sylvie twisted around.

The Zorka had overturned the banquet tables, spilling all the food and drinks to the ground. The ones clustered by the surrounding tents cheered. Then they all surged into the clearing, straight for the stage—and Sylvie.

CHAPTER NINE

Rurik
Obudai Island, Hungary

Despite the surly people in the crowd, Rurik thought he had the situation under control—until Yuri caved and the people near him upended the tables. Then everything went to hell faster than a lightning strike.

The mob that Rurik had penned between two tents— with spread arms and colorful epithets of what he'd do to them if they tried to pass—cheered the tables' demise and scattered, only to circle around and barge through the gap on Yuri's side while other rioters mowed Misha down and stampeded into the clearing.

Rurik hurtled through milling bodies, aiming for the stage. Dmitry and Viktor took up positions on either side of Alyosha. A chubby old lady flung herself in front of Zora's wheelchair and was holding a cane like a baseball bat. But if the crowd attacked, they'd be overwhelmed.

Rurik shoved people out of the way. In seconds, he reached the platform and planted himself in front of it, glaring at the throng.

"Ow!" One of the brides lay on the ground and jerked her hand out from under his shoe.

He pulled her up. Her veil flew off, and he recognized the pretty Skomori bloodwalker from the scissors incident. Tears streamed down her face. She tried to run after her veil, but he pulled her back. "Get on the stage with the others," he said in Romanian. "And stay behind me."

She shook her head, sobbing out words that included "she hates me" and "cast out."

He had no time to figure out what she meant before the horde surrounding the stage closed in.

80

One of Bartelli's sons, a teen trapeze artist with a quick temper and inflated ego, grabbed the bride's arm. "Skomori witch! Go back to hell!"

Rurik's fist lashed out and connected to the boy's jaw with a resounding *crack*. The teen dropped like a stone. Damn. Rurik should have pulled the punch. The kid would be out of work for weeks now. Though it would be a pleasure to have the loudmouth's jaw wired shut for the duration.

All across the clearing, circus people encircled the Skomori men and women, yelling and shoving them toward the parking lot.

A young Skomori man with white-blond hair stood his ground, sheltering two bloodwalker women behind him. Minko and two of his riders attacked with riding crops. The leather whips rose and fell, and the women squealed, covering their heads.

Fury burned in Rurik's veins as the bullies ganged up on the defenseless Skomori. Then his attention snapped back to the stage when two fire-eaters rushed him. He kicked the legs out from under one—careful not to break bones this time—and then clipped the other on the jaw hard enough to send him staggering away.

Someone leaped onto the rear of the stage, and Rurik shouted a warning. Viktor turned from Alyosha's side to meet the invader with a punch to the gut. Dmitry finished the job by grabbing the guy's shirt, spinning him around, and booting him back into the mob.

Alyosha jumped onto the ground and stormed toward the center of the clearing.

Refusing to abandon the women onstage, Rurik let the man pass. Alyosha always knew what he was doing.

Dmitry and Viktor bounded after him, but he raised his hand. They halted ten yards away, like well-trained dogs.

"All of you!" Alyosha let loose in a voice so loud it seemed impossible it could come from such a small man. "You bring shame on the circus. Shame on the Zorka clan. Shame. On. Me."

The attackers hesitated. Fists and riding crops paused mid-air. Insults and shouts trailed off.

"The Skomori aren't the ones causing trouble. You are!" Alyosha thundered.

"They shouldn't be here," a brave voice rang out.

"They brought the police," another sputtered.

"One wedding makes no difference to the police." Alyosha gave a derisive snort, but then stabbed a finger at those around him. "It's your actions that will attract their attention."

The circus people eyed each other with uncertain frowns.

"We'll stop—when the scumbags leave!" Minko loomed over the Skomori near him, his whipcord muscles coiled as tightly as the riding whip brandished in his hand. "They have no right to be here."

"And what rights do *we* have?" Alyosha swept his gaze across his employees. "Do you forget how outsiders treat us? They applaud our shows, but if we walk into their shops, they kick us out. Call us thieves and panhandlers. We've all been persecuted—simply because we're different from them."

A few acrobats and roustabouts mumbled agreement. The tightrope walkers stared at the ground. Others weren't silenced so easily.

"They're bad luck, and we have enough problems."

"And the biggest is our pay!"

"We get treated like slaves, and you throw the Skomori a party!"

Ivan's tall form appeared at the edge of the crowd. He pushed his way through, his gray hair dull in the fading light. "Who cares about the Skomori?" he called out. "Let them marry and be gone."

For a second, Rurik could almost feel the tension decrease—until Ivan spoke again.

"I lost another cyclist today. The second in two months. Why? Because he"—Ivan pointed a finger at Alyosha—"isn't paying worth a damn!"

Alyosha's jaw muscles twitched.

Ivan paced in a circle around the ringmaster. "We work our asses off—for what? The tour schedule is wrecked, the publicity is bad, the money is shit!"

Rurik stared open-mouthed at Ivan, stunned he'd joined the rebellion against Alyosha.

"My salary is *lower* than shit!" Bartelli spat on the ground.

"And why are we in Hungary so early?" said Bartelli's oldest son. "We should be in Zagreb. Lots of money in Zagreb."

"Where are the customers?" a woman horseback rider said.

"No advertising. No customers. No money!" Ivan shouted.

A blood-red flush crept up Alyosha's face.

Rurik caught Ivan's eye and gave a little shake of his head. Attacking the one man who could control the mob was a stupid and dangerous move. But Ivan plunged on.

"And *who* is in charge of advertising?" Ivan faced the ringmaster. "What's the matter? You getting too senile to remember how it's done?"

Alyosha clenched his fists, and his body began to tremble, his complexion flaming so bright he almost glowed in the dark.

"Maybe you need to retire, old man." Ivan folded his arms across his chest.

"Yeah. Hire someone who can do the job. And one who comes up past my belt buckle," said tall Minko with a grin.

Scattered chuckles rose from the crowd—and Alyosha exploded.

"Have you forgotten who I am?" Alyosha roared, spittle flying. "I am Alyosha Zurenko! From the number one circus family in Russia. My brother Kazimir runs the Moscow Circus School, and my brother Vladislav owns the St. Petersburg *Zorka Cyrka*. I could fire all of you! One word from me, and my brothers would have you blackballed from every major circus. You think money is hard to come by now? I can make sure you never make any again!"

A hush fell over the circus people. They shifted and jerked as if ants were crawling on them.

"I'll tell you what's going to happen. You'll go back to your homes—*now!*—and get ready for tonight's performance, and thank *me* that you still have jobs."

The son of Bartelli opened his mouth, but his father

cuffed him to silence. Being blacklisted in the close-knit circus business was a serious threat, one none of them could take lightly. With a few resentful glares at Alyosha, the circus people turned away and trudged back into the maze of tents.

Ivan strolled past Rurik. "I know all about Kazimir and Vladislav," the cyclist said in a low tone. "But the others needed a reminder."

Rurik relaxed, a little smile pulling at his lips. Trust the crafty old cyclist to have goaded Alyosha into playing his trump card.

"See you after the show." Ivan gave Rurik a wink and left the clearing.

"Now, let's get on with this!" Alyosha said, stomping back to the stage. After a quick word with Viktor and Dmitry, they pushed Zora's wheelchair to the back of the platform and carried it away. The woman with the cane tried to follow, but Alyosha stopped her. "Stay here. You need to finish this." Alyosha pointed at the huddled clusters of Skomori. "You! Come here. My wife is ill and must leave. But there were supposed to be three weddings today, and by God, there will be!"

The bloodwalkers and Skomori men approached the platform slowly.

"We have another bloodwalker elder to officiate." Alyosha beckoned the heavyset woman forward as Rurik retreated into the shadow of the arch. "Cosmina Yurchenko will conclude the ceremony. The last bride and groom—get up here."

Like an enraged father at a shotgun wedding, Alyosha hustled the pretty blond bride into a kneeling position and demanded the groom step up and take his place at her side. After exchanging the required promises, the Yurchenko woman pronounced them married.

Rurik felt a strange twinge in his chest when the girl allowed her hands to be bound by the hulking Skomori man.

"Rurik!" Alyosha shouted. When Rurik reached his side, he pointed behind the stage. "Get that oil drum, bring it here, and light the timbers in it so the brides can burn their blasted veils. Then get them all out of here and make sure the box office opens on time."

"Yes, sir," Rurik said. As he did Alyosha's bidding, he couldn't help but watch the bloodwalker girl—the one who'd worried about his injuries in the wardrobe trailer, the one who hadn't shrank in fear at the sight of him. He wondered if she'd be happy with her new husband.

He squashed flickers of jealousy. It was none of his business after all. Most likely, he'd never even see her again.

* * *

Strings of fairy lights dangled over the path to the big top, mimicking the stars that hung across the night sky above.

After a quick check to make sure no buskers lingered to waylay customers on their way to the concession carts and no teens huddled together passing liquor bottles or joints between them, Rurik walked around the giant tent to the back entrance. The music of the plate-spinning act blared through the canvas walls. They used a fast-paced tune to build excitement and give the illusion the two women performers were racing to complete a thrilling feat. All the acts had music that suited them: waltzes for the horses, a cheerful calliope melody for the clowns, trumpets for the fire-eaters, and hard rock for the motorcyclists' "Globe of Death." Rurik and his parents had used classic Tchaikovsky for their feats of strength and balance. The Markarov strongmen used rap music for theirs.

He entered the clearing behind the tent, greeted by the bitter scent of smoke. The rose-decorated arch remained at the end, but maintenance had removed the overturned tables and the food and flower mess that littered the ground. At the center, a gritty haze surrounded the oil drum. It still crackled and spat sparks, the packed newspaper and wooden kindling inside had been overkill for burning three little veils.

Rurik paused beside it and looked down at the flickering flames, recalling the final time he'd seen the blond bloodwalker—and what she'd said to him.

After she'd found her green veil stuck on a nail at the

bottom of the arch, she'd joined the other brides around the bonfire for some ritual where the new husbands took the veils, pronounced their wives' childhood over, and tossed the fabric into the blaze. The blond girl's husband let go of her "leash" for a minute as he tried to get close to the fire without getting burned.

As soon as his back was turned, the girl hurried to Rurik's side, peering up at him through enormous blue eyes. "Go to the RV. The camper the brides changed in. It's at the very end of the rows. There's..." She broke off, her teeth pulling at her plump lower lip as if she was afraid to say more.

"Did you leave something?" he said . "I can go with you if you're afraid to go back alone." He'd make damn sure none of the Zorka did anything to her.

"No. It's...there's something there. Very bad. Please"— her fingers clung to his forearm—"go...search under the sink. It's a matter of life and *death.*"

The way she said the last word sent a chill through Rurik. He opened his mouth to ask her what she meant when her husband suddenly appeared at her shoulder.

"What's this? How dare you speak to this oaf!" The man grabbed up the length of leather binding her wrists and jerked her hands from Rurik's arm. His grating voice sank to an ominous pitch. "You're mine now. When we get home, you're going to get a reminder of proper behavior."

The hackles rose on Rurik's back, and all his muscles tensed. He barely stopped himself from bashing in the man's face . There was nothing worse than a man who bullied women or children. But they were Skomori and lived by the old ways. No matter how twisted and sick.

As the girl's new husband dragged her away, she looked back over her shoulder and mouthed, "Go to the RV."

Rurik had no time then. Getting Yuri and Misha to escort the Skomori off circus grounds, organizing the clean-up crew, and making sure the ticket takers received their cash drawers kept him busy. He stared at the fire's dying embers and promised himself that as soon as he picked up the box office receipts and put them in the safe, he'd go and check that camper.

An engine snarled from behind the tents. Ivan rode through the clearing on a brightly painted motorcycle. He waved at Rurik and paused at the rear entrance, letting the girls who performed the plate-spinning act trot out of the opening.

Alyosha's voice boomed over the loudspeaker system. "Now you will see a stupendous feat all the way from Moscow! The amazing Ivan and his Globe of Death will shock and thrill you—" The rest was drowned out as Ivan gunned the motor and roared into the big top.

Rurik ambled after him, picturing every move of Ivan's show since he'd seen it from the wings countless times. The cyclist would blast into the center ring and pop wheelies for the crowd as his giant round cage was lowered from above. Then he'd speed along the outside ring, flying by the customers' faces, as the roustabouts fastened the twelve-foot diameter globe to the ground, and opened the big, hinged door that dropped to become a ramp. After riding his bike up and into the bottom of the cage, the roustabouts would close the ramp and Alyosha would lock it, making a big deal of there being no escape from the "Globe of Death."

What followed would be the cyclists—now only Ivan—speeding in a circle inside the ball until centrifugal force allowed him to zip around horizontally or vertically and not fall off his bike. With three riders on different routes barely avoiding crashing into one another, it was very impressive. With one rider, not so much.

At the rear entrance, Tania, the box office manager, handed Rurik the bag with the night's proceeds. Marva stood inside the canvas flaps, her show over, but staying close with the first aid kit in case a performer or audience member needed help. She nodded at Rurik with a tired smile. As he turned to leave, he noticed Dmitry and Viktor hanging back in the shadows, watching Ivan drive his cycle into the globe. Odd, since their strongman show had finished half an hour before.

Rurik tucked the cash bag under his arm and made it halfway across the clearing when screams erupted from the tent. He raced back and dove through the tent flaps, his gaze flashing across the arena.

In the center ring, the door to the cage had fallen open, and Ivan's cycle jack-knifed into it. Bits of metal glinted from the sawdust. A loose tire rolled toward the audience. Inside the globe, Ivan lay sprawled, his body freakishly twisted.

Marva dashed across the ring and into the cage, yelling for the roustabouts to bring a stretcher.

Moving Ivan might be bad, but all the performers knew that if they had an accident, they'd be removed quickly and quietly from the audience's view. Only then would an ambulance be called. The show came first. Always.

The audience's murmurs rose to a clamor of alarm as the workers ran toward the globe with the stretcher. Rurik started after them. Strong hands grabbed his arms. Dmitry held him on one side, Viktor the other.

"You can't go out there," Viktor said.

"The customers are scared enough," Dmitry added. "Seeing *your* face will make it worse."

Rurik shook them off, but swallowed his anger. They were right. The last thing the audience needed was to see him. It seemed to take forever for Marva and the men to belt Ivan onto the backboard and carry him to the exit.

Ivan's eyes were closed inside his helmet, his head held in place by an orange neck brace. One wrist was bent back too far. His shin bone stuck out from the shredded leggings of his costume.

Rurik grabbed Marva's arm as she passed. "How bad is it?"

"I can't tell." She wiped sweat beading on her forehead. "A broken leg, dislocated wrist. Probably a concussion. There might be internal bleeding. We'll call an ambulance and get him out to the parking lot."

Rurik's jaw tightened. Another circus rule—no emergency sirens where the audience could hear them.

"Don't worry," Marva said. "I'll go with him and call as soon as I know anything."

Alyosha came running up. "Marva! Get him a private room. The best doctors. Spare no expense."

She nodded and hurried after the stretcher.

"You, get that globe out of the ring!" Alyosha yelled at a couple of the remaining roustabouts. He turned to the Indian fire-eaters standing nearby. "Get ready. You're on as soon as it's clear."

The exotic-looking men in brilliant gold costumes began to check the scimitars strapped to their backs and bottles of fuel hanging from their belts.

Alyosha dashed back toward the ring, raising the wireless microphone to his lips, already beginning the spiel that introduced the next act.

Rurik exited the tent, sucking down lungfuls of bracing night air, his mind dissecting the accident.

Of the hundreds of times Ivan and his cyclists had performed their show, the cage door had never fallen open. Not even in practice. Ugly suspicions about the clowns' threat to Ivan crossed Rurik's mind. And about Alyosha. How angry had the old man been about Ivan's nasty comments?

Rurik shook his head. Accidents happened. People were injured. Sometimes killed. That was life in the circus.

Feet pounded across the clearing. Pavel and Anatoly Markarov, the sons of Dmitry, sprinted up, breathing hard. Miniature copies of their father. All muscle, compacted into shorter, and if possible, nastier versions.

"It's under control," Pavel said to his father. "The riders and a bunch of others helped us put it out."

"Put what out?" Rurik said.

"The fire." Dmitry shrugged like it was no big deal. "One of the empty campers caught on fire. It wasn't hooked to any propane tanks, so there was no real danger. We were..." He exchanged a quick look with his brother. "We were here to tell Alyosha about it, but...it seems his plate is full with the accident."

"So it's out now?" Rurik said to Pavel. "No damage?"

The young man laughed. "Well, I wouldn't say that. It's totally wrecked. But no one was using it, and Alyosha has insurance. No problem."

Rurik didn't like any of the Markarovs, but he particularly disliked Pavel. The boy had a sly attitude and a twisted sense of humor. "When the hell did this happen?

89

Why didn't you come get me?"

Dmitry stepped in front of his son, his chin jutting. "We didn't need *you*. We take care of things just fine. That's why Alyosha depends on us more than you now."

Before Rurik did anything he'd regret, like introducing pompous Dmitry's head to his own asshole, he spun and headed past the performers' tents toward the RV portion of the camp.

At the very back stood the smoking remains of the old camper. Sides blackened. Roof caved in. Tires still smoldering. The smells of soot and burned plastic turned the air toxic. A few performers still had small garden hoses trained on the wreck. Steam joined the smoke spiraling into the night sky.

Another of the circus's rules: unless the big top was on fire, no one was to call the fire department. Like all other problems, they handled fires internally.

Rurik sighed and walked away, only to stop and turn back again.

This was the RV the bloodwalker brides had used—the one the girl had begged him to search.

His eyes shrank to slits. Whatever she thought was in there was gone now. Burned to ashes.

But the unused camper wasn't hooked to the electric line. It had no propane tanks.

The fire hadn't lit itself.

Someone had burned down that RV on purpose.

CHAPTER TEN

Sylvie
Miskolc, Hungary

> *After laying out the corpse and removing its clothing,*
> *pour a thin line of honey around the body. It will trap*
> *the lice leaving the cooling flesh and keep them*
> *from using you as their new, warmer home.*
> *~ The Bloodwalker's Book*

Sylvie whipped the rolls out of the oven, transferred the steaming buns onto a plate, and slid it onto the table next to her husband's half-finished dinner.

The single bulb over the kitchen table barely lit the one-room apartment, but she had no trouble reading the expression on Miron's face.

"Now you give me rolls?" Miron's lips curled in a sneer. "Are you stupid? My stew's finished."

The tiny stove didn't have space to cook everything at once. But she kept her lips buttoned. She'd learned.

"Damned sorry excuse for a meal. Stew, baked vegetable *ghivetch*, cabbage noodles, and biscuits." He slapped the table. Utensils and glasses rattled. "Where's the soup? Where's the rice? You couldn't even make *mamaliga*. That's served on every table in Romania!"

She'd made *mamaliga*, a corn meal porridge, two nights before. It hadn't met with his approval. She almost let an "I'm sorry" slip out, but he viewed apologies as back talk and would get even angrier. She dropped her gaze to the floor, focusing on the lines of splintered wood between her shoes.

After a moment, he shoved his chair back, and the tension in her shoulders eased. Every night he went off

91

for a few hours and returned smelling like cigarette smoke and beer. But he always arrivedin a better mood . He didn't spend time criticizing—too interested in something else.

Miron shrugged on a jacket. "What's this?" he said , pointing at a canvas bag under the coat rack.

"It's my...um..."

He grabbed it, crossed to the bed, and upended the contents onto the covers.

Darting to his side, she saved the cotton wadding before it bounced onto the floor, but the ball of twine fell off and rolled under the wardrobe.

"What is this junk?" He pawed through candles, towels, a bottle of baby oil and one of vinegar, a large jar of honey, and a pack of upholstery needles.

"It's my bloodwalking bag. In case...someone needs me."

"You mean the things you use to prepare a body?"

She nodded.

"Fah!" He threw the things down as if they'd contaminated him. "Are you an idiot? You live in a city now. They have funeral homes for this. No one will come to you. You can't even speak their language."

"If I had a Romanian-Hungarian dictionary, I could learn to—"

"No!" His yell made her jump. He loomed over her, his breathing heavy, nostrils flared, and a glint in his eye she hadn't seen since the night he brought her home and "taught" her proper behavior. "I told you never to speak to anyone. Not the customers. Not the tradesmen. Not the neighbors. What do you do if a customer asks a question?"

"Point to the sign with your mobile phone number on it," she whispered.

"And what do you do when you need something from a store?"

"Wait until you come home and give you a list."

"And I bring everything you need, right?"

"Yes." She bowed her head. He took direct eye contact as a challenge.

"That's right. Now, throw this shit away. No wife of mine is going to be known for handling the dead." His footsteps stomped across the floor. "And stop bringing feathers and rat fur into the house. Only morons follow those filthy Skomori traditions." A moment later, the front door slammed, and she heard him trotting down the stairs.

The breath she'd been holding exploded from her lungs. Slowly, her heart rate returned to normal, and the shaking in her limbs stopped. She gathered up her bloodwalking tools. Her fingers lingered on the things, feeling their weight, their well-worn edges. The candles smelled good, though aroma wasn't what they were used for. Bloodwalkers used those to—

No. That was all over now.

She took everything to the garbage pail and hesitated only a second before dumping it in.

To be free from bloodwalking. Free from Skomori rules. It was what she'd always wanted, wasn't it?

But seeing her things in the trash left her feeling sad and lonely.

Every day she had the strangest feeling that little parts of herself were drifting away, and soon there'd be nothing left.

* * *

Sylvie stretched the dress shirt over the padded board and lowered the pressing panel. Steam shot out from under it, and another bead of sweat trickled down her forehead. Almost without thought, her hands lifted the handle, repositioned the shirt, and lowered the press again. Front. Back. Sleeves. Cuffs. Collar. Then over to the folding table. Insert the plastic cutout. Whip sleeves and sides over, and then fold in thirds from bottom up. Stack at the end with all the others.

She couldn't even remember whose laundry she was doing anymore. The fat lady with bad breath. Or the hatchet-nosed woman who glared at the laundry scale, willing the number to stay low. Or maybe the elderly woman whose heavy-lidded expression was always dazed and distant.

That woman's rheumy eyes gave Sylvie the shivers and reminded her of Mrs. Costiniu—and her first solo bloodwalk.

Ninety-year old Mrs. Costiniu had passed peacefully in

her sleep. It was the last peaceful thing she ever did.

As Sylvie worked on her, Mrs. Costiniu's lips kept drawing back over her teeth in a gruesome smile. Thinking the problem was the woman's dentures, Sylvie removed them. But then the mouth kept dropping open. Following bloodwalker technique, Sylvie put a rolled-up towel beneath the old woman's jaw, forcing her mouth closed, and continued with the preparations.

The next hurdle was that no amount of pressing and massaging would make the eyelids stay closed and she'd forgotten the twine used to sew them shut. Trying to fix the problem took Sylvie too long. Rigor mortis set in. The entire body stiffened. Mrs. Costiniu's eyes dried out with one looking left and one looking right. And only then did Sylvie realize that without the dentures, the mouth closed too far—the woman's chin practically disappearing under her nose. Trying to push the dentures back in proved impossible. So, with her chin and mouth pinched tighter than a draw-string pouch, Mrs. Costiniu stared cockeyed at her family during the whole wake.

That was the beginning of the cruel gossip that followed Sylvie for years.

At least running the laundry machines wasn't hard. It had taken Sylvie less than a week to learn everything, although Miron had taught her for only a day before disappearing, leaving her to figure out most of it on her own.

With an arthritic groan, the dryer finished its last cycle and rattled to a stop. She moved to the table next to it and wiped it with a towel before setting the dry clothes on it. Between the heat and the humidity, a wet sheen coated every surface in the shop. As she folded undershirts and briefs, her eyes escaped to the one window in the back. Covered with iron bars. The little garden behind the store was a nasty tangle of weeds and bushes, but she loved to look at the green hues. They reminded her of Romania.

The shop's bell jangled as someone pushed the front door open.

Unusual, since it was almost six, and customers mostly came in the morning.

She walked to the front on stiff legs, surprised to see a man at the counter. Another stood in the doorway, and a large truck was parked by the curb outside.

The man at the counter, middle-aged with sagging jowls and scruffy beard, handed her a pen and a clipboard with a form on it. He said something she didn't understand and pointed to an empty line at the bottom of the slip.

Outside, a third man opened the truck and muscled a huge box to the edge. They were delivering something. She clutched the pen. Her heart thumped. Sign it or not. The wrong decision could land her in trouble with Miron. She stared at the slip, unable to decide.

The man reached around the clipboard and tapped the empty line with a dirty fingernail. His sour perspiration rose up her nose, even stronger than the scent of laundry soap from the washers. His blue coveralls were wrinkled and stained. On his chest, a sown on patch displayed a name. Emil Lupescu.

Lupescu was a Romanian name.

She took a chance. "You're delivering something to the shop?" she said in Romanian.

Lupescu's bushy eyebrows rose, and he replied in Romanian. "A dry-cleaning machine and an automated pressing-folding system. Ordered by Mr. Miron Florescu. They're both pretty big. Don't know how we'll get them in there." He cast a dubious glance at the rear of the store, its tight space already crammed with several industrial-sized washers and dryers.

If Miron had ordered the equipment, it must be all right. She signed her name and handed back the board. Lupescu gave her a receipt but frowned at his copy and said, "This says to use the loading dock entrance on the side, but you got stores on both sides. Is there a loading dock in back?"

She shook her head.

He sucked on his lower lip, glaring at the bill, and then peered at the number painted on the open door. "Oh, hell. This is Florescu Laundry at Six Szechenyi Street. We need the Florescu Laundry at number *Sixty*. That's eight, nine blocks down. Sorry, ma'am." Shaking his head and muttering, he left. Moments later, the men closed up the truck, and it rumbled off down the street.

She had no idea Miron had another store. That must be where he spent his days.

At six, she closed up and ran upstairs to start dinner, but as she cut and chopped, she couldn't help wondering what the other shop was like, and why it was getting costly new equipment while her shop's machines were always leaking and shorting out the fuses.

* * *

After Miron finished his dinner and left the apartment, Sylvie stared at the slip left by the delivery man until she couldn't stand it anymore. Number Sixty should be easy to find. She only wanted a glimpse of it, and Miron wouldn't be back for hours.

She sped along the cobbled bricks of Szechenyi Street, avoiding the light spilling from shop windows and pooling under streetlamps. By following the tram tracks in the center of the road, her black dress melded with the darkness, concealing her.

The farther down the street she went, the more her surroundings changed.

Sprayed graffiti no longer marked the stone façades of buildings. Windows were cleaner, brighter, and displayed fancier merchandise. Even the streetlights were prettier, painted in shiny black enamel. They had antique gas lamp frames at the top, creating a glowing head shape as if tall tuxedoed waiters gazed down to survey the crowd.

Flowers decorated everything—blooming from planters on the sidewalks, urns beside doorways, and even in baskets hanging from streetlamp poles.

Gone were the smells of damp plaster, mildew, and garbage. Replaced with the perfumes of flower blossoms and well-dressed pedestrians.

But Sylvie had underestimated the length of city blocks. Twenty minutes had passed since she'd snuck out from her building. If she didn't find the other laundry shop soon, she'd have to turn back. The risk of Miron coming home early was too great.

And then—there it was. A giant store taking up the whole corner of the next street.

Fluorescents blazed inside, shining through the front windows and lighting the sidewalk. Three stone steps led up to its double-doored entrance. Over it, a sign read "Florescu Laundry and Dry-Cleaning."

The buzz of a circular saw drifted onto the street along with a faint cloud of dust from the open doors. Carpenters worked on new countertops, heavy platforms for the machines, and hammered paneling onto inner walls.

Then her gaze swept upward, and her lips parted in awe.

The apartment above the shop spanned two floors. French doors opened onto wrought-iron balconies. Fancy carved shutters hung beside tall windows. Inside, workmen were painting walls and the trim on elaborate corner moldings. In a large front room, two men stood on scaffolding, lifting a glittering chandelier to the ceiling.

A crystal chandelier.

She'd never seen one in real life, only on TV.

The apartment was glorious—a palace!

Excitement stirred her blood. This was what Miron was doing every day. Preparing a new store and a new home for them. Of course he wouldn't tell her about it. Men in her village never shared their business plans with their wives. He was going to surprise her with it.

For the first time in a week, she smiled.

But she had to get back. Keep Miron from finding out she'd spied. Act amazed when he finally brought her to see it.

She headed back, elation making her float past the well-dressed couples who strolled along the avenue.

She'd been too critical of her husband. Too self-centered. It must have taken a lot of money and work to open a place like that. His demanding attitude was just the result of exhaustion and stress from the pressure. She promised herself she'd be more patient and supportive.

Halfway home, she thought she heard footsteps dogging her own, but when she looked back, she didn't see anyone following. Nonetheless, the tiny hairs on the back of her neck stood up. Sour saliva flooded the back of her mouth.

This was the city. Crimes were on the news every night.

People were dangerous here.

She sped up, almost running on the uneven cobblestone sidewalk. Dodging pedestrians and eyeing the shadows behind her.

The dark entrance to her building came into sight. Only a little farther.

From the corner of her eye, she glimpsed a form following her. Someone running. Gaining on her.

She flew toward her building, but as she passed an alley, a weight hit her in the back. Rough hands grabbed her shoulders and shoved her into the alley. Her shoes slid on the grimy cobblestones. She tore loose and spun around.

A black figure filled the mouth of the alley.

She cringed away, a shriek strangling in her throat.

"Sylvie!" A girl's voice hissed through the darkness. "We have to talk."

A face coalesced from the dimness. Skin pale. Circles under her eyes. A peasant's *babushka* covering her hair.

"Ada's dead," Liana said. "Murdered."

CHAPTER ELEVEN

Rurik
Bratislava, Slovakia

From the expansive parkland of Budapest's island, the circus moved to a cramped dirt lot next to a busy Lidl department store in Bratislava, the smallest site on the entire tour. Rurik always considered it a minor miracle when they managed to squeeze into it every year.

After a week of good weather, the circus's final day saw the clouds open up, turning the dirt lot into a swampy mess.

Rurik slogged through muck that oozed up to his ankles. With every step, the mud tried to suck the boots off his feet. Plus, the clay-type earth was as slick as motor oil . Deep ruts left by their trucks' wheels had become mini ravines. You slid down one side, splashed into the brown puddle at the bottom, and then had to climb up the other side. Or you just gave up and waded through the gritty water at the bottom and followed the furrow to where you wanted to go.

The humidity stayed close to a hundred percent. Sweat ran down Rurik's face, neck, and shoulders, and pooled in the small of his back. In minutes, his security shirt was soaked through and stuck to him like a wet washcloth.

Only a few performers ventured outside their tents and RVs. They wobbled over the treacherous ground with irritation stamped across their faces. Most stayed inside.

But for all that, the venue was perfect from Rurik's point of view. The killer couldn't slip through his defenses this time. The site's unusual features made it completely secure.

A ten-foot high, chain link fence surrounded the entire

lot, and there were only two gates. One on the main street, guarded by either him, Yuri, or Misha in eight-hour shifts. The other on a side street, which Rurik had chained closed and padlocked.

No way was the killer getting past him this time.

The walkie-talkie hanging off his belt crackled.

"Rurik? This is the front gate. Over," Misha said.

Rurik answered him, "Go ahead."

"Irina and Tasha Markarov at the checkpoint. Going shopping." Static buzzed for a second. "Oh... *Over.*"

Rurik had ordered Misha and Yuri to get his permission before letting anyone out of the compound. Irina was the elderly mother of Viktor and Dmitry. Tasha was Viktor's wife. They definitely didn't fit the killer's profile. "Okay. Let them go."

"Roger that. Over and out!" Misha's puppy-like enthusiasm carried over the static, bringing a half-smile to Rurik's face. The kid loved the new walkie-talkies and copied military jargon he'd heard in movies.

So far, Rurik's plan to cage the killer had worked. During their week in Bratislava, there had been no reports of missing children on the news. In a few hours, they'd put on the final show, and Rurik was determined to keep the killer penned up that night, too.

"This is the front gate. Over," Misha said.

"Yes?"

"Marva's back—with Ivan! She's driving around to the side entrance and needs you to let her in. Over."

"Okay. Got it."

Rurik started off at a run toward the side gate, but the waterlogged ground soon slowed him to a clumsy walk.

Since the accident, Ivan had been laid up in a Budapest hospital with a concussion, dislocated shoulder, sprained wrist, and a broken leg, which had required surgery and put him in a wheelchair. Alyosha had visited him twice during the week before announcing his discharge and that Marva would bring him home in the handicapped-equipped van they used for Zora.

Passing the roustabouts' tent, Rurik shouted for Pyotr. The brawny, blond Russian yanked on rubber boots and waded after him.

Rurik unlocked the gate, let Marva drive in, and fastened it shut again.

"Glad you brought help," Marva said, leaning out the window and nodding at Pyotr. "No one can push a wheelchair through this mess."

"Rurik," Ivan shouted from the back of the van. "Get in and drive! Marva will just get us stuck in this mess."

"Don't worry about me," Marva said over her shoulder. "I'm not the one who fell out of my own Globe of Death."

Ivan clamped his mouth shut, moustache bristling.

True to her word, Marva expertly guided the van through the rain-soaked ruts to within ten yards of Ivan's door. Rurik tipped an imaginary hat to her.

"Oh, please." She grinned. "Try hitching a twenty-foot trailer full of barking dogs to your RV, and then backing it into a slot, like I do. Every. Week."

After lowering the hydraulic platform with Ivan's wheelchair to the ground, Rurik and Pyotr grabbed it on either side and carried it to the RV. Marva ran ahead and opened the door. Getting it inside was a challenge, since the narrow doorway wouldn't fit both the men and the chair, and Ivan flatly refused to be carried.

"No one's picking me up like a damn baby. I'd rather spend the night out here in the rain!" Ivan bellowed.

"Glad to see time off has improved your temper," Rurik said.

Pyotr went in first, guiding the wheels up the stairs while avoiding Ivan's long cast, which covered his leg from thigh to toes.

Rurik lifted the entire thing, his muscles bunching, legs straining from squat to erect in a power-lift. Bands of sinew squeezed his abdomen, and he could hear the beat of his heart thrumming in his ears as he mounted the stairs. With an explosive release of breath, he set the chair in the cabin. "What the hell did you eat at that hospital? The other patients?"

"Ha ha." Ivan rolled his eyes. "You lie in bed for a week with nothing but Hungarian soap operas to watch and you'd be stuffing your face, too."

"I gotta go," Marva said from the doorway. "I stocked your fridge and moved your plates and glasses down so you can reach them. But as far as the bathroom goes, you're on your own. I'll check on you after the show."

"Thanks," Ivan mumbled as she left, followed by Pyotr. Rurik started for the door when Ivan said, "So? How's the search going? You've been here a week. Did you find the clown costume yet?"

Rurik turned back with a grimace. "Couldn't search. We're crammed in so tightly everyone can count the freckles on his neighbor's ass. But I've locked the place down. There are only two exits, and no one leaves unless I say so."

Ivan frowned. "But how do you know? Someone could say he's going for a walk, disappear, and grab up some little kid somewhere."

Rurik cocked his head. "I thought you didn't believe someone in the circus could really do something like that."

"I didn't." Ivan eyebrows slashed down over his blazing eyes. "Till I started searching all the trailers, and then some bastard messed with my equipment and tried to kill me!"

Rurik shook his head. "I examined the cage's hasp. It wasn't filed. All the screws were in place. It just slipped loose."

"I know my equipment, dammit!" Scarlet mounted Ivan's cheeks.

"You don't think it was an accident?"

"Like bloody hell."

"I'll take that as a no."

"Tell me what you're doing to catch the sonuvabitch!"

"Well...the back gate is locked, and we're covering the front entrance."

"Who's we?"

"Misha takes four to midnight, I take the midnight shift, and Yuri takes day."

Ivan made a rude noise. "Yuri. He's as helpful as tits on a bull." He slipped a finger into the top of his cast and scratched at his thigh. "But people must be going out for supplies."

"There's a store next door. People go and come right back. The only people who've been out longer were Viktor Markarov—to drop off one of the vans at the garage, and he walked back in half an hour—and Alyosha and Pavel Markarov went twice to Budapest to visit you. That's it. No one else."

The color seeped from Ivan's face. "Well, shit. I'd never have believed..."

"Believed what?" Rurik said alarmed at the shock clouding Ivan's eyes.

"Alyosha and Pavel. They lied to you. They didn't come to see me in the hospital. Not once. It's them! One of them is the clown—and he tried to kill me!"

* * *

Rurik paced across the front entrance of the lot, an hour into his midnight shift. His anger and frustration grew with every step. As much as he wanted to, he couldn't bring himself to question Alyosha. It was as good as accusing the man of lying—the man who'd been his only benefactor for the last ten years.

Pavel Markarov, however, deserved no such respect.

Rurik had confronted the kid when the Markarovs finished their performance. But flanked by his father, uncle, and brother, Pavel swore he'd gone to Hungary with Alyosha. He blamed Ivan, saying he must have been loopy from the pain meds and just didn't remember. Rurik knew Ivan better than that, but realized Pavel would never confess in front of his family. Rurik would have to wait and corner him alone. But Rurik hated waiting.

Hanging around after his shift ended, Misha dogged Rurik's steps, keeping up a one-sided conversation about his father's time in the military. "In training, my father ran every day, at least two miles. Even when it was fifteen below zero."

"Uh-huh," Rurik said. If Pavel was the killer, Alyosha had to know. Why would he keep quiet about it?

"And he trained with a PP-2000. Best machine gun there is."

"Mm-hm," Rurik mumbled as he paced across the entrance. Although the thought made him sick to his stomach, he had to consider the two were working together. There had only been one kidnapper at Istvantelek depot, but the other could have been waiting in a van close by.

"It has one of those laser sights, like the one Aleksey Dmitriev used in *The Interceptor*. Did you see that movie?"

Rurik swung around. "Do me a favor. Go check on Ivan and make sure he doesn't need anything."

"Sure." Misha grinned. "Be right back." The teen jogged away, slowing when he crossed into the mud beside the big top.

Left to his own thoughts, Rurik folded his arms and stared morosely at the empty park across the street. The smells of soggy grass and oily asphalt in front of him combined with cooked food, manure, and wet dog fur from the circus in a disgusting mix. Of those, the dog hair actually smelled the worst.

Even when he tried, he couldn't picture Alyosha as the killer. Rurik had grown up with him. If the man had shown any perverse attraction to children, Rurik would have known. Or heard rumors. A man doesn't get to be sixty-five and suddenly become a child-murdering maniac.

A long, frustrated breath streamed from his nostrils. When he thought about the suspects, one unnerving truth kept swimming to the surface no matter how hard he tried to push it down.

Alyosha *did* fit the size of the killer.

But so did almost a dozen others, including Pavel. Imagining *him* as the killer was much easier. That little bastard was lazy and arrogant and—

"Rurik!" a voice yelled over the walkie-talkie. Ivan? "Come to my RV. Quick!" Definitely Ivan.

Rurik raced into the big top to avoid the sodden ground outside.

Small security floods at the tops of the poles shone down, banishing the shadows from the center ring, but leaving plenty more lurking at the edges. As he ran through, they slid around him with a life of their own.

"What's going on? Ivan?" he yelled into the radio. No one replied. He hurtled across the ring and reached the exit in seconds.

Behind the big top, twenty tents spread in several rows across the quagmire. Lights glowed inside more than half. Above their canvas roofs, Rurik could just make out the tops of the RVs, lined up in two rows.

"Talk to me," Rurik said as he plunged between the tents, slipping and sliding through the muck.

A scream rose at the back of the encampment.

Rurik emerged from the tents and turned down the line of RVs, laboring through the worst of the mud.

Ivan's camper lay in the second row at the end. Light beamed from its open door. A figure stood in silhouette, a broom raised in both hands like a weapon.

Rurik vaulted onto the stairs.

Marva gasped and scrambled out of his way. "Oh my God. I thought you were the creature."

At the kitchen table, Ivan sat in his wheelchair. Face white. Eyes huge. Misha's walkie-talkie clutched to his chest. Mud and dirt smeared his hands and shirt, and more caked his white leg cast. "'Bout damn time. Someone broke in and tried to kill me—tried to rip my leg right off!"

"It was a monster, covered in mud—all mud—from head to foot!" Marva panted, still gripping the broom like a bat. "I hit it. Kept hitting it. But it never flinched. We would've been killed if Misha hadn't come in."

"It was a man not a monster," Ivan said. "Misha jumped on his back. Walloped him good, but he was strong. Threw Misha over his head." Ivan brought a fist down on the table. "The boy landed right here. And then the muddy sonuvabitch came after me *again!*"

"Ivan chucked a glass of vodka in its eyes. It stopped attacking, and Misha kicked it right in the chest."

"Where are they?" Rurik demanded.

"It ran off, and Misha chased it."

Rurik leaped from the RV and headed back the way he'd come. "Misha?" he called.

"Stop!" a voice shouted from somewhere ahead.

Rurik barreled forward, looking at the tents on one side and between the RVs on the other.

Twenty yards ahead of him, a lumpy and misshapen figure broke from cover between two campers. Slathered in mud from head to foot, it blended with the ground, looking as if a section of earth had suddenly come to life and reared up on thick legs. It paused and glanced at Rurik, the whites of its eyes glinting in the darkness, before it dashed across the open space and vanished into the line of tents.

A skinnier form chased after it. Misha. The kid splashed into a puddle and tumbled to his knees. "Get it!" he yelled toward the tents. "It attacked Ivan."

Rurik couldn't see who he was yelling at, but answering shouts erupted from the cluster of tents.

Lights flickered on in some RVs. Doors banged open. "What's happening?" someone yelled. "Who's there?"

Rurik sloshed toward Misha, staring between the tents' canvas walls as he passed. A flash of movement caught his eye—a brown form loping awkwardly toward the big top. The same uneven gait as the clown at the train depot. It was definitely the killer.

Now Rurik would finally catch the bastard.

Rurik bolted after him and tried to leap a rut but overshot, sliding and landing face first in the next ditch. Dirty water drenched his pants and shirt. His fingers sank into the ooze as he clawed his way to his feet. A second later, he was up and running again. Every step narrowed the gap to the dirt-covered figure.

"Misha! Get up here!" The killer was headed to the front of the circus—and the now unguarded main gate.

Rurik picked up his pace.

"There it is!" Two people hurtled between tents and tackled Rurik. All three toppled into the mud.

"It's me, Rurik! The attacker's aiming for the front gate. Head him off." Rurik struggled to his knees. Water flowed inside his boots. He dragged himself up and took off again, water squishing between his toes.

When he burst out of the tents, he spotted the killer in the shadow of the big top.

The mud-covered man hesitated, swiveling his head toward the street beyond the fence and back to the jumble of tents that had provided him with cover.

Rurik threw himself toward the big top, seeking to catch

the mud-man before he could get to the gate.

But he switched direction, swerving to the side. He scurried across murky ravines and then dove back into the tent rows.

Rurik chased after him, water spraying from under his feet.

Circus folk spilled out of their homes. They got in Rurik's way, craning their necks, trying to see what was going on.

Shouts rang out.

"We got him!"

"Here!"

In the next row of tents, Rurik came upon two men holding another on the ground. But when he pulled them off, Minko poked his head up, spitting mud from his mouth. The horseman was tall and skinny—definitely not the killer.

"That's not him." Rurik straightened, his gaze skimming the area.

Movement was everywhere now. Flashlights beamed in the darkness. Shapes filled the paths between tents. A pack of pursuers sloshed past, heading toward the big top. Others ran to the RVs, stumbling across the furrowed swamp. People slipped in the oozing muck and flailed at the bottom of water-filled ruts.

"I got him!" someone yelled, followed by a scream.

Rurik raced toward the voices and found Misha, bent over, out of breath.

"I thought I had him," Misha wheezed. "I grabbed him. But it was only Mrs. Donovan."

Great. Misha had caught the camp's cook. Rurik rushed on to the RVs.

The whole camp was up now. Men and women shouted from camper doorways or struggled in the narrow alleyways between vehicles.

Pyotr and a few roustabouts appeared, carrying baseball bats. "We saw the guy heading for the equipment trailers. We'll flush him out!" He and his friends charged toward the rear of the compound.

Another group had planted themselves in front of Ivan's RV, swearing to protect the man as he sat in the doorway, recounting the blow-by-blow of the attack to anyone who'd listen.

The more people sloshing around in the mud, the more impossible it became to tell friend from foe.

Enraged, Rurik climbed an RV bumper and yelled across the camp, "Go back inside. Everyone! Get inside *now*!" He ordered two of the men "protecting" Ivan to guard the front gate. Then he demanded that Ivan and Marva lock themselves inside the RV. Finally, he bellowed for Misha and Yuri until they answered and helped him herd everyone back to their homes.

Soon, except for Rurik and his two deputies, nothing in the camp moved, and it was silent as a grave.

The mud-man had melted into the night.

Refusing to give up, Rurik began a door-to-door search, certain it would turn up his quarry—he'd be the man with the most mud in his home. Dirt would still cover his hair and face. Or some short, bulky person would be just stepping out of the shower.

The killer was trapped inside the compound. Now Rurik just had to find him.

Rurik, Misha, and Yuri started with the RVs nearest to Ivan's and made their way across the rows.

After the first seven or eight campers, Rurik knew his plan wasn't going to work.

Every home had muck tracked into it. Half the people wore muddy clothes or were just changing out of them. The other half were washing up, water glistening on wet arms and faces.

He paid special attention when he got to Alyosha and Pavel. Those two bore no sign of mud except for their shoes, and they weren't soaked from a fast shower.

Rurik's teeth ground together, grit from dirty water crunching between them.

Although he'd succeeded in keeping the killer penned up on the lot and not allowing him to take any more children, Rurik was no closer to discovering his true identity or stopping him for good.

CHAPTER TWELVE

Sylvie
Miskolc, Hungary

*Preparing a body can take hours,
so remember to bring a thermos of tea and some
sandwiches.
Don't worry about relatives' surprise at finding you eating
beside the body and ignore suggestions about wearing
gloves.
They don't understand. Bloodwalkers never get sick. Ever.
~ The Bloodwalker's Book*

Sylvie shivered in the alley, adrenaline filling her veins until she shook so hard she was afraid pieces of her might fall off. First, being chased through the streets, and then the dreadful news about Ada. Her heaving breaths refused to slow. She pressed a hand to her forehead, willing herself not to faint.

Liana tightened her headscarf under her chin, her features so shadowy they looked almost menacing.

"Ada's dead? Are you sure?" Sylvie said weakly.

"Of course I'm sure. I was standing right there," Liana hissed. "They almost got me!"

"But... I don't understand. Someone killed Ada and tried to kill you, too?"

"Keep your voice down!" Liana threw a nervous glance behind her before grabbing Sylvie's elbow and steering her away from the streetlights. Deeper in the gloomy alley, the air reeked from the smell of garbage. Rats burrowing in the trash looked up. Instead of fleeing from the newcomers, they bared their teeth, red eyes glowing with malice, ready to fight for their small, filthy kingdom. "I think someone followed me from the station."

Sylvie's gaze darted to the street. People hurried down the sidewalks, intent on where they were going. No one looked at Sylvie or Liana.

"I'm the only witness," Liana said. "It makes sense they'd try to finish the job."

"You saw Ada get killed?"

"Well...not exactly. I was in her house, and she was right outside. Okay, not *right* outside, but at the end of this long garden. One minute, she was plucking some tarragon or parsley or whatever for dinner. The next she was lying on the ground. Then I saw someone in the trees behind. Just a blur. But I swear it looked like..." Liana cast another quick glance at the street.

"Who? Did you recognize them?"

"I..." Liana shook her head. "Too dark. I thought Ada had fainted or something, but when I went into the garden, she was lying there with a knife this long"—Liana held her hands a foot apart—"sticking out of her head! Her eyes were still open, but she was gone. Just...gone."

Sylvie's stomach rolled at the image of sweet Ada with a knife in her skull. "You didn't see who stabbed her?"

"Maybe I saw something in the trees...maybe not. It was fifty yards from the house. When I looked closer, no one was there. At least that's what I thought. But when I ran into the cemetery to find her husband—"

"To where?"

"The cemetery." Liana gave an irritated huff. "Weren't you listening at the wedding? Her husband and his father are custodians of Rulikowski Cemetery in Oradea."

"Oh...right." Sylvie remembered now. Zora had been pleased the family were grave diggers, the traditional vocation of Skomori men. The wedding was only a week ago, yet it felt like ages. Her life was so different now.

"I went to the gravesite and brought her husband and his father, but when we got back—it was gone."

Sylvie gasped, her hand flying to her mouth. "Ada's body was gone?"

"No, not her. The knife!" Liana leaned forward, her eyes boring into Sylvie's. "You know what that means? Someone was there. They took it! If I hadn't run away so fast, I bet they would have killed me, too."

"But who did it? Couldn't you see anyone in the trees or—"

"No!" Liana said it too harshly, too quickly. "I told you it was too far away."

"Did the police search?"

"You don't think I hung around, do you? I already have Claudiu trying to track me down—as if I'm ever going back to his stupid dairy."

"You left your husband? But you *can't*. You'd be..." Sylvie couldn't say it.

"Cast out?" Liana arched her brows. "Yeah, the day before Ada died, that horrible Cosmina woman found out I left Claudiu and was hiding out at Ada's—I bet Ada's husband called her—and she showed up and told me I had to go back to him. Said I had to be a *good wife*." Scorn dripped from her voice. "Follow bloodwalker rules. Obey my husband. Live a respectable life. Blah, blah, blah. Or else I'd be cast out. You know what I told her?"

"No." Sylvie's fingers knotted together. Being cast out was the worst thing possible. Not even your own family could acknowledge you. It was a living death.

"I told her I didn't want to follow anyone's rules but my own. And I'm not interested in *obeying* a man. Just think about it, Sylvie. Women do everything in the house, raise the kids, cook and clean, even help with their husband's business. But *he* controls the money and decides what to spend it on." Her lip curled, baring white teeth in a face almost as malevolent as the rats'. "I'm the one who earned the money for my dowry. But when I wanted to upgrade the house with a dishwasher, a new TV, and decent furniture, what does he say? 'No.' Then he spends *my* money buying cows and dumb milking machines."

Sylvie swallowed, thinking about Miron's new store and equipment. "But...you're married. What he does benefits you, too."

Liana snorted. "Let me tell you something about that. Just because some old lady says you're married doesn't make it so. It's not *legal*. Your name isn't on any papers, not the house or land or anything. According to any country's government, you're not married. "

Sylvie's mouth fell open.

"Cosmina said I had to go back to Claudiu or be cast out. So I told her I wasn't going to spend years being a good little wifey and wait for the bloodwalker's curse to get me like it got *her!*"

"Wait—what got her?"

"The bloodwalker's curse. It's what happens to old bloodwalkers. Sure, we never get so much as a cold when we're young, but when one of us hits fifty or sixty, we start getting really sick. Our bones get weak. They break like twigs. Why do you think Zora's in that wheelchair? Or Cosmina hobbles around with her cane? The curse cripples us. Most bloodwalkers over sixty get bedridden and then just die. Zora's the only one her age left. It's a miracle she's still alive."

"How do you know all this?" Sylvie's mother had never even hinted to her about it.

"All the old ones know. It's supposed to be some big secret. No one's allowed to talk about it. But when my grandma got crippled, she told us before she died, and she was only fifty-eight. Cosmina got really mad when I mentioned the curse. Cast me out then and there! Told me no one in my village would speak to me anymore or let me stay with them. Told Ada she had to throw me out, too... but of course Ada didn't. Except...she's dead now..."

"What are you going to do?"

Liana raised her chin, eye sparkling fiercely. "I already did it. I found an apartment in Debrecen, and I can make plenty of money telling fortunes in the park. And it's only sixty miles south of you, Sylvie. Just an hour by train."

"Not far... But how did you even know I lived here?"

"Your mom has the address. She gave it to my mom. And naturally, my mom still calls me...even if I can't live with her anymore. By the way, your mom's a little mad that you haven't called her."

"I...I'm not allowed to use the phone," Sylvie said in a small voice.

For a moment, Liana just stared. "Not *allowed?* Your

husband doesn't let you talk to family or friends?"

"No...it's just..." Thinking about Miron made Sylvie realize how late it was. Miron would be coming home soon, and if she wasn't there, she didn't want to think about what would happen. "I don't need to talk to people from home. Or here, since I don't speak the language. And I'm sorry about Ada, but I have to get home."

"I don't speak the language either, but I bought this"— Liana pulled a Romanian-Hungarian dictionary from her purse—"and I'm picking it up quickly."

"I'm not allowed to have one."

Liana's lips mashed into a tight line. She snatched out a pen, scribbled something inside the dictionary. "Here. Take mine. I put my phone number and my address in Debrecen inside. Remember, it's only an hour by train. You can visit anytime." She slid the dictionary into Sylvie's hand, pressing Sylvie's fingers closed over it with her own firm ones. "If you want, you could stay for longer than just a visit. I mean, if you decide this life isn't for you, come find me." Her lips twitched into a lopsided smile. "We can be outcasts together. It'll be fun! I'll teach you to read fortunes, and we'll make lots of money."

Sylvie didn't know what to say. Being cast out was no joking matter. She'd never willingly choose the loneliness and misery of that life. Liana just wanted company because she felt more alone and scared than she'd admit.

From the mouth of the alley, a harsh voice called. "Sylvie?"

The hair on Sylvie's arms stood on end. "It's my husband!"

Pulling up the ends of her scarf, Liana scrunched her face and started dabbing her eyes.

Miron stalked into the alley. He peered at Liana, but his gaze shot to Sylvie as if daring her to explain.

Sylvie's mouth worked but nothing came out.

"I'm sorry to come unannounced, sir," Liana sobbed and sniveled into her scarf, keeping most of her face covered. "It's bad news from home. I promised her mother to bring the message, but I'll return to Romania now." Her fake crying grew muffled as she slipped past Miron and

113

hastened onto the street.

"I'm sorry," Sylvie began. "I know I'm not supposed to—"

"Not here," he cut her off. Grabbing her arm, he forced her down the sidewalk till they reached their building's entrance. "Get upstairs." He remained at the door for a moment, looking up and down the street.

She scrambled up the steps and burst into the apartment, belatedly realizing she still clutched the dictionary in her hand. As Miron's steps thudded up the stairs, she held the book over the trash. No, he might see it there. A split second before he entered, she dropped the book on the floor and kicked it under the stove.

He closed the door quietly, which was somehow more unnerving than if he'd slammed it. "What news?"

"Uh—someone died," Sylvie said.

"Who? Your mother?"

"No. One of the brides at our wedding."

"What does that have to do with you?" He stepped closer to her, a fire kindling in his eyes.

"N-nothing."

"Then the woman should have given the message and been on her way, but you went outside with her. Why would you do that? Just to spite me?"

Sylvie backed up until she ran into the sink.

"I told you not to talk to people." Miron began rolling up his sleeves. "I told you never to go outside. Easy rules. Simple to understand. But you're too stupid to remember them. You'll soon start listening when I talk to you."

The first blow came so fast Sylvie crashed into the table before she knew what happened. "I'm sorry. I'm sorry. I'm—" The second blow lifted her off her feet and flung her across the room. She tumbled into a heap by the bed.

Pain pounded in her skull. Her vision blurred. She blinked, trying to clear her watering eyes. When she opened them again, Miron was coming. Sliding off his belt. Letting the buckle swing like a pendulum.

Desperate, Sylvie crawled under the bed.

A savage grip closed on her ankle and hauled her out.

CHAPTER THIRTEEN

Rurik
Kosice, Slovakia

The circus's new location in Mestsky Park presented security problems. Big ones. The park spanned fifty acres in the middle of the city. Open on all four sides, it provided easy access to streets and nearby neighborhoods.

No way to lock it down.

Even if Rurik's deputies, Misha and Yuri, helped to patrol the circus and grounds, the killer could find a place to slip out.

Although Rurik hated to admit it, he needed more people to keep watch over the circus, search for the costume, and patrol the surrounding park.

Ivan suggested asking Marva, Pyotr, and his cousin Vadim to help. So Rurik recruited the three of them, Misha, and Yuri and brought them up to speed on the whole story—the four children's disappearances, the attempted kidnapping at the train depot, and the button from the clown's costume.

Each of them swore to tell no one else.

Rurik had no trouble keeping that promise. He had no girlfriend asking about his day. No friends invited him to dinner. No buddies joined him to tip back a beer and swap stories. When most of the camp viewed you with fear and loathing, no one wanted to talk to you.

But the others had friends, families. The smallest slip and word could reach the killer, warning him of their plans.

Rurik had scrutinized the circus's eighty members, ruling out most of the performers because of gender or size. Crew members were harder to nail down. Workmen came and went, many of them staying less than a month before grabbing their paychecks and disappearing.

Luckily, all the employees—the roustabouts, truck drivers, carpenters, technicians, and kitchen staff—had gathered at the edge of camp to hoist the mammoth big top.

The perfect time to observe each one.

Rurik shaded his eyes from the sunlight glinting off the circus's four metal towers, each looming ninety feet above the park. Between them, the big top's pinnacle cap hung suspended from cables that winched it halfway into position.

The wind caught the canvas, billowing it out from the trusses like the sails of a huge ship—a *gigantic* ship considering the big top's canvas was 70,000 square feet. With 120 support poles, 300 metal stakes, and 3 miles of metal cable to hold everything in place, setting up *Zorka Cyrka* required 10 hours of back-breaking work. It was like building a small city at each new venue.

Workers crawled over the framework and heaved support poles into position while Rurik watched, slowly adding fifteen of the shortest, stockiest men to his suspect list.

"Hey, Rurik!" Misha trotted over, pulled along by four dogs from Marva's act that strained at their leashes. All wore grins, including Misha. "I thought you'd already be at Ivan's meeting. You forget?"

"No, just deciding whose homes to put on the search list." Rurik turned away from the workers lashing sections of the tent together and headed for Ivan's RV.

Misha fell into step with him and lowered his voice. "I thought of something. I need you to come to the dog trailer for a minute."

The dog trailer was in the opposite direction. "Just take the dogs back, Misha, and you can tell me at the meeting." Rurik started walking away.

"Wait, this is important. It's about the clown costume."

Rurik swung around. Now Misha had his full attention. "What about it?"

Misha shook his head. "Not here." He led the way to a

long trailer with "Marva's Marvelous Mutts" painted on the side. Converted from a horse carrier, the lowered tailgate formed a ramp, and Rurik followed Misha inside.

Along the walls of the trailer, six dogs in cages barked as if they hadn't seen their four brethren in years. The ones on leashes joined in the Welcome Back Bark-Off until the noise reached a deafening level. Leashes twirled around Misha as the excited canines leaped up and down so much he barely managed to get a white poodle into its cage.

A spotted pointer pulled free and romped toward Rurik, his tail whirring back and forth. Rurik reached down and rubbed the dog's ears.

Designed to fit six horses, the twenty-foot trailer now carried ten large cages. Noses pushed against wire mesh, and liquid-brown eyes begged, *Pet me!! Pet me!!*

Misha put away two border collies and collected the pointer from beneath Rurik's hand to load him into his cage. "See this one, here?" Misha walked to the end and crouched in front of a cage with a long-haired dog. Its gray, black, and white splotches made it look like a patchwork Franken-dog. "This is Campion. He's a Hungarian Mudi."

"What's this got to do with the clown costume?"

"Campion was trained for search and rescue before he retired. He's a tracker. That button you pulled off the costume has to have the smell of the killer on it, right? Campion could lead us right to him."

"With a thousand other scents in this circus?" Rurik stared dubiously at Campion's gray muzzle and lolling tongue.

"Yeah. Search and rescue dogs can sniff out anything. I hope so anyway. So what do you think? Is it a good idea?" Misha's eyes had the same pleading look as the dogs.

"It's a very good idea," Rurik said. "At the meeting, you can ask Marva. If she says it'll work, we'll do it first thing tomorrow morning."

"Super! Campion will make a great detective!"

Rurik doubted the dog could sniff a button and then lead them to the killer, but he was desperate enough to try anything.

Misha walked out with Rurik and lifted the ramp to

form the tailgate, leaving the upper doors open for air.

When they reached Ivan's RV, voices clamored from inside. Too many for the few people that should have been there.

Rurik mounted the steps to find the camper stuffed with people. They sat in every available chair and crammed into the open spaces, including the driver's compartment. There were close to fifteen. He crossed his arms and scowled.

Ivan shrank under his glare but then shrugged. "People brought some friends. I gave them the whole story. They want to help, and they promise not to tell anyone else."

Oh, hell. Rurik rubbed a palm over his face. Fifteen people couldn't keep a secret no matter what they promised.

Once the killer knew their plans, he'd be twice as hard to catch.

* * *

At midnight, Mestsky Park was officially closed. Although with no gates, no fences, and no security guards, it seemed pretty open to Rurik.

He paced through the park, a giant 400-by-600-yard expanse, and came across a few drunks snoring on benches, a couple strolling in the moonlight, and another couple who were going at it, judging by the moaning and panting coming from behind some bushes.

Staying off the paths, he prowled the shadows beneath maples and hornbeams. Black locust trees must have been nearby, too. It was too dark to see their clustered white blooms, but he recognized the bubblegum odor that flavored the air. Sickly sweet. Like fruit in a bowl too long. Brown. Rotting. The sugars slowly fermenting.

His walkie-talkie crackled, and Misha whispered, "I think I spotted something."

"Where?" Rurik tensed, muscles coiled like a jungle cat.

"Near the gazebo."

Rurik sprang across the grass but kept within range of a path's lampposts. They cast a weak light, but enough so that he wouldn't run into tree trunks.

"I'm almost there," another voice said over the walkie-talkie. Maybe Pyotr.

Six people patrolled the park beyond the perimeter of

the circus, but it was hard to distinguish one from another in the dark, or through the static of the radios.

Barks erupted from somewhere ahead.

Klondike. Marva had suggested Misha take her American Eskimo dog with him. The white ball of fluff wasn't very intimidating, but he was much younger than the "tracking" dog, loved to chase things, and had a good set of lungs that could be heard anywhere in the park.

When Rurik reached the gazebo, it was empty.

Footsteps pounded up behind him. "Where is he?" Pyotr said .

Klondike barked again, the sound moving deeper into the woods.

"Come on." Rurik raced away from the gazebo, homing in on the noise. Pyotr's steps thudded behind him. The trees were far enough apart to show flashes of movement about fifty yards away.

Someone fled between the trunks, wearing baggy white clothes emblazoned with the diamond-shapes of a harlequin design and a three-pointed jester's hat.

The clown.

No jingling came from the hat like at the train depot. The killer had cut off the bells. Clever.

A small white form shot across the grass. Klondike bayed like a hunting dog and pulled a stumbling Misha behind him.

Ahead of them, the figure glanced back, showing a white-painted face with a big grinning red mouth.

Fire leaped in Rurik's veins, and he kicked into high gear. This time, the bastard wouldn't escape.

Dashing away, the clown veered into a clump of bushes and out of sight.

Klondike darted through the trees and plunged into the shrubbery, dragging Misha with him.

More barks. Followed by growls.

"Hey! St—" Misha's voice cut off. The dog yelped.

Seconds later, Rurik hurtled through the bushes, and skidded to a stop.

Misha lay curled on the ground, eyes closed, Klondike's leash still twisted around his wrist. The dog whined and licked the boy's face.

A glimmer of white caught Rurik's eye. The clown darted through trees thirty yards away. Gaining more of a lead every second. His uneven lope was taking him toward the edge of the parkand the houses beyond.

Rurik took a half-step after him, every instinct urging him to chase down the villain—just like Klondike had. But also like the dog, Rurik couldn't leave Misha. The boy was his responsibility. He turned back and bent over Misha, praying the boy wasn't dead. At his touch, Misha groaned.

Pyotr arrived, his blond hair a windblown mess, huge chest heaving.

Rurik pointed at the clown's receding back. "He's heading for the street. Cut him off!"

Pyotr dashed for the street, a hundred yards away.

"Misha? Can you talk?"

No response.

Grabbing his walkie-talkie, Rurik shouted, "We spotted the clown. Heading for Stefankova Street. Get over there—don't let him out of the park!"

"On the way."

"Right by me—I see him!"

A hand closed over Rurik's fingers. Misha squinted up at him. "I'm okay... Go. Get him!" Misha said, voice dazed but stable.

Rurik didn't have to be told twice. He leaped up and charged through the trees, aiming for Stefankova Street. It ran along the entire side of the park, leaving the killer plenty of places to escape.

Every few seconds, the clown vanished from view behind the trees. But each time he reappeared, Rurik had gained ground.

On one side, Pyotr neared the street and began angling toward the running clown. Voices and the crack of breaking underbrush came from Rurik's other side. Black forms sprinted beneath the trees along the street, racing to head off their quarry.

White silk rippled as the killer slowed, his head jerking left and right. Then he spun around and reversed direction. Straight back toward Rurik.

They charged each other like freight trains.

At the last moment, the clown swerved.

But Rurik anticipated it. He veered, launched himself in a flying tackle, and slammed into the clown. They crashed to the ground and rolled in a tangle of limbs.

The clown struggled to rise, squirming desperately. The white silk slipped through Rurik's grip. The clown lurched to his feet. Rurik jumped up beside him.

Clenching his fist, Rurik put all his strength into an uppercut. It connected—should have knocked the guy into orbit. Instead, the bones of Rurik's knuckles cracked against a jaw as hard as lead. Pain lanced up his arm.

The punch's force sent the clown tumbling backward. He rolled though the shrubs but popped up a second later.

A black form darted in from the side. He swung at the clown's face. When the blow connected, it left the clown unfazed, but the man bellowed in agony. He clutched his hand to his chest.

The clown bolted, and Rurik chased him. They wove between the trees.

Pyotr suddenly appeared and leaped into the clown's path.

The clown barely slowed. Swinging his arm like a club, he bashed the big roustabout on the head and kept going.

Pyotr dropped like a stone—directly in front of Rurik.

Rurik tripped over him and hit the ground hard. He rolled and came up on his knees.

Someone banged into Rurik from behind and fell on top of him.

With zero time for tenderness, Rurik shoved the body off and climbed to his feet.

The clown was much farther away now. Barely visible. Heading back toward the circus.

Rurik shot after him, relieved they'd managed to herd him away from the street. *No more children for you, shithead.*

With air burning inside his chest, Rurik fumbled for his walkie-talkie. Pain sliced through his fingers. He gritted his teeth and used his other hand to grab it, clumsily hitting the talk button. "He's going back to camp. Guard your posts. Stay alert."

He'd left four people guarding the encampment at its compass points. No way for the clown to get back in without being seen.

Rurik's leg muscles cramped. He slowed, certain his radio would surge to life any second with the news the clown had been spotted and captured. But dead silence reigned.

Minutes later, Rurik emerged from the trees and into the clearing housing the circus. The big top rose before him. A black mountain, blotting out the night sky. He jogged toward it.

"Who's there?" shouted a nervous voice.

Rurik spied a figure in the gloom beside the tent. Yuri. "It's Rurik. Aren't you supposed to be on the west side?"

"I was...but there's nothing but tennis courts over there, and you said the clown was coming through the woods, so I came over here."

"You didn't see anyone? Wearing white?"

"No, boss. Just you."

Rurik lifted the walkie-talkie. "Who's guarding the north side?"

"I'm here. Vadim."

"Did you see anything?"

"Uh-uh. No one's come through here. And Bogdan is on the east side. I can see him, about fifty yards away. No one passed us."

"Who was guarding the south—the big top?"

"I'm not sure..." Vadim replied.

"Oh, that was Lazlo. I told him..." Yuri trailed off, peering around Rurik to the sound of scuffling feet drawing near.

Rurik glanced over his shoulder. Several people left the tree-line. Limping. Staggering. Bedraggled.

The furry white dog trotted forward, tugging at his leash.

"Klondike, cut it out. I'm not fooling. My head is killing me." Misha groaned.

Rurik's eyes bored into Yuri. "What did you tell Lazlo?"

"He had to take a piss, so I told him I'd keep watch till he got back. He's been gone pretty long though."

"Lazlo? Lazlo!" Rurik yelled into the walkie-talkie.

"What?"

"Where are you?"

"I'm in my tent. Yuri relieved me. Said I could go home."

Yuri shuffled backward a few steps. "No...I didn't say that. He must have misunderstood..."

Rage erupted inside Rurik. His hands itched to strangle the fat, lazy security guard. He took one step toward him when Klondike abruptly threw back his head and howled. Its gut-wrenching sorrow froze Rurik on the spot.

Misha's jaw dropped. Pyotr and the other two men glanced around, eyes wide.

Screams came from inside the encampment.

Rurik and the men tore around the side of the big top, following the cries.

When he reached the equipment trucks and trailers, he found the source.

Near the dog trailer, Marva sagged between several circus women. Only their support held her upright. Horrible wails issued from her throat. Klondike howled again. The sounds twisted together into a tragic harmony.

Light spilled from the rear of the dog trailer. Rurik dashed to it and ran up the ramp. At the top, he reeled back.

Blood coated everything. The walls. Ceiling. Floor. The cage doors had been ripped off. Each cage was empty. There wasn't a dog to be seen. Only pieces of them. Fur, gristle, and bone lay in wet heaps, up and down the length of the trailer.

One head, the black and gray head of Campion, the tracking dog, was placed atop a cage, face pointed toward the entrance. His brown eyes open. His tongue bitten in half. Blood dripped from his severed neck onto the bottom of the cage.

Rurik couldn't breathe through the stench of blood and shredded bowels. His stomach constricted. It ate at him, like razors slicing his innards. Bile rose, and he swallowed, forcing it down.

"Oh my God!" Misha said from behind Rurik. The boy backed away, squeezing his eyes shut.

Rurik wished that he could blot out the image before

him so easily. But he knew he'd carry it with him forever.

CHAPTER FOURTEEN

Sylvie
Miskolc, Hungary

*The life of a bloodwalker is never easy. As your family
grows, you may find your responsibilities conflict.
Always tend to your own home and hearth first.
Husbands anger easily.
The dead are patient.
~ The Bloodwalker's Book*

Sylvie squatted on the bathroom floor, raised the meat
cleaver, and whacked the tail off a dead rat. That was the
last one. She needed three tails to braid into a harmony
charm. A small one—easy to hide in the shadows above
the bed.

She tossed the three rat corpses out the window, and
they landed with thumps in the overgrown garden two
floors below. It hadn't taken long to find the decaying rat
bodies in the tangled weeds. They were everywhere in this
city.

It would have been nice to slow boil one, peel off the
skin and fur, and keep the skull for a "never get lost"
talisman—rats had an unerring sense of direction—but
the smell of rancid meat would alert Miron.

Sylvie turned from the window and caught sight of her
bruises and cut lip in the mirror. With her bloodwalker's
constitution, the injuries were already fading, all except
the ones on her ribs, the ones that bore the imprint of the
belt buckle. Those were still ripe as plums.

Miron had felt awful the morning after the beating. He'd
apologized. Begged her forgiveness. Told her he'd drunk
too much and would never do it again.

As long as she followed his rules and didn't make him angry.

It wasn't unknown for spats to spin out of control in the Skomori community. Sometimes a woman needed a strong hand. The topic was never discussed openly. Other wives sensed when something was amiss. They'd bring pans of fresh baked food and pretend not to notice the marks. Sylvie's mother often delivered a harmony charm secreted inside a towel-wrapped plate of cookies. Things always went back to normal after that.

Although husbands brought in the money, every Skomori clan member knew it was the wife who was responsible for keeping the family together. It wasn't the men's fault. They simply weren't equipped to provide the love and care needed to make a family happy and harmonious.

The wife needed to step up—while *appearing* to step back.

Deception. Another necessity best left to women.

Sylvie didn't like the idea of hiding things from her husband and being sneaky wasn't something she was good at—like trying to hide her weaknesses from Zora had ended up in a prophesy-of-doom rant and touched off a riot—but the peace and stability of her home was at stake. She had to use every weapon at her disposal, including bloodwalker ways, to save it.

The front door creaked. Alarm flared inside her. It couldn't be Miron. It was only six, and he never came home before seven.

"Sylvie?" Miron called.

Black plague take it! Sylvie flung the cleaver out the window, where it landed next to the dead rats, and then looked around for a place to put the rat tails. "I'm in here," she answered, glad she'd been smart enough to hide in the bathroom in case of a calamity. "One minute."

She unscrewed a powder container's lid and dumped the tails in. Miron would never look there. But he'd notice the rust-colored blood smeared on the floor. She grabbed a handful of tissues, wiped up the stains, and then flushed them down the toilet. Bits of gore and fur still clung to her fingers and nails. She doused her hands under the faucet and scrubbed quickly before opening the door.

Miron stood by the coat rack, hanging a plastic case with a suit inside. Sweat beaded his temples, and his hair stuck to his neck in curly tendrils. He whirled toward her, eyes rolling like a cow on its way to slaughter. "Here," he said, pulling a package from a shopping bag and shoving it at her. "Take that downstairs and press it."

She eyed the tailored dress shirt, pristine white under its plastic wrap. Egyptian cotton. Beautifully stitched. Expensive.

Miron rummaged through the kitchen, opening and closing the cupboard doors. "Where the hell is the shoe polish? Why do you move everything?"

"I think it's..." She faltered as he entered the bathroom. What if there was still blood on the floor. Or tufts of gray fur. Or tail pieces.

Dashing to the bed, she ransacked the nightstand. "The polish is here!" She held up the round tin until he emerged and took it from her. No suspicion in his eyes. No questions. No anger.

Safe.

He glanced into the long mirror on the wardrobe and ran a hand through his hair. "I should have cut it. Does it look too long?"

"No. It's fine," she said, gambling that was the answer he wanted.

"Why are you still here?" He sat on the bed and kicked off his shoes. "I gave you the last two days off work because you were...sick. The least you can do is press a shirt when I ask you."

"Right away." She grabbed the shirt, ran to the door, and scooped the store keys from a shelf before hurrying downstairs to the shop.

After turning on the pressing machine, she waited for it to heat while wondering what was going on. New shirt. New suit. Polishing his shoes. It had to be some kind of a party.

Of course! She smiled to herself. The other store must be having its grand opening. Her village in Romania had few shops, but the owners always threw lovely parties for openings or renovations. Food and music. Gifts from friends. Romanian țuică spirits and homemade wines that even the ladies were allowed to drink.

Sylvie would love to go. It hurt a bit that Miron hadn't invited her.

After carefully removing the plastic, pins, and collar stays from the shirt, she began pressing the high-quality cotton.

Maybe Miron didn't want her to go because people would stare at her bruises and cuts.

That didn't seem fair. It wasn't her fault.

The new store would probably look spectacular—all lit up, everything decorated and shiny.

While ironing the French-style cuffs, she suddenly decided she would go. Miron wouldn't find out. She'd do what she did last time: stand across the street and watch. No one would see her. She'd stay well back and hide her puffy, bruised face.

An image flashed into her mind of the man from the circus. The one with the scars. People would stare at features like that. The poor man probably couldn't go anywhere without attracting horrified glances.

If someone from the party saw her, face swollen and cut, they might think she was scary looking, like him.

She'd have to find a hiding spot in the darkest shadows.

One way or another—she was going. She'd watch the festivities even if she couldn't share in them.

Finding a hanger, she dutifully took her husband his freshly-ironed shirt.

* * *

Sylvie was right—it *was* the store's grand opening.

The party illuminated the building's upper floors and was far grander than Sylvie expected. She slinked into the darkened doorway of an antique shop across the way and gazed up, her eyes devouring the scene like a starving dog gulping a rabbit.

Sparkling lights, music, and laughter streamed out the apartment's open windows and spilled into the night as if the entire building was an overflowing champagne bottle. Women in long dresses and men in suits mingled in the large salon, the foyer, and the dining room. Some strolled out onto the balconies, glasses in their hands and jewels glinting from tie-clips and necklaces.

On the street, a trolley clanged past, its overhead wires buzzing with electricity. No one got off. The people at this party alighted from cars. Big, stately ones that dwarfed the sidewalk. Women glided up the stairs in the highest heels Sylvie had ever seen. Their escorts sported slicked back hair that shone with gel.

Sylvie squinted into the lights, trying to spot Miron in the throng, but couldn't find him. Perhaps he was at an inner door, welcoming people as they arrived. As she should have been.

With eyes half-closed, she imagined herself in an evening gown, her hair styled by the best salon in town, jewelry glittering on wrist and neck. It would be heaven.

The music changed into a celebratory march. People began applauding in the large salon. A cart, loaded with a four-layer cake, passed the balcony, wheeled out by two uniformed waiters. Men and women cleared the floor, parting to reveal a platform at the back of the room. Two throne-like chairs commanded center stage.

Miron sat in one. A beautiful girl sat in the other. She looked regal, her black hair piled on her head in romantic coils, her ball gown the pink of a new dawn, its strapless style leaving her shoulders scandalously bare.

Above them hung a banner that said, "*Eljegyzés* – Miron & Gizella."

Who was Gizella?

Sylvie's brain asked the question, but her heart already knew. It tumbled down to her shoes and landed with a thud that shook her entire body.

She didn't know what "*Eljegyzés*" meant, but it must be congratulations, or happy engagement. Or happy wedding. Those were the only reasons a man and a woman sat on a stage at a party.

Miron was getting engaged. To someone named Gizella.

And apparently Sylvie could go to hell.

"*Hogy van?*" An elderly woman stopped on the sidewalk in front of Sylvie.

It took Sylvie a second to recognize Mrs. Kovács, one of the customers from the laundry shop, but she had no idea what the woman had said.

Mrs. Kovács turned to two equally old women behind her and rattled off a few sentences.

"*Örvendek,*" each woman said to Sylvie, inclining their heads.

Mrs. Kovács pointed across the street to the luminous windows. "*Miron és Gizella ünneplik, hogy össze fognak házasodni.*" Her blindingly-white dentures gleamed inside a broad smile.

Sylvie stared, her heartbeat galloping inside her chest. How could Mrs. Kovács smile at her? The woman knew Sylvie ran the shop, must realize she lived upstairs with Miron, was his *wife*. Did she expect Sylvie to be happy her husband was getting engaged?

"*Miron húga,*" Mrs. Kovács told her friends and pointed at Sylvie.

The others nodded and beamed. "*Gratulálok, Miron húga.*"

Their confusing words and toothsome grins demolished Sylvie's composure. The darkness that had sheltered her grew thorns and pierced her heart. She bolted, racing down the street. Strangers scattered from her path. She ducked her head, avoiding curious gazes. Wind-whipped tears trickled down her cheeks.

It seemed only seconds later when she staggered up the stairs to her apartment. Inside, she got down on hands and knees and pulled out Liana's Romanian-Hungarian dictionary from under the stove.

Sylvie's fingers rifled the pages.

"*Eljegyzés*" meant engagement.

That was horrible enough, but when she looked up *húga,* it got so much worse.

Miron húga meant Miron's sister.

He must have told all his customers that Sylvie was his sister. That's why they were congratulating her on Miron's engagement.

That rotten , flea-infested jackass.

This was too much. She'd tried, really tried. Done

the best she could to be a good wife. But Miron was no husband.

She couldn't stay, knowing their marriage meant nothing to him. She had to leave. Now.

After packing her few belongings, she ran down the stairs to the shop. Secreted behind cartons of washing soap was her bag of bloodwalker things. She'd decided to keep them after Liana's visit. It was lucky Liana had left her the dictionary, and she wished she'd thanked the girl before she returned to Debrecen.

Still, she and Liana were worlds apart. Sylvie had good reason to leave Miron. She wouldn't be cast out like Liana. Wouldn't have to live a lonely, shameful life in Debrecen.

Sylvie opened the cash register and scooped out all the Hungarian *forints* inside. It was a thick wad and would easily pay for a taxi ride to the train station and buy her a tichrot back to Romania.

In seconds, she was on the street, flagging down a taxi.

At the station, she purchased a ticket and walked onto the platform. It was empty. Eerily deserted. Miles of track stretched both ways, disappearing into the infinite night. The wind grew cold and gnawed at her skin.

All alone, in desolate silence, she realized the enormity of what she was doing.

By leaving her husband, she *did* risk being cast out.

The elders might not listen to her reasons. They might not even believe her. If Miron denied he was engaged to another woman, she couldn't prove otherwise. The elders could force her to go back to him.

A shiver rattled her backbone, and her teeth chattered. Suddenly, she wasn't sure she'd made the right decision. Running away might be a biggest mistake she'd ever made.

Hoping for advice—maybe even encouragement—she found a pay phone and dialed her mother.

"Hello?" her mother answered.

"Mommy?" Sylvie choked out the childhood name. "I-I have to come home. I left Miron. He's horrible. A liar."

"What? You're leaving your husband?!" her mother's voice screeched down the line.

"I have to. He got enga—"

"Have you lost your mind? You will *not* throw away your future after everything I did to secure it. Whatever the problem is, I'm sure you can work it out. I'll call Aunt Cosmina, and she'll come talk to you and Miron—"

"No! It won't work out. He's marrying someone else!"

Nothing. Only the sound of breathing.

"I bought a ticket," Sylvie whispered. Then more forcefully, "I'm coming home."

"You must be wrong. How can he be marrying someone else?"

"I saw them getting engaged. He had a big party."

"Listen to me, Sylvie. This is not the way to handle things and you know it. We do not leave our husbands for every little transgression. You must contact an elder. They'll go to his family, get Miron to solve the problem, and everything will be fine."

"I don't want to talk to an elder. Besides...Miron hits me!" Her strident words echoed down the platform and faded into the gloom.

"Sylvie, stop acting like a child. I'll call Aunt Cosmina, and we'll take care of this. Don't worry, we know how to handle these things. He will *not* marry someone else. You are his wife, and that's the way it will stay."

The idea of going back to Miron, to his lies and nasty temper, and suffering while some faceless elders and parents negotiated her future made Sylvie's stomach shrink into a little ball of despair. And what would Miron do to her if he found out she revealed his secret to others? "Mommy, please. I have to come home. I can't stay here."

"No," her mother said in a steely voice. "Do not come to Romania. You must act like an adult and fix your problems, not run away. Stay in Hungary. If you come home, I...I won't let you in."

Sylvie gasped. It was as if her mother was suddenly a stranger—like she didn't care at all.

"Did you hear me, Sylvie? I said *stay in Hungary!*"

"I heard," Sylvie said dully and hung up. Exhaustion and misery dragged at her as she shuffled back down the platform to the ticket window. "I need to return this." She handed the ticket to the man behind the counter.

"Do you want cash or do you want credit toward another ticket?"

What did *Sylvie* want?—this complete stranger wanted to know. He was the only one who cared enough to ask.

She wasn't a hundred percent sure what she wanted. She only knew what she *didn't* want—returning to Miron.

Straightening up, she raised her chin.

"I want a ticket. To Debrecen," she announced.

CHAPTER FIFTEEN

Rurik
Kosice, Slovakia

Blood dripped from the corners of the dog trailer. Rivulets trickled down the ramp, covering the grass in a spreading stain. The odor of death hung in the air like a foul mist.

Half the circus members—performers, roustabouts, and almost forty others—stood in a loose circle around the vehicle. The lights of Mestsky Park angled through branches, the dappled beams twisting across faces, revealing expressions of shock and rage.

For the first time, Rurik didn't hesitate, going straight up to every onlooker and questioning them. And for once, the horror on their faces wasn't because of him.

After an hour of canvassing witnesses, he still hadn't found anyone who'd seen the killer.

"When you heard the barking, did you look outside?" he said to Miriam, the circus's contortionist.

"I heard them, they were making such a racket." The slim brunette gulped, deepening the stark hollows between her collarbones. "But I can't see the trailer from my RV. I figured Marva would take care of them. And after about five minutes, they all stopped barking..." She shivered and wrapped her arms around herself.

Everyone reported hearing the dogs but assumed Marva would see to them. However, she'd been on the other side of camp, in the Bartelli tent, taking care of a trapeze artist who'd sprained his wrist. It had been Minko, checking on his horses, who'd seen the open dog trailer and the carnage inside.

By that time, the clown was gone.

Rurik's gaze combed the crowd, trying to locate Yuri.

Since the tracker dog's head was displayed so grotesquely in the trailer, the killer must have known about him. But only people at Ivan's meeting had heard Misha's questions about the dog and their plans to give him the button in the morning. Someone at the meeting had talked. Not only had Yuri been there, but he'd abandoned his post just when the killer returned to camp.

Coincidence? Rurik doubted it, and he was determined to find out more. Except Yuri wasn't answering his walkie-talkie.

Miriam leaned closer and whispered, "But something strange *did* happen a little later."

Rurik's attention snapped back to her.

"I heard a crash outside. When I looked, someone had fallen over my lawn chairs. It was one of the clowns."

"Who?" Rurik's breath snagged in his throat.

"I couldn't tell. I only saw him from the back, and then he ran off. I thought it was weird he was in costume when the show was over hours ago. Do you think he saw Marva's dogs get killed...or..."—her eyes widened—"did he do it?"

Rurik shook his head. Actually, he was sure the clown did it. But there was no evidence. No witnesses.

At least Miriam had seen the clown at the RVs. That proved he lived in one. Unless he was just circling to confuse his pursuers.

"Thanks," Rurik said. "If you remember anything else about the clown, come tell me." As he walked away, he rubbed his forehead in frustration—and a bolt of pain shot through his hand. His two middle fingers had swollen as big as bratwursts. They needed ice and a splint, but he'd be damned if he'd give up now.

Hoarse sobs followed him everywhere, burrowing into his ears. Marva. Surrounded by friends, she peered out at him, her eyes bloodshot—and accusing.

He dropped his gaze. Her dogs were her children. Irreplaceable. Their death was his fault. The clown had slipped through his fingers in the park and escaped. Rurik believed the circus was sewn up tight, but there had been a gaping hole—a hole by the name of Yuri.

"Vadim," Rurik yelled when he spotted Ivan's cousin.

"Have you seen Yuri?"

Vadim shook his head, his perpetually gloomy expression and droopy eyes even more pronounced after the disaster.

"How about before the attack on the dogs?" Rurik said . "Did you see Yuri walking around?"

Vadim frowned and shook his head. "Such a tragedy. The world is a terrible place. Nothing's safe anymore. No, I didn't see Yuri, but about half-an-hour before the dogs barked, Pavel stopped at my guard post and asked where Yuri was. I sent the lad past the trucks to Yuri's post. If you want to know where Yuri was during the attack, you should ask Pavel."

Pavel Markarov. The name made Rurik want to hit someone, preferably Pavel. The obnoxious young strongman was the right size to be the clown. If he'd been seen half-an-hour before the attack, that left enough time for him to change into costume and lead the chase through the park before circling back to kill the dogs. He could have found a way to get Yuri to leave his post. It wouldn't be hard. Knowing Yuri, a twenty would do it.

Rurik had to find Pavel and Yuri. He needed answers.

A figure pushed through the onlookers, and Rurik's father wove unsteadily toward him. Although he was as tall as Rurik, the ex-strongman's shoulders sloped and his flesh hung slack. The odor of vodka arrived before he did.

"So," his father said. "It's truethen." He glanced around him and rubbed his nose, its broken veins swollen and red. "I can smell those dead mutts from home." His loud, slurry words carried. Across the crowd, Marva looked around. "Their blood and shit is stinking up the camp."

Marva's face flamed. She stepped toward him, but others held her back.

"What do you want?" Rurik clasped his father by the arm and pulled him away from the crowd and Marva's ferocious gaze.

"Came to warn you. You better find out who did this." It was unusual for his father to notice anything beyond the rim of his shot glass. "I saw the boss pacing outside his RV, smoking. You know what that means."

Alyosha had quit years ago, only sneaking cigarettes

when he was very upset.

"People say a clown did it. You better get your ass to the Italian's tent and find out what they know." He paused and a loud burp rumbled from his throat. Rurik turned his head from the alcohol fumes. His father blustered on. "You gotta at least *look* like you're working. You can't keep taking handouts from Alyosha for doing nothing."

Anger sparked inside Rurik's belly, building with every word.

"First, you question those shit-kicking clowns. If they don't confess , you treat them *hard*. Just like Leonid Alexi Petrov"—he thumped his chest with each name—"would do it!"

Rurik's rage grew into an inferno. He clenched his hands, his broken fingers sending agony up his arm. He thought he was beyond caring what his father thought. Too old to be surprised by anything the man said or did. But apparently, there was no age limit on a child being hurt by a parent's opinion, no matter how warped.

"I do my job and do it well!" Rurik couldn't keep the snarl out of his voice. "I know it can't be the clowns. But you're right. Hard questions need to be asked. But not of the clowns. Of Alyosha *himself*." He turned on his heel and set off toward the RVs.

If he couldn't find Yuri or Pavel, he'd confront the man who'd lied about visiting Ivan and find out where he and Pavel had really gone.

"No, Rurik. Wait!" His father stumbled after him and snatched at his shoulder. "Don't be crazy. You can't ask Alyosha anything. What if he gets angry? We need him—" He tripped and staggered off to the side, arms windmilling. His words faded as Rurik left him behind.

Maybe Rurik was crazy to go up against his boss. Alyosha had saved him from going to jail. Rurik owed him for that—and a lot more.

But the memory of Marva's accusing eyes spurred him on.

Alyosha's RV stood at the end of the last row. The ringmaster paced in front of it, a cigarette clamped between his lips. Next to him, the circus van outfitted to take Zora's wheelchair sat parked.

Dmitry and Viktor Markarov hauled a trunk out of Alyosha's RV, their muscles bulging as they lifted it to the edge of the van's roof. Dmitry's sons, Pavel and Anatoly, knelt atop the vehicle and hoisted the trunk before tying it down.

The strongmen halted their work when they caught sight of Rurik.

"Why're you here?" Dmitry said . "You got dead dogs to deal with."

Rurik's gaze latched onto Pavel. The young man's cold expression betrayed nothing as he stared down from the van roof. Rurik wanted to yank him off and make him talk. But if he went after the kid now, the family would surround and protect him like water buffalo heading off a lion. He'd get no answers that way.

Instead, he turned to Alyosha. "Can I talk to you? In private?"

"Hmm?" The ringmaster blinked at him. "I... Of course, my boy." He tossed the cigarette away and gestured to the RV.

Alyosha mounted the stairs, and Rurik followed.

Inside, Rurik recoiled as odors clawed at his nose. It was like walking into a butcher shop—the pungent smells of disinfectant and ammonia couldn't disguise the stink of rancid blood. He coughed at the stinging aromas: layers of sickness and decay mixed with antiseptic and medicines.

At the other end of the vehicle, the open bedroom door revealed a bed. A tank of oxygen sat at its foot. Two hospital stands were hung with plastic sacks of blood and a clear liquid. Thin lines hung from them and trailed beneath the swathes of mosquito netting screening the bed. Behind the curtains, a dim form shifted. Misshapen. Ugly. Barely resembling a human.

Rurik jerked his gaze away, and the heat of shame mounted his cheeks. He had no right to judge the appearance or illness of another person. He'd spent months confined to bed when recovering from his lightning-inflicted injuries. Some considered *him* barely human.

No, he couldn't judge Zora, crippled and deteriorating,

or Alyosha who had to tend to her.

But Rurik still needed answers.

He hardened his resolve and faced Alyosha. "In Bratislava, you left with Pavel to go visit Ivan twice. But Ivan says you never came. Bad things have been happening in this circus. Bad things on the whole tour. I have to ask where the two of you were."

Alyosha's head rose, outrage glittering in his eyes. "How dare you! You're nothing without me. Just a...a scarred has-been..." He trailed off, his eyes suddenly filling with remorse. His whole body sagged, deflating like the big top coming down on closing day. "I'm sorry. I didn't mean that. You have a right to know. I didn't visit Ivan. I...have a personal issue I'm dealing with. No one knows. Not even Pavel. He just helped take me out of the camp a few times, then he'd get out at the garage where the other circus van was parked. He'd take care of circus business in that one while I traveled in the other."

"Traveled to where?"

"Budapest, Vienna, Prague..." A pall of exhaustion spread over Alyosha's face. "It's Zora. She's sick...dying... Even when she gets oxygen, transfusions, and medicines, they only slow the disease. I've been to doctor after doctor, showing them the files, the x-rays, and the blood tests. No one can help." The old man's eyes brightened. "But now I've found someone in Vienna! A doctor who agreed to take her case. I was going to leave in the morning, but the tragedy with Marva has upset Zora too much." He waved a hand in the direction of the bedroom. "She's been ranting about evil portents. A cursed bride. How death follows wherever she goes. I decided it's better to leave now."

Alyosha paused and lowered his voice. "I hope you understand why I lied. No one can know the truth. I can't show weakness. The people would lose faith in me. And I've worked too hard for too many years to let that happen." He clutched Rurik's arm. "Please keep it quiet. I'm telling everyone I'm going to Russia to scout new venues for the tour. Two days is all I need, and when I return, everything will be better. Okay?"

Considering the smell of rot in the vehicle, Rurik thought

Alyosha was fooling himself. Zora was past helping. But as he stared into the man's watery blue eyes, he couldn't blame him for trying to save his wife.

Besides, as Alyosha clung weakly to Rurik, he knew that the man just didn't have the strength or the weight to be the clown. When Rurik tackled the killer in the woods, their mass had been nearly identical despite the clown's small stature. More importantly, Alyosha was miserable; he didn't have the rage necessary to fight off pursuers and rip dogs to pieces.

Rurik would stake his life on it—Alyosha wasn't the clown.

Rurik nodded at the ringmaster. "I won't tell."

Alyosha smiled and squeezed his arm. "You have a good heart, Rurik. If I wished for a son, I'd want one just like you."

Ironic, considering Rurik's own father didn't give a damn about him.

Footsteps clumped up the stairs, and Dmitry and Viktor halted behind him.

"Everything's loaded," Dmitry said to Alyosha. "Is she ready to go?"

"Yes." Alyosha led them into the back bedroom.

Rurik seized his chance. He charged out of the RV and went straight to Pavel, now standing behind the van with his brother.

Rurik loomed over the kid. "I know about the trips Alyosha took from Bratislava. You weren't with him. Where did you go those days when you were supposed to be visiting Ivan?"

Pavel glared at Rurik. "What's it to you? You're not—"

Rurik grabbed Pavel's shirtfront with both hands. His broken fingers ground together but his anger was far hotter than the pain. He lifted Pavel, holding him suspended in the air and said, "I'm done playing. Answer my question."

"Hey!" Anatoly sprang to his brother's defense and hauled at Rurik's arm. Both young Markarov men were well-muscled, but Rurik was taller and broader. Fifteen generations of strongmen and the strange effect the lightning had had on his bones—making them abnormally dense—made him both less and more than human.

Pavel squirmed like a fish on a hook and gurgled, "I... er...only business. I went...Budapest...business."

"Bullshit. The circus was over. What were you *really* doing?" Rurik tightened his grip, drawing the shirt closer around Pavel's throat.

"N-nothing. Swear!" Pavel rasped.

"Get off!" Anatoly pummeled Rurik in the ribs, but the blows couldn't get past layers of rock-solid muscle. Then the kid grabbed Rurik around the waist, trying to wrestle him off his feet.

Encouraged by his brother's attacks, Pavel began fighting back. Swinging his fists. Aiming clumsy blows at Rurik's head.

Pavel's weight, the tensed muscles under Rurik's fists, the ineffectual battering—it all matched the clown.

Rurik stared into Pavel's piggish eyes and read the lies lurking there.

Time to up the ante.

Rurik lowered Pavel, keeping one hand wrapped in his shirt collar. His other hand whipped out and punched Anatoly in the face.

The young man staggered back and fell on his ass. His hand flew to cover his nose.

Then Rurik shook Pavel, snapping his head back and forth like a ragdoll. "Tell me what you were doing. And tonight—why were you looking for Yuri?"

"All right, all right," Pavel squealed. "I was there to—"

"What the hell?" Dmitry shouted at Rurik from the RV stairs with Viktor. They held Zora's wheelchair between them. But Dmitry stumbled on the last step, falling to one knee.

Viktor gasped, clinging to the chair as it began to tip.

Zora's shrouded body swung sideways. From beneath the black veil, a moan of alarm spiraled higher and higher. Her arms flailed—gray-skinned arms with veins roped around them thicker than tree roots, ending in hugely swollen wrists and joints.

"Zora!" Alyosha sprang from the door. He threw his arms around his wife, stopping her fall. When the Markarovs regained their grip, he turned a livid gaze at Rurik. "What are you doing? Let him go!"

Rurik grudgingly released Pavel.

"He's crazy!" Pavel tottered away from Rurik and pointed at his brother, sitting on the grass. "He gave Anatoly a bloody nose."

Under five angry glares, Rurik crossed his arms and refused to back down. "Things are serious. People have gotten hurt. I need the truth."

"Then why don't you ask instead of acting like a gorilla?" Dmitry made his way past with Viktor, the two carrying Zora's wheelchair to the hydraulic lift at the back of the van.

"All right. I need to know where Pavel went during the two days he was gone. And where he was tonight before the dogs were killed."

"Not your business, asshole," Pavel spat.

"He was with me tonight," Anatoly declared, his voice wet and phlegmy from the bloody nose. "The whole night."

"Liar," Rurik snapped. "Vadim saw Pavel near the dog trailer looking for Yuri half-an-hour before the dogs were killed."

"Maybe I met Yuri. So what?" Pavel said. "I had nothing to do with what happened to Marva's dogs!"

"Of course he didn't," Viktor said in a calm voice. "None of us would ruin an act and jeopardize the show that way. *Zorka Cyrka* is family. Everyone knows that."

"Not everyone," Rurik growled. "Someone is our enemy, and I think it's Pavel."

"You see?" Dmitry said to Alyosha, flinging a hand in Rurik's direction. "He hates my family. Always been jealous of us. He'll never cooperate. Never abide by my new rules."

"New rules?" Rurik said in shock, turning to Alyosha.

"Rurik..." Alyosha scratched at his chin. "I'm sorry, but I'll be gone for a while, and Dmitry pointed out that you've been unreliable recently. Got into trouble at the train depot. Almost got arrested. Brawling with the clowns. While I'm gone, Viktor is in charge of the circus and..." Alyosha sidled toward the van door, and his gaze avoided Rurik's. "And Dmitry is taking over as Head of Security.

From now on, you work for him."

Rurik's heart stuttered. Unbelievable. Alyosha was as good as firing him. He could never work with the Markarovs. They were untrustworthy. Possibly murderers.

He leaped after Alyosha who swung into the driver's seat and pulled the door closed. "But I'm close to discovering who did this. You can't—"

Alyosha gunned the motor and shook his head at Rurik while Viktor shut the back doors. A moment later, the van pulled away, leaving Rurik breathing exhaust fumes.

Dmitry stalked up to him, chest thrust out. "As the new Head of Security, here are *my* rules. No more playing cop. No more searching people's homes. No more questioning anyone. And"—he jabbed Rurik's chest with his index finger—"no talking to my sons. Ever. If you screw with me, you and your papa will be kicked out of here faster than he can swig down a bottle of vodka." He angled his head, giving Pavel a sidelong grin. "And we all know how quick that is."

Laughing, the Markarovs joined ranks and headed off in the direction of their tent.

Pavel looked over his shoulder, lips curled in a smirk.

Rurik couldn't move, but inside, he was reeling. How could Alyosha do this to him? He'd given Alyosha and the circus all he had—every minute of his life—since he'd been born.

The van roared out the Mestsky Park entrance and turned onto the city streets.

Alyosha, the man who'd been a second father to him, had taken away everything and put the most dangerous suspects in charge of the circus.

The van's taillights disappeared into the blackness, and with them, Rurik's last hope of catching the killer.

CHAPTER SIXTEEN

Sylvie
Debrecen, Hungary

> *If anybody in your town gets hurt, do not try to give them first aid. Just because you know where the vital organs are doesn't make you a doctor. Your job comes later—when they're dead.*
> ~ The Bloodwalker's Book

"**I** see danger in your future. You will go on a perilous journey. Dark forces will be all around you, and you will... see death?" Sylvie couldn't remember what else she was supposed to say.

"No, no." Liana rolled her eyes. Again.

They'd been practicing for over an hour, and Sylvie had been the recipient of nothing but sighs and eye rolls. The sighs were getting louder, and Sylvie was certain that sometime soon Liana's eyeballs would roll so far back in her head they'd never come out again.

"People like to be told something scary," Liana said. "But you have to end with something good. Make them happy. Then they'll come back and pay for another reading. Try again."

Sylvie squirmed on Liana's threadbare couch, trying to keep the springs from digging into her rump. "I...um...can see danger in your future—"

"No! You have to sound confident or no one will believe you." With an angry grumble, Liana swept up the paper plates and take-out bags from the coffee table, crossed to the kitchen, and tossed them onto the overflowing garbage pail.

The mountain of refuse shifted. Napkins, plastic

utensils, and leftover food pattered onto the kitchen floor, adding to the dirt and stains already there.

Liana's home in the Debrecen apartment building was more spacious and newer than Miron's, but everything in it was tattered and grimy as if the things had been bought second hand and no one ever bothered to clean. Liana certainly never did. Old perspiration on the couch Sylvie slept on had made the fabric into a cross between animal hide and wax. And no telling what the original color of the rugs and curtains had been. They'd faded to bluish gray—the color of despair. Sylvie could feel the misery and unhappiness, a third resident, hunched in the corner, silent but creeping ever closer.

"Keep trying or you'll never get it." Liana maneuvered past the garbage landslide to a closet and pulled out a multi-colored peasant dress.

"I see danger in your future. You will take a perilous journey, but find...at the end...something that will make your life much better." Sylvie grinned.

"Don't grin like a fool!" Liana shook the dress at Sylvie. Fake gold coins sewn on the skirt clinked together. "You're an *all-knowing* fortune teller. Take it seriously and the customers will, too." Liana stripped down to panties and a bra and slid the dress over her head.

Sylvie averted her eyes from the leopard-print undergarments. "I'm sorry. I just can't seem to come up with...fibs."

"Naturally, Miss Perfect has trouble lying," Liana mumbled, head inside the brightly-colored dress. She smoothed it down, tugging the bodice lower until a lewd amount of cleavage showed. "Well, get over it! Our money won't last forever, and there haven't been as many people in the park as usual. Every day I have to stay later."

"If you bring groceries, I can cook. You don't have to keep buying from restaurants." And expensive ones at that. Between Liana's fondness for lavish foods and her commissioning a fortune-telling costume for Sylvie, the money Sylvie had stolen from Miron's shop was almost half gone—and it had only been three days.

"You mean make food?" Liana stuck out her tongue.

"That's for poor people. We'll do very well once you start telling fortunes, too. Stop being such a wimp. The time for following Skomori rules is over! I don't care if you made twenty *Farmece Arkana* potions—you're not one of those snobby bloodwalkers anymore." She snorted. "It's not like they don't do the same thing I do."

Sylvie's eyes widened. "My mother would never make up fortunes to tell people! No bloodwalker would do that."

"They *all* do it. There are no ghosts giving them messages. My grandmother told me the truth, and my mother admitted it. All they do is listen to village gossip, watch how everyone acts, and then apply some common sense. That's how they figure out what 'messages' to give."

"But..." Sylvie slowly shook her head. "My mom *knows* things... *Secrets*. Like when our neighbor's daughter got pregnant, my mother knew who the father was even when the girl denied it. And once, money got stolen from the cattle feed store, and she told them to look in the old mill— and it was there! How could she know that unless the dead were telling her things?"

Liana shrugged. "She heard a rumor. Or maybe she noticed the culprit had grain from the mill on his boots. It's not hard to find clues if you watch people real close. And your mother's been in that village since she got married— twenty years or more. You can't hide secrets in a small place where everyone knows everyone."

Sylvie opened her mouth to argue but closed it again. There was no point. She knew her mother really *did* see spirits, but Liana would never admit it. Easier for her to claim everyone was a liarso she didn't have to feel bad about being one herself. In fact, her fortune-teller act depended on the fact she was so good at lying—and at taking people's money.

Sylvie could never do that.

Except...now she kind of had to. The thought made her insides twist in shame.

"Stop thinking everyone's so honest because they're *not*," Liana continued. "Didn't you learn anything from that asshole husband of yours? If you want to succeed, you have to be as sneaky as everybody else. Screw your stupid principles! I can't keep going out to work while you sit here because you're too good to lie." She turned to the mirror and slashed red lipstick across her mouth.

Sylvie hung her head. It was true about Miron. He'd lied from day one, and she never suspected. And the laundry customers often tried to cheat her when they paid their bills. Just because she didn't know their language, they thought she was too stupid to do math.

The world was a bad place. If she wanted to live in it, maybe she had to be equally bad.

Liana walked to the front door, high-heels clicking on the floor. "Lock this when I leave. You can't be too careful. I swear, some weirdo tried to follow me home last night."

Sylvie slouched after her, nodding.

Liana stepped into the hall but quickly spun around, her eyes pinned to Sylvie's. "I—uh—I'm sorry for what I said. You're learning fast. Really. Soon you'll be telling fortunes as good as I can ." She smiled stiffly and fidgeted with her purse strap. "You'll still be here when I get back, won't you?"

Sylvie watched Liana's lower lip tremble, palpitating like a bird's breast. Beneath the proud-peacock attitude Liana usually showed the world, she was just a baby chick, far from her home, unsure and anxious. Sylvie dredged up a smile. "I'll be here. Don't worry."

"Good!" A whoosh of breath accompanied the word. "I'll bring back something really nice from the bakery on the corner!" Humming to herself, Liana sauntered down the hallway past three or four other apartments and clip-clopped down the stairs.

Sylvie shut the door and twisted the deadbolt before staring around her and wrinkling her nose at the filthy apartment. It was disgraceful. And depressing.

Her mother's Bloodwalker Book had a saying. "Cleaning your home is as important as cleaning a corpse's mouth with vinegar and packing the throat. It may not be fun, but you'll thank yourself when you have no burps of gaseous rot hanging in the air."

She might not be much of a bloodwalker and be awful at telling fake fortunes, but she could clean like a pro.

And busy-work would keep her mind off whether her mother knew about her running away. Whether Aunt Cosmina had officially cast her out. Or if Miron was searching for her.

Or if she truly had nowhere to go but this dingy little apartment. Forever.

A shudder rippled down her back. She grabbed a sponge, found a bucket, and set to work.

After two hours, the kitchen and bathroom revealed actual colored tiles hidden under the speckled mold and dirt, and the living room's coating of dust had floated into the air and out the open windows. Sylvie wanted to clean the floor, but the apartment had no mop. A towel would have to do.

She shoved the furniture out of the way, rolled up the rugs, and was halfway through swabbing the parched wood with a damp towel when someone hammered at the door.

Sylvie's breath bottled up in her throat. No one knew she was there, and she wanted to keep it that way.

"Hey, Liana! Open up!" a woman shouted in Romanian.

Sylvie still hesitated—but it was obviously someone who knew Liana. It might even be the seamstress with the new dress. Finally, Sylvie crept to the door and opened it, revealing a woman so old that her stooped back folded her into a question-mark shape.

In a slouchy housedress with a faded rose pattern and white hair stiffer than a boar's bristles, the elderly woman glared at Sylvie. "I knew it! That young tramp rented the flat for one person. *One!* You tell Liana that I don't care if she's a fellow Romanian—if there are two people living here, the rent is double."

"Double?" Sylvie didn't even know how much the rent was, but double-price sounded unfair. "But I'm just visiting...and I'm very quiet."

"Hell's bells! You're making enough noise for six people. The tenants under you are complaining. And of course 'double.' If there are two of you, you use twice as much gas and water." She squinted into the apartment and tsked at the wet floor. "Look at that water you're wasting! You're lucky I don't charge you triple!"

"But it's just this once. And the floors were very dirty."

"Why do you think I have rugs in here? Just put them out the window, beat the dust out of them, and you're done." She shuffled away, her bedroom slippers making scuffing noises down the hallway. "Washing the floors," she grumbled under her breath. "Crazy girl."

Sylvie finished the floors anyway and then put the furniture back as quietly as possible, not wanting any more complaints from the neighbors or the landlady.

Liana would be pleased with how good the place looked. She'd be less pleased when she heard the rent had doubled.

There was no way around it. Sylvie would have to start earning money. She'd have to become a street-corner fortune teller, and if she didn't lie well enough to make customers happy, she'd be a failure—just like she was at being a bloodwalker, and a wife.

Her stomach growled. The sun had set an hour ago. Liana always came back near sunset, saying the police patrolled the park at night and might arrest her if she loitered, thinking she was a drug-dealer or worse.

While waiting, Sylvie worked on her "spiel" as Liana called it, thinking up interesting fortunes to tell and trying to make her voice sound confident.

Her mother always sounded confident when she gave townspeople messages from their dead relatives or advice on problems. No one ever doubted her. Too bad Sylvie hadn't inherited any of her mother's abilities.

A whine echoed out in the hall. It sounded like a scared dog. Or someone in pain.

Something hit the door with a thud. Sylvie jumped.

Scratching noises came from the other side.

Perhaps it was a dog. Maybe sick. She rose and moved to the door, but didn't turn the lock.

Wet, raspy breathing filtered through the wood.

"Hello?" she called. "Who's there?"

No one answered. Cities were filled with criminals. But what if it was a victim, needing help? Sylvie knew too well what it felt like to be a victim. But just in case, she grabbed a small knife from the kitchen before slowly releasing the lock.

Liana swayed in the doorway, her face pale as moonlight. Blood trickled from the corner of her mouth. It followed the curve of her chin and fell onto her straining chest in thick, wet drops.

Her jaw worked but only a whine emerged. The sound ramped up to a gurgling shriek. Her eyes rolled back in her head. She pitched forward onto her face.

A long dagger stuck out from between her shoulder blades.

Sylvie gripped Liana's arm, shaking her, trying to rouse her. "Liana! Liana!"

A dry, crackling exhale wheezed from Liana's mouth.

A death rattle. Sylvie had heard them before, when a family knew the end was near and called her in to attend the passing before preparing the body. It was the last expulsion of air when the heart ceased to beat.

"Liana?" Hopelessness dulled Sylvie's voice.

As if someone had turned on a tap in the bathtub, thick blood flowed out of Liana's mouth. It spread across the newly washed floor and pooled around Sylvie's feet.

Doors opened in the hall. Hurried footsteps sounded. People peered through the doorway. Gasped. Shrieked. Ran away. But some stayed, their eyes wide and greedy, drinking in the horror that had taken place right in their own building.

The landlady appeared moments later and elbowed her way past the onlookers. Her gaze flew from Liana to Sylvie and back again. She pointed at the knife still clutched in Sylvie's hand. "Murderer! I'm calling the police!"

Sylvie had completely forgotten she was holding the slim knife. She sprang up, dropping it on the floor. "No! I had nothing to do... She came like this... I'd never hurt her!"

Her neighbors' expressions changed from curiosity to fear. They shrank away.

"Look!" Sylvie pointed at the murder weapon, still planted in Liana's back. "There's the dagger that did it. I didn't kill her! I didn't!"

More feet ran up the stairs. More gawking forms filled

the doorway. They jabbered at each other in Hungarian, their words alien and unintelligible.

Sylvie tried to talk to them, but as her desperate voice rose, their eyes narrowed. Their fingers pointed. Their faces pinched shut with condemnation.

Sylvie panicked. She raced across the apartment, collecting her things. Bloody shoe prints followed behind her, marking the floor with little oval shapes that aimed at her—like signs saying, "Here's the murderer!" She stuffed everything into her bloodwalker bag and made for the door.

The neighbors wouldn't let her pass.

She tried to shoulder her way through, but they refused. Pushing her back. Yelling things. Keeping her caged.

They only broke ranks when the police arrived. Instead of listening to her, men with hard eyes and harder hands gripped her arms.

She kept trying to explain, defend herself. She never gave up. Not when they put her in handcuffs. Not when they marched her downstairs and shoved her in a cramped car. Not when they dragged her down a barred corridor and threw her into a damp, concrete cell that stank.

She never stopped shouting at them. But no one listened.

CHAPTER SEVENTEEN

Rurik
Kosice, Slovakia

The afternoon sun reflected off windshields, glaring into Rurik's face as he made his way down the line of RVs, hands in pockets, feet scuffing the earth. The meeting with Ivan and the others had started an hour ago. Yet when he arrived at Ivan's camper, he hesitated outside the door, wishing he had somewhere else to be. Anywhere else. But, except for hiding out in his RV, he had nothing to do. The Markarovs had taken over the whole circus.

He knocked and when someone called, "Come in," he opened the door and trudged up the steps.

Inside, Ivan rolled his wheelchair back and beckoned Rurik toward the kitchen. Seated at the table, Misha and Vadim gave him overly-cheerful smiles.

Fakers.

Rurik slid into a seat and glanced around. The place looked different.

When Ivan first returned from the hospital, Marva had visited every day, helping him, cooking, and cleaning.

She was there now, facing them from the passenger seat in the front, but engrossed in her laptop, fingers smacking the keys. Her red hair hung in greasy strands. Gray showed at the roots. Beneath exhausted eyes, loose skin drooped. She'd aged ten years in just days.

The RV showed the same neglect. Unwashed dishes on the counters. Dirty clothes piled on the backs of chairs. Syrupy smears on the tabletop that stuck to Rurik's elbows.

The worst was that Marva didn't even acknowledge him. She hadn't spoken to him since the night her dogs were

152

killed. Now, her gaze bored into her laptop, and she didn't even glance up.

Ivan poured a shot of vodka and slapped it down in front of Rurik. "Maybe some of this will wipe that sour expression off your face."

Rurik didn't touch it. He wasn't like his father—couldn't afford that long fatal spiral. But staring at the liquid, as transparent as ice, capable of numbing your body and freezing your feelings, he understood for the first time how it was a temptation his father couldn't resist.

"Come on." Ivan huffed and leaned forward to scratch under the top of his cast. "Don't tell me you're letting the Markarovs get to you."

"Rurik, everyone's on your side." Misha sat forward, his brown eyes earnest, his uniform hanging loose on his spare frame. "Especially after the scene in the mess tent. That was harsh."

Only three days after Alyosha left, Dmitry Markarov, the new "Head of Security" and Rurik's boss, had formally fired Rurik. In public. In front of half the performers and roustabouts gathered for dinner in the mess tent. Dmitry, like the attention whore he was, made a big show of listing Rurik's supposed transgressions, taking away his official keys, and banning him from the box office.

"That was just Dmitry's first step." Rurik's distracted tone forced the others to draw closer to hear him. "He's going to kick me and my father out of camp."

Ivan waved a dismissive hand. "Even dimwitted Dmitry wouldn't do anything that drastic. That family of bullies will only be in charge till Alyosha gets back. And firing you and keeping you from doing searches was a bonehead move. It just makes them look guilty."

The others nodded in agreement.

Rurik's finger traced the edge of the shot glass.

Ivan was too optimistic. Alyosha was already two days late. The longer he stayed away, the easier it was for Dmitry and Viktor to continue their power grab. It was only a matter of time until they became brave enough to throw Rurik and his father out. And unless someone had a job opening for the ugliest man on earth, Rurik was shitoutta-luck.

He rubbed a finger along the warped planes of his face. He'd never hated his scars more than he did in that moment. He hated a lot of things in that moment. "Did you find Yuri yet?" He scowled at Misha.

The kid shook his head. "He hasn't been bunking in the roustabout tent. Not since we found"—his gaze skated over Marva, and he lowered his voice—"the dogs. There's a rumor Alyosha fired him."

"Bullshit." Ivan poured himself a shot of vodka and knocked it back. "He knows you're looking for him. He's just slinking around, bedding down in some girlfriend's place till he thinks the heat's off."

"What girlfriend?" Rurik said.

Ivan shrugged. "Pick one."

"Dammit!" Rurik's fist banged the table. Vodka sloshed over the glass rim, and Marva's eyes flicked up from her laptop. "He was the last person to see Pavel that night. He knows something! Maybe he saw Pavel changing into the clown costume and that's why he's hiding out. Misha!" His sharp growl made the boy flinch. "Go visit all his girlfriends—every girl in camp if you have to—and find him!"

"I—uh—sure," Misha said.

"Now!" Rurik's tone propelled Misha up from his seat and out the door.

"Pavel is an ass , I grant you that. But not a psycho." Vadim, Ivan's cousin, ran his nails over the white stubble on his chin, creating a sandpaper noise. "When he asked about Yuri, I figured it was about money. That's all the kid's interested in. He wouldn't do anything worse than betting too much on a game."

"I think he would." Rurik leaned forward, the tabletop creaking under his elbows. "I think he's dangerous. Remember that RV that burned? Pavel and Anatoly supposedly saw the fire first and put it out. But I was there when they told Dmitry and Viktor, and those two weren't even surprised at the news. They knew about it. And Pavel and Anatoly treated it like a joke."

"Oh, come on. The little monsters were probably in

there getting high and accidentally set the place on fire."
Ivan chortled.

"I think they did it on purpose," Rurik said, tone icy.

"Why?" Ivan lifted his shoulders. "Who'd want to burn
down an empty RV?"

"Because there was something important in it," Rurik
said. "Remember the bloodwalker wedding? The brides got
dressed in there. One of them said something to me before
she left. She told me there was something hidden inside,
under the sink. A 'matter of life and death' she said."

Ivan wrinkled his nose. "You can't trust those Skomori.
They all marry their cousins. Freaks."

"But I got a good look at her veil. It had paint on it.
Grease-paint. The colors a clown would use."

"You think the clown was using the RV to change in?"
Vadim's bushy gray eyebrows pinched together.

"Well, I'm sure she didn't bring the veil from home
looking like that. So it happened here. In that RV."

"So maybe she found the clown's makeup or his
costume?" Ivan said.

"Or maybe she found something worse." Rurik
remembered the missing child from Budapest. "Like a
little girl's bloody dress."

"Or a little girl's bloody body." Marva's words cut through
the air like a broadsword and immediately silenced the
group. "There's something you don't know about my dogs."
Her bloodshot eyes glared from a waxen face. "I helped
bury them, and Campion wasn't the only one the killer
singled out. Fifi, my smallest poodle, was pulled apart and
had *teeth marks* on her leg. The killer chewed on her!"

Vadim's face screwed up in disgust.

"And remember when Ivan was attacked? The killer
went after his broken leg."

"Sure as hell did!" Ivan said. "He tried to pull it off. So
the clown's a cannibal?"

"No, he didn't eat the flesh. He ripped off the meat and
gnawed on a bone. One bone. Where Fifi had a hairline
fracture." She stood up, carrying the open laptop, and
approached the table. "Look here." She slid the laptop
onto the table, bumping the vodka glasses aside.

Rurik studied the screen and frowned at diagrams of bones and bone marrow.

"I was a nurse for ten years before I started working in the circus. There's one thing that Fifi's leg, Ivan's leg, and little children have in common." She paused as if she expected someone to know the answer. They stared at her blankly. "Osteoblasts. They're bone growing cells. Your body produces a lot of them if you break a bone—or if you're a child."

"So...the killer wanted to tear off my leg to get these cells? That's crazy." Ivan poured himself another shot.

"No, it's not." Marva snatched away his drink. "I'm not letting you sit here and swill booze. You're all just talking and doing nothing." Her voice cracked. "Someone killed my babies. I'm going to figure out who and make sure he gets what's coming to him!" Behind a sheen of tears, her eyes sparked with fury.

The men exchanged uncomfortable glances and mumbled in agreement.

"I've been researching what osteoblasts can be used for. In a healthy person, they can be used like steroids. Making a person *stronger*. And who would need that? A *strongman*." Marva's gaze swept across them. "I think Rurik's right—Pavel is the killer. But I want proof. Somehow, we have to search the Markarov tent."

"Don't know how you'll do that." Vadim's face soured. "Those Markarov women are always in there."

"Then we have to think up something!" Marva insisted. "A search is the only way to find proof Pavel's the killer. The clown costume. A child's clothes. Anything. And once we do, he's gonna pay." She raised Ivan's vodka and downed it in one go.

For the first time in days, Rurik felt a smile curve his lips. They were going to get Pavel Markarov and his whole rotten family.

They'd pay all right. For what they'd done to him. For Marva's dogs. Most of all, for the children who'd vanished into their clutches.

Hope streamed into Rurik, clearing his head, energizing his senses, filling him with purpose again.

All he needed was a plan. And just then, one crystallized in his mind.

* * *

As the music blasted from the big top, accompanied by the roar of applause, Rurik crept around inside the Markarov's tent, rummaging through drawers, delving into closets, and looking under beds.

The Markarov's tent was the biggest in camp except for the big top and the mess tent. It was even larger than the roustabouts' sleeping quarters, which housed twenty cots and footlockers.

Rurik had often wondered why the Markarovs didn't buy a couple of RVs. They could have afforded it. But once inside the mammoth tent, he understood. It was as big as a small house, with a living room and kitchen in the center, and four separate bedrooms at the corners. They even had furniture. Having four strongmen to put up poles, hammer stakes, and then lug in chairs and beds probably made it easy to set up.

Great for them.

Not great when you had to search the entire thing.

Rurik had been through every inch of the bedrooms. Pavel's and Anatoly's bedroom had been first on his list. He'd uncovered their porn videos, drug stash, and a bunch of cell phones, likely dropped by audience members and collected by Pavel and Anatoly from under the bleachers after performances.

He couldn't honestly fault them for that. There was no such thing as a "Lost and Found" box in the circus. Anything lost became the property of the finder.

However, Rurik's careful search hadn't revealed a clown costume, bloody clothing, or anything linking them to the children's disappearances or the dog killings.

Rurik slammed the last cabinet of the kitchen closed and stared around the interior. The evidence had to be there. He just wasn't looking hard enough.

Time was ticking.

The four Markarov strongmen were performing in the big top—but their show only lasted another five minutes. Viktor's wife Tasha and his mother Irina had been lured away by Marva to a fake baby shower, or engagement party, or some woman's thing Rurik didn't understand.

If he didn't leave soon, the Markarovs would return and find him. That would undoubtedly be the last straw, and Rurik and his father would find themselves kicked out on the street before dawn.

In the far corner, Rurik spotted a portable shower room. Beside it sat a gas water heater. But that wasn't the interesting part. There was a big barrel of water as high as his waist with a plastic cover. He rushed to the tank and pried off the lid. A plastic package floated in the water.

Excitement kicked his heart rate into overdrive. This was it!

"You're wasting your time in here." Madame Nadia's voice almost gave Rurik a heart attack. The elderly costume-maker ambled into the living room and sank into a chair as if she owned the place. Her gaze swept the interior and returned to stare at Rurik. "The Markarovs aren't the ones you're after."

"This isn't the time," Rurik growled. "Get out."

She returned his glare, her eyes shriveling into slits.

Short of throwing the old lady out, Rurik had no choice but to ignore her. Finding out what was hidden in the package was too important.

He untied the top of the bag and peered in, certain of what he'd see.

But he was wrong. It wasn't the clown costume. It was money.

Bills filled the bag. Hundreds of them, neatly banded in packs of 5000 Euros apiece. There must have been a hundred thousand in there. Didn't the idiot Markarovs believe in banks?

"Shit!" he spat.

"Told you." A smug smile stretched the wrinkles on Madame Nadia's face. "By the way, I saw Tasha and Irina leaving Marva's RV. They'll be here any second."

Adrenaline jolted through Rurik's chest as he struggled to retie the plastic bag.

"What's going on in here?" Tasha's shrewish voice rang out as she and her mother-in-law, Irina, stepped into the tent.

"Where have you two been?" Madam Nadia's tone was even sharper. "You tell me you want a dress mended, but when I come, you're not here. So I have to go through the trouble of looking through your closets for it."

Rurik could feel the Markarov women's eyes needle his back as he slid the bag inside the tank. He blocked the action with his body, but couldn't resist glancing over his shoulder. They stared but weren't running at him, screaming and pointing.

"I'm exhausted from searching, and then what happens?" Madam Nadia's strident voice pulled the women's attention back to her. "I get this terrible pain in my chest, and I think it must be the end. Lucky for me, Rurik was passing and heard me calling for help." She turned his direction and gave him a sugary smile. "He put me in this chair and is getting me a glass of water."

Rurik snatched a cup from a basin of dirty dishes on the ground and filled it from the water tank's tap. As he walked to Madame Nadia's seat in the living room, Tasha and Irina's stares stabbed into him, probing for secrets.

"Here you go." He handed the drink to Madame Nadia.

Tasha leaped forward and jerked it away. "You can't do that!"

He straightened his shoulders, bracing for a confrontation.

"That tank in back is for washing up. Fresh water is here." Tasha headed for a case of bottled water on the kitchen counter.

"Never mind," Madame Nadia said, extending her hand to Rurik. "Rurik will walk me home. My medicine is there." She allowed him to pull her to her feet and tucked her gnarled fingers into the crook of his arm. As he led her out the door, she called over her shoulder, "You ladies can bring me the dress tomorrow morning. Assuming I don't die before then."

Outside, she peered around and steered him away from other performers returning to their tents. Near the equipment trucks, out of earshot of any of the camp inhabitants, she spoke. "You've never paid attention to me, always written me off. But I know a lot more than you think! I know about the children."

Rurik practically choked, swinging around to face her.

"This has been going on longer than you know. Way back to when I was a child in the Ukraine. It's the bloodwalkers," she hissed. "It's always been them. Dirty evil creatures! They'd sooner die than have one piece of truth pass their lips."

Rurik's shoulders sagged. Just the old feud between Zorka and Skomori again. Nothing but hatred and blame for imagined wrongs. He resumed his pace, pulling her with him in the direction of her tent.

"You don't know what they're really like, but I do! I know all about the bloodwalker's curse. All about how they try to keep it under control."

Great. Now she wanted him to believe in curses. Magic spells and secret potions would probably be next.

The woman rattled on about witches and the history of the Ukraine and Russia while he nodded and kept saying, "Mm-hm."

Crickets abruptly fell silent as Rurik and Madame Nadia passed the oldest truck in camp. It belonged to Alyosha and stored his calliope organ, a priceless antique used in circuses sixty years ago, before there were such things as sound systems. Alyosha loved it. Refused to store it anywhere, always traveled with it, even if it hadn't been played in years.

Suddenly, Madame Nadia's babbling faded as he focused on something shocking.

As quickly as Rurik could, he escorted her to her own tent, said goodnight, and promised to return and listen to her entire tale in the morning.

Then he sprinted back to the calliope truck, running the shadowy pathways like a wolf on the hunt.

At the rear of the truck, he inhaled deeply. There it was. A smell he recognized. One that made the inside of his stomach curdle.

He pulled a flashlight from his pocket—one he'd used in the darker spaces of the Markarov tent—and shone it over the truck's rear sliding door.

At the bottom corner, a stain caught his eye. Something crimson had leaked from inside and run down the bumper, leaving a slick trail.

He crouched and felt the grass. The earth was damp. He pulled up a clod of dirt and rubbed it between his fingers. It left red blotches on his skin.

The calliope truck was leaking blood.

CHAPTER EIGHTEEN

Sylvie
Debrecen, Hungary

*Since the time of the Black Plague, we have walked in
Death's shadow.
We collected those felled by his touch in order to protect
the living.
Even now, influenza and other diseases may endanger
your village.
The weak shall perish. The strong shall survive. All you
can do is watch, and wait, for the storm to pass.
~ The Bloodwalker's Book*

Sylvie paced back and forth in her small jail cell. With every impatient turn, a few locks of hair slipped loose from her crocheted cap. Soon, half her hair dangled in her face. She wrenched the cap off with a jerk. Bobby pins flew in all directions.

Although past midnight, the lights burned in the corridor outside the jail cells. The cell walls blocked her view of the other inmates, but she heard them. One woman cried, her hoarse sobs echoing down the row. Another moaned and prayed. A third was throwing up.

A fitting soundtrack for the worst day of Sylvie's life.

She flung herself onto the mattress and wished for sleep. Even a moment of respite from the day's events would be welcome.

A sharp pain pricked her ankle, and a moment later, it began to itch. Fleas. The bed was infested. Lurching upright, she began to pace again. Her cage seemed to get smaller by the minute. Squeezing the oxygen from her lungs. Pressing her down. Crushing her.

Drab green paint covered everything: the walls, the floor, the bars, the metal bed frame, and the wire mesh covering the light bulbs. The paint had worn away on the walls and floor, leaving dull, gray cement. At the front of the cell, the iron bars had corroded from the humidity. Rust bubbled to the surface, blistering the paint until it resembled green leprous skin dotted with brown scabs.

A web of cracks fissured one wall, cutting through paint, plaster, and concrete alike. The foundation had sunk, and her cell—probably the whole building—tilted slightly toward the back.

And the stench...

Sylvie was used to horrid smells. Her nostrils had been assaulted by everything from burst intestines to decayed, maggot-ridden flesh. Once, she'd helped collect a body from inside a pig sty, where it had been covered in so much manure and mud even the pigs wouldn't go near it. But she'd never smelled anything like the jail.

Its "toilet" consisted of a small hole at one end of the cell that dropped to a channel beneath. At one time, maybe an underground stream had carried the waste away, but now there were no gurgles of moving water. It was blocked up somewhere. What lay beneath the jail cells was a lake of feces.

Sylvie wasn't going near that thing. She'd hold it in until it came out her ears.

Shoes scuffed in the hallway. Her heart jolted as a shadow fell across her cell bars.

A fat guard with a walrus mustache and heavy-lidded eyes stuck a key in the door. Pulling it open, he muttered something in Hungarian and jerked his head toward the hall.

They'd realized their mistake and were letting her out! Excitement burst inside her and she cannoned out of the cell, practically running down the guard.

His warning shake of the head, jowls flapping, slowed her down. Making sure she remained behind him, he headed down the corridor.

Matching his glacial pace, she followed him into a large room where a dozen policemen sat at desks. A few eyed her. Most didn't bother to look up. In ponderous steps, the guard continued down another hall. Finally, he waved her into a medium-sized room with half a dozen chairs pushed up against the walls.

A gray-haired man, skinny as a stray dog in winter, sat at the far end of the room, at a table piled high with papers and folders. He leaned over a document, his spider-like fingers clasped around a pen, his brow beetling in concentration as he wrote. He didn't acknowledge her entrance.

She figured she must have to sign something before they formally let her go. She seated herself on a nearby chair.

The guard suddenly came to life, stomping across the room, yanking her to her feet, and shoving her toward the empty space at the center of the floor.

All her hopes of release vanished. Reality hit her in the gut. The man must be some kind of judge or prosecutor—and she was about to be charged as a murderer.

Without knowing Hungarian, she couldn't explain anything. Couldn't defend herself. The jail would be her home forever. Her back bowed, her body ten times heavier than when she'd walked into the room.

The old man glanced up. He gave her the once over and sniffed, as if passing judgment. But then he grabbed a tissue and blew his nose. A cough rattled in his chest. He spat into the tissue before mumbling an order to the guard, his voice thick and wet.

The mustached guard nodded and disappeared, returning moments later with a woman in a policeman's uniform.

Square-jawed and intense, the female officer whipped off her cap, tucked it under her arm, and marched up to where Sylvie stood.

"I'm Officer Dobos," the woman said in Romanian to Sylvie. "I will be translating for Prosecutor Bruhn, and you will answer all his questions."

Fresh hope dawned inside Sylvie. With the woman's excellent command of Romanian, her round face and blond hair, she could have passed for one of Sylvie's Romanian neighbors. But instead of being a friendly face, her hard expression held about as much warmth as an icicle.

Sylvie's smile died before it reached her lips.

The prosecutor rummaged through a pile of folders, picked one out, and opened it. He said Sylvie's name and asked something in Hungarian.

"Your papers say your name is Sylvia Annamaria Dinescu. Is that correct?" Officer Dobos said

"Yes," Sylvie answered.

"State your birth date, age, and Romanian identity card number." After Sylvie did as instructed, the woman said , "Are you married?"

"No," Sylvie declared. As far as she was concerned, she wasn't and never had been.

"Any children?"

"No." And at this rate she'd never have any.

The prosecutor wiped his nose again and asked a new question.

"Your ethnic background is...Skomori?" the woman said.

"Yes."

The prosecutor leaned back in his chair and gave Sylvie the stare. The same nasty look all *Baran* gave to Skomori—as if they were something slimy that crawled out of a cemetery grave.

Sylvie's cheeks grew hot.

For hundreds of years the Skomori had tended the dead—preparing bodies, sewing shrouds, making coffins, carving headstones, and digging graves—and the *Baran* had used their services gladly. But then funeral homes and mortuaries opened. Now it was better to hand your loved one off to a stranger, who'd drain their blood, fill them full of chemicals, spray their hair in place, paint their faces to look pink and healthy, and wire their lips into serene smiles.

And they thought the Skomori were the disgusting ones.

"The victim? She was Skomori, too?" Officer Dobos said

Sylvie wondered if Liana's being cast out counted and decided it didn't. "Um...yes."

"You were living with her? Or do you have your own apartment somewhere?"

"No. I mean yes." Best not to mention her time in Miskolc. "I was just visiting from Romania."

"And you knew the victim from Romania?"

"No." Sylvie's voice hitched, and her eyes began to sting. She wished they'd stop referring to Liana as "the victim." It was a callous term. Too formal. Too final.

"Then how do you know her?"

"We met in Budapest at our wedding ceremony."

"I thought you said you weren't married?"

Black Plague take it! Worst liar in history. Sylvie's mind raced as her mouth took off on its own. "I'm not married. No... It was...an engagement. Just a promise ceremony, really...I...we didn't wear white dresses or anything. And we didn't sign papers. That means it's not legal, right?"

Officer Dobos raised her brows, but she translated for the prosecutor.

He listened for a moment before cutting her off and launching into a long speech. Above gaunt cheekbones, his eyes narrowed. One eye twitched. He pulled out a paper and read from it, the page crinkling in his grip. When he finished speaking, he slapped the paper down and glowered at Sylvie. His eye twitched again.

Officer Dobos rounded on Sylvie. "Witnesses in the building say they heard thumping sounds from the apartment and then loud voices. You and the victim were having a fight. What were you fighting about?"

"No" Sylvie said, aghast. "That's wrong. Liana left in the afternoon. I cleaned the apartment...I guess I made noise. But the landlady came to talk to me. She can tell you Liana wasn't there."

"People heard voices. If the victim wasn't there, who were you talking to?"

"No one. Only me. I was practicing."

"Practicing what?"

Darn it. This was getting harder by the minute. Sylvie couldn't admit she was pretending to be a fortune-teller and making things up. That would make the police suspect everything she said.

"It was just... Well, I was..." she mumbled, playing for time, her gaze darting between the prosecutor and Officer Dobos. Liana's words came back to her. *If you want to succeed, you have to be as sneaky as everybody else.* She wondered what policemen would find believable and harmless.

It's not hard to find clues if you watch people real close.

The prosecutor's nose was red and runny. It gave her an idea.

"I was making a medicine for my cold." She covered her mouth and gave a little cough. "I boiled lemons, honey, and garlic. If you stand over the pot breathing it in, and then talk loudly, it will clear your chest. It's an old cure, but it worked on me." She gave him a tentative smile.

The prosecutor pursed his lips as if considering. Another tissue appeared in his hand. He dabbed at his nose before aiming another lengthy monologue at the officer.

"When the victim came home, you attacked her—"

"No, I didn't!" Sylvie interrupted, but Officer Dobos continued on like a bulldozer.

"—and killed her. Witnesses saw you standing over the body. You had a knife in your hand. It is obvious you murdered her. However, the prosecutor says that if you sign a confession now, you will save the court time and money. He will make sure your sentence is lenient."

"But I can't confess." Sylvie's voice rose. "I didn't do it!"

"If you don't confess, the court has no other option but to prosecute you. He will ask for a life sentence. Your best option is to confess now."

Sylvie gasped. Life! Didn't they care about the truth? Anger ignited inside her. Her skirt bunched in her fists. "I will not confess to something I didn't do." She shouted, "*Nem!*" At least she knew "no" in Hungarian.

The old man's face flushed. His eye began twitching as he yelled at her in incomprehensible Hungarian.

"*Nem.*" She repeated, standing her ground. Never in a million years would she confess to killing poor Liana.

The prosecutor's harangue devolved into a coughing fit. He jammed a tissue over his mouth. Above his clenched hand, both eyes were twitching now, jolting his whole face into spasms. He flung out a hand at the door.

"You are excused. Come," Officer Dobos said, leading the way to the exit.

As soon as she was in the hall, Sylvie spoke quickly. "Please, can I use a phone? To call home? No one even knows I'm here."

The woman gave a short laugh. "The crime is all over the news with the picture from your ID. I'm sure your family knows all about it by now."

Sylvie gagged at the thought of her mother hearing it on the news. What would she think? Her only daughter, running away from her husband. Probably being cast out. Branded a murderer. She caught the officer's arm. "I swear on my life I didn't kill my friend. Can't you let me call my mother?"

"I'm sorry. It's not possible," Officer Dobos said curtly, shaking off Sylvie's hold.

Inspiration struck. Sylvie dropped her voice into a bloodwalker's gravelly tone. "Your mother would be ashamed of you. She'd want you to do what's right and help a fellow countryman."

Officer Dobos's eyes widened.

It was a just guess. "Dobos" was Hungarian, meaning the woman's father was Hungarian, so she probably got her Romanian looks from her mother. Judging by the woman's startled reaction, Sylvie's guess had hit home.

"My mother's...dead," the officer murmured.

"Not to me." Sylvie raised her chin, assuming the haughty expression she'd seen so often on her mother's face. "I'm a Skomori bloodwalker, and you know what that means. The dead talk through me. I can see your mother. Despite death, she remains close—you often feel her presence." Her unblinking eyes drilled into the woman's, desperate for her gamble to work. "She expects you to help an innocent Romanian."

The officer chewed her lip. After a quick glance around, she bent her head closer and whispered, "All I can do is give you some advice. *Don't* confess. Other witnesses say your friend was attacked in front of a bakery. They say a short man threw a knife. The forensic team found blood *outside* your building, and they have the weapon. It's a special throwing dagger with carvings on it. Definitely not the one people saw you holding."

"But..." Sylvie rocked back on her heels. "But if everyone knows this, why am I still here?"

"Because they don't have the man that did it... They have you."

CHAPTER NINETEEN

Rurik
Kosice, Slovakia

Rurik examined the rear of Alyosha's calliope truck, his flashlight beam traveling up the line of dried blood from the bumper to where it disappeared beneath the roll-up door. A solid-looking padlock fastened the door shut. The key to it was on his security ring...the one Dmitry Markarov had taken.

As far as Rurik knew, no one had opened the truck in months, maybe years. Alyosha always kept it closed, saying the calliope shouldn't be exposed to dust or pollution. He was rabid about it.

But the blood leaking from under the door meant someone had been in there—or someone still was.

Curiosity fought with possible repercussions from Alyosha.

No contest.

Rurik trotted down the line of trucks till he reached Minko's pickup. The riding master kept a toolbox in the open bed that held a tire iron.

Back at the calliope truck, Rurik jammed the iron rod behind the hasp holding the padlock in place. Hiking his foot up on the bumper for leverage, he pulled. The nerves in his arm jangled from his broken fingers. He gritted his teeth.

The hasp broke with a gunshot's bang. Unhooking it, he tossed it and the tire iron in the weeds.

The door squealed along its tracks as he rolled it up.

The stink of rotted flesh sent him staggering backward.

"Hey!" The white silk of a clown costume materialized from the blackness behind Rurik.

170

Rurik's heartbeat accelerated. He crouched, ready to attack.

"Markarov say you no search. So what you doing?" said the man as he strutted up.

Rurik relaxed. It was only Antonelli, the chief of the clowns. An idiot, but not the killer.

"*Madre di Dio!* What is that smell?" The disgust in Antonelli's tone contrasted with the cheery smile painted on his face.

"Go back to your tent. This doesn't concern you." Rurik swung up into the truck. His flashlight lit up the large calliope organ sitting against one wall. The beam glinted off metal and polished wood, making the instrument shimmer in the darkness.

Above a piano-style keyboard, twenty tall pipes rose into the gloom, each a different height and made of brass that shone like gold. The ancient steam engine that powered the instrument lurked in the back of the truck, charred as black as the coal that fed it.

Rurik remembered seeing the calliope in action when he was little—Alyosha playing the keyboard with a big grin on his face, each pipe belting out its particular toneand clouds of steam jetting from the tops like fiery dragon's breath. Painted red with gold-leaf trim, it had been an impressive sight.

Rurik ventured farther inside, aiming his light along the track of the blood. It led to the calliope. He flashed the light over the great organ, along its sides, behind its pipes, and then into the back corners of the truck.

The light revealed nothing. No body.

While Rurik was relieved not to find a child's decomposing body, he knew something terrible had happened in there.

"Why is smelling so bad? Like sausage factory in here," Antonelli spoke from right behind Rurik's shoulder.

"I'll deal with this. You go home," Rurik said sternly, but the man regarded him with a stubborn pout before he turned to the wall opposite the organ.

"Hey, Luigi," Antonelli called. "Look at these *giornali.* From your day, eh?"

Rurik glanced outside and ground his teeth together.

Like multiplying rabbits, the entire clown crew had appeared on the grass behind the truck. They jostled around and pushed green-costumed Luigi up onto the floor. The elderly clown grunted and rubbed his back before shuffling over to join Antonelli. "I can't see. Rurik, shine that light over here."

Like he was working for them now. "You have no business being—" His words cut off as he followed their gazes. Yellowing photographs and newspaper clippings were taped to the wall. The wash of his light revealed a photo of a clown in a white costume. Three red pom-poms ran down its front like buttons, matching the one he'd pulled off the clown at the train depot.

He shouldered his way between Antonelli and Luigi and examined the image up close. Elizabethan ruffle around the neck. A jester's hat with bells hanging off the pointed ends. It was definitely the costume the killer wore.

The face, however, was covered with makeup.

He thrust a finger at the picture. "Who is this?"

"That harlequin style is old. From forty, fifty years ago," Luigi said and shrugged. "I can't remember that far back."

Antonelli moved down the line of clippings. "Ah-ha! Alyosha here and the clown, too."

Rurik's light flew to the new picture. It was the same clown, face covered with white makeup, wearing the unmistakable costume . Next to him stood a man Rurik would never guess was Alyosha. With a full head of black hair and a mustache, the short man smirked at the camera. Two wide bandoliers crisscrossed his chest. Instead of carrying ammunition like a soldier, a dozen large daggers stuck out of the leather belts.

Luigi sauntered up next to Rurik and gave a wolf whistle. "Now this I remember. She was a looker back then."

"Who?" Rurik squinted at the stunning blonde dressed as a showgirl with her arms around both Alyosha and the clown.

"That's Zora! Quite a doll, eh? She was Alyosha's assistant when he worked as a knife thrower. She'd be strapped on a board, it would spin, and he'd throw knives at her. He was a big draw, used to make all the ladies in the audience swoon."

Rurik's brows rose. Of course no one started out as a ringmaster, but he had no idea Alyosha used to be a knife thrower. And Zora was gorgeous. Mile long legs and the face of an angel. No wonder Alyosha had fallen for her.

Another two clowns climbed into the truck, making it creak on its axles.

A prickle of alarm raised the hairs on Rurik's neck. The last time he'd been in a truck with these jerks, they'd done their best to beat him senseless. He watched them warily.

One of the clowns popped off his round plastic nose and began sniffing. Like a hound, he walked from one side of the truck to the other, testing the air and muttering.

"This *giornale* has writing about old circus." Antonelli leaned closer and read in a halting voice, "In the Pushkov Circus, Alyosha the Great displays amazing feats of knife-throwing skill with his wife, Zora. Also appearing, the clown, Maximilian Markarov."

A collective gasp went up from the clowns, followed by dead silence.

"Did you say Markarov?" Rurik said, his hackles rising. "The same family as our strongmen?" He knew those evil bastards figured in this thing.

"Maximiliano," one clown whispered. "*Il tragico pagliaccio.*"

"The tragic clown." Luigi shook his head. "He was Viktor and Dmitry's father."

"Where is he now?" Rurik said.

"Murdered. Stabbed to death." Luigi crossed himself. "It happened many years ago."

"*È qui! È qui!*" The clown who'd been following his nose pointed at a large, red, trunk-sized bench with a padded leather seat shoved under the keyboard.

Rurik stepped toward it and squatted. It nestled so snuggly inside the calliope, he hadn't noticed it. He dragged it out to the middle of the floor. Its weight and size could easily conceal a body. He pried at the top, but it wouldn't open. After examining all sides, he could find no lock, no handle, no way to open it. But a dark stain colored the lower corner of the box.

Shining his light on the floor, Rurik trailed the line of blood from the empty spot where the bench had been to the door of the truck and out onto the bumper. He turned and glared at the wooden box. The source of the blood was in there, but there was no way to open it. He'd have to lift it and smash it on the ground outside. Although having whatever was inside spill out for all to see wouldn't be good.

Antonelli's small eyes met Rurik's. "We hear rumors," the man said. "Children missing, maybe dead. And a clown doing it. Very bad for us. We want truth, same as you." He raised his voice. "Michelangelo!"

"*Si?*" A small person, barely three feet tall, peered over the bumper. Rurik recognized him from the clowns' act, but the little man was new, kept to himself, and Rurik hadn't spoken to him before.

Antonelli said something in Italian, and another clown boosted Michelangelo into the truck. He waddled over to the bench and cracked his knuckles.

"He was magician assistant before," Antonelli said. "He good at puzzles. Give him flashlight."

Rurik handed it over and stepped out of the way.

"Is this where the party is?" a woman said from outside, laughing.

Rurik glanced over his shoulder, displeased to see Miriam the contortionist and two other female performers approaching the truck.

Above the line of tents, the big top loomed dark and silent. The show had just ended. No telling who might amble past.

"No party here," Rurik growled, but the girls kept staring inside. He dropped to the ground beside them, trying to block them from looking and herd them off, along with any other gawkers that might show up. "Nothing to see. On your way." He aimed his scariest glare at them.

"But I just want a peek. Always wondered what was in this truck." Miriam shook back her long brown hair and pointed past him. "Look, Evie. An old organ!"

"Does anyone play it?" Evie winked at him. "How about a polka? I've got some great schnapps here!" She held up a bottle of liquor, and her feet pranced in a mock polka until she staggered into Miriam. Apparently, Evie had a head start on the schnapps.

From the truck at his back came a loud click, a thud, and startled exclamations. He whirled.

One side of the box had fallen outward, disgorging its contents onto the floor.

A man's body lay sprawled. Above it, wadded into a wrinkled bundle, was the white clown costume. Dried blood and bits of fur clung to the fabric. The corpse's face was swollen and tinged brown with decay, but even without seeing the man's security uniform, Rurik recognized Yuri.

The girls screamed. Miriam clapped a hand to her slim throat. Evie dropped her liquor bottle, and it shattered on the ground.

Rurik ducked as Michelangelo hurtled out of the truck as if fired from a sling shot. "*Mio Dio, mio Dio!*" the small man shrieked as he ran into the maze of tents.

Another clown tumbled out behind him and bent over, spewing vomit onto the grass.

"Markarov," someone inside the truck hissed.

Antonelli, Luigi, and the sniffer-clown all stared at the costume.

"Maximilian Markarov." Antonelli shook his head and his gaze sought out Rurik. He stepped to the edge of the truck and lowered his voice. "There is fur from Marva's dogs. Someone wear costume, and Yuri see him, and he kill Yuri." His look hardened. "This truck always locked. How you open?"

Rurik grabbed the broken lock and tire iron from the weeds. "I had to use this. *Dmitry Markarov* has my keys," he said. In the back of his mind, a little voice reminded him that he'd still had the security keys when Yuri disappeared. He ignored it. If he shined suspicion on the Markarovs—where it belonged—they'd have to come clean about everything.

Alerted by the screams, other performers and roustabouts emerged from between the tents. Miriam and the girls met them as they came, giving hysterical accounts of the organ hiding a dead man. A few curious people pushed forward to peer inside and then backed away just as quickly.

Rurik knew he should get rid of them, but his attention kept returning to Yuri's body. Guilt stuck in his throat. He'd assumed Yuri was hiding in camp, not going to work to avoid him, basically being his typical weasely self. But all the time Rurik was thinking nasty thoughts about Yuri, the man had been here. Dead.

Luigi grabbed the costume and stalked to the end of the truck to stand beside Antonelli. "We found Yuri in this truck—murdered!" he said to the onlookers. Gasps and exclamations rippled through his audience. "And this bloody costume was hidden with him." He held it up for everyone to see. "I recognize this. It's from the Markarov family. And Dmitry is the only one with keys to this truck."

"He killed Yuri?" a trapeze artist said.

"Oh my God!" a woman cried.

"And Marva's dogs, too," Antonelli yelled. "He kill them all!"

"He'll answer for this!" a roustabout said. "Come on!" He took off along with half a dozen onlookers toward the Markarov tent.

Rurik watched them go, satisfaction swelling his chest. Without Alyosha to protect them, the Markarovs would be forced to talk—one way or another.

Misha jogged up to Rurik. "Is it true? Yuri's dead?"

Rurik nodded.

"Holy shit!"

"Does everyone know?" Rurik said.

"Michelangelo is running through camp, yelling the news."

"But Marva doesn't know yet, does she?" Rurik didn't think Marva could handle seeing the remains of her beloved dogs splattered across the clown costume. She was hanging on by a thin thread as it was.

A murmur of voices rose to a crescendo. Roustabouts appeared from the tents, dragging Dmitry Markarov with them. The crowd split apart, letting the men haul Dmitry to the truck.

Still in his strongman's leotard and tights, Dmitry

struggled in their grip. "Are you crazy?" he yelled, kicking at his captors. "I'll fire you all!"

"Shut up!" A roustabout cuffed him in the face.

"This"—Luigi shook the bloodied costume at Dmitry—"belonged to your father. You must have kept it, yet here it is with Yuri's body, hidden in this truck. Who killed Yuri?"

"I did nothing to him," Dmitry yelled, one eye reddening and beginning to swell. "You're all wrong. You'll regret this!"

"*You* keep your father's things," Antonelli yelled. "*You* have keys to this truck. *You* kill Yuri and hide him inside!"

"No!" Dmitry eyed the livid faces ranged around him, and his bravado turned to a sniveling whine. "Believe me, I had nothing to do with it."

Rurik barged up to him. "You aren't surprised he's dead. Or that your father's costume is with him. Obviously, you already knew about it." He pressed his advantage. "And the RV that burned? It had the clown's makeup inside, didn't it? You sent your sons to burn it. Admit it!"

"Tell us the truth!" Riding Master Minko stretched his long arm over those holding Dmitry and socked him on the ear.

"Beat it out of him!" someone in the crowd shouted. "Bossy sonuvabitch deserves what he gets."

"Okay, okay," Dmitry whimpered. "We did burn the RV. But Alyosha ordered us to do it."

"Ha!" Luigi snorted. "You accuse a man who's not here to defend himself."

"But it's true! He said circus receipts were down and he needed the insurance money. He's the one who ordered my sons to get some things out of it, and then burn it."

"Pavel should be here, too," Rurik yelled over the crowd's mutterings. "I questioned everyone in camp. He's the last person to see Yuri on the night the dogs were killed. And that's the last time anyone saw Yuri alive. Either Pavel killed Yuri or he knows who did!"

"No!" Dmitry bellowed. "It wasn't my son! It was Alyosha. He's to blame for everything! He gave Pavel money to pay Yuri so he'd leave his post that night. But later, Alyosha called us to his RV. When we got there, Yuri was on the floor. Dead. Alyosha said Yuri threatened him. Attacked him. He said he killed Yuri in self-defense and wanted us to help hide the body. *He* was the one who opened this truck. It was his key. And he knew how to hide the body inside the bench of his calliope. *He* did that!"

"Alyosha wouldn't kill anyone," exclaimed Miriam. "I can't believe it."

"You're a liar!" Antonelli shouted.

"This costume tells a different story," Luigi yelled, the white fabric wrinkling in the old man's fists. "It's not Alyosha's. It proves a Markarov killed the dogs. Admit you did it and then killed Yuri to keep him quiet!"

The crowd surged forward. Fists rose and struck blindly at Dmitry who sagged to his knees.

For the first time, Rurik felt a twinge of doubt. He wanted the truth—but not a mob beat-down. Things were going too far. He raised his arms, shouting, "Calm down!"

A shot splintered the air. The equipment trucks rang with the echoes.

Onlookers ducked reflexively. A few squealed in alarm.

Craning his neck, Rurik looked over people's heads to see Dmitry's brother, Viktor, along with Dmitry's sons, and the rest of the Markarov family striding down the line of trucks. Viktor, his wife Tasha, and Anatoly held rifles. Pavel lagged behind, nervously peering around. He looked like he'd rather be anywhere else on the planet.

"This has gone far enough!" Viktor shouted. "Let my brother go. Now!"

For a second, nothing happened. Then the mob edged away from Dmitry.

The roustabouts holding Dmitry ducked behind his large form, using him as a shield.

"A man is dead! Someone has to answer for it," Minko said.

Rurik eased his way forward, putting himself between the guns and Dmitry's captors. He held his hands aloft, his voice firm. "No one's getting shot tonight. But we're not just letting him go either. That clown costume in the truck—a Markarov family costume—is damning evidence. And I *know* the man who wore it has done more than kill

Marva's dogs. More than kill Yuri. I caught him in Budapest as he was kidnapping a child. I saved the child—that time. But other children have disappeared on the final day of our shows in Gemona, Kranj, and Maribor."

"Oh my God!" Miriam raked a bony hand through her hair. "Dmitry's a kidnapper too?"

"No!" Rurik's forceful voice silenced the babble. "I fought the clown twice, and Dmitry is too tall. He says this is all Alyosha's doing, but the man I fought is too heavy to be Alyosha." He lowered his head, his narrowed eyes skewering Dmitry's sons, Pavel and Anatoly. "One of you is. And you'd better tell me who because no one's leaving here until I find out."

"And I find out!" a voice cried. Marva barreled her way through the circus performers. An old Walther pistol glinted in her hand.

Rurik recognized the World War Two trophy from Ivan's collection. It should have been locked up. The antique gun was as likely to blow up as to fire. "Take it easy, Marva."

She came to a stop, swaying slightly, and aimed the gun at Pavel.

Pavel froze. His mouth hung open, eyes wide, looking like he was about to piss himself.

Viktor and Tasha swung their rifles toward Marva while Anatoly kept his on the men holding his father.

"Come on, Pavel. Admit you killed my babies!" Marva took a step forward. Her eyes had the near-sighted squint Rurik knew too well. The glazed look of a drunk. The pistol wavered in her hands. "Or tell me it was your brother. I'd be happy to shoot either or both of you."

Tension radiated across Rurik's shoulders and burned up his neck like fire. He could reason with the Markarovs, but no one could reason with a drunk. He'd tried too many times with his father.

Marva had no idea what she was doing. One accidental jerk of her finger and Pavel might be hit. Might die. Even if the Markarovs didn't shoot her immediately, there were too many witnesses here. Someone would talk. Then she'd go to jail for a long time.

Rurik couldn't let that happen to the woman he loved

like a second mother.

"I'm waiting!" Marva yelled. Her finger tightened on the trigger.

Rurik launched himself at her. His arm swung up just as the pistol fired. Answering shots boomed from behind him. Pain lanced into his side. He knocked the gun from Marva's hand and drove her to the ground, landing on top of her.

Screams and shouts came from everywhere.

Beneath him, Marva locked her horrified gaze on his. "I-I didn't mean to shoot. I just wanted to scare him. Did I kill him?" Her eyes glittered with tears. She squirmed, pulling her arm out from under him and holding a bloody hand in front of her face. "Oh my God! Did they shoot me?"

Rurik tried to answer but couldn't draw a breath.

A moment later, hands hooked him under his armpits and hauled him to his feet. Once up, he stared into the faces of Misha and Antonelli.

Misha looked at Rurik's shirt and a spreading patch of red. His eyes bulged. "You're hit!"

Antonelli lifted Rurik's shirt and shrugged. "Meh. Is shallow. Enter and exit. Bounced off your ribs. You strong like bull. You live."

Rurik dragged his gaze away from the blood streaming down his pant leg and scanned the area. No Dmitry. No Markarovs. He drew a full breath to speak and was shocked by the pain that exploded across his side. Through gritted teeth, he said, "What the hell happened to them?"

"Shooting start. Everybody jump on ground," Antonelli said. "When we get up, whole Markarov family gone. Good they go. Those *bastardi*"—he spat on the ground—"no work here anymore. No work in any circus."

Rurik's only suspects, captured and lost. He smacked a fist into his palm, then regretted it as agony burst along his ribs again. Lesson learned. No sudden moves, no deep breaths, he ordered himself.

The sound of retching came from behind him. Marva had made it to her knees, but was bent over, throwing up in the grass.

"Misha," Rurik said. "Take Marva home. Return the

gun to Ivan and tell him to lock the damn thing up. Antonelli, tell everyone we're not doing a final performance tomorrow. We're leaving for Oradea, Romania, first thing in the morning. Someone may have heard the shots. The sooner we're out of here the better."

"What about...him?" Antonelli cast a look back at the calliope truck.

"I'll handle it." Rurik straightened his shoulders. It felt good to take control again. He belonged to the circus, and it belonged to him.

He was still staring at the truck when someone tapped his arm. He looked down into the pale face of Miriam.

"You weren't kidding about the children, right?" she said . "Three gone, on our tour route?"

"Four, actually. There was one in Budapest, too."

"I think it's five now." She pulled over a short, disheveled woman that Rurik recognized as one of the cook's assistants. "Tell him what you told me," Miriam said to her.

The woman sucked in a breath, her hands twisting in her apron. "It was early this morning. He came to my tent. Said he wanted to take my daughter, Anushka, to Saint Elizabeth's Cathedral and to see the Singing Fountain. Said it would be fun for her. She got all excited... She's only nine." The woman's breath hitched, and tears dribbled down her cheeks. "I said yes. I mean, he's her godfather. I trusted him. But he never brought her back."

"Who?" Rurik said , fear stabbing into his gut. "Who took your daughter?"

"Alyosha."

CHAPTER TWENTY

Sylvie
Debrecen, Hungary

> *Keep an eye out for suspicious deaths. Bruises on the*
> *neck and red eyes*
> *when the person supposedly died in their sleep. The*
> *narrow slit of*
> *a knife wound when the person supposedly fell down the*
> *stairs.*
> *We do not judge. That is for God. But we must report it.*
> *~ The Bloodwalker's Book*

"Hé! *Felkelni!"*

The harsh words broke through Sylvie's dream—a lovely one where she'd been sipping tea in her home's cozy kitchen. It took a few seconds to process where she was, but the ugly surroundings and the uglier smell brought it back quickly enough.

Silhouetted in the door of her cell was a guard. Behind him, an orange sunset battled its way through the dusty windows of the hall. He wasn't the fat walrus-faced one of yesterday. This one was lean and clean-shaven.

"*Kifelé!*" came another sharp order.

Since the guard had the door open, she guessed she was being called back for more questioning. Maybe the prosecutor thought twenty-four hours in a flea-infested cell would change her mind about confessing.

If so, he'd be very disappointed.

The twenty-four hours, and a few exhausted naps on the cot, merely strengthened her resolve to fight. She wasn't much of a fighter...wasn't very good at it. But she'd have to get good or spend the rest of her life behind bars.

She traipsed after the guard, rubbing grains of sleep from her eyes.

Instead of going through the policemen's office like last time, he led her the opposite way—toward the double-doored entrance of the station. Her sleepiness vanished instantly.

Through the glass, the cars in the parking lot glittered in the sunset's glow. If she were outside, a ride to the station and a train ticket could have her home in an hour. Her mother would surely have a change of heart after all that Sylvie had been through. She could be in her kitchen actually drinking tea before nightfall.

Her walk curved slightly, edging toward the doors.

But the guard grabbed her shoulder and pulled her back, delivering her to a counter in front of a locker room.

Then he walked away. Left her there alone. She couldn't believe it.

Her gaze bee-lined to the exit, and she heard its promise of freedom as if someone had whispered the word right into her ear.

She could escape if she was fast and smart. Maybe she could get away without being caught. With a life sentence looming in her future, it would be worth the risk.

She took one step toward it. A quick glance down the hall showed no one looking. With her shoulders curled forward, she took more steps, light on her toes, trying to be invisible.

"Sylvia Annamaria Dinescu?" a man said from behind her.

She spun, alarm coursing through her.

A blond man across the counter crooked his eyebrows in a puzzled expression. "You not go without your paper, yes?" He held out her Romanian ID card.

His Romanian was bad, but at least understandable. He said "go" like it was a natural thing, like he expected her to leave.

She darted back to the counter and grabbed her ID card, holding it tightly in both hands in case he changed his mind.

He bent down and lifted a canvas bag into view.

Her bag! The one with all her bloodwalker things and the clothes she'd hurriedly dumped inside before she got arrested. She snatched at that too, only to find his hand gripping the handles and refusing to release it.

She knew it was too good to be true.

"First, you sign." He shoved a document across the counter and tapped an empty line at the bottom.

The Hungarian was unreadable.

Her mouth clamped into a hard line. It was a trick. They were pretending to let her go, asking her to sign something that would turn out to be a confession.

She shook her head.

"No sign. No property," he said with a shrug.

She eyed him. He appeared indifferent, more like a bored employee than someone trying to trick her. "But... what is it?"

"Sign paper, you received property from police."

"Not a confession?"

His eyebrows rose again. "You release now. Bail money... *fizetve*...paid."

Released on bail? But who...?

Her mother! Excitement zipped through her veins. Her mother must have heard about her on the news and came to the station with money. She was a powerful bloodwalker. She could make anyone listen to her.

If her mother paid her bail, that must mean Sylvie was forgiven. She could go home. Her lips curved into a grin. She scribbled her signature, collected her bag, and headed for the exit.

Emerging into the orange sunlight, her grin widened. Her head tilted skyward. She took an extra-long inhale of breath, sucking in clean oxygen to banish the putrid smells of the jail. She was free! The horrible roller-coaster of events that tortured her had finally ended. She'd never felt more grateful—or wanted to go home so badly in her life.

Blinking back tears of relief, she looked around for her mother.

But her mother wasn't on the sidewalk. Or in the parking lot.

Maybe getting out had taken a long time, and she'd already gone to the train station.

Sylvie set off, crossing the lot and aiming for the main street beyond. This part of Debrecen wasn't familiar. Short, gray office buildings lurked behind webs of trees. No shops she could see, but the wide road was busy. A taxi could take her to the station—but that would require money. She fumbled her bag open, scrounging beneath the candles, towels, and big jar of honey. A few Hungarian *forints* winked at her from the bottom. She scooped them up while hurrying between parked cars.

"Sylvie?"

She looked up and almost dropped the bag.

Miron stood in front of her, wearing sunglasses and a strange smile on his face, especially strange since she'd never actually seen him smile.

She shuffled backward, all her joy draining away, replaced by fear.

"What? Not happy to see me?" Miron said . "Would you rather go back inside the police station? Wait for your trial?"

"No..." her voice came out breathy and barely audible. "But I don't want to go back to Miskolc."

"Then you'll be happy to know I'm taking you home. I spoke to your mother. Under the circumstances, she's willing to take you back." He reached for Sylvie's elbow, but she flinched back out of reach. "Oh, come now, don't be childish. Especially after I went to the trouble of borrowing a car just to take you home." He swept a hand toward a large light-blue sedan in a nearby parking space. Faced with her lingering silence, he heaved a sigh and put his hands on his hips. "Look, I'm just as happy to have you go back home as you are. This hasn't worked out for either of us. The elders and I reached an agreement. I'll give you an annulment, and you won't be cast out." He grinned. "See? It's all taken care of. Oh, and, of course, I keep your dowry."

An annulment and not being cast out were great news. If she could believe it. She studied him, searching for hints of rage beneath his passive exterior. But his posture was relaxed, and the smile lingered on his face while he waited patiently for her to decide. Maybe he really *was* happy to take her back home. With a new fiancée, he probably didn't want her back in Miskolc. And she doubted he paid her bail out of generosity. He'd want her mother to repay it, in addition to foregoing the dowry. Miron was nothing if not greedy.

In the end, her desperate desire to go home won out— she just wanted to put this whole awful part of her life behind her. So she got into the car with him.

At the beginning of the drive, Miron remained calm, taking them directly onto the highway toward Romania. But when they crossed the border twenty minutes later, things changed. He shifted uncomfortably in his seat as the Romanian forest thickened around them. Instead of turning on the headlights to combat the shadows lengthening across the highway, his fingers drummed on the steering wheel. He kept adjusting his rear-view mirror, peering into it and frowning.

Sylvie stayed silent, watching the road markers pass, knowing her village was only half an hour from the border. Soon, she'd be home and never have to see Miron again.

He loosened his collar and cranked the A/C to full, but dampness still glistened at his temples, and the stink of flop-sweat filled the car. Suddenly, he sped up, rocketing down the asphalt.

Sylvie clutched the armrest with one hand, her other hand gouging her canvas bag, her eyes straining to see in the gray dusk.

Moments later, he abruptly turned off the highway, and the car jounced down a dirt road.

"This isn't the way!" Sylvie's voice blared like a siren in the confined space. "The turnoff to my village isn't for thirty miles!"

"Well, excuse me if I have to take a leak," Miron snapped. After driving two hundred yards down the bumpy track, he pulled over and turned off the engine.

Sylvie's belly squirmed, and she sat ramrod stiff against the seat back. This was wrong. Protected by dense woods, he could do anything—beat her up, rape her—no one would hear her scream.

In the fading light, his teeth glimmered in a smile. "You know, Sylvie, you should have just stayed working at my store. I'd have given you money. Taken care of you. But no. You couldn't follow the rules." He pulled the keys from the ignition and got out of the car. A second later, the trunk popped open.

Sylvie's heart began to race. He could do worse than beat her up or rape her. She clicked the locks closed and looked around for anything she could use as a weapon. Her fast search revealed nothing but empty cigarette packs under the seat and papers for the car in the glove compartment. She dug inside her bag. Her bloodwalker things lay jumbled. Candles, twine, needles. Then her hand closed on the scissors. They were small, but they had a mean point.

Knuckles rapped on the glass by her head, and she gasped.

"Why don't you stretch your legs before we get back on the road?" Miron said. A plastic poncho now covered his shirt, and one hand was hidden behind his back. When she didn't answer, he tried the door and found it locked. Dipping a hand in his pocket, he pulled out his keys and jingled them outside the window. "You never were too bright, were you?" He unlocked the door.

She clicked the lock closed again. Every time he unlocked the door with the key, she re-locked it with the button.

But he was faster. Finally, he yanked the door open, seized her by the hair, and dragged her out.

She swung wildly with the scissors. The blades slashed through the plastic poncho but missed flesh.

He swore and flung her in the dirt, face down. Planting a knee in her back, he grabbed her wrist and pried the scissors away. "I got lots of money from your dowry—couldn't have opened my new shop or gotten engaged without it. Too bad all that money came with such a *bitch!*" He smacked the back of her head, jamming her nose into the gravel. "With you on the news, people are gossiping. I'm inches away from losing my fiancée *and* her father's money. But if you disappear, I can fix it. Soon, it'll be like you weren't ever there at all."

He hauled her up and pulled her bag from the car. "You should have thrown this away when I told you to. Now you'll have to carry it."

She clutched her bag and winced at his tight grip on her upper arm.

He forced her off the road and into the forest.

"Please! You can marry anyone you want," she begged. "I'll go away. I won't tell anyone."

"Who do you have left to tell? Your bloodwalker friends are dead. The news says someone's killing them off with a long dagger. Kinda like this one." He held up a hunting knife, long and shiny.

"You killed Ada and Liana?"

He snorted. "Of course not, you idiot. Why would I bother myself with bloodwalker bitches? But if you're found dead of a stab wound—just like them—it'll look like the same killer struck again." His lips tautened in a smirk.

Her knees weakened. She stumbled over a root and fell. Beneath her, the rumpled leaves gave off an earthy scent. Fresh and vital. The forest had always smelled good to her. Now the odor reminded her of a newly dug grave.

He hauled her up again, but she struggled this time. "Stop that!" he yelled, shaking her roughly. "If you keep it up, I'll just stab you here and drag your body farther from the road."

She quieted, realizing she needed to devote all her energy to planning an escape.

He marched her deeper into the woods—and to what she knew would be her burial plot unless she could get away or talk him out of it.

She took a deep breath. "You paid the bail to the police . They will remember you." She kept her tone low, doing her best to sound assured, like a real bloodwalker. "If you do this, you'll be caught!" But her voice cracked, her tongue sticking to the roof of her dry mouth. Instead of sounding authoritative, she sounded weak and scared.

"Who's to say I didn't bring you back to Miskolc and then you ran away? You did it once already."

Her hand snuck into her bag, searching for anything she could fight with.

"If you disappear, no one will think it's my fault. After all, I'm just your employer. It's not like we're really *married*." He laughed.

Anger flamed inside her. She grabbed the first thing she found. The heavy glass jar of honey. She lunged at him, smashing it into the side of his head.

He went down like a felled tree.

For a second she could only stand over his body, all her limbs shaking from fear and anger. *Oh my God. Oh my God. Oh my God.* The panicked words ran through her brain over and over. At last, instinct overcame hysteria. She took off back toward the car, blundering over roots and scratching herself on branches. But when she reached it, she remembered he had the keys. She would have to go back for them.

She turned and faced the black woods, mustering her courage.

Twigs snapped and underbrush crashed from inside the border of trees.

A chill slid down her spine. Miron wasn't dead. He was coming after her.

The highway at the beginning of the road was her only hope. She had to flag down a car before he caught her.

She sprinted away, flying down the dirt track. But the highway was farther than she remembered. After a few minutes, her breath burned in her lungs while twilight strangled the last rays of sunlight. She careened over ruts. Her arms flailed for balance. If she fell in a ditch or twisted her ankle, she was dead.

As she raced the final fifty yards to the highway, the headlights of a vehicle speared the darkness. But it was on the other side of the median strip. A car heading to Hungary. It whizzed past.

No lights approached on her side of the road.

Footsteps pounded the dirt road, growing louder. She could hear Miron's wheezing breath.

She leaped onto the pavement and ran toward home. So very far away. Maybe she could outrun him until a car came. Or maybe she was better off hiding in the woods? She had no idea what to do. Adrenaline kept her racing forward.

Bright lights flashed on behind her. She glanced back and was momentarily blinded by the beams.

An engine gunned. Tires squealed. The headlights zoomed down the highway, bearing down on her. She staggered sideways and screamed.

At the last moment, the vehicle swerved away from her. It sailed up onto the shoulder.

There was a sickening thud. A body flew through the air. It landed nearly thirty feet past her down the shoulder.

The car screeched to a stop. Its headlights shone on Miron. Back twisted, arms splayed out, head bent at an impossible angle.

He was dead this time.

Wasn't he?

What if he wasn't?!

She had to get away from him. Fast.

The vehicle turned back onto the road.

"Stop!" She waved it down, and the driver pulled over next to her.

It wasn't a car after all. It was a white van. She opened the passenger door. "Please! I need help..." She trailed off, realizing the man in the driver's seat looked familiar.

"Climb in, my dear! I've been looking for you. You've had quite a scare, but that's over now. I know just where you want to go."

Now that she heard the voice, she recognized him. She climbed up into the seat, knowing she was finally safe. "Thank you! Thank you so much, Mr. Alyosha."

CHAPTER TWENTY-ONE

Rurik
Western Carpathian Mountains, Romania

Rurik down-shifted, slowing the calliope truck as it rumbled around a curve. Trees loomed in the headlights, the thick forest beyond them dark and impenetrable.

When the curve straightened out, he jammed the brake pedal down. The air-brakes hissed as the truck swerved onto the shoulder and skidded to a stop.

In a flash, he leaped out and planted himself in the middle of the pitch black road. It was dangerous—probably foolish—but he was pissed off.

A minute later, an RV rounded the bend. Its headlamps glared into Rurik's face.

Brakes screeched. The large vehicle shuddered, but slowed, and pulled in behind the truck—as Rurik knew it would. He stalked up to the RV's door, jerked it open, and bounded up the steps.

Four pair of eyes blinked up at him like shamed children.

Ivan leaned back in his wheelchair beside the kitchen table, and Marva was curled up on the table's bench seat. In the front compartment, Misha was on the passenger side while Pyotr, the roustabout, sat behind the wheel.

"Jesus, Rurik!" Pyotr yelled. "What if I didn't stop in time?"

"You stopped. Now *stop following me*. Go back to the circus where you belong." Rurik crossed his arms, sleeves straining over his biceps the same way he strained to keep his anger in check. They'd argued about who'd go with him back at camp. Rurik thought he'd won until he'd hit the isolated roads outside Oradea, Romaniaand noticed headlights trailing him.

"For all you knew, we were the police!" Pyotr slapped the steering wheel. "Then you'd be caught with the truck—and the body!"

"If the police wanted to pull me over, they would have. They wouldn't trail me for forty miles, like a wife sneaking after her cheating husband."

"You can't just leave us behind!" Ivan growled. "We don't care how dangerous it is... Yuri was our friend." When Rurik raised his brows, Ivan squirmed. "Well, maybe not friend exactly..."

"He was *my* friend," Misha said quietly. "He helped me a lot when I first got here and always invited me out with his buddies ."

"He lived beside me in the roustabout tent for the past ten, twelve years." Pyotr shrugged. "Maybe we weren't best buds, but I could count on him if I needed something."

"It doesn't matter if we were his closest friends or not," Marva said. "We're circus. We're family. And none of us should go to our graves without some caring words spoken over us."

Rurik sighed. It was hard to argue with her sentiments—but he had to. For the good of everyone. "You want to do the right thing.I get it. But this isn't a social event. If the police catch me burying Yuri, I'll go to jail. If they catch you, you'll all *go. To. Jail.* Can I make that any clearer?" He played his ace card. "Marva, I've already taken a bullet to save you from making a mistake that'd get you arrested. Was it for nothing?"

Marva's hand flew to her mouth. She flushed, and the wrinkles in her face cinched tight. Her gaze fell to the tabletop.

"And Ivan?" Rurik transferred his attention to the motorcyclist. "Don't look so smug. Whose liquor did she drink and whose gun was she waving around when she went out and almost killed someone?"

"Hmmph." Ivan inspected his fingernails, trying to appear unfazed, but he didn't meet Rurik's gaze either.

Rurik turned back to Misha and Pyotr in the driver's compartment. "I know the two of you want to pay your respects, but the best thing you can do for Yuri is to gather his things and collect money to send to his parents. Even if they haven't seen him in years, they're the ones who deserve to get something out of this mess.

"Plus, all of you should be in camp, making sure Alyosha or the Markarovs don't sneak in and do more damage. It's terrible enough that Anushka's missing. We can't let them get anyone else."

They all looked thoroughly crestfallen.

"Promise me you'll turn this RV around and go back. I need to do this alone, for everyone's sake."

Misha nodded reluctantly.

"All right, Rurik," Pyotr said.

"Good. I'll see you in a few hours." Rurik jogged down the steps.

He waited in the calliope truck until he saw the RV turn around. Something bright on it flickered. He squinted and made out Ivan's motorcycle on its rack at the rear of the vehicle. Its chrome wheels and dual-exhaust pipes shimmered like flames between the red brake lights. The gleam diminished along with the taillights as the RV vanished down the road.

Rurik slipped the truck into gear and headed into the foothills of the Western Carpathian Mountains.

Every once in a while, he caught sight of headlights behind him and wondered if Pyotr had disobeyed him. But after changing to smaller roads and climbing farther into the mountains, the lights disappeared. In fact, all lights disappeared, even lights from occasional houses. Almost no one lived this far from Romania's cities, which was exactly what Rurik wanted.

He found a stretch of road with a shoulder wide enough for him to park well off the pavement. Duct tape went over the truck's front and rear reflectors, further concealing it from motorists who might pass by.

He rolled up the rear door and coughed as bleach vapors seared his throat. The inside of the truck had been thoroughly washed and cleaned. Yuri's body lay encased in a blue, plastic tarp tied with ropes. Rurik took a shovel fitted with a strap and hitched it across his back before pulling Yuri's body to the edge of the truck floor. He hoisted it onto his shoulder, grunting from the bullet wound in his side and the fact that *blini*-loving Yuri weighed close to 300 pounds.

Rurik clicked on his flashlight and entered the forest. The area he'd chosen was densely packed with trees and shrubbery. Good for seclusion, but it made walking slow and treacherous.

Insects chittered and buzzed around him. Once, he heard the scream of a lynx. The big cat would probably steer clear, since he was much larger than its normal prey. Bears were another matter. Romania had a huge bear population, and he didn't relish meeting one in the dark.

He tramped over bushes, roots, and fallen trees for ten minutes before he felt he'd gone far enough from the road. Then he put the body down, balanced the flashlight on the branch of a tree, and started digging.

Sweat dripped into his eyes, rolled down his back, and soaked his clothes. It took him a long time to hit the six foot mark. Any less and wild animals might dig up the grave. Poor Yuri had had enough abuse already.

The encased body made a wet thud when it hit the bottom. Rurik dug the shovel blade into the loose dirt and began filling it in. Dirt and rocks spattered on the plastic like the dull beat of rain on a roof.

A yell pierced the forest. Rurik stopped and listened, goose bumps rising on his flesh. After half a minute of silence, he decided it must have been the lynx.

Once dirt filled the grave, he cast the shovel aside and stood for a moment, giving the dead man the respect he was due.

Regardless of Yuri's faults, he didn't deserve to be murdered or buried in the woods. But if the stab wounds on his body were revealed to the authorities, they'd descend on the circus like a swarm of wasps—and everyone would get stung.

The same held true for the disappearance of the little girl, Anushka. No one had alerted the police, and no one would.

Rurik raked a hand across his brow and flung the sweat droplets from his fingertips. "Dammit to hell." Alyosha wasn't the clown, yet he'd taken Anushka, and Rurik had no idea why. Nothing made sense. The cursed puzzle was driving him crazy.

And without involving the police, there seemed no way to solve the problem.

But he wasn't giving up. When he got back to the circus, he'd put out the word to other circuses to keep an eye out for Alyosha and the Markarovs.

And then what? Sit back and wait?

No, dammit. The situation demanded more. He'd tell every circus member to send messages to their friends and family. Everyone they knew in Eastern Europe would be looking for the Markarovs and Alyosha.

Rurik bowed his head and said a prayer. For Yuri. For Anushka. For the other children who'd gone missing.

Twigs and dead leaves crunched in the distance. Something was coming from the direction of the road. More brush crackled. Getting closer.

Rurik snatched up the shovel, hoping for a lynx and not a bear.

A glow grew behind the trees. Then a light beam glittered, shining through branches.

A muffled voice said in Russian, "See anything?"

"Not yet," came the reply.

Obviously not the Romanian police—it had to be Ivan and the others. They'd followed, determined to say a farewell to Yuri and share the blame with Rurik if he got caught.

With a shake of his head, Rurik drove the shovel into the earth and leaned on the handle, waiting for them to arrive.

The light swung in wide arcs over the area, and finally zeroed in on his face. The tromping footsteps moved closer until the light became painful.

Rurik held a hand up to shade his eyes. "Okay, you found me. Now say a quick good-bye 'cause we have to get out of here."

The light clicked off. When Rurik's vision adjusted, he found himself facing four rifle barrels.

"Out for a nighttime stroll, Rurik?" Dmitry Markarov

sneered. "Just you and a dead body?" He and his brother, Viktor, along with Pavel and Anatoly ringed the gravesite, aiming rifles at Rurik's chest. They were careful to stay back, well out of reach of his fists.

But he knew no one had followed him on the road for the more than half an hour before he parked. "How'd you find me?"

"Tracked you," Dmitry said. "Pavel and Anatoly have a nice little business with phones and other tech gadgets, including tracking chips."

"You bugged the truck?"

"No. Him." Dmitry jutted his chin at the dirt heaped upon the grave. "In the tarp. Not everyone in camp is against us. We still have loyal friends."

"So, why are you here? Getting rid of the one who knows where the body's buried?" Rurik said . They'd always despised him, and even his heavy bones couldn't deflect a barrage of bullets.

"We just needed to know where Yuri was," Viktor said. "No Markarov is going to prison for this. If the police come after us, we'll deliver Yuri's body to the forensics experts. They'll find the knife wounds...and we know where that knife can be found."

Rurik's chin sank a little. "With Alyosha."

"Right."

Rurik hated to think it—so much easier to blame Pavel—but Alyosha had taken Anushka, the little girl from camp. No denying that.

"Okay. You know where Yuri is. Why're you still here?" Rurik said.

"You'll find out soon enough. You're coming with us." Dmitry motioned him forward with his rifle muzzle.

Rurik's hand tightened on the handle of the shovel. One or two men with a gun, he might take. Three was even money. Four was a fool's game.

"I'll take that." Anatoly cat-footed up and snatched the shovel away. "Get moving."

Reluctantly, Rurik waded into the underbrush, watching his captors from the corner of his eye.

He'd be patient. Wait. One of them was bound to slip up

sooner or later, and when they did—there'd be hell to pay.

CHAPTER TWENTY-TWO

Sylvie
Western Carpathian Mountains, Romania

Always take care when you evacuate a corpse's bowels.
Place plenty of towels under the backside and press gently
on the groin. What starts out as a thin ooze can quickly
become a torrent, and then you'll find yourself in a
much worse pile of shit than you imagined.
~ The Bloodwalker's Book

As Alyosha's van accelerated onto the highway, Sylvie collapsed in the passenger seat, exhausted from running and her narrow escape. Her arms wrapped around her bloodwalker bag, hugging it to her chest, a security blanket against a world gone crazy.

No matter how she tried, she couldn't seem to take a full breath. Her lungs expanded only enough to give her rabbit-like gulps of air. Her heart beat as fast as a rabbit's, too.

Soon, Miron lay miles behind her...his dead body anyway...but she couldn't stop thinking about him. About what he'd tried to do to her. It defied belief.

Miron was a cheater, yes. A liar, yes.

But a killer?

She never dreamed he could hate her that much. What had she done wrong? She'd been a respectful wife. Never disagreed or argued. But her mere existence threatened the life he'd wanted. A life he never intended to share with her to begin with.

Even now, it wasn't really over. The police would find his body. Would they figure out she was there? Blame her for the accident?

If it really had been an accident.

She stole a glance at Alyosha. His thick silver hair shone in the dash lights, every strand in place. The old ringmaster stared out the windshield. Smiling. As if nothing had happened. As if he hadn't just killed a man.

The van had swerved—she'd seen it—deliberately running onto the highway shoulder and striking Miron.

Accident? Not likely.

How could Alyosha act so blasé? Happy even?

He was a Zorka. They were hard, mean, and indifferent to suffering. Nothing like the Skomori.

Except for Miron. He was Skomori but much worse than a Zorka.

Suddenly, she felt ashamed for thinking badly about the Zorka. Without the Zorka man in this van, she'd be dead on the side of the road instead of Miron.

Alyosha caught her gaze, and his smile widened. "You're the final one."

She cocked her head. "The final one what?"

"I mean..." He cleared his throat. "It's good you're *finally* here and out of trouble. After the horrible tragedy of the other two brides' deaths, I knew the *Baran* would try to pin the murders on a bloodwalker. But you? That's ridiculous!

"Of course I felt it was my duty to get you released from jail. But when I arrived, I saw you drive off with your husband." Alyosha's lip curled. "That devil! His parents heard of his two-timing and washed their hands of him. It seemed highly unlikely he'd care enough to get you out of jail. I wanted to catch up and talk to you, but he was driving so fast. I lost him for a while. Luckily, I didn't give up."

Yes, lucky he'd been there at the perfect moment. Almost too lucky.

"Now, don't worry about a thing," Alyosha continued. "We've called a meeting of the bloodwalkers. Your mother and the other brides' mothers will be there, too. We'll get to the bottom of all this nastiness."

"We?" she said . The Zorka man couldn't call a bloodwalker meeting by himself, he'd need... A chill ran across Sylvie's neck.

"Zora and I." He tipped his head at the back of the van. "And our god-daughter, Anushka, who's staying with us."

Sylvie twisted around in her seat.

In the back of the van, darkness swam and swelled. Then, like ink bleeding slowly through paper, a form coalesced. A hunched figure in a wheelchair. A veil blocked the face and shoulders. Reddened eyes glinted through the lace.

Zora. The oldest of the bloodwalkers sat so still it was like she'd been mummified. She didn't even seem to breathe.

Zora. The woman who'd warned everyone at the wedding that Sylvie would bring death wherever she went.

She'd been right.

First Ada. Then Liana. Now Miron.

Near the wheelchair, a little girl sat with her back pressed against the side of the van and her knees drawn up tight to her chest. Large eyes overshadowed a pale face. A face that looked strained. Scared.

"Hello, Anushka," Sylvie said with an encouraging smile.

The girl didn't reply. Didn't turn her head. But her lower lip trembled.

Sylvie's stomach dropped, leaving a whirlpool of blood draining into her gut. For the second time in one night, she felt the world shift out of balance around her. This was wrong. All wrong.

"Don't mind her," Alyosha said. "She's tired from the trip, and"—his voice dropped—"she's not quite right in the head, poor thing."

"Oh," was all Sylvie managed as she turned to face front again. That child was frightened, not mentally challenged. Any idiot could see that. And if the girl was "staying" with Alyosha, why weren't they at the circus instead of wandering the Romanian countryside? Sylvie's mind churned, taking her back to her wedding day at the circus. Images boiled up. The RV she'd been in. The plastic-wrapped body of a child. Butchered and gnawed on. Imprints of human teeth on the broken bones.

Now, another little girl. Far from her home. And scared.

The circus belonged to this man. Did he really not know what was going on there? Or was he part of it?

Sylvie wondered if she was overreacting. After all,

without his help, she'd be dead.

But Liana had warned her that people were never what they seemed, and reality supported her pessimistic view more and more.

If this man had something to do with the dead child at the circus, then the young girl here was in danger.

Did Zora know? During the wedding ceremony, she'd mentioned monsters eating the young. But even if she knew, there was no way she could stop him. Crippled, bound to her wheelchair by the bloodwalker's curse. She was a victim, too.

If anything happened, Sylvie would be the one who'd have to stand up to him.

Half her mind balked, telling her she was jumping to wild conclusions—until a lighted sign skimmed past her window. It read "Huedin," the city nearest her village. The van sped right by the exit.

"That was the turn off," she said, the words chafing her suddenly dry throat. "That road leads to my home."

"What?" Alyosha stared at her vacantly before waving his hand. "Oh, that's not where the meeting is. It's up in the mountains near Mediaș, in a tiny town you probably never heard of called Bǎjenie. It's only thirty minutes away. Your mother will be so happy to see you." He reached over and patted her knee. She forced herself not to cringe.

He was lying. Just like Miron.

Despite what Alyosha thought, Sylvie knew Bǎjenie well.

It was a horrible place, set up by the government in the thirties to give homes to Ukrainian refugees fleeing Soviet starvation. *Holodomor* her mother called it—the hunger plague.

Desperate, skinny immigrants with nowhere to go were shipped in by the truckload, given clapboard homes, and set to work in two new factories. One factory made carbon black for dyes, a powdery ash that crept into everything, like coal dust from mines.

The other factory was a smelter, burning ore to make lead. But lead was even viler than carbon black. The poison mineral seeped out of the vats and snuck into the ground, the water supply, and the blood of the workers.

When Communism fell in the eighties, the factories were closed. No one lived in the polluted place now. Even the animals stayed away.

Her mother's grandparents had been refugees. Their terrible stories about it had made her mother hate the place. She'd never go to a meeting there.

For the second time in as many hours, Sylvie wished for a weapon. Searching for one wasn't possible with Alyosha just feet from her.

A plan formed in her mind. When Alyosha stopped the van, Sylvie would grab the girl and run. The man was close to seventy. He wouldn't be able to catch them.

But what if he had a gun or a knife?

She definitely needed a weapon. Her hand slipped into her bloodwalker's bag, and like moles in the dark, her fingers nudged blindly over the contents. Candles, matches, packing cotton, a ball of twine, needles, and a bottle of lilac oil for massaging corpse's eyes closed.

All useless as weapons.

The only sharp things were the needles. Big, long ones used for sewing through flesh and tendons. One sticking out of its paper package jabbed deep into her fingertip. Her eyes bulged, but she didn't betray herself by gasping.

Maybe she wasn't as weaponless as she thought.

Working with one hand so Alyosha couldn't see, she pulled the needles from their cardboard holder and stuck them into the ball of twine. Not straight in, like a porcupine—too likely to fall out that way—but slid in sideways, so both point and thread-hole poked out on either side.

The van ate up the miles to Bǎjenie while Sylvie jammed needles into the twine. Working by feel alone, she stabbed herself often. Her fingertips grew sticky with blood. At last, half the ball bristled with needles while the other half was empty so she could hold onto it.

When the van rolled into the desolate town, she was surprised to see streetlights working. But all the houses were dark, many little more than shells with caved in roofs and leaning walls.

Alyosha pulled into a gravel driveway. The van's headlights swept across a lawn of dead, brown grass. Only the toughest of weeds could survive in the poisoned town.

"You stay here," he said and shut off the engine. "I'll be back in a moment." He opened his door and got out.

Quick to seize her chance, Sylvie leaned over the center console and said to the girl, "We have to go. Come to the front."

The girl stared at her vacantly and didn't move.

Maybe there really was something wrong with the child, but no way was Sylvie going to make a run for it and leave her behind. Sylvie pulled her bag's handles over her shoulder freeing her hands in case she had to carry the girl . Clambering onto the center console, she squeezed between the seats into the back of the van and took the child's arm. "We need to leave. This way."

The girl resisted for a second, but then scrambled to her feet.

Sylvie prodded her over the console and onto the front passenger seat. "There"—Sylvie pointed at the door—"pull the handle. Quick! We're going home!"

The girl turned back and said, "H-home...?" The word stuttered to silence as she looked past Sylvie. Her eyes grew huge. Her mouth dropped open.

"No, little one," came a raspy voice, as brittle as a snake slithering over dried leaves. "You *can't* go home. Neither of you can."

Sylvie spun, squinting into the dark.

The light from one streetlamp barely pierced the gloom. But it was enough.

Zora rose from her wheelchair. She leaned forward, and a leathery hand darted out and captured Sylvie's wrist. As the elderly bloodwalker stood, her veil caught on the arm of the wheelchair and slid off, revealing a face from a nightmare.

Zora's oversized forehead jutted into a cliff over her eyes, like a prehistoric caveman's. Her cheekbones stuck out on either side, bulbous and too large for her skull. Her lower jaw was also monstrously overgrown, protruding and giving her the underbite of a bulldog. Her skin stretched tightly over her face and seemed ready to split open from the strain.

Her head bumped the van's ceiling. Tilting it down to make room, she straightened her hunched back. Her joints cracked as her collarbones widened, revealing shoulders broader than a man's. With a sigh of relief, she extended legs covered by tight sweat pants, each one turned outwards from her pelvis like a lizard's. One muscular leg was shorter than the other.

"Stupid wheelchair," she grunted.

"Run, Anushka!" Sylvie shouted.

Zora's bloodshot eyes narrowed. She tightened her grip on Sylvie's wrist and drew back her other hand into a fist.

The back door of the van wrenched open, and Alyosha leaned in. "Zora!" he said. "Gently!"

Sylvie cringed, waiting for the blow. Her fingers dove into her bloodwalker bag.

"Don't kill her," Alyosha continued. "Just break the bones. We need her alive for as long as possible."

"Only break." Zora grinned, lips sliding back over long teeth. The skin of her cheeks tautened over unnaturally big jaw muscles.

Her fist sailed forward, but Sylvie ducked. The blow whipped through the air above her. She yanked the ball of twine from the bag and straightened up. With all her might, she slashed it across Zora's face.

The needles ripped through skin already membrane-thin. The flesh tore open from Zora's temple down to her jaw. Muscles and tendons gleamed. Blood spattered onto Sylvie's skin.

Zora screamed and covered her shredded face.

Freed from her grip, Sylvie sprang into the front seat, reached past Anushka, and flung open the door. But overbalanced, she tumbled out from the seat, knocking Anushka down. Both landed on the ground.

Zora's shrieks rose behind them.

Jumping up, Sylvie grabbed Anushka's hand and bolted. But only twenty yards down the street, she had to slow—the little girl's legs couldn't keep up with hers. If she picked the girl up and tried to carry her, she'd barely manage a jog. Tough love, she decided, compressing the small hand in hers and pulling Anushka harder.

After another twenty yards, she looked back.

The van bounced on its suspension as Zora hopped from the back. She started after them, head bobbing with every uneven stride.

As lopsided as the gait was, it would still be fast enough to catch Sylvie and Anushka soon. They needed a hiding place.

Sylvie's gaze shot to the nearby homes. Roofs sagged, walls had fallen in, and porch floorboards gaped with holes. No sanctuary there.

On the other side of the street, a field of bare earth stretched off into the distance. A clanking sound came from a row of four or five mammoth machines. In the street lamps' dim light, the machines dipped up and down like giant birds pecking at seeds on the ground. Although the machines were big, they wouldn't conceal the girls.

Clouds rolled across the moon. Humidity congealed in Sylvie's puffing lungs.

A storm was coming.

Zora was coming even faster.

Sylvie had to find somewhere to hide.

CHAPTER TWENTY-THREE

Rurik
Western Carpathian Mountains, Romania

Crammed in the rear seat of the Markarovs' pickup truck, Rurik eyed two of his captors, Viktor and Anatoly, who wedged him in from either side. The truck's cab was wide, but not wide enough for iron-pumping strongmen. Their shoulders fought for space, elbows dug into Rurik's ribs, and their hips pressed closer than he wanted any man's to be.

Dmitry wrestled with the steering wheel, taking turns too fast, and mashing Rurik between the two Markarovs. In the passenger seat, the vinyl squeaked every time Pavel shifted positions or cracked his neck. He kept fidgeting, nervous as a high flyer without a net. Something ate at him, and his gaze never left the dark Romanian road ahead.

In contrast to their glittery strongmen costumes, all the Markarovs now wore black long-sleeved shirts and black pants. With some cammo face paint, they could pass for a military special ops unit.

The truck's nose pointed like a hunting dog's as they climbed into the mountains. Rurik swallowed against the pressure building in his ears.

Wherever they were taking him couldn't be good. They hated him too much.

Escape was the best option, but with his knees jammed into the front seats and the roof brushing his head, trying anything in the small space would be like fighting in a straightjacket. Not to mention all the Markarovs had rifles close at hand.

The air-conditioner blasted cold air onto Rurik's face.

The sweat at his hairline turned icy, and gooseflesh rose on his forearms, yet perspiration continued to soak his back where it leaned against the seat. With every mile, the humidity increased, and the odor of stale BO filled his nostrils. Too many men in too tight a space. Rats in a cage.

Rurik's hands fisted, and pain shot through his broken fingers.

He breathed out, controlling his anger and impatience. So far, losing his temper hadn't gotten him any answers. Not about Pavel's trips with the van. Not about the clown's true identity. Not about the fate of the missing children.

Time for a new approach.

For once, he'd play along. Throttle back his rage and desire for vengeance. Pretend he didn't want to bash in their heads.

In the headlights' glow, the terrain changed. Flatland opened up on either side of the road. The trees thinned out, retreating from view almost as if they were scared to enter the part of Romania that lay ahead.

When the climb finally leveled off, Rurik bent forward and peered through the windshield. Along the heights of distant ridges, lightning flickered, illuminating miles of straight plateau ahead of them.

Anxiety brewed inside him, and acid bubbled up the back of his throat.

They were heading into a storm. One with lightning. On a plateau with no trees or anything else to get between him and a million volts. Like shit wasn't bad enough already.

"We aren't stopping here, are we?" Tension barbed his tone.

"Pavel?" Viktor said.

In the front, Pavel leaned toward the window and scanned the fields that rolled past. "Not here. It's a few more miles," he mumbled.

"What's in a few more miles?" Rurik said . What the hell did the Markarovs want on a plateau in the middle of nowhere?

"It's the girl. The one that's missing, okay?" Pavel said in a petulant voice. "We heard Alyosha took her, and...I think I know where."

Rurik's shoulders yanked free from the men pressing his sides. "If you know where she is, why haven't you gotten her and brought her back?"

Pavel slumped in his seat.

Dmitry caught Rurik's gaze in the rearview mirror. "It's not that simple. Pavel knows where the girl is—or thinks she is anyway—but if we bring her back, there'll be too many questions about how we found her. Why we knew where she was. We'll all look guilty."

"Because you are guilty!" Viktor snapped. Strange, since Viktor was the older and usually the calmer of the two brothers.

Rurik studied him. It never occurred to him that Viktor would be the weak link in the chain that bound the Markarovs together. Maybe Rurik could use it to his advantage. He counted to ten—only made it to five—before saying mildly, "You know where this child was taken? Or all the children?"

"See? You blame us for everything, just like the others—but you're wrong!" Dmitry's voice boomed in the small space. "We had nothing to do with this child or any others being taken!"

"Bullshit!" Viktor said. "You knew what was going on. You just decided to look the other way."

"I did what I had to do to protect my sons and our jobs!" Dmitry yelled.

Viktor lurched forward, thrusting his face inches from his brother's ear. "Our jobs were safe until you started this shit! Now look at us. No work, no home, probably blacklisted from every circus. Great job you're doing protecting us."

"Stop fighting!" Pavel shouted, wrenching around in his seat to face Viktor. "It's my fault, okay? I'm the one that helped Alyosha. *Not Dad!*"

Rurik raised his brows. Now, they were getting somewhere. Keeping his voice soft and non-threatening, he said , "And what did you help with?"

Pavel blew out his cheeks. He sat in silence, head hanging like a broken tent pole. Then he began to speak, quietly at first. "It all started back in Budapest. Alyosha asked me to burn down the RV. He offered a lot of money. But first, he wanted me to get some stuff out of it: towels, makeup, and...a package." His face screwed up as if he was suddenly nauseous.

"I waited till the bloodwalker brides left, and then I went in. I got the towels and makeup, and there was a suitcase there. I thought that was the package. But then some crazy girl appeared and wouldn't let me have it. When I brought the towels and makeup to Alyosha, he got real mad. Said he needed a *plastic* package out of there. So I went back. Searched. Found it..." He shook his head, locks of hair flicking around his ears. "Man, that thing stank. It...it was like bones and pieces of meat, but all rotten."

The blond bride, Rurik remembered, asked him to look in that RV. Was that the package she wanted him to find? But rancid meat didn't prove anything. His attention veered back to Pavel as the kid continued.

"So I took it to Alyosha, then did like he said—I burned down the RV, and he paid me. When we moved to Bratislava, Alyosha said I could earn more money by making a delivery for him. He wanted a box taken to Romania. He gave me a map and worked it out so we left camp together before I switched to another van."

Sneaky bastards. Rurik's pulse rose with his frustration. Alyosha had duped him so easily. With effort, he curbed his irritation, determined to keep Pavel talking so he could learn the whole truth. "And once you left camp?" he prodded.

"Well...halfway to Romania I knew things were messed up. That box was stinking up the whole van, and it smelled the same as that other package. I just wanted to get rid of it. So I went to the town Alyosha circled on the map. The whole place was creepy. Deserted. But there was a house where he said, and it had his name on the front. So I went in.

"I was supposed to take the box down to the basement and put it in a big freezer. The house was a wreck—broken windows, rotted floors—but I found the door that led to the basement. Downstairs was different . There was a living room, kitchen, bedrooms. Way newer than the rest.

Like he built a whole house underneath the old one. And no one knows it's there.

"In the kitchen, I found a long freezer. Inside it were more boxes like the one I had. And...well...I opened one up." A violent shudder rocked his body. "There was...meat inside. But I looked close...and saw a whole hand. Little. A child's. I pulled out more boxes and found a boy's head!" Pavel groaned and buried his face in his hands.

Unbelievable. Alyosha was the killer after all... Yet something didn't jibe, but Rurik couldn't put his finger on it.

He leaned closer. "Then what happened?"

"I..." Pavel scrubbed his sleeve across his eyes. "I dumped everything back in and ran out of there like my tail was on fire. Never looked back. Never said anything. But..." Pavel shivered. "I couldn't stop thinking about it, so I told Dad. He said I should pretend it never happened. Keep my mouth shut."

Rurik's slow simmer boiled over. He glared at Dmitry in the rearview. "Keep his mouth shut? What were you thinking?"

"He was thinking about the money!" Viktor's eyes blazed. "I've seen the stash get bigger and bigger over the last weeks. You said it was from the boys' mobile phone business, but it was payoffs from Alyosha!"

A flush darkened Dmitry's cheeks. "But I didn't know for certain what was going on," he protested. "Back then, I hadn't heard about any missing children on our tour route. And now I'm doing something, aren't I? I'm taking us there to fix things."

Rurik clamped his mouth shut before he exploded. He'd love to lay into Dmitry and Pavel. They'd known about the dead bodies and done nothing. It was their fault Anushka had been taken.

But a little voice in the back of his mind told him he was partly to blame. When he realized children were being taken, he should have told others. Raised the alarm. Instead, he'd kept silent, determined to catch the killer by himself. And he'd allowed his relationship with Alyosha to cloud his judgment.

It wasn't just the Markarovs' fault. There was plenty of blame to go around.

Pavel bent toward the windshield. "Hold it. Slow down. I remember seeing the pipeline beside the road here. It goes on about a mile, and then it goes across some fields to these oil pumpers. Where it leaves the road is the beginning of the town."

Rurik followed his gaze, seeing a two-foot wide pipeline that paralleled the road, held in place by U-shaped braces. Strange to think some company drilled an oil field up in the mountains.

Across the plateau, lightning burst in wicked streaks along the lower foothills. Only heat lightning. No rain yet, and too far for the thunder to travel. But it would start soon. When the storm rolled down the plain, it would come like a juggernaut, aiming straight for them. Straight for him.

Pins and needles prickled across his scalp. "Are you sure the girl's here?" Rurik said , his voice hoarse.

"It's obviously his hideout. Buried in the ground like that. Hidden under the original house," Pavel said. "He thinks no one will find it. And believe me, no police would ever look there. The town's trashed . Looks like no one's lived in it for fifty years." He pointed. "There! The pipeline turns. If we keep going, we'll go straight into the town. You can just see the first house under those streetlamps."

"Then we stop here." Dmitry parked on the shoulder. "Everyone out."

"Why don't you just drive in?" Rurik said . Being on rubber wheels would protect them from electrocution. "If Alyosha still has the circus van, we should be able to find it and know for sure if he's here."

"Because as dangerous as he is, there's someone else who might be even more dangerous."

"What...?" Then Rurik got it—what he should have realized before. "You mean the clown. Alyosha might have a freezer full of bodies, but he isn't the one I stopped from kidnapping the child in Budapest. He isn't the one who fought us in Metsky Park, and he isn't the one who killed Marva's dogs."

Viktor jumped from the truck and pulled Rurik out. Dmitry motioned with his rifle for Rurik to go first.

Rurik leveled his gaze on Dmitry. "You know who the clown is, don't you?"

"Maybe." Dmitry shoved Rurik into a walk. "And it sure as hell isn't one of us, like you keep saying. I brought you here to see what's really going on and tell the people at the circus that the kidnapping and murders weren't our fault."

"Then whose fault is it? Who is the clown?" Rurik demanded. Alyosha might be involved up to his neck, but the clown was the killer—the real one Rurik was after.

Pavel matched strides with Rurik and spoke in a low tone. "Sometimes when I went to Alyosha's RV to collect money, I heard noises from the back bedroom. Like closet doors sliding closed. Windows being pushed open. Zora isn't crippled. She can move."

"And she weighs more than any of us," Viktor added. "When Dmitry and I have to carry her chair, it's backbreaking. It feels like she's made of iron."

"You're our witness, Rurik," Dmitry's voice growled from the darkness. "We don't know if the girl's alive or what Zora and Alyosha are doing with her. All we know is they're not just a little old man and his crippled wife. They're a lot more dangerous."

A tortured scream ripped across the town. Unearthly. Inhuman.

Three hundred yards down the road, two figures flashed under a streetlight, running. They vanished a second later, lost in the blackness between the lights.

One shape was small. The size of a nine-year-old girl.

Rurik took off after them.

CHAPTER TWENTY-FOUR

Sylvie
Bājenie, Romania

> *Bloodwalkers are gifted with exceptionally strong constitutions, but the price we pay is an early death. When your time comes, do not fear it. Do not run from it. Death and bloodwalkers are old friends. The kind of friends that don't lie to each other.*
> ~ *The Bloodwalker's Book*

Sylvie rushed down the dark street, the blustery wind lashing her long skirt against her legs. She held onto Anushka with one hand, using the other to keep her bag from bouncing off her shoulder. She should've left it behind. The weight slowed her down. But she was confused, overwhelmed. Her thoughts spun like a tornado.

Was that really Zora or some bizarre deformed man?

They needed to find a hiding place before they collapsed with exhaustion.

The creature had risen from the wheelchair, joints popping and bones clicking . It seemed to expand with every breath. Impossible.

Sylvie picked up the pace, her legs pumping harder.

That face! What lay beneath the veil was hideous. Unnatural. It didn't even resemble a woman but a demonic denizen of hell. Sylvie mentally kicked herself. No time to wonder what Zora had become. Just find a hiding spot.

A line of derelict houses lay on her right, with doors falling off hinges, windows with no glass, roofs full of holes, front porches caved in, and the walls' timbers so cracked and rotten she could see right through them.

On her left, barren land—open as far as she could see.

If they dashed across the field, were there trees to hide in on the other side? Too dark to tell. The field could be a half mile long or three times that.

After another fifty yards, Anushka began to lag, dragging against Sylvie's hold. With a shake of her head, she mumbled words Sylvie couldn't understand.

Sylvie's gaze flew past her to the shadowy street behind them.

The beast—Sylvie couldn't think of it as Zora—loped down the center of the street, evading the glow from the streetlamps as if it feared being burned. It ran with its head down and its legs splayed out. The longer leg catapulted it forward while the shorter one faltered with each step, its knee bending wrong, sickeningly out of joint. Its eyes caught the lamplight and reflected it, glittering in the dark like a cat's.

Despite its hunched and hideous gait, the creature gained on them.

"Come on, honey. We can't stop!" Sylvie said, tightening her grip on Anushka's puny fingers. The girl would never make it across the fields to the forest. Carrying her would slow Sylvie down. They'd both get caught. They needed to find somewhere nearby. Fast.

In the distance, lightning arced from the clouds and lit up the sky. It illuminated a row of mountains—and the skeleton of a dinosaur.

Sylvie squinted. The next flickers revealed not a dinosaur, but a derelict factory, three stories high. The top two floors were only bare girders, the building's skeletal remains standing stark against the heavens. But the first floor looked intact. And big. Plenty of hiding spots.

Sylvie dashed headlong toward the factory's ruins.

Glass from broken windows littered the ground and crunched under her shoes. Light from the streetlamps revealed a collapsed wall—a quick way into the building. She pulled Anushka over a heap of dislodged masonry. Bricks tumbled from the pile, clattering onto the concrete floor and echoing across the vast space.

Sylvie peered back outside but couldn't see Zora yet. The woman was probably a minute behind them, but their panting breaths sounded like trumpets. Once Zora got there, she'd locate them in seconds.

Sylvie crept farther in, pulling Anushka with her. Muted light from the street shone across half the area. Hardly enough for her to see anything, but possibly enough for Zora to spot their pale faces.

Lightning strobed through the open ceiling. In those split seconds, Sylvie saw the layout.

A giant fifty-yard square of open space, interrupted by about eight wide pillars. Dotted around the factory floor were other odd shapes that the burst of light hadn't given her time to see clearly. They could be anything from the hulks of old equipment to piles of garbage. Like a gaping black mouth, the entrance to a corridor lay in the nearest wall. The lightning hadn't shone from inside it. The corridor must still have a roof. Maybe the whole wing did.

Perhaps there was a darker hiding place in there. Darker meant safer from Zora.

Sylvie hurried into the dim hallway.

The first thirty feet featured small rooms on either side, like offices. But they had no doors. No protection there. She continued another ten feet, and the hall abruptly turned a corner. When she rounded it, the light from the streetlamps vanished completely.

She halted, and Anushka banged into her hip. For a second, Sylvie despaired of going forward into pitch blackness. The floor might be damaged. They could fall into a pit.

Then a streak of lightning—blessed lightning—shone through a window in a room to her left. It was a large room, bigger than the office spaces. Broken tables and chairs littered the floor. One wall glinted like metal.

The light flickered into the hallway , revealing more offices on her right. Thankfully, these had doors.

The lightning faded too quickly. Back to being blind, she waved her hand in front of her. As faint thunder rumbled in the distance, her fingers found the wall and the first door. The knob wouldn't turn. Locked. Feeling her way down the corridor, she came to a second door, also locked. And so was the third.

A rattle of bricks hitting cement echoed down the passageway from the factory.

Sylvie stopped dead.

Zora! She'd followed them into the factory.

No time to check all the doors. Sylvie would have to find safety immediately.

She whirled and stumbled back to the large room. With no lightning to direct her, she smacked into something. A table, lying on its side. Only the dimmest of outlines was visible. She shuffled, letting her toes guide her past the table, and ended up tripping over a chair. It spun away with a clatter. She froze, holding her breath. Zora had to have heard that. How long before she came looking?

A moment later, another jagged bolt of lightning lit the room. The metal wall turned out to be a row of lockers with rusted doors hanging off their hinges. Tables and chairs lay jumbled across the floor. Along the length of one wall was a counter, beneath it some large cabinets.

Hiding inside those was her only hope.

She picked her way through the debris, keeping Anushka close, and opened a cabinet. The rotted wood of the door cracked apart and fell to the floor with a dull thump. Inside, her fingers found shelves that left no room to hide.

In the corridor, something scraped against the concrete floor.

Backpedalling, she swept Anushka with her behind the nearest overturned table. She sought the girl's white face in the dark and held a finger to her lips. Anushka might not understand Romanian, but at the symbol for quiet, she nodded.

Scrapes and a strange tapping grew louder. Shuffle, tap. Shuffle, tap. Shuffle, tap.

It must be Zora, feeling her way in the dark and tapping the walls.

If Zora found them, Sylvie would have to fight. She shoved her hand inside her bag, searching for the twine ball stuck with needles. Her fingers probed every corner. It was gone. She must have dropped it while running from the van.

Damn, damn, damn.

Only matches, candles, massage oil, and cotton left. And a few of her clothes. Light an apron on fire? Throw it at Zora?

With her luck, Sylvie would catch herself on fire first.

The shuffle-taps got closer. Louder.

A voice whispered, "Tereza? Where are you?"

Tereza was Sylvie's mother's name.

Sylvie peeked over the edge of the table but couldn't see anything in the blackness of the hall.

"T-Tereza?" the voice whimpered—a female voice, but not the raspy croak of Zora. "Emilia? Where are you?"

Emilia was Liana's mother's name. Were the other bloodwalkers here after all?

If they were, there was hope! Sylvie's mother always knew what to do. She'd figure a way out of this mess.

Lightning blazed for a second, illuminating a fat gray-haired lady in the doorway, hunched over a cane. The woman gasped, her eyes squinting in the sudden brilliance.

It was Aunt Cosmina, the only bloodwalker who'd been nice to Sylvie at the wedding, giving her the beautiful and expensive veil. She'd also done her best to quiet Zora when the old woman had pronounced the horrible curse on Sylvie.

"Aunt Cosmina," Sylvie whispered. "I'm over here."

"Who is that?" Aunt Cosmina's voice quavered. "Tereza?"

"No, it's me, Sylvie Dinescu."

Aunt Cosmina waddled into the room. With a grunt, she tried to get past a broken chair but soon gave up. "These old legs don't work anymore..."

Sylvie stood up and rounded the corner of the table. Anushka scurried after her, clinging to Sylvie's hips, face pressed against her wool dress.

"How did you get here?" Aunt Cosmina said.

"Alyosha brought me. And Anushka. Then Zora..."

"Shush! Keep your voice down. Zora's gone crazy. Your mother and the others are hiding in here. In one of the offices. I left because I heard a scream. I thought I could reason with Zora—but she's too far gone. She's searching through the equipment in the factory. I snuck back here, but now I can't remember where they are. It's so dark..."

There was safety in numbers. If Sylvie and the other bloodwalkers banded together, maybe they could fight Zora and get away. Sylvie scooped a candle from her bag and lit it with a match. "Let's find them. Hurry!"

"This way." Aunt Cosmina shuffled off, her cane making hollow clunks on the floor with every step.

Sylvie kept pace, lighting the way to the end of the hall.

"Here! Last door." Aunt Cosmina pushed the door open and entered. "Tereza? You'll never guess who I found."

Sylvie stepped into the room, her stomach shimmying in excitement, a smile leaping to her face. Seeing her mother again would be wonderful. Her mother always knew what to do. She could take charge of any situation. She'd fix everything.

In the center of the room, a long metal desk sat with chairs stacked on one side. But nothing moved. No one spoke.

"Mama?" she said, venturing toward the desk. A pair of shoes stuck out from behind it. As she got closer, legs and a long skirt came into view, and then another pair of shoes lying beside them. She dashed the final steps—and suddenly she was looking at her mother, lying on the floor. Eyes closed. Skin paper-white. A gaping wound slashed across her throat.

"Mama! Oh my God!" She leaped forward and dropped to her knees beside her mother's body. The candle fell from her nerveless fingers, and she wrapped her mother in her arms. Her mother was cold. So cold.

Sylvie's heart stuttered against her breastbone, like a misfiring engine. A flurry of shivers shook her from head to toe until she was sure she'd disintegrate into tiny pieces. Her breath hitched in her chest, and her eyes blurred with tears.

The candle hadn't gone out when it hit the floor. Its wobbly flame shone across two more bodies. Liana's and Ada's mothers.

"They're dead!" Sylvie shrieked at Aunt Cosmina.

"Yes... A pity." The old woman straightened, no longer leaning on her cane, her tone indifferent. "But none of them would shut up about the bloodwalker's curse. Kept blabbing about how Zora was still alive while all their own relatives never made it past sixty. Then your mother has to go and tell them about her Ukrainian grandparents. How they survived the Soviet starvation genocide in the thirties by eating their neighbors—till they were thrown out of the Ukraine and had to come here. Your mother knew the bloodwalker's secret; that the only way to survive the bloodwalker's curse is to eat the bones of the young."

"What?! That's insane. Bloodwalkers don't eat people!" Sylvie cried.

"You do if you want to live," Aunt Cosmina said. "Children are best, but anyone will do if they have broken bones that are healing. There's something in the cells—they make bone. When a bloodwalker gets old and her limbs weaken, it's the only solution." Her voice turned low and spiteful. "I offered your mother and the other mothers a choice. A chance to *live*. All they had to do was keep quiet about Zora...and the child's body your mother found in the circus RV."

Sylvie gasped. Her mother hadn't found the body. *She* had. Her mother had sworn Sylvie to secrecy but apparently told Aunt Cosmina about it. Had her mother known it would be dangerous? Is that why she hadn't mentioned that Sylvie knew, too?

"If word got out, other bloodwalkers might put it together with Zora's unusually long life. They might have heard about the cure from your mother. The younger bloodwalkers are less than sympathetic. But let me tell you, once your body weakens and your bones buckle and fracture when you take just a step, once you're lying in bed in pain, waiting to die, you'll do anything to stop it."

"Not anything," Sylvie said, her voice rough. "Zora's life isn't better than death. She's become a monster."

"Indeed." Aunt Cosmina sniffed. "Well, the mothers of the brides felt as you do. They refused to keep quiet. Liana's mother *told* her everything, and so did Ada's. Naturally, when I warned Alyosha, he decided to take care of the problem. Or *problems*. That little man is frighteningly good with a knife." A dark chuckle slithered from her lips. "Only you remain, my dear. And sadly for you, your death won't be as quick and merciful as your mother's. You're still young, and if your bones break, they'll begin producing the lovely cells that will make an old bloodwalker's body grow strong and tough. And I, for one, am looking forward to that." A feral smile slipped onto her face. She whirled into the hall and slammed the door shut.

Sylvie lunged after her, but heard a metallic click as she rammed into the door. It didn't budge.

When she tried the knob, it was locked.

CHAPTER TWENTY-FIVE

Rurik
Bājenie, Romania

Rurik hurtled over the collapsed wall of the abandoned factory and skidded to a stop. Streetlights behind him threw his shadow across the debris-strewn floor. His gaze skimmed the area. No way to tell its true size; darkness obscured everything beyond the first thirty yards.

Dmitry pounded up behind him, sucking wind. "Did you see where they went?"

Rurik shook his head. The running figures—the slim woman and the child—had been two hundred yards away. Too far for Rurik or the Markarovs to catch them before they disappeared into the giant building.

The same with their pursuer. The misshapen thing had lurched down the street and into the building after the girls, its lame, clumsy movements all too familiar from the train depot, the "mud-man" chase, and the woods of the park.

The clown.

Without its white suit, it had merged with the shadows when it entered the factory. Rurik couldn't spot it or the girls.

Viktor wobbled over the collapsed wall and beckoned Rurik and Dmitry to him.

Seconds later, Pavel and Anatoly bounded in, knocking bricks across the floor and earning a scathing look from Viktor . The boys tiptoed over, their rifles locked in tense grips while their gazes zigzagged through the crumbling factory.

"We need to split up," Viktor said in a low voice. "Two of you go right, two go left, and I'll stay here to make sure no

221

one leaves...and that no one else gets in."

Rurik nodded, knowing he meant Alyosha. When they'd run past the circus van, its doors stood wide open. Nothing inside except the wheelchair—empty.

That proved two things: Zora didn't need her wheelchair and could have been the deformed hulk they'd seen on the street. Also, knowing Alyosha's attachment to her, he probably lurked somewhere close by.

"Anatoly," Dmitry whispered. "With me." He and his older son turned right and snuck along the inside wall of the factory.

"Come on." Tossing a sullen expression at Rurik, Pavel headed left and led the way between the nearest wall and a row of huge pillars.

Rurik didn't like being paired with Pavel, either, but this wasn't about them. It was about saving Anushka and the other girl.

Pebbles and dirt crunched under his boots. He bent his knees, softening his steps, keeping his ears pricked for any sounds that would betray Zora or the girls.

Streetlamps shone on the pillars and abandoned equipment but created deep, black shadows behind them where anyone could hide.

Rurik rolled his shoulders, easing tense muscles. The clown had proved a dangerous opponent—more than a match for Rurik's strength. He eyed Pavel's gun and wished he were armed.

But could he really pull the trigger on Zora or Alyosha?

Alyosha had done a lot for him over the years—paid the family when Rurik was injured by the lightning and couldn't perform, looked the other way when Rurik's father showed up drunk to performances or missed them altogether, and gave Rurik a job as security guard even though his face frightened the public.

However, by taking Anushka, the ringmaster had betrayed the circus, betrayed everything Rurik respected about him. He'd lied and murdered Yuri. Perhaps others.

Rurik's gratitude and loyalty to his old friend ended now. The massive concrete pillars rising from the floor connected to a network of steel girders crossing the air thirty feet above. No one could be on the girders, too narrow, but each thick column was a potential hiding place.

Rurik kept his eyes on them as he crept past. Nothing moved. But as he went deeper inside the building, a sharp, acidic odor rose around him. Not strong, since a stiff wind blew through the place, but enough to make Rurik wrinkle his nose. It was a strange smell, like...

A flapping sound came from the rafters above.

Rurik tilted his head.

In the upper levels, movement flashed. Wings fluttered. A blur of feathers jetted from one girder to the next.

Ah yes. Birds explained the strange smell. Or rather, bird crap.

The wind gusted, whistling through the rafters and rattling chains that dangled from them. Rurik squinted, spying hooks attached to the chains. Probably a pulley system for hauling loads across the building. The chains and hooks had rusted. Bits flaked away, slowly disintegrating under the watchful eyes of the avian inhabitants.

Lightning shot across the sky and blazed into Rurik's eyes. Instinctively, he backpedaled and rammed the factory wall, cracking his head. His pulse thrummed in his ears. His throat closed up. Breathing strangled.

Thunder exploded like an artillery barrage.

Rurik gulped air. By the time his heartbeat calmed, he felt like an idiot.

This was no open field—not like the one where he'd been struck by lightning at seven. Nor was it one of the big top's towers, where he'd been unjamming a cable when struck at seventeen. In fact, he was safer in the factory than outside. Its tall girders would take the brunt of a lightning strike and ground them straight to the floor. As long as he stayed away from metal, he'd be safe.

He turned to go after Pavel and smacked his shoulder on something protruding from the wall. A ladder, bolted to the bricks, leading up to the girders. Made of metal. He leaped away as if burned.

Marshaling his nerves, he gave the ladder a wide berth. Twenty feet away, Pavel waited by a tall mysterious mound.

Up close, it wasn't all that mysterious. Just stacks of wooden pallets, the kind used to carry material with a forklift. But there were a ton of them, forming a pile twelve feet high by twenty feet on a side. Streaks of green mold stretched over the rotten wood like fat fingers trying to claw their way out. Bird droppings speckled everything with white blotches. The moldering pile stank of mildew, fungus, and the ammonia smell of bird crap.

Pavel gestured to catch Rurik's attention. He pointed at himself and motioned around one side of the mound, then at Rurik, and motioned around the other side. After Rurik's nod, Pavel padded off.

Rurik was tempted to let Pavel circle the damn thing alone. The Markarovs had all the rifles. Rurik didn't have shit.

But the two girls had nothing to protect them either. They had to be found.

He headed along the stacks of pallets, treading as silently as possible. Halfway around, the back of his neck prickled. He looked behind him. Nothing. But he couldn't get rid of the feeling that someone was watching.

When he turned the corner, he caught sight of Pavel rounding the other side.

With a squawk, something flew out from one of the pallets. It darted straight at Pavel, all panicked motion and whirring wings.

With a yelp, the kid leaped backward, tripped, and fell on his ass.

The frightened bird soared into the rafters.

Rurik sauntered over and gave Pavel a hand up, but couldn't keep the smirk off his face.

"Yes, very funny," Pavel hissed. "Pavel falls on his butt while Hero Rurik comes to his rescue. Does it make you happy?" he said , brushing off his pants. "Knowing everyone screws up while you're always perfect?"

"Perfect?" That was the *last* word Rurik would use to describe himself.

"Don't act dumb. The whole camp thinks you're a saint. Never make a mistake. Always helping people. Meanwhile, when my father gets promoted to Security Chief, all they do is bitch. 'Bring back Rurik. He's straight with everyone. We trust him.' Blah, blah, blah. Even the girls. I've been after Miriam the contortionist for six months, but she only has eyes for you."

Rurik's jaw slackened. The people in the circus trusted him? Even liked him? And Miriam...? No. Rurik gave his head a shake. Ridiculous. He saw fear and disgust in their eyes when they looked at him. He'd always seen it. And he didn't blame them. Who could look upon his terrible scars and see anything but an ugly monster?

Pavel was crazy and wasting time.

Rurik focused on the task at hand. "If I were running from Zora," he said quietly. "I'd go to the darkest place with the most cover."

"Huh?"

"There." Rurik tipped his head to the hallway behind him.

Pavel glanced over Rurik's shoulder and grimaced. "I dunno. Black as a cave in there."

"You want to wait for your father?" Or maybe Rurik should take the rifle and let piss-ant Pavel go hide in the truck.

Pavel made a rude noise. "Like he gives a shit about me. He hates me. Always has." He lowered his chin and clasped the rifle tighter. "Come on."

Rurik followed in Pavel's footsteps until they reached the hallway. Then the hairs on his nape stood on end. He spun around, gaze flashing over the factory interior.

The only thing he saw was Viktor, still guarding the broken wall thirty yards away. Dmitry and Anatoly weren't visible, undoubtedly still combing the other side of the factory.

Near Viktor, shadows shifted. Something was silhouetted in the streetlamps outside.

Rurik narrowed his eyes.

The shadow vanished.

Nothing else moved.

The wind increased to a shriek, whirling through the girders above. Loose feathers spun in little cyclones. Rurik decided the shadow was probably just trash, blowing around outside, and turned back to Pavel.

"Here." Pavel handed Rurik a mobile phone.

"What's this for?" Circus people didn't use cell phones. Too expensive for constant travelers.

Pavel clicked the screen a few times and a thin beam of light shot out the top of the device. "See? Now, you go first."

Figured.

They trekked down the hallway, shining the tiny light into the rooms that lay on either side. Occasional flickers of lightning helped guide them, though tiny shivers ran across Rurik's limbs every time his enemy bared its electric teeth.

When the corridor turned, the light from the factory was lost, but the phone light illuminated office doors. Rurik tried every one he came to. All were locked.

At the last locked door, they hit a dead end.

Rurik looked back the way they'd come, wondering how the girls and Zora had managed to disappear so completely. Maybe they'd run straight through the building and out the other side. If so, they could be anywhere. "Sunuvabitch," he muttered.

"You know, this thing isn't my fault," Pavel whispered. "I wanted to tell someone. Dad wouldn't let me."

"You always do what your father wants?" Rurik said .

"I do when he reminds me every day that I killed my mother," Pavel said through clenched teeth.

Rurik faced Pavel, brows lifting in disbelief. "I remember her passing, but that was when I was a child. You must've been a baby. How was that your fault?"

"My blood. It's the wrong type. She got sick when she got pregnant, and then died when I was born... And no one lets me forget it."

Rurik found that hard to believe. Dmitry treated his sons the same. Maybe Pavel's own feeling of guilt made him imagine what others were thinking.

Huh. The idea expanded in his mind, creating a surprising revelation. Maybe if you felt one way about yourself, it was easy to imagine everyone felt that way, too.

The door squeaked behind them. Rurik wheeled around, shining his light on the doorway, expecting to see someone standing there.

No one. The door remained closed. But the squeak came again. And again.

A thin whisper drifted through the door. "Hold the light up. No, like this." In Romanian.

Rurik curled his hand over the phone, blocking its light. Sure enough, a dim glow showed beneath the door. It wasn't Anushka. She spoke Russian. It might be the blond woman with her.

The small squeaks resumed. It sounded like a rusty screw being turned.

He put his mouth near the wood and said in Romanian, "Hey! Is someone in there?"

A sudden scrape. Then the light vanished, replaced by complete silence.

Rurik glanced at Pavel, whose eyes shone wide in the dark.

"Anushka?" Rurik said in Russian. "It's Rurik and Pavel. Your mother sent us to find you. Are you in there?"

"Yes! Yes!" The cries flew out on the wings of sobs. "Please help!"

Rurik closed his eyes for a second, thanking God. "Move back from the door. I'll break it down." He turned to Pavel. "This'll be loud. Keep a good watch behind us." He stepped back a pace. Hitting the door with his shoulder was out. His ribs were too damaged. But his feet still worked. He took a good breath before slamming his boot into the wood beneath the lock.

The door crashed open. A small figure burst from the room and wrapped her arms around Rurik's hips.

"Rurik! I want to go home now. Please!" Tears wet Anushka's cheeks.

Another figure appeared in the doorway. The phone light revealed a young blond girl with brilliant blue eyes. His heart stuttered. It was *her*. The bride. The one who'd told him to look in the RV.

The one who hadn't been afraid to gaze on his mangled face.

And now, she was doing it again. Looking up at him, without horror or pity. In fact, she was beaming.

"It's you!" she exclaimed. "Thank you!" Such relief flowed across her features that he couldn't hide an answering grin.

Footsteps thudded down the hall behind them.

Rurik pivoted, stepping in front of the girls.

Viktor charged around the corner, his rifle at the ready.

"It's just us!" Pavel held up a palm. "Don't shoot. I found her!"

Sure you did, thought Rurik. "We've got them, but we haven't seen Zora. You?"

"No," Viktor said. "I heard the crash and got worried." He peered around Rurik's side and smiled at Anushka. "Don't worry, little one. We're getting you out of here now." He reversed his steps and led the group back down the hallway.

When they reached the entrance to the factory floor, a voice boomed, "Hold it right there, boys. You can't leave just yet."

With a microphone or without, the ringmaster's stentorian tones were unmistakable.

Rurik scanned the dimness, looking for any sign of Alyosha.

"It seems you have something that belongs to me. Two things, really. I'm a reasonable man. You wouldn't leave without compensation."

Rurik's gaze bored into every shadow, but the voice seemed to come from all around.

"We're not interested," Viktor said. "The girls are coming with us."

"But you haven't heard my offer. I know Pavel will be interested. And Dmitry, too. Twenty thousand Euros. And all you have to do is walk away."

"No!" Rurik shouted.

"Don't be rash, Rurik. You haven't heard my final offer yet." Alyosha's voice turned dark with menace. "You take the twenty thousand and leave the girls to me. Or none of you are getting out of here alive."

CHAPTER TWENTY-SIX

Sylvie
Bājenie, Romania

*There was once a bloodwalker whose village was
inundated by a flood.
Many perished. With her neighbors hurt or mourning, her
strong sense of
duty forced her to begin recovering bodies herself. One
was lodged in a
tree. Despite her long skirt and vertigo, she climbed the
tree and pulled
him loose. The branch cracked. She and he crashed to the
ground
at the same time. He was no worse for wear. She broke
her back.
The villagers found her a week later, dead from exposure.
A sense of duty is a virtue. Foolhardiness is not.*
~ The Bloodwalker's Book

Sylvie ran down the dark hallway following her rescuers. The big scarred man—Anushka called him Rurik—stopped short, and she thumped into his back. All three men bunched up in the corridor entrance.

From somewhere on the dark factory floor, Alyosha shouted. She couldn't understand his words, but Rurik said "*Nyet!*" in an angry voice.

Sylvie sidestepped, trying to see around him. The route to the exit looked clear. Yet the men still shouted back and forth. Wasting time. Aunt Cosmina or Zora could show up any second!

She clutched Rurik's sleeve. "We have to go," she whispered.

"Stay back," he said, not even looking at her.

The arguing continued. Unbelievable. Why were they even listening to the old man? They had rifles...at least, two of them did. And Alyosha hadn't been armed when she saw him in the van.

But Alyosha was Zorka. In fact, all her rescuers were Zorka. Circus people. Untrustworthy.

A trickle of suspicion became a flood when she glanced at the young rifleman beside her and suddenly recognized him.

The thief from the RV! He'd stolen the towels and makeup and fought with her for her suitcase.

She flinched back, thumping into the hard bricks of the hallway.

Was he just a thief—or was he helping the killers?

What if the men weren't really rescuing her at all? What if they were just luring her out and planned to hand her over to Alyosha or Zora?

Thunder rumbled. Answering shivers ran down her back, her limbs rattling together like dice in a cup.

All the Zorka could be in it together. The men trapping and killing children. Then Zora eating them to sustain her new physique. And Alyosha—so jovial and normal seeming—was the worst of all. He'd kill anyone who got in the way.

Like her poor mother.

Her eyes blurred with tears, but she scrubbed the back of her hand across them. No time to mourn. Time to act.

Flush against the wall, Sylvie squeezed past the men and poked her head out of the corridor. On her right, the collapsed wall lay only thirty yards away. No one blocked it. She reached back, her questing fingers grabbed onto Anushka's small, cold hand.

A woman's voice sounded from her other side.

Sylvie's gaze snapped left.

Three figures approached from the rear of the factory, fifty yards away. Too dark to make out who. No time to wait and see.

Just as she tensed, ready to make a dash for it, lightning speared down from the clouds. The factory floor lit up as if by floodlights.

Three people stood out in bold relief at the rear of the factory. Two men carried rifles, wearing black like the ones next to her.

The other was Aunt Cosmina.

The men walked beside the old bloodwalker as if they knew her. As if they were friends.

The circus people *were* all in it together. And they were walking straight toward the hallway—toward her and Anushka.

Her fingers clamped tighter on Anushka's hand. No time to lose.

She took off, pulling the girl along with her.

The collapsed wall and the streetlamps beckoned. Plans raced through her mind.

Outside, she'd find a car. Aunt Cosmina must have one nearby. The men must have one, too. Or maybe the keys were still in Alyosha's van. As soon as Sylvie found a vehicle with keys, she'd jam the accelerator to the floor, speed out of the horrible town, and never look back.

Halfway to the collapsed wall, a figure burst out from behind a pillar.

"She's mine!" Zora planted herself between the girls and the opening. Streetlamps outlined her grotesque silhouette. Her deep voice scraped her throat like a meat grinder. "You're more trouble than you're worth, little bloodwalker. I knew I smelled death on you! But it's going to be your own death." She lurched forward.

Gunshots rang out. Anushka screamed.

Sylvie dropped into a squat, hauling Anushka down with her.

After only a few steps, Zora fell to her knees and toppled forward.

Relief streamed through Sylvie. The horrible old bloodwalker was dead.

Then Zora's hands pressed against the concrete. Slowly, she began climbing to her feet.

Sylvie's breath turned ragged. Staying in a crouch, she turned and scuttled back the way she'd come, Anushka in tow.

The thief from the RV and the older man aimed their rifles over her head.

She swerved around them as they fired, the explosions deafening. Anushka's nails dug into Sylvie's palm, almost drawing blood.

Rurik appeared at her shoulder. "Get inside!" Another pair of shots shattered the gloom as he latched onto her arm and pulled her toward the corridor.

Anushka broke away. The little girl covered her ears and ducked her head. A scream boiled from her throat, loud as a siren. She reeled away from the shooting toward the rear of the factory—where Aunt Cosmina and the other two men were.

Anushka was running straight into the arms of her enemies.

"No!" Sylvie broke Rurik's hold. Adrenaline surging, she flew across the floor and caught Anushka before she got far, wrapping her arms around the girl and propelling her toward the relative safety of the wall.

"Look at me!" Zora's terrifying bellow resounded from the entrance. She threw her arms wide. "Look at me! You cannot kill me with little pieces of metal. I'm stronger than metal!"

Lightning flashed. The fiery incandescence revealed just what Zora had become.

Gray skin stretched drum-head tight over a body that was broader and thicker than any man's. Her domed skull bulged. A bullet glinted, jutting from her forehead, the wound leaking blood. Her rounded chest protruded outward beneath wide collarbones. The T-shirt covering it had bullet holes in it, too. From her burly shoulders to her heavy legs, every bone in her body seemed double or triple normal thickness. It was as if she was wearing a suit of armor on the *inside* of her skin.

The woman thumped her chest with her fist. "Bone plates. This is what bloodwalkers can become—supermen—ten times stronger than any of you!"

The RV thief lost his nerve. His gun shook, and the muzzle lowered. But the tall man next to him sighted down his rifle barrel and fired twice.

Zora staggered backward but didn't go down.

From the middle of the factory floor, a dark shadow separated itself from a pillar. With a *shriiingg* like a broken guitar string, he loosed something that streaked through the air. Metal glinted for a split second. With a cry, the man who'd fired fell backward. A large dagger stuck out from his stomach.

Sylvie's eyes bulged. The dagger's size and shape looked just like the one that killed Liana.

Aunt Cosmina hinted that Alyosha was good with knives, but Sylvie never imagined he could throw them with such deadly force. That was how Ada died, too—struck by a knife thrown hard enough to pierce her skull.

"Uncle Viktor!" the RV thief shouted. "Rurik, help!" He and Rurik grabbed the wounded man's shoulders and dragged him into the hallway.

A shouted curse rang out from behind Sylvie.

One of the riflemen with Aunt Cosmina raised his gun and aimed at Zora.

Another dagger erupted from the blackness. It spun across the factory with a high-pitched whine and slammed into the man's chest. He stumbled back a few steps and looked down at the knife, puzzled, as if unable to fathom what it was. Slowly, his knees buckled. He fell to the concrete.

The younger man with him shouldered his gun. Before he could fire, Aunt Cosmina lifted her cane and smashed it into his head. He crumpled.Aunt Cosmina jumped over the fallen man. With no sign of a limp, she barreled toward where Sylvie and Anushka cowered against the wall.

Sylvie jumped up, but couldn't get Anushka to her feet before the old woman caught them.

Digging one hand into Sylvie's dress-front and the other grasping the little girl's arm, Aunt Cosmina called out, "I have them, Zora! You see? I'd never let you down."

Sylvie struggled, but the fat bloodwalker was stronger than she looked.

"But I get a part!" Aunt Cosmina yelled. "This time, I want my full share!"

Sylvie drew back a fist, and with all her strength, she

belted the old lady in the face.

Aunt Cosmina stumbled back. Blood trickled from her mouth. She coughed. A red-stained tooth spattered onto the ground. "You *bitch!*" she screamed. Curling her fingers into claws, she stormed toward Sylvie.

But a meaty hand landed on her shoulder and wrenched her around.

Rurik glared at the old bloodwalker. "I hate to hit a woman, but..." He slugged her.

She flew ten feet across the floor. Her chunky body thwacked the concrete and rolled to a stop.

Sylvie expected her to jump back up, but apparently, she wasn't a Super-bloodwalker yet. Maybe Zora kept the special elixir to herself.

Rurik stepped toward Sylvie. "Get in the hallway. We'll protect—"

A metal pipe whizzed through the air behind him and smashed into his skull.

He staggered sideways and fell to one knee.

In the murky light, Zora relaxed her grip on the pipe and grinned. Oversized teeth gleamed in her gray face. She advanced on him and raised the pipe again.

Sylvie winced, unable to look. Without Rurik, there'd be no one to help her and Anushka. She had to get away. Right now. "Anushka?"

The little girl was gone.

Sylvie's gaze darted around her. No glimmer of blond hair or pale face. At the back of the factory, the two riflemen lay where they'd fallen, one struck by a dagger, the other out cold from Aunt Cosmina's cane.

On the other side, the RV thief hid in the hallway with the wounded man.

No Anushka.

If she ran onto the factory floor, Alyosha would catch her. Sylvie sprang away from the wall but made it only two steps when a muffled whimpering halted her.

It came from above. She whirled and looked up.

Hanging twenty feet in the air, Anushka clung to a metal ladder fastened to the wall.

Sylvie gasped. What was the girl thinking? Who ran *up*

to get away?

The child's choked sobs answered her—Anushka hadn't been thinking. She'd seen death on all sides and panicked. But she couldn't have chosen a worse spot. There weren't any floors above them to hide on, just open space. Flickers of lightning revealed only a web of steel beams. Nowhere to go.

A glance over Sylvie's shoulder showed Rurik hadn't been so easy to kill. The huge man regained his footing. He warded off another blow from the pipe, but he swayed drunkenly, unable to attack Zora back.

"Anushka," Sylvie called. "Come down!"

Thunder roared, and the sobs got louder. The little girl had her arms wrapped around the rungs like tree roots.

With no choice, Sylvie gathered up her long skirt and began to climb. If she could bring Anushka down quick enough, they could still escape while Zora was distracted.

The ladder rungs, corroded with rust, scraped Sylvie's palms. The fabric of her skirt kept snagging on rough patches and tangling with her feet. Despite how many times she yanked her skirt loose, climbing proved to be impossible. In desperation, she hiked the hem all the way up and grabbed it in her teeth. Skirt above her knees, she raced up to Anushka and had almost gotten her loose when the little girl looked below and shrieked.

Zora. The deformed monster scaled the ladder. Her bizarre legs angled knees-out, like a giant toad. She tipped her head back and bared her teeth in a wicked smile. "There isn't anywhere to go, my little darlings. Not anywhere that Zora cannot catch you!"

Anushka scrambled farther up the ladder.

Black Plague take it! Whether wounded or dead, Rurik hadn't won the battle with Zora. Now only Sylvie was left to protect them. Going higher was foolish, but staying and fighting on the ladder was more risky.

She climbed. Rung after rung flashed past. Her breaths came in urgent pants, half-smothered by the wool skirt clenched in her teeth.

Brilliant lightning flashes lit up the sky. Desperate for an escape route, Sylvie peered around.

Iron girders connected to the wall next to the ladder, twice—at forty feet up and seventy feet up. But the beams were only about eight inches wide. Perhaps she and Anushka could crawl out onto one. Then they'd have a chance to make it across the huge factory to the opposite wall where there was probably another ladder.

Probably...

Anushka passed the first beam at the forty-foot mark and kept going.

Damn! Even worse, Zora was climbing the ladder faster than Sylvie expected.

But could her hulking, misshapen body balance on a girder?

Sylvie clambered up the ladder as fast as she could. Storm gusts whipped her hair into her face, ripped at her clothes, and forced tears from her eyes.

The ladder ended just above the second beam. No choice. Sylvie and Anushka would have to go out onto the highest girder.

From there, they'd have to make it across.

And hope Zora couldn't follow.

CHAPTER TWENTY-SEVEN

Rurik
Bājenie, Romania

Rurik floated in an ocean of silence and solitude.

Someone shook him, and an angry whirlpool swept him upward.

He struggled against it, but the shaking continued.

He finally slivered an eye open.

A figure beside him rippled as if still underwater. Pavel? Yes, Pavel. Why would Pavel be in his RV? Rurik tried to sit up, but pain smashed through him, all his nerves ramming so many alarm messages into his brain he almost passed out again.

"Come on! Snap out of it!" Pavel's gaze flicked right and left, and he hunched closer. "Only the two of us are left. If you take a rifle, maybe we can shoot our way clear."

Only two of them? That sounded wrong. Rurik sat up more slowly this time. Dizziness swamped him. He clenched his teeth against nausea churning in his belly. Deep breaths helped, and slowly, details came into focus around him.

Fifteen yards away, Dmitry and Anatoly sprawled under a mountain.

What? Rurik rubbed his eyes. No mountain, just the big stack of pallets. Beside it, the two Markarovs lay, unmoving. A dagger gleamed dully from Dmitry's chest. He wouldn't be getting up. Anatoly, dead too? Maybe. Rurik couldn't see a dagger though.

No one else around. Not Zora or Alyosha. Not even the old woman he'd knocked out.

The girls! He'd been trying to protect them. Where were they?

237

If the world would stop spinning, he'd get up and find them. He'd promised to get them to safety, and by God, he was going to do it.

But his body wouldn't cooperate. A jackhammer pounded on his skull. His stomach swirled one too many times. He leaned over and threw up.

"Come on!" Pavel hissed. "We gotta get back to the hallway!"

"Where are th-the girlsh?" His jaw felt like he'd been kicked by a mule.

"I'll only answer if you get up. *Now!*"

With Pavel's help, Rurik rose and limped to the corridor.

Inside, Viktor lay on his back. "You look like shit," he said to Rurik.

"You're no b-beauty contest winner, old man."

Viktor chuckled, but a wet cough replaced it. A gray hue crept over his face. His body shivered in the dimness. The dagger still protruded from his abdomen. Only a hospital could remove it safely.

They needed to get to the pickup. But first, they had to find everyone.

"The girls...not with you?" Rurik said to Pavel.

The kid shrugged.

Had Zora and Alyosha gotten them? Rurik's hand shot out and grabbed Pavel's shirtfront, dragging him nose to nose. "Where are they?"

"Take it easy." Pavel squirmed backward. "They're safe."

"Safe whe..." Pain rocketed through Rurik's skull. Spots floated in his vision. He staggered against the wall. Pavel slipped away like a greased eel. Rurik bent his head forward, rubbing his fingers across his sticky scalp. A lump the size of a walnut protruded from the back of his head. Behind his ear, blood ran from a long, deep cut. Both he and Viktor needed a hospital. "Shit. Didn't know a pipe could cut through skin."

"The bitch with the pipe didn't get you," Pavel said. "Alyosha threw another dagger. Pure luck you turned your head and it glanced off. Musta packed a wallop, though, 'cause you went down like a log."

Alyosha. A heaviness crushed Rurik's chest that had

nothing to do with his injuries. After the years they'd spent together, the idea that Alyosha could kill him without a second thought hurt more than any wound.

He pushed away from the wall. No time for self-pitying bullshit. Alyosha wanted them dead? Okay. The war was on.

"Where are the girls?" Rurik hoped a menacing glare would compensate for his slurred speech and the fact he was now seeing two Pavels. "Don't make me come over there and kick your ass."

"Whoa." Pavel held up a palm—two palms in Rurik's skewed vision. "I told you they were safe. From Zora anyway. After you got knocked out, Zora woke up that fat lady, sent her running outside. Then she went up the ladder."

"The what?" That ladder led to the rafters. Why would Zora go up there?

Pavel rolled his eyes. "For some stupid reason, Anushka and that blond woman went up a service ladder on the wall. Zora went after them."

Rurik's heart froze mid beat. "*What?!* Are they still up there?"

"The girls got to the top and crawled out on a beam. But don't worry." Pavel waved a dismissive hand. "They're safe. Zora can't get them. She's too big to fit on those girders. She'd fall."

"You're wrong." Rurik knew something Pavel didn't. People with dense, oversized bones were incredibly stable. Large body mass, low center of gravity. Immovable as bedrock.

"Naw." Pavel paced to the end of the hallway and peered up. "Like I said, she couldn't... Oh, shit."

Rurik lumbered forward and pushed past Pavel, his gaze zipping up the ladder. No light reached the rafters seventy feet up, but lightning flickered behind the clouds, revealing silhouettes.

On the topmost beam, he picked out two small forms. The girls cowered at an intersection where two horizontal girders crossed, and a vertical support beam thrust up between them. They hugged the upright one, apparently too scared to go farther.

A bulky shape inched out from the ladder. Zora crouched on the metal beam, walking on all fours, moving her hands forward to grip and then sliding her feet after. She advanced slowly, but once she got used to it, she'd speed up. Then she'd get the girls.

Lightning sliced through the air. Rurik flinched back. The bolt streaked over the factory and slammed into a streetlamp outside. Sparks and glass exploded, showering onto the road. Thunder crashed as if giants were applauding the show.

The sounds pierced Rurik's aching skull. Every instinct told him to stay inside the hallway. Instead, he lunged onto the factory floor and leaped onto the ladder.

With every rung he grabbed, his broken fingers screamed in pain. With every step, his pounding head, bruised ribs, and cut scalp yammered for him to stop.

Yet the physical pain paled next to the fear. Being up high and getting struck by lightning was his worst nightmare.

At least until now. Watching the girls fight with Zora and maybe fall to their deaths while knowing he'd done nothing to help them would be far worse.

If he didn't have the balls to do something, if he stayed on the ground like a coward, he'd rather be dead anyway.

The higher he climbed, the more the wind whipped at him, trying to pry him from the ladder.

His foot missed a rung.

He fell, scrabbling for a hold. His arms locked around the ladder. He clung, his heart hammering, and made the mistake of looking down.

The dark factory floor seemed to gape like an open mouth, waiting for him to fall into it, and it would swallow him straight to hell.

Outside, the streetlamp continued to burn, its live wires sparking and spitting. White spots danced in Rurik's eyes. Vertigo hit him.

A scream jerked his attention up, and he tore his gaze away from the blaze. The chaotic flickers of electricity illuminated a grim scene above.

Zora was halfway to the girls.

The blond woman had seen her and was trying to make Anushka let go of the upright and brave the next length of girder. The child wailed and held on tighter than ever.

Planting his feet on the rungs, Rurik forced himself to climb.

When he reached the top, he hooked an elbow around the last rung and stripped off his boots. Something he'd learned from tightrope walkers and slack-liners. They needed to feel the surface for balance.

He braced himself and stepped onto the girder.

As if laughing at his foolish decision, lightning bolts speared from the clouds in rapid succession. An acrid odor burned the air.

The storm had engulfed the entire plateau. The derelict factory was the highest structure for miles, its beams sure to attract strikes.

He refused to think about it.

His toes curled over the edges of the beam. He sank into a crouch, his arms out for balance. Wind battered him. He slid one foot forward and pulled the other up behind.

Zora still clutched the metal, moving on all fours.

Staying upright, he'd make better time. He'd get to her before she got to the girls.

Unless he fell.

He pushed forward, narrowing the gap between them. He had the element of surprise. She couldn't hear him over the storm. When he reached her, there'd be no mercy— he'd push her off.

He was barely three yards from her back when she suddenly rose up.

Her head cocked to the side. On her almost bald skull, wisps of gray hair as flimsy as cobwebs twisted in the wind. "I smell broken bones. And delicious osteoblasts trying to repair them." She looked over her shoulder. Her deep-set eyes blazed when she spied Rurik. "Your bones are almost as good as the children's. I wonder how they'll taste when I lick the marrow clean." She pivoted to face him. A wind gust struck her, and she wavered. Her arms flailed.

With the smallest push, she'd be over the side.

Rurik stepped forward.

Lightning hit a girder on the other side of the factory. Fire erupted. Molten metal spat out like comet tails. The factory lit up under the blast of electricity.

Rurik cringed. Lost his balance. He wobbled above empty space. One arm shot down, fingers clawing for purchase. He closed his hand around the edge of the beam.

Anchored in place, his mind whirred in reverse, rewinding back to the brilliant flash, and what he'd seen below as he lost his balance.

Very near where the girls were, the huge pile of pallets sat on the floor. Big enough to land on, rotten enough to give way and cushion a fall.

Rurik had lost fights to Zora already. In his present condition, he had to accept he might not win this one. If anything happened to him, he owed the girls their chance at freedom.

"Anushka!" he shouted in Russian. "You must be a big girl now. Like a great tightrope walker. Take the beam that goes to the back of the building. Halfway, you can jump down. Wait for the lightning. You'll see a big brown hill on the floor. It will catch you—just like the net for the trapeze shows. You'll be okay. I promise." If praying like hell counted as a promise. He repeated the instructions in Romanian.

Zora glowered. "You'd best worry about yourself, Rurik. Lightning seeks you out like a lover." She edged forward, her face pulling into a snarl. "It's the only thing that'll have you. Being up here is tempting fate." Her voice deepened into an imperious tone. "You'll be struck, Rurik. The lightning's third try will succeed. You will die."

Something about the confidence and wickedness of her voice burrowed into his psyche. A shiver stole over him. Without thinking, he shuffled backward a step.

She accelerated, closing the gap.

He sank into a deeper crouch.

Her hand darted out swifter than a striking snake. She shoved him off the edge.

His feet slipped one direction, but his center of gravity pulled his chest the other. He slammed belly first into the beam, folding over it like a dishrag. But his heavy legs weighed him down. He slid, the beam scraping up his chest. His feet pedaled empty air. At the last second, his hands grasped the girder.

He hung suspended seventy feet above the factory floor.

Zora peered down at him. "I hate to lose your delicious marrow, but I know Pavel and Anatoly are still alive. They're younger than you. Once their bones are broken and begin to repair themselves, they'll make a great meal."

The woman was as twisted inside as out.

He'd been a fool for imagining himself as a monster for so many years. Yes, monsters existed. But *he* wasn't one of them.

The electrical fire on the street flared up, and his eyes pierced the darkness, searching for the girls.

The older one had straddled the beam that crossed to the back of the factory. She used her hands to grip in front and slide her butt along. Clever. And Anushka grew brave enough to follow. She was a true circus girl. A trouper. If they could just make it twenty feet, the giant mound of pallets would be right under them.

Meanwhile, he had to buy them time. Tightening all his muscles, he began to pull himself up. His biceps and deltoids burned. He sucked in deep breaths, feeding oxygen to his straining muscles. His body inched upward.

A blow hammered his knuckles. He grunted as the bones crunched.

Above him, Zora raised her anvil-like fist and clubbed his hand again.

Pain exploded in his already damaged fingers. His hand went numb. His grip loosened. His fingers slipped off the girder. He swung sideways, hanging by one arm.

"If it's any consolation, the drop onto concrete will probably kill you instantly," Zora said. "But maybe your osteoblasts can be saved if I chop you up and freeze you quick enough."

He kicked desperately. Something brushed his legs, clanking and rattling. The chains. Fastened to this part of the beam were thick chains with hooks.

His only hope was to grab onto them and hope they

were well anchored.

Lightning flashed. His gaze flew to the girls.

They'd made it to the middle. Joining hands, they nodded together as if counting. Then they tipped off the side and plunged straight down.

A crash reverberated through the building as the wood exploded with the impact.

Rurik scanned the pile's wreckage.

There! The transformer fire illuminated the girls among the jumbled pallets. They sat up and began climbing out.

He laughed in a crazed moment of relief.

Zora screamed in rage. "You bastard! They were mine!" She straightened, jerked her leg up, and stomped on his hand.

He gritted his teeth against the torment. His free arm waved through the air, feeling for the chains. He caught the rusty links, but his broken fingers refused to close around them. He scissored his legs, struggling to catch the chain between them.

One ankle met metal, and he swept it in a circle, trying to wrap the chain around it. Almost. No. Lost it. Again—

The world exploded.

Everything around him blazed white.

In the second before the flash blinded him, he saw Zora struck. Her body pulsed with a million volts of electricity.

Her mouth wrenched open in a scream. Fire shot out between her gaping lips.

As the lightning surged into the metal girder and sped through the structure, it passed into Rurik.

Zora and Rurik toppled into space.

CHAPTER TWENTY-EIGHT

Sylvie
Bājenie, Romania

*In the time of the Black Plague, the number of dead bodies
often became so great that they were burned instead of
buried.*
*Some families couldn't accept the necessity. They hid their
dead in closets, attic rooms, cellars, or below baseboards.
They said it was out of love—but it was selfishness.
They paid for it. The sickness claimed them, and
they joined their loved ones in death.*
~ The Bloodwalker's Book

Sylvie squirmed across the mound of pallets on her belly,
the wood shifting and creaking ominously under her.

Anushka, smaller and lighter, reached the edge and
slid out of sight while Sylvie crawled slowly, feeling the
pile shudder every time she placed a palm or knee on the
rotten boards. With a sudden crack, the boards splintered.
Her hands and knees plunged through, landing on slime-
covered planks below.

Mold and mildew oozed between her fingers. Farther
down, she felt feathered skeletons, sitting in a soup of
decayed flesh. Just like when she prepared Mr. Movilă's
body after he'd spent a week in the lake. Loose as an
over-boiled chicken, his flesh practically fell off his bones.
But he never smelled as bad as the mildew and powerful
ammonia odor that wafted up from the rotted woodpile.

Sylvie withdrew her hands , dug her fingers into the
flaking wood in front of her, and pulled herself out of the
hole. Flattened on her belly like someone on thin ice, she
inched her way to the edge of the pile and swung her legs

over. From a few yards below, Anushka's pale face peered up from the shadows. Sylvie gathered her courage to jump when a small landslide broke free under her, sending her hurtling down. She hit the concrete floor and sprawled in a heap of kindling.

A large hand closed on her wrist.

She jerked away, her eyes straining in the darkness. If Alyosha caught her, she was as good as dead.

But the man was a stranger and wore black, like the other riflemen.

Anushka stood at his side. "Anatoly." She pointed at him, nodding. "*Thevareesh.*"

Sylvie didn't know the word, but since Anushka wasn't running away shrieking, he was probably okay. Sylvie extended her hand, and he pulled her up from the debris.

Suddenly, an explosion rocked the factory. Burning embers showered onto the floor at her feet. She jumped back, her gaze flying to the high girders.

Three stories up, electricity sparked and sizzled on the metal. Two shapes glowed inside the white fire. Rurik and Zora! One stood atop the beam, the other hung beneath, but it was too bright for Sylvie to tell who was who.

The electrical fire sputtered out—and both people fell.

A roar of thunder swallowed Sylvie's horrified shriek.

Halfway to the floor, one of the bodies stopped—and hung in midair as if by magic.

Closer scrutiny and another lightning flash revealed a chain had wrapped around the person's ankle, tethering them to the girder.

Sylvie made out jeans and a checkered shirt. Rurik! Just as she thanked heaven he was safe—the chain snapped.

Rurik plummeted to the factory floor.

At the last second, Sylvie turned away. Death didn't scare her, but Rurik was different. He'd given her and Anushka time to get off the beams. He'd saved them from Zora. All at the expense of his own escape.

He was a great man. She didn't want to look at his corpse.

Anushka and Anatoly rushed past her to the two bodies lying atop one another on the concrete. Anatoly dragged

Rurik's off, kneeled beside it, and listened to his chest. With a curse, he began pounding his fist onto Rurik's breastbone.

Sylvie edged closer, but shied away and paced the floor, her woolen dress bunched inside curled fingers. What could she do? She didn't know CPR.

Smoke curled through the air like questing serpent. The odor of burned flesh singed Sylvie's nose, growing stronger.

She stopped, her gaze creeping to the body of Zora.

The woman would never surrender to death willingly. She could rise any second, like some demonic phoenix.

But the once mighty bloodwalker lay with her legs twisted, her body smashed and broken. Splintered ends of her caved-in ribs jutted out the sides of her smoldering T-shirt. Her deformed skull had shattered. The skin of her face was burned black and seared onto her blocky cheekbones. Wisps of smoke drifted from her open mouth.

She looked as if a building had fallen on her.

When the chain broke, Rurik fell forty feet and landed on top of her. Her giant plates of bone and muscle had cushioned his fall as much as the pile of wood had cushioned Sylvie and Anushka, but his weight had crushed her like a tin can.

Zora was dead. And it was because of a man who now lay fighting for his life.

Ashamed of her squeamishness, Sylvie darted over and kneeled across from Anatoly. She took one of Rurik's hands in hers.

It wasn't cold. There was still a chance.

As Anatoly tried to revive Rurik, she closed her eyes and wished Zora's curse died with her. Death *had* followed Sylvie, taking Ada, Liana, and Miron.

But not Rurik. Please not him, too.

Two people stumbled up to them. The RV Thief, supporting an older man, the hilt of a dagger protruding from his abdomen. His chalky skin stood out in the dark, and shivers quaked his shoulders. If he went into shock, death wouldn't be far behind.

The RV Thief exchanged heated words with Anatoly

in Russian. Anatoly called him Pavel, and the two kept repeating one word she knew—"auto."

Auto meant they had a way out of the horrible place. Alyosha and Aunt Cosmina still lurked somewhere. Escaping before they came back was crucial.

But Rurik deserved a chance. Every moment they waited could save his life.

She squeezed Rurik's hand and bent her head to his ear. "You saved me," she whispered. "Don't let the lightning win. You're tougher than that. A true hero."

A second later, Rurik coughed and sputtered. His eyes cracked opened. His bleary gaze drifted across her. "Angel," he breathed.

She shook her head, her cheeks heating. Considering her disaster-filled life, an angel was the last thing she was. "I'm just Sylvie."

Anatoly gripped Rurik's shoulder and spewed a bunch of Russian at him, fast and urgent. After feeling Rurik's legs, hips, and arms, he nodded toward the exit.

Rurik struggled to push himself into a sitting position. His face went white, pain written in every taut line. He sent Anushka to recover his boots from under the ladder, and then it took both Anatoly and Sylvie to help the big man up.

The group set off toward the collapsed wall.

Frantic to leave the factory and the whole evil town behind, Sylvie tried to hurry them along, but Rurik limped and the wounded man could barely shuffle. When they passed the hallway, she dashed in to pick up her bloodwalker's bag where it had fallen, forgotten, in her mad dash to escape.

Stepping back onto the factory floor, she came face to face with a bloodwalker—one even more deformed and over-developed than Zora.

The woman leaned toward her, the skin of her face parchment thin, and she sniffed. "Young. Fresh," she said in a gravelly voice. "No osteoblasts, but we'll fix that."

With a cry of terror, Sylvie dashed around her and chased after the group.

They'd only made it halfway to the exit when they'd

been stopped.

Five figures stood on the tumbled-down bricks of the opening. The glow from the streetlamps emphasized their grotesque forms. Postures curved. Arms hanging to the knees. Heads cocked sideways or bent low in front of hunched backs. Crooked spines, wide hips, uneven legs. They were just like Zora—only bigger.

Anatoly and Pavel had their rifles up, pointing at the new bloodwalkers. They said something in Russian, their harsh words sounding like a threat.

Someone chuckled near Sylvie's ear.

She spun. The one from the hallway leered at her.

"Little children playing with toy guns... But the same lead that poisons this place feeds us its strength. We have no fear of bullets."

Sylvie retreated until she backed into Rurik and Anushka. She reached for the girl's hand.

"Zora?" Alyosha rushed into the factory, stumbling onto the mound of bricks. His hair stuck out from his head in wild tufts. He pushed between the five creatures and called for his wife again and again. His voice grew higher and more hysterical with every try. Finally, he shouted at Rurik. "Where is she?"

Rurik glowered at the old man and remained silent.

Then Pavel spat out a line in Russian and thrust his chin over his shoulder to where the body lay.

Alyosha bolted to his wife. At her side, his legs gave way. He dropped to his knees. His hands poked and prodded the still form. He picked up one of her hands and stroked it. His lips repeated her name, but this time, his voice grew quieter with every questioning plea. Finally, he sat back on his haunches. He threw back his head. A moan ripped from his throat. Pure desolation. A wolf howling at the moon at the loss of his mate.

Sylvie shivered, but a warm hand closed overtop of hers.

Rurik leaned close. "We'll fight them. Do as much damage as possible. You take Anushka and run. The car's at the entrance to town. The keys are in it. Don't stop. Don't look back."

"You'll follow?" She searched for hope in his eyes but

found none, and then she understood. He and the men would distract the bloodwalkers even if they had no chance of winning, even if they were captured or killed. It would be Sylvie and Anushka's only chance to escape.

"Youuu!" Alyosha's word seethed with hatred, his gaze locked on Rurik. "You did this. You couldn't let it alone. You followed us here. The lightning came seeking *you*, not her. You're the one who deserves to die." Jerking a dagger from a bandolier across his chest, he drew it back and cocked it over his shoulder.

"Stop!" The word bellowed across the factory, echoing with such power the walls trembled. Bricks fractured. Mortar dust spurted into the air.

Vibrations came up through the floor, jarring Sylvie's legs.

Pavel shook his head and pawed at his ear.

Alyosha recoiled and lost his grip on the knife. It clattered to the ground.

At the rear of the factory, three figures shambled from the dimness. Their heads dipped before bent backs. Their barrel chests were so enormous their arms couldn't hang straight down but stuck out like crab legs. They moved in a bizarre side-to-side motion as if all their bones had fused together.

Their strange gait would almost have been funny, but when they drew closer, the light shone on their faces—and they had none.

Gooseflesh rippled up Sylvie's arms.

The creatures' foreheads had grown so large that they covered their eye sockets and most of the nose. Their mouths and nostrils were mere slits, like a lizard's. Under bald scalps, their malformed craniums bulged with crags and lumps.

"We do not simply kill here," the one in the center said in a bass voice so deep it sounded male. "If any had a right to, it would be me. Zora was my daughter, but she was spoiled and foolish. She risked too much by living in the outside world. And she was selfish with her victims. Never shared. Not even when she was a little girl."

The bloodwalker beside Sylvie sniggered.

Zora's mother jerked her flat face in the direction of the sound.

The laughter cut off, and the bloodwalker shuffled a few steps back, head bowing.

"I am Klavdia. I don't want harm to come to any of you." Zora's mother paused. An inhale whistled through the slits of her nose. "But since the days of the great starvation in the Ukraine, survival has always come first. You *will* die, but be kept alive long enough to feed the community. Get their weapons!" she ordered.

The bloodwalker beside Sylvie lunged and snatched the rifle from Anatoly's hands before he could react.

From the entrance, two bloodwalkers darted in and grabbed Pavel's gun. He fought for it. An attacker clubbed him across the face. He reeled backward.

In the scuffle, Pavel lost his hold on the wounded man with the dagger in his belly. With a feeble cry, the man sank to the ground.

Both Pavel and Anatoly leaped at their attackersand fought to reclaim their weapons.

Rurik pressed Sylvie's hand. "Now!"

She pulled Anushka closer, her gaze racing over the factory. Three bloodwalkers still blocked the exit. Too many. She and Anushka would be caught. Maybe she could make it past the blind ones. There had to be an exit behind them somewhere.

Just as she got ready to bolt, a sudden movement in her periphery sent alarm bells zinging through her.

It was Alyosha. His baleful glare at Rurik hardened into something deadlier. Disregarding Klavdia's order, he whipped another knife from its sheath and stepped forward, his gaze lasering into Rurik's, his face twisting in malevolent determination. He drew back, poised to throw.

Without hesitation, Rurik lurched in front of Sylvie, ready to take the knife aimed at him.

CHAPTER TWENTY-NINE

Rurik
Bājenie, Romania

Rurik faced down Alyosha, the naked hatred in the ringmaster's eyes biting into him like an arctic wind. He jerked his arms up to block his chest but knew it left other targets—neck, head, belly—open to a strike. After surviving the lightning three times, his luck had run dry.

At least the girls huddled behind him, safe.

Alyosha threw his dagger, and a gunshot blasted from the rear of the factory.

Alyosha staggered. Blood bloomed on his chest. The knife clanged off the floor at Rurik's feet and skidded into the darkness. A ragged wheeze escaped Alyosha's lips. He toppled to the ground.

Marva appeared behind him, a gun in her hand.

The bloodwalker leader, Klavdia, swiveled her head toward Marva. Her lipless mouth widened. With a snake-like hiss, she bared long teeth. The two women at Klavdia's sides pulled her away. They crab-scuttled past the hallway and aimed for the wall opening.

Rurik couldn't believe the blind creatures could see where to go—could see anything at all. No eyes. Virtually no face. It must be hell on earth.

They deserved it.

Misha and Pyotr fanned out behind Marva, each carrying an antique gun from Ivan's collection. They strode forward like gunslingers, arms outstretched, firing at the bloodwalkers surrounding Rurik and the Markarovs.

The bullets hit the creatures with dull thwacks. They rocked backward but didn't go down.

Anatoly and Pavel Markarov struggled for their rifles

but were clearly outmatched by the heavier bloodwalkers.

The three creatures guarding the exit lurched onto the factory floor, heading for Marva and the newcomers.

Rurik turned to Sylvie. "This is it. Go!" He shoved her toward the broken wall, and then headed for Anatoly.

Halfway there, a bloodwalker barreled into him. Fists like stone savaged his head and ribs.

His ears rang. He ducked down only to surge up again, aiming a punch at the creature's diaphragm. It was like hitting concrete. The impact reverberated up his arm. His nerves blared with pain.

She swung at him again, but two bullets slammed into her ribs. She staggered sideways.

Pyotr charged forward, chest out, nostrils flaring. He emptied the full magazine from his TT-30 pistol into the creature.

She cringed from the onslaught, but when the gun clicked empty, she turned on him like a rabid dog. Teeth glinted in over-sized jaws. Her fist flashed out at Pyotr's head.

The tall roustabout dodged. Taking his gun in both hands, he struck a double-armed hammer blow into the bloodwalker's face.

No effect.

She back-handed him.

He flew through the air, and Rurik heard the "Oof" when he landed.

Rurik pivoted, his foot lashing out in a powerful side kick to the bloodwalker's abdomen.

It knocked her off her feet. But she rose again.

They all did.

Fury added to the adrenaline flowing in Rurik's veins. The damn bloodwalkers were like tanks. Nothing could stop them.

All around him, a wild melee raged. His friends dodged in and out. Their fast reactions saved them from many blows. But some landed. Misha hurtled backward from a strike, pitched into Anatoly, and they both went sprawling.

A high-pitched scream raised the hairs on Rurik's neck.

Anushka and Sylvie hadn't made it out. In front of the

opening, one bloodwalker held the little girl by the arm while Sylvie kicked and fought to free her.

He ran toward them, despair crushing him. Nothing he'd done mattered. His preternatural strength, the one thing he'd always depended on, had failed him. Failed everyone. The creatures couldn't be defeated. His friends would tire, run out of ammunition. They'd be captured.

But nothing on earth would make him abandon Anushka to that fate.

He tackled the bloodwalker from behind. The force broke her grip on Anushka and drove her to the ground. She and Rurik tumbled across the floor.

He jumped to his feet first. "Get out," he yelled, his voice carrying across the factory. "Run! Get to the car!" He didn't wait to see who followed his order. Scooping Anushka into his arms, he punched an oncoming bloodwalker in the face and charged through the wall opening.

Outside the factory, he leaped across the uneven ground. Clods of dry earth and broken glass crunched underfoot. He stumbled repeatedly, favoring one ankle, the other swollen from the fall.

Sylvie caught up to him and pulled ahead, her long skirt hiked up past her knees. She hit the street at a sprint, long blond hair flying in the storm gusts.

He staggered onto the asphalt a moment later and flung a glance over his shoulder.

Marva and Pyotr dashed from the factory. Misha followed close behind, cradling his arm. Of the Markarovs—Anatoly, Pavel and the wounded Viktor—there was no sign.

Rurik would go back for them, but not till he put Anushka in the car and sent her and Sylvie on their way.

But then Sylvie stopped in front of him.

He opened his mouth to yell at her before he saw what lay ahead. His desperate run faltered. He skidded to a halt.

Misshapen forms filled the street. Over twenty of them. They lumbered out of houses and across dead brown lawns.

It seemed Alyosha and Zora weren't the only ones with secret below-ground hideaways.

Every house lining the left side of the street disgorged

its occupants. Through gaps between homes, he saw the next street and the next. Bloodwalkers spilled onto the roads. Some broke into a run, others shuffled. They all turned toward the factory.

No way to get past them all. Rurik and the others were cut off from the pickup. But Ivan's RV had to be nearby.

At the farthest house down the street, Rurik spied the white circus van where Alyosha had left it. Behind it sat Ivan's RV, but it was under attack, too. Three bloodwalkers hammered on its door and windows. Another one climbed the front bumper and beat on the windshield.

Now, thirty creatures blocked the street. And more came tromping across the ground from every corner of town.

The only place left was the oil field.

"Come on," he shouted to Sylvie. They had to take their chances on the dark plateau. If they were fast—and lucky—they could circle around and make it to the Markarov's pickup at the end of the road.

Scrubby weeds whipped against his boots as he plunged across the open land. After a few minutes, his breath clawed at his chest. His ribs twinged with each inhale, and every stride stabbed him as if broken glass ground between his ankle joints.

The streetlights fell behind. Shadows lengthened. Small dips and ditches became inky pools of blackness. Treacherous. After he tripped over a jagged furrow and almost dropped Anushka, Rurik had to slow.

Forked tongues of electricity flicked from the clouds as the storm rolled across the plateau toward a distant line of trees. It was as if the damned storm was following him onto the open field. For Anushka's sake, he'd have to hand her off to someone else.

At least he'd reached halfway across the field, about 150 yards from the street. Good time to circle back and head for the truck.

He stopped and set Anushka on her feet.

She twisted around, cocking her head at a rhythmic clunking and banging that sounded from dead ahead. "What's that?" she said, her voice trembling.

"Oil pumping machines," Rurik guessed, though he

couldn't see them clearly. "They won't hurt you."

Sylvie and Pyotr reached them, their arms slung under Marva's shoulders, helping the wheezing older woman along. Misha followed, his jog unsteady, his head lolling.

But that wasn't all.

Bloodwalkers poured across the street and onto the field. Almost forty now. The rough terrain slowed them. They wobbled over hillocks and blundered into ditches, but they came on unfazed, intent on finding their prey.

Shouts carried from the factory. Two figures ran from the building, hauling a third between them. A few bloodwalkers chased them. Even slowed down by Viktor, the Markarov boys were outrunning the slow, awkward gait of the creatures.

Until some of the bloodwalkers on the field saw them and changed direction.

"Oh my God!" Marva said and clapped a hand over her lips.

Too far away to give assistance, they watched helplessly as a pack of bloodwalkers hemmed the Markarovs in.

Rifle shots peppered the air, sounding like small firecrackers. Bloodwalker fists flew. Arms pinioned up and down like jackhammers.

A body was lifted overhead. He struggled, shrieking, arms flailing.

A bloodwalker reached up and twisted one arm brutally. It snapped at the elbow and hung loose. Another of the monsters went down on one knee. Her cohorts slammed the boy—back first—onto her extended leg. When she stood, the boy flopped onto the ground like a ragdoll. His shrieking trailed off to groans.

Rurik winced. Broken back. Paralyzed. Whoever it was wouldn't walk again. But the monsters didn't need victims who could walk.

Sylvie grasped his wrist. "We have to go on to the forest. They'll catch us if we stay in the open!"

She was right. The remaining bloodwalkers had fanned out across the field in a flanking movement as clever as an army's. They blocked the way to the pickup and peered into the blackness, ready to catch anyone they flushed out from hiding.

Rurik gave Anushka to Pyotr while Sylvie helped Marva. After seeing what happened to the Markarov boy, the group doubled their speed across the field.

Even Rurik ran faster toward the forest—and toward the lightning that flickered above it. Talons of light arced down, sinking claws into the tops of trees. His stomach flip-flopped at the sight of his electric enemy, but considering who chased him, death by lightning was preferable.

The clanking grew louder. A pumper came into view. Then another. Their twenty-foot tall mechanisms glimmered as they moved. Titanic metal birds, their tops bobbed up and down drawing oil from the ground as if it was a struggling worm.

They passed three more pumpers before they neared the woods.

Once inside the protective line of trees, Marva collapsed.

"I can't..." Marva clutched her chest. "I can't go any further." Her voice cracked. "I'm sorry. You go on without me..."

Sylvie doubled over, gasping for air. "Too far. Need a break."

Rurik squinted over his shoulder. At the far end of the field, the streetlamps lay strung out like a row of fairy lights. Blocking them, shadowy forms weaved across the ground. Still coming. Some closer than others. But they searched slowly, beating bushes, examining ditches. They hadn't reached the halfway point or the machines yet.

"The women and Misha can go on," Pyotr said to Rurik. "We'll make a stand here. Slow the monsters down. Confuse them."

Misha swayed on his feet. "I-I don't feel so good."

Rurik turned the boy into the dim light cast by the streetlights. White bone stuck out from his forearm. A dark spot spread across his shirt where he cradled his arm to his chest.

Shit. Compound fracture. Blood loss. Misha was in no shape to go anywhere, much less lead the women through the forest.

But Pyotr was right about one thing. Someone had to

keep the bloodwalkers from reaching the woods. Someone had to make a stand. But fighting them one on one was fruitless. He needed to think of something that could stop them all in their tracks.

Suddenly, he knew just how to do it.

CHAPTER THIRTY

Sylvie
Bājenie, Romania

Your bloodwalker bag is more than a collection of supplies.
It's an extension of you. It must be clean, neat, precise.
With as much attention as you show the dead bodies you
prepare, you must care for the bag's contents.
Without those items, your work will suffer.
Then you're not a bloodwalker.
You're a ghoul.
~ The Bloodwalker's Book

Sylvie kneeled next to Anushka and the old woman, dried leaves and twigs poking into her shins. Her lips pulled tighter than the sewn lips of a corpse as she fought to keep huffs of frustration from escaping. She needed to convince the group to go farther into the forest and hide, but she couldn't speak their language. Besides, the woman was still breathing hard and her hands shook as if with palsy. Sylvie prayed she wasn't having a heart attack.

And she wasn't the only sick one.

The skinny boy refused to sit with them. He stubbornly stayed on his feet and propped himself against a nearby tree, but she heard low groans issuing from between his clenched teeth.

Their little group was exhausted except for the man who Rurik had called Pyotr. He'd been pacing back and forth ever since Rurik had sprinted onto the field.

It was insane. Rurik would never be able to fight off all those bloodwalkers by himself, even if he promised her he had a plan. Although she didn't know what his plan was, considering what he'd taken with him, it seemed risky.

259

Foolhardy, if she was being honest.

First, he had asked them all for matches. When she pulled a pack of them from her bloodwalker bag, he'd taken the whole sack in his hands and scrounged through it. She'd gnawed on a fingernail when he dumped out her candles, packing cotton, the bottle of lilac massage oil along with her spare clothes. But when her underwear landed in a heap, too, her stomach tied itself in a knot. Bad enough having a stranger rummage through her bloodwalker supplies, but now Rurik knew she wore the ugliest white cotton undies in the entire world.

Maybe not important in the grand scheme of things, like being eaten by bloodwalkers, but embarrassment was fear's smaller, chubby cousin. The one who tagged along when he was least wanted and you could never get rid of.

Thankfully, Rurik didn't seem to notice her undies, so when he picked up the packing cotton and oil bottle, she snatched the underwear behind her back. If there'd been more light, she knew everyone would see her face flaming red as a radish.

With a sharp nod to himself, Rurik had whispered, "Molotov," under his breath before shoving the cotton and oil in his waistband and running off.

But there was only one bottle. He couldn't slow the creatures down with one Molotov cocktail.

Her nails ripped off loose threads from the end of her sleeve as she strained to follow his movements in the dark. The flashes of lightning gave her occasional bursts of clear vision, but she still had no idea what he was up to.

On the field, he slowed and stopped at one of the pumping machines. He seemed to be working at something. In the next flicker of lightning, she saw what he was trying to do—and gasped in horror.

He struggled to turn a wheel that would open the pumper's valve.

She leaped to her feet. He must think this was an oil field. Maybe he wanted to release the oil, flood the field, and light it to stop the bloodwalkers. But she knew the area. And on the drive into town, she'd seen the warning signs put up by the Romanian company.

The company didn't pump oil. They pumped natural gas!

Sylvie bolted onto the field.

If Rurik opened the valve and tossed the lit cotton and oil at it, the pumper would explode. If the others ruptured, they would take the town, half the plateau—and Rurik with them!

Outside the protection of the trees, the storm lashed at her long skirt and flung dirt in her face. More than 200 yards lay between her and the pumpers. Unseen dips and humps made her stumble, but she had to warn Rurik and she couldn't risk yelling. The bloodwalkers would hear her.

She fell into a ditch, knocking the breath out of her lungs. Ignoring the pain, she scrabbled up the other side and took off again.

Her tired legs ached. A stitch jabbed her side. Her heartbeat banged a mile a minute. But she had to get to him.

A shout carried across the field. A bloodwalker stopped to point.

Rurik had been spotted.

The town's streetlamps dimmed and brightened as contorted shapes changed direction. The bloodwalkers massed toward the pumpers, picking up speed, scenting a victim was close.

Sylvie plunged onward, faster and faster, in adrenaline-fueled panic.

Thirty yards. Twenty.

But Rurik wrenched the big wheel, opening the valve. He frowned and peered at the machine.

"No," she shouted, staggering up to him. "Close it. Quick!"

"Where is the oil?"

"It's not oil—it's gas!"

His jaw dropped.

"Close it! Even the lightning might set it off. It could destroy everyth—" She broke off as arms grabbed her from behind. Over her shoulder, she glimpsed a bony face, gray skin, and burning eyes. A bloodwalker wrapped her in a steely grip.

261

Two more bloodwalkers rushed past, aiming for Rurik.

Sylvie writhed and bucked. One frantic kick connected with the creature's knee. With a cry, the bloodwalker sagged and relaxed its hold. Sylvie wriggled away. But within two steps, she ran into another dark, twisted shape. It grabbed at her, but she bobbed down and evaded it.

A horde of the creatures reached the pumpers. They surrounded Rurik and Sylvie.

Rurik shoved one to the ground and kicked another's feet out from under it. But two more attacked him. One jumped onto his back.

A bloodwalker caught Sylvie by the arm. She yanked away and heard a shredding sound as her sleeve tore off.

Other bloodwalkers leaped onto Rurik, hitting him, punching him, trying to bring him to his knees. In another minute, they'd pin him to the ground. They'd get Sylvie, too. Then both of them would be at the creatures' mercy— and the creatures had none.

Sylvie's fear turned to anger.

Bloodwalkers were a sisterhood. They were supposed to help one another. These beasts had corrupted everything that bloodwalkers stood for.

Her teeth gnashed. Her fingers curled into fists. It was too much. No one should have to put up with what she had. The nasty gossip in her village. The wedding fiasco. Miron's beatings. And the horrible things Cosmina, Zora, and Alyosha had done to her and others.

They'd killed her mother, dammit!

Sylvie shook with outrage. Pent up pain and anger combined inside her and detonated like a bomb. A new strength exploded in her veins.

"*Stop!*" The shout burst from Sylvie's lungs and filled the night with a deep, dark sound. A noise so powerful it was both beautiful and hideous. The sound encompassed her misery, her despair, and her hope. It shattered her soul and then fused it back together again.

Her bellow reverberated off the metal pumpers. It ran up and down their structures. Sonic vibrations harmonized. Their discordant clanking grew into a strident roar.

It blasted into the air and rocked the ground.

A deep rumble entered Sylvie's chest, sending tingles through her limbs.

The wave of sound boomed across the field. All the bloodwalkers flinched, their deformed faces twisted in pain.

They cowered.

From the middle of the pack, Rurik rose up and flung off his attackers. He caught sight of Sylvie, standing frozen in shock, and dove at her. Before she could open her mouth, he slung her over his shoulder and raced into the darkness.

Sylvie's world bounced upside down. The wind tangled her hair in her face. Her limbs still echoed with the jarring vibration.

Rurik leaped furrows and hillocks while her stomach slid up her throat with each of his bounding strides. Finally, he came to a deep ditch and jumped into it, laying her down and stretching out beside her.

Above the other side of the ditch, she spied the inky tops of trees churning in the wind. The forest was only a hundred yards farther on. What hadn't Rurik kept running? If he had, they'd be safe by now.

But then she saw them.

Like sentinels, the three blind women from the factory—Zora's mother Klavdia, and her two cohorts—prowled the open area before the forest. With bird-like jerks, their heads angled up, down, and then sideways.

Sylvie thought they were listening, but as one passed closer, she heard the distinct whistle of its slitted nostrils flaring. Inhaling. They were sniffing out their prey.

Several more patrolled the darkness, searching for the escapees in the surrounding dips and gullies. If Rurik had run to the woods, he'd have led them straight to the rest of their group.

"I know you're out here," Klavdia called. "I heard you running. I can smell you. Your friends are close by, too. One is injured. Smells so sweet. When the wind changes, I'll know exactly where you are."

The threat sent a shiver down Sylvie's back. Her gaze shot back the way they'd come, wishing it was clear.

Bloodwalkers milled around the pumps, poking at the equipment. One pointed at the valve Rurik had opened. She tried to turn it, but as heavy as the bloodwalkers were, and as armor-like as their bones had become, none had the muscle mass of Rurik. However, if enough of them got together, they'd eventually turn it off.

Would that be good or bad?

Sylvie didn't know anymore.

Rurik shifted next to her. He took the bottle of oil, the cotton, and the matches from his pocket. His eyes met hers. "They'll find us soon," he whispered. "There's only one chance. I have to blow the gas. If we stay down in the ditch, we might survive. I won't do it unless you agree." Concern deepened the lines of his face, turning his scars into a jagged trail of pain and fortitude.

Sylvie's nails dug into the earth. The choices were bad and worse. Stay and be discovered, then be tortured and eaten. Or fight back in a suicidal blitzkrieg. If they didn't survive, at least they'd take a lot of bloodwalkers with them. Anushka and her friends could get away.

"Okay," Sylvie said. "Do it."

Rurik quickly twisted the packing cotton and shoved half of it into the oil bottle. When he struck the first match, the wind blew it out. The second one, too.

Sylvie moved closer and cupped her hands around his when he struck the match for the third time.

It lit. The wick of the Molotov burned.

He quickly mumbled something in Russian that sounded like a prayer. He jumped up, drew back his arm, and threw the bottle. A split second later, he dropped down atop her, covering her body with his.

Sylvie braced herself for the blast.

And waited.

Nothing happened.

Seconds ticked by.

No explosion.

They poked their heads up.

By the pumper, bloodwalkers formed a knot, stamping at something on the ground.

They'd caught the Molotov. They'd put out the fire.

Sylvie and Rurik's last chance was squelched under the feet of the monsters.

They couldn't try to run back to the forest. The others' lives depended on it.

All they could do was wait until the beasts discovered them.

CHAPTER THIRTY-ONE

Rurik
Bājenie, Romania

Rurik flattened himself in the ditch beside Sylvie. Rocks and weed stalks jabbed through his thin clothing, seeming to spear every bruise on his battered body. He didn't dare shift position. The bloodwalkers would hear.

Dry grass rustled and snapped as Klavdia and her cohorts searched nearby . The sounds of their shuffling grew closer.

Sylvie's breathing quickened. Soft puffs fanned his face, but he had to give her credit, she didn't move a muscle.

Lightning strobed across the field. He shut his eyes against the brilliance and prayed no one happened to be looking in their direction. But even if no one discovered them that second, it was only a matter of time.

They were trapped. Nowhere to go. No way out.

Sylvie's hand found his, her small fingers entwining his thick ones and tightening as if she clung to a ledge atop a building. He didn't blame her. Anyone in the pile of shit they were in needed comfort. Truthfully, at any other place or time, holding hands would have felt great. But not when he had to concentrate on the bloodwalkers and come up with a new plan to evade them.

He silently cursed the plastic bottle of oil. If it had been glass, it would have broken on impact, spilling fuel everywhere and bursting into flame. The bloodwalkers couldn't have put it out.

Thunder cracked overhead. His heart gave an answering jolt, and he worried about Marva and the others in the woods. By now, Pyotr should have realized the bloodwalkers' search would eventually lead them to the trees. He should be moving the group, guiding them through the forest to safety.

It would be bad enough if Rurik and Sylvie were caught, but he couldn't stomach the thought of all his friends dying, too. Especially little Anushka. Saving children was all he'd ever wanted. As long as Anushka got away, then he'd done one thing right.

Dry dirt crunched nearby. Sylvie's eyes widened, and a tiny whimper fled her lips.

He froze, determined to make no sound that might give them away. But as he lay, commanding every tense muscle, every heartbeat, and every breath to rigid silence, he noticed the stench of blood and sweat seeping off him. Klavdia or one of the others would smell it, or perhaps even his broken hand and ribs, just like Zora had.

The only thing in their favor was that the lightning had tapered off. On the other hand, if the lightning had kept up, it might have struck the pumpers and finished the job he'd started. It figured that the one time in his life when he actually wanted lightning, the damn storm was moving off over the forest.

Faint thunder rolled, but as the rumble dwindled, he heard something else—something that chilled his blood.

The whistling sound of one of the creatures inhaling through its slitted nostrils. The snuffling grew louder.

He held his breath.

Next to him, Sylvie shivered and curled closer.

He silently let go of her fingers and laid an arm over her. Through the fabric of her dress, he felt the rapid beat of her heart.

Footsteps closed in from his other side.

"Fee-fi-fo-fum..." The voice's sing-song sent goose bumps skittering across his neck. "I smell the bones of circus scum."

Pebbles skidded down into the hollow.

He looked up. Outlined against the gray clouds, black figures bent over the lip of earth hiding him. Despite the darkness, he swore he could see them leering in triumph.

"Run!" he yelled. Jumping to his feet, he charged up the slope and slammed his shoulder into the nearest bloodwalker. She pitched backward and hit the ground hard. But another appeared beside him and swung.

The blow took him in the side of the head. Pain rattled his skull. His vision clouded. But he didn't need to see—the enemy was everywhere. He hit and kicked the stone-hard flesh on all sides of him.

A heavy weight smashed into the back of his knees. He fell forward, catching himself on his hands. Behind him, Sylvie screamed. Adrenaline surged in his veins. He pushed back to his feet and struck out at everything within reach.

Bloodwalkers poured from the darkness. The steady rain of blows took their toll. Dizziness made him stagger. He didn't know how much longer he'd stay conscious.

The beasts knocked Sylvie down, pummeling her helpless form as she lay on the ground. Rage filled him. He roared, letting loose with all the energy he had left. Punching. Chopping. Kicking.

A different roar overtook his. A speeding engine.

The strikes to his body faltered. He blinked and dragged a forearm across his face, clearing blood from his eyes.

From the main street of town, lights stabbed through the darkness. A vehicle bounced and juddered over the rutted field. Its headlights flared toward the sky one second and down into dirt the next. Wide-set headlights. Bigger than the pickup.

Ivan's RV!

What the hell was Ivan doing?

Bloodwalkers chased it and jumped on the back. One crawled onto the roof.

The engine raced, and its wheels spun in the loose soil. With every dip, Rurik heard its undercarriage crash into the ground. But it came on, aiming straight for the gas pumpers.

The bloodwalkers in its path converged on it. They threw themselves at the front bumper. Some hung on. Others were mowed down.

"Get to it! Stop it!" a bloodwalker next to him screamed. "The gas!"

The creatures around him charged toward the pumps.

Across the field, more bloodwalkers made it onto the back of the RV. They climbed onto the roof, swarming it like ants. Others leaped onto the front bumper. They beat on the windshield with heavy fists. The glass shattered and gave way. It bowed into the cabin. The creatures clawed their way inside.

But Ivan didn't stop. Didn't even slow.

Rurik's jaw dropped as the vehicle continued its suicide run at the giant pumping machines.

It sideswiped the first in the line. The shriek of angry metal seared the air as an anchored piling came loose. The seesaw mechanism on top of the pumper tipped crookedly. Its sharp end ripped down the side of the RV, rupturing the cabin like a can-opener. Bloodwalkers screamed as the giant blade sliced through them.

Flames spurted from inside the RV. Black smoke billowed out its open windshield.

Regardless, it surged straight for the next pumper.

The one where Rurik had already loosened the valve.

Rurik whirled around. Sylvie sat on the ground, blood streaming from her mouth and chin. He swept her with him as he leaped back into the ditch.

A huge crash split the air. Then a much bigger blast nearly deafened Rurik.

The ground heaved. A wave of super-heated air shot over his head.

The fireball swept over the hollow, igniting everything. The grass. His clothes. His hair. His scalp blared in pain.

Rurik squeezed his eyes shut against the heat. The blaze scorched him from top to bottom. But he held his breath so the fire wouldn't destroy his lungs.

A moment later, dirt hit him. Rocks and pebbles rained down. A barrage fell atop him until it seemed like the entire field was dropping on his back.

Something whacked into his skull, and he blacked out.

When he woke, he couldn't breathe. His face was mashed into the ground. Dirt filled his mouth and nose. It pinned his arms and legs.

Sylvie must be close, but he couldn't move to reach her. Buried under rubble, he couldn't even be sure which way was up.

He struggled, spitting to clear his mouth. His lungs strained, trying to inhale, but there was no oxygen. His hands clawed at the packed earth. His heart throbbed in his ears. Little by little, his efforts slowed. He weakened. Suffocating.

Rough hands scraped at his back, then at his head.

Someone grabbed his shirt and hauled him up.

Dirt and rocks sluiced off him. He sucked in a huge gulp of air and coughed.

A large dust cloud from the explosion clogged the air. He grabbed the bottom of his shirt and dragged it over his mouth and nose, taking giant breaths, filling anguished lungs.

The hands released him. He rubbed his eyes and peered around.

Next to him, Pyotr scrabbled at the ground, digging down.

Sylvie! She must be still trapped.

Rurik dropped to his knees. His big hands scooped up earth like steam shovels. When his broken fingers wouldn't close over the rubble, he jammed them into the dirt anyway, using his palm to fling it over his shoulder.

He touched the wool of her dress and grabbed it. One-handed, he used all his strength to pull her from her grave.

She came up sputtering and gagging. But alive.

Rurik steadied her against him as he stared around.

All over the field, things burned, making the haze glow orange. Weeds and grasses flamed like candles as far as he could see. Fiery debris had fallen on the houses in the town. The decayed wood blazed to life, and the fire jumped from house to house, sweeping through everything in its path.

Big charred lumps, barely recognizable as human, lay all around him. Some still smoldered, greasy black smoke spiraling upward. Many of the victims had been blown apart. Bits of bodies, scorched black, lined the field like little rocks of flesh.

Except for him, Pyotr, and Sylvie, nothing moved.

Where the gas pumpers had stood was a crater fifty

yards across.

Of the RV, only a part of the chassis remained. The rest was gone.

Pyotr shook his head. "Crazy bastard. Never afraid of anything. Even at the end."

Rurik averted his gaze, unable to put into words how much he owed Ivan or how much he would miss him. Keeping an arm around Sylvie, he turned and they walked toward the forest. The outermost trees had been blown down by the blast. Limbs sheared clean off the trunks. Several still blazed.

"Is everyone all right?" Rurik said to Pyotr.

The man nodded. "When we saw the RV coming, we took off, deeper into the woods. The fire didn't reach us."

As they passed the end of the blackened fire line, Marva, Misha, and Anushka ran out from the woods to meet them.

"Ivan?" Marva said , peering from Rurik to Pyotr, her features pinched with dread. "You didn't find him?"

Pyotr shook his head.

"But did you look? Maybe—"

"Marva," Rurik said quietly. "No one could have survived that."

Marva's eyes squeezed shut, her face crumpling like a tissue. "That stupid, brave...horrible...wonderful man." When she opened her eyes again, tears slipped out, following the empty chasms down her cheeks.

Rurik took a shaky breath. "Ivan was true circus through and through. He'd do anything to help those who needed it. He'll never be forgotten."

Pyotr leaned close to Rurik and whispered, "Do you think Ivan got them all? Are they all dead?"

Rurik eyed the destruction. "Yes."

As if to prove him wrong, a strange buzzing noise rose from the smoky field. It became a chainsaw-like growl.

The group peered into the haze. Sylvie's mouth dropped open. Anushka darted behind her and peeked around the woolen skirt, her knuckles between her teeth.

Rurik strained to see through the smoke. Tension scraped over his skin like claws. It had to be over. No bloodwalker could have lived through that.

271

The sound escalated, and a dark shape whizzed around the crater and aimed for them.

A motorcycle, painted with red flames, bucked and rolled across the ground. When it reached them, it swept into a sideways skid and came to a stop.

Ivan yanked off his helmet.

Marva rushed over and hugged him.

"Now don't fuss, woman," Ivan grumbled, but his eyes crinkled and he kept his arms wrapped around her.

"What did you do?" Rurik's mouth widened into a grin.

"I thought I was a goner for a while the way the ghouls kept hammering on the camper, but they all went into the field after you. I watched and saw what you tried to do with the Molotov. Good thinking! The problem was, you just didn't have a big enough one. But I did! A whole Molotov cocktail on wheels with plenty of gas to blow it sky high. So after getting the bike off—and setting a little fire in the kitchen—, I aimed the RV at the machines, tied up the steering wheel, and jammed the wheelchair on the gas pedal. Then I gave the old girl a kiss good-bye and let her rip!"

"But your leg...the cast..." Marva eyed his bare leg where the white cast used to cover him from ankle to hip. A belt tied the knee to the fuselage, padded with a towel.

"Oh, yeah...I had to cut the cast off. My damn leg hurts like hell,"—he grinned—"but I've never felt better in my life!"

CHAPTER THIRTY-TWO

Sylvie
Pașnita, Romania

> *Bloodwalkers are all related by birth, united by*
> *knowledge,*
> *and linked by powers entrusted to us. Yet we are all very*
> *different.*
> *Each bloodwalker must find her own voice, own path, own*
> *life.*
> *For only God and Death know our true destiny.*
> *~ The Bloodwalker's Book*

Sylvie read the last entry in the Bloodwalker's Book and smoothed the crinkled vellum of the final page, wondering how many hands had touched it, how many eyes had read the words over the years. Although her mother had taught her from it since she was young, she'd never been allowed to hold it. It was a sacred thing—too important to be trusted to the hands of a child.

With the death of Sylvie's mother, it had become hers.

And the notes, too. Some of her ancestors had jotted down advice and experiences on sheets of paper and tucked them inside the book, the way old women did with recipes.

Sylvie bent her head, savoring the smell of the dusty old pages—and rose-scented perfume. Her mother, the toughest, most practical woman in the whole village, had written her comments on rose-scented stationery. Sylvie hadn't even known she liked roses. But after reading her entries, it turned out there was a lot about her mother she didn't know.

Despite an unshakable façade of confidence, her mother

273

hadn't been a perfect bloodwalker in the beginning either. In cramped letters on the pink paper, she'd confessed her doubts, her failings, and her fears.

Sylvie wished her mother had shared her insecurities. Then Sylvie wouldn't have felt so incompetent, so alone. But the woman clung to her pride, her beliefs of right and wrong. And she was stubborn.

Her intractable personality showed in her last note—one about Zora.

After overhearing Aunt Cosmina's conversation with Zora and finding out about Ada's and Liana's deaths, I have no choice but to go to Băjenie. No subtly worded threats from Cosmina can sway me from this path or keep me from learning the truth. Emilia and Martine have vowed to go with me. They have nothing left to lose—their daughters are dead. Mine is still alive. But at least by ordering her to remain in Hungary with her husband, I can tell myself she's safe. I don't know what we'll find in Băjenie. If it's what I suspect...what my grandparents warned me about...then God help us all.

Sylvie wished her mother hadn't gone to Băjenie. Wished she hadn't been so determined to find the truth. Wished she'd let Sylvie come home and somehow stop her from going. Wished...

Tears pricked Sylvie's eyes. Months of crying, yet the salty well of sadness never ran dry.

Her mother never backed down from anything. One way or another, she'd have gone to Băjenie. Nothing Sylvie said would have stopped her. That was her path, her life, her destiny.

Just as it was for all the others who perished in the poisoned town.

After the gas field explosion, Băjenie had headlined the news for weeks.

When the authorities found Sylvie's mother's body in the factory, they'd come asking questions. However, Sylvie no longer found it difficult to make people believe the things she said. Or didn't say. An excuse about her mother foraging for Skomori charms in the area—delivered in a cold and confident bloodwalker voice—was all it took to send the police on their way. Plus, there were so many other bodies that no one claimed or admitted to knowing. After several months of investigation, the police decided it was best to brand the whole thing an accident.

The government announced that a settlement of illegal squatters, in league with child traffickers, had perished in a fire on the gas field.

The nation gasped in shock, mourned, and then went on about their business. No one really wanted to know the truth. They liked believing their world was safe and predictable.

The kitchen timer rang, startling Sylvie from her reverie. The roast! She'd forgotten all about it, and she hadn't even started on the *mamaliga* yet. Plus, it would be an hour's walk to the town store to buy fresh fruit for dessert.

With care, she placed the leather-bound Bloodwalker Book into its hiding place in a cupboard before dashing over to pull the beef from the oven.

Not overcooked, thank goodness. Medium rare. Just the way Rurik liked it.

She checked the clock before starting to chop the vegetables. How could she get so behind? At this rate, nothing would be done in time. The knife missed the carrot and cut her finger.

"Dammit!" Blood oozed from the wound. She ran it under cold water. Her whole hand trembled. Closing her eyes, she took a deep breath.

Keep your wits about you, and everything will be all right. Her mother's words on the day they'd arrived in Budapest for the wedding.

But how could Sylvie be calm today of all days? She'd been looking forward to it for two months.

After they escaped the town, Rurik had visited her every weekend while the circus toured Romania and the nearby countries of Moldova and Ukraine. But when the show traveled farther north to Poland, Belarus, and Russia, it was too far for him to drive. Their only contact had been by phone.

But now the circus was heading south again, passing through Romania on its way to Bulgaria and Serbia.

He'd said there was something important about this visit. Something special. Her stomach fluttered every time she thought about it. Today, everything had to be perfect.

Squawking came from the chicken coop. She sighed , knowing what it was even before she looked. Her neighbor's dog, Bruno. Always getting into trouble.

Her fingers flew to her apron and began untying it before she realized she didn't have time to chase the rascal around the yard, flapping her apron at him.

She flung open the kitchen window and took a deep breath. "Bruuuunoooo!!" Her gruff bellow resonated through the kitchen. Glasses clinked in the cupboards, and silverware rattled in the drawers. In the yard, the chickens fell silent. A flock of birds erupted from a nearby tree.

Bruno stopped dead, glancing at the window with the whites of his eyes showing. Tucking his tail between his legs, he raced off.

Sylvie smiled to herself. Funny that Rurik and his friends had never admitted what she'd done back at the field. They remarked on how lucky Sylvie and Rurik had been that the storm's thunder had caused the pumpers' weird vibration and startled the bloodwalkers.

Sylvie never told them any different.

CHAPTER THIRTY-THREE

Rurik
Satu Mare, Romania

Rurik hurried toward the circus parking lot, yanking at his tight shirt collar for the tenth time. It had to be the wrong size. It felt like it was cutting off the blood to his brain.

He pulled the van keys from his pocket and shoved them at door lock. Missed. Stabbed again and missed. And then fumbled them into the grass.

When he bent to pick them up, he heard the telltale rip of threads from under the suit's arm. Dammit. First time he'd worn a suit. Who knew they were so flimsy?

"You'll never get there at this rate." Marva joined him at the van with Misha at her heels. She lifted Rurik's arm, peered beneath, and tsked under her breath.

Misha bent and retrieved the keys.

"It's a small rip," Marva said. "No one will notice, but stop moving so much. Today, you're not a strongman. You have to be a ballerina."

A ballerina? More likely an elephant.

"You have to be suave and graceful if you want things to go well."

Rurik did...but it was getting more unlikely by the minute. He leaned on the van door and tried not to throw up.

"Looking a bit green there, Mr. Circus Manager." Ivan ambled over from his RV, a newer, better model than the one destroyed in the explosion. Ivan himself was a newer and better version. He walked without a cane or a limp, and ever since Marva moved in with him, he seemed to smile a lot more.

Three months of recuperation had been good for him. Rurik reminded himself to put Ivan back on the schedule for that week's performances.

If Rurik managed to live through the day.

Ivan took a flask from an inside pocket and held it out. "A little of this will give you courage."

"Stop that!" Marva batted it away. "You don't want him showing up with vodka breath. What will the poor girl think?!"

"You don't seem to mind it," Ivan winked at her.

A flush rolled up Marva's cheeks, and she gave a befuddled cough before transferring her attention back to Rurik. "Let's just make sure you have everything. Keys?"

Rurik snatched them from Misha and jangled them at her.

"Wallet?"

He patted his back pocket and nodded.

"Breath mints?"

His fingers dug a roll of mints from his suit jacket. He grinned and waved them with a flourish.

"Chocolates?"

His smile fell. "I—um—I think I left them in the RV."

Marva rolled her eyes. "Misha! Run and get them. Quick!"

"Yes, ma'am." He saluted like a soldier, but his eyes were laughing as he dashed off.

"Now...can I see it? Just one more time?" Marva said.

Rurik knew what she meant. From his inside jacket pocket, he pulled out a jewelry box and opened it. Sunlight shimmered off the ring inside.

"Ohh..." Marva clasped her hand to her chest and looked like she was about to faint.

Why were women so weird about these things?

"It's *so* beautiful."

Rurik looked at it, glittering in the afternoon sun, and secretly admitted it *was* beautiful. Normally, he never could have afforded such an expensive engagement ring, but the circus people—everyone from the performers to the roustabouts to the concessioners—had taken up a collection for him when Marva had revealed his plans.

Misha rushed back to the group, holding out a box of Swiss chocolates. Pyotr strode along behind him.

Rurik paused to look at his friends. *Friends.* The word still didn't feel real. But *they* were real. They'd stuck by him through everything. Even when he'd been wrong. Like on the night he'd buried Yuri. They'd obeyed him and left, but passed the Markarov pickup on the road. Suspicious, they'd followed and seen the Markarovs force Rurik inside at gunpoint. Although Dmitry's speeding had left them behind, they'd arrived in the abandoned Romanian town and armed themselves with pitiful vintage guns to go into battle. For him.

It was humbling.

And now that he'd taken over the management of the circus, everyone treated him differently.

Or perhaps, they'd always treated him well, but he just hadn't been able to see it.

Pyotr stepped forward and shook his hand. "Good luck."

Ivan and Misha followed suit.

Marva wrapped her arms around him—or as far as she could reach around his barrel chest—and whispered, "I know she'll say yes."

Rurik wished he could be so sure.

He managed to open van's door this time, and a few minutes later, pulled onto the highway leading to Sylvie's house.

It was an hour away, but it seemed only seconds passed before he found himself parking outside the white fence surrounding her home.

He stepped out. Yanked at his collar again. Cupped his hand over his mouth and breathed into it. Not too bad. He shined his fancy shoe tips on the back of each calf.

But then he stood, feet glued to the road at the end of a flagstone walkway, gazing at the cozy house and garden.

He couldn't do this. He needed more time. Time to prepare a speech or something. Some way to let her know how much she meant to him. Some way to convince her to say yes.

Waiting would be better. Smarter. In a month, the circus would go to Italy to spend the off season. He'd come back then.

No, no. Waiting was for cowards. If you wanted good things in life, you had to go get them.

He *could* do this.

As he started forward, his knees shook with every step. He was so nervous, he'd rather have faced the whole field full of bloodwalkers than go up to that front door.

His feet slowed and stopped. After being struck by lightning three times and surviving, maybe he'd used up all his luck. Maybe he was pushing it. Expecting too much out of life. Maybe—

The door opened. Sylvie rushed out, hair flying in the sun, beaming in that way she had, with a smile that said he was the greatest thing on earth.

She flew down the walkway to him.

As he stretched his arms out to catch her, he decided he wouldn't want to face a whole field of bloodwalkers.

Just one would do.

His bloodwalker, Sylvie.

~ The End ~

About the Author

L.X. Cain lives a stone's throw (if you throw it really hard) from the beautiful beaches and turquoise waters of the Red Sea. Despite the scenic delights, she's an indoor gal *cough* couch potato *cough* and spends most of her time happily tapping away on her laptop, coming up with thrilling story ideas to entertain you!

Contact L.X.Cain at:
Blog: www.lexacain.blogspot.com
Facebook: www.facebook.com/lx.cain
Twitter: www.twitter.com/LXCain